STARLINGS

STARLINGS

ERINNA METTLER

REVENGE INK

British Library Cataloguing in Publication Data
A catalogue record for this book is available from the British Library

Revenge Ink
Unit 13 Newby Road, Hazel Grove, Stockport Cheshire, SK7 5DA, UK

www.revengeink.com

ISBN 978-0-9565119-2-8

Copyright © Erinna Mettler 2011

Typeset in Paris by Patrick Lederfain

Printed in the EU by Pulsio Ltd.

To the Mettler Boys: Rob, Noah and Gillespie

I weary for desires never guessed,
For alien passions, strange imaginings,
To be some other person for a day.

Amy Lowell, *The Starling*

THE VIEW TO THE WEST PIER

The seagulls see everything. They swoop down from on high with their little beady eyes and consume it all. They see how typical the day is and also how different from the last; a slight rise in the temperature, an altered colour in the cloud, more or less food on the city's pavements. They see it and they take it in.

On this day in early July, it isn't raining exactly but there is moisture in the air, oppressive clouds in the skies above cover all but the uppermost traces of blue. There is a warm humid breeze, passers-by have shed their jackets and jumpers and are walking along the front bare-armed. People seem happy, thankful to be by the sea before the holiday season starts with gusto and the beach resembles Benidorm in August.

The West Pier Playground is fairly empty. It's the same as any other inner-city playground except — suggested by its name — it is nestled alongside Brighton's famous pebble beach just in front on the old West Pier. Today there is plenty of room, outside the school holidays all children over the age of four are tucked safely away in their classrooms. Most of the brightly coloured benches, bagged by 9am in August, stand unused. Various yummy-mummies perch at the tables nearest the sandpit, all high-heeled boots, ironed hair and designer sunglasses. They sip at their Beach Café soy-lattes only half-watching their toddlers clamber around the climbing frames and play areas.

In one corner of the playground is a wooden castle; flat turrets and towers in primary colours reach up into the sky. It has a slatted drawbridge, walkways, arched windows and two slides. There is a crawl space underneath — the bane of many a parent's life, as they search around the playground, calling out their child's name in ever-increasing panic, until the little poppet emerges from under the castle and demands ice cream.

Today the main inhabitants of the fairy castle are Oscar and Arabella. Arabella teeters along the drawbridge, closely followed by her younger brother Oscar. She stops at the end and turns to face him.

'I'll be the princess and you can be the dragon.'

'Na! I princess.'

She pushes out her bottom lip, considering if it's in her interest to back down.

'OK. We'll both be princesses and fight the dragon.'

She lifts her arm and points an imaginary sword at the invisible beast.

'Take that, dragon!'

Oscar copies his sister and almost falls off the walkway. They clamber along the battlements swords raised, then jump down onto the sandy floor, and disappear into the dungeon beneath.

If you stand by the main gate to the playground, look towards Oscar and Arabella's castle and out to sea, the wreck of the West Pier looms behind. Its black skeleton, like an apocalyptic vision, dropped a little way off the coast as a warning of what is to come. Part of the old walkway remains, snapped off and sloping towards the waves a few hundred yards short of its destination; it is as if a giant has stepped on it with a heavy-booted foot and broken its connection.

Broken and unconnected — that's how Andy Watson feels right now. He stands at his window on the twelfth floor of Ocean Heights, looking down with birdlike stasis at the beach and the Pier beyond.

Andy has been out of prison for six months now, and in that time he has barely exchanged a word with anyone other than Winston, his parole officer. Andy used to be a teacher — before. Now he sweeps the streets in the early hours; a job he knows was arranged for him so that it would minimize his contact with people. *Start off slowly,* Winston had put it.

The sound of children squealing and laughing drifts up above the hum of the traffic and the waves. Andy has wondered many times since his release why they let him come back here — to his old place — opposite a children's playground. He has questioned why they didn't make it a condition of his parole that he couldn't live here. He has decided that — though it could be seen as monumental stupidity — it is actually because they want him to fail; they want him to fail so that they can lock him up again.

He used to live here with his wife and two little girls — before. Then the boy did what all the others didn't, and told someone. The little bastard had more strength of character than he'd anticipated, went to the police, even taped a video for the court, and looked straight into the camera — straight into Andy's eyes — as if the camera wasn't even there. Andy got five years. Prison isn't good for anyone, but when you've messed with little boys, you get singled out for special treatment.

When the door clanged shut on his cell with a snap of its metallic locks, Andy was gripped by an almost unendurable fear. He felt tiny, like a specimen on a microscope slide, filed away for future reference. On that first sleepless night, as he lay on his bunk chewing his nails until they bled, listening to the asylum noise around him, he vowed never to be sent back. Andy kept his head down, took the physical and mental abuse, showed *genuine remorse*, and was released a year early. He thought he'd lived through the worst four years of his life — but now he's not so sure.

As Andy looks out of his curtainless window, he tries to avoid the playground and concentrate on the West Pier. When he went to prison it was still relatively intact, by the time he came out, two fires had turned it into a wreck. It reminds Andy of himself — an empty burned out husk, only existing because nobody has the guts to get rid of it. He's had a lot of time to think about the Pier; it's the first thing he sees when he looks out of his window. It's become a bit of an obsession. They say the Pier will be gone in a couple of years, some grand plan to replace it with a modern tower. *People never learn. Why the hell would anyone want to build a tower these days?* Despite the glossy brochure the council posted to all the residents, Andy's unconvinced; in the past year it's been one scheme after another. He's sure none of them will get off the ground and the old Pier will stay, disintegrating year on year, until it disappears from view beneath the waves. Maybe it will outlive him.

The faint sound of children singing Happy Birthday assaults Andy's ears. Sweat springs to his upper lip. As he presses his palms against his ears, interleaving his long bony fingers behind his head, his eyes catch on the playground below. There is a cluster of children around one of the tables, golden heads crowded together, someone dressed as a clown is cutting a cake.

Is it God, or the Devil testing me? Or some other force?

He grabs the telephone from the chair and dials the number he has used so often he knows it by heart. It rings a few times, a woman answers. She's new — it isn't a voice Andy has heard before — it is a voice that is soft and filled with sympathy.

'Hello? Samaritans. How can I help you?'

'You've got to make them stop. It's only the beginning of summer and I know I won't last if they don't stop!'

'Ok. Ok. You sound very agitated. Try and stay calm. What's your name?'

'Andy.'

'Ok, Andy. Is someone trying to hurt you?'

Andy laughs out loud. *Stupid Bitch!*

'No. They're not going to hurt me! But I might hurt them.'

He listens to her questions. As usual, he feels the need to unburden himself — the words come out in a torrent — when he is done her voice has changed, the initial sympathy is gone, replaced by a tone of judgement. She'll be of no use to him. He cuts her off mid-sentence.

A wasp buzzes against the window pane. It's been there for a couple of days, butting incomprehensibly, trying to reach the open sky. It is angry — but it is dying. Dehydrated from the heat, it languishes on the glass, and moves its yellow feelers robotically; trying to take whatever sustenance it can from the grease on the window. Andy watches it intently, repulsed as it lifts its striped abdomen and rubs at it with sticky black legs.

What are they for anyway? All they do is eat, fly and sting. They have no purpose, they don't even make honey.

Andy remembers that when he was 11 years old, his father found a wasp's nest in the attic. The house had been plagued by the insects all through the summer holidays, whichever room you went into there would be at least one droning at the windows or flitting around the light bulbs. On the weekend before school started, Andy broke the trellis at the front door climbing up it to retrieve a shuttle-cock. His father went into the attic to get his tool-box and first heard, then saw, the nest in the eaves. He got onto the council pest-control office but was told the waiting list was so long that he might as well wait until they died of cold in the autumn.

At night Andy was sure he could hear the buzzing through the ceiling. He lay awake in the encroaching chill, picturing the nest above his bed — a ball of writhing, stinging insects separated from him by a layer of plaster and floorboards. At the point of slumber he imagined he saw shadows on his wall — giant feelers and opaque wings. After a few nights he began to think of it less and less — in any case, he had other things on his mind, like the sound of footsteps on the landing outside his room. *Would he pass by, or would the handle turn, and the bedroom door creak open in the dark?*

That Christmas his father asked him to help bring the artificial tree down from the attic. They saw the desiccated nest clinging to the roof beams. '*Watch!*' said his father laughing, and poked at it with a broom handle. Andy flinched, half expecting to be engulfed by a thousand black buzzes; instead the nest disintegrated into grey dust on the floor, leaving only a round of paper frills against the rafters.

Sounds of childish joy rise into Andy's consciousness from the playground. He puts on his denim jacket and picks up his keys. Then, as an afterthought, he turns back to the window, places his left thumb over the wasp and squashes it against the glass. There's a sharp stab of pain as his skin touches the venomous sting and he pulls away. The wasp sticks to the window, twitching out its last moments of life. Andy leaves the flat to take the coffin-like lift to the street below.

As Andy's door closes, another opens down the hall. It's the old lady from 12C — he thinks her name is May. She shuffles out of her flat, then sees Andy and shuffles back in slamming the door behind her. Before — when he lived here as a respectable married teacher — May had made a fuss of his girls, buying them eggs at Easter and presents at Christmas. They would exchange small talk in the hallway and he would do little jobs for her like changing light bulbs she couldn't reach. These days if they happen to be in the corridor at the same time, she does one of two things: if circumstances allow it she does what she has just done and goes back inside until she is sure he has gone, or, if she has already set off towards the lift, she stares blankly ahead as if not focussing on him will cause him to disappear. Andy isn't sure which of these two actions he prefers — which he finds least hurtful. Sometimes he has to fight the urge to get into the lift with her — just to make her squirm for the ride down. He wonders who changes her light bulbs now and pictures her as she sits in the darkness, lit only by the glow from her television.

Today Andy takes the lift down alone. It judders along slowly, passing each floor uncalled, the lights inside dimming as if it's going to break down. Confined spaces make Andy nervous and he presses his fingernails into the flesh of his palms. Finally the door rattles open onto the tiny dark hallway of the ground floor. Lit by a single blinking tube-light, this gloomiest of hallways depresses Andy even more than the rest of the building. Before — when he lived here with his wife — they'd made the best of it. The flat was all they could afford and they looked on the bright side — it was near the beach and very central — they painted the rooms in the bright colours of a shared future. The children were conceived there and grew from babes to schoolgirls. Now the rooms in Andy's flat have yellowing chipped walls and dirty windows, the niceties of family life have all been removed.

Ocean Heights used to be a council block, full of families. Built during the sunny optimism of the 1960s it must have once been a nice place to live. Most of the two bedroom flats are now privately owned and rented out to a transitory community. Andy is one of the few long-term residents — aside from his enforced absence — he has lived here for nearly ten years.

Now, apart from May, the only face he recognises is the man with the dog. He was there when Andy and his wife moved in. Andy knows his type from prison: skin-short hair, tattoos, gold teeth, arms heavy with chunky bracelets and rings. His dog is a pit-bull called Cassie; despite its ugliness it's a friendly sort of beast. The man walks the dog twice a day, at 6am and at 6pm. Andy hears its claws on the tiled floor outside his flat, and its snuffling, choking breath as it strains for freedom on its chain. The man with the dog frightens him — on the occasions Andy has met him in the corridor, he has been greeted with a nod so terse as to be almost imperceptible. This acknowledgement of his existence is terrifying; it says — with unmistakeable certitude — *I know what you are.*

In a city of a quarter of a million people, these are Andy's only dealings with humanity. To his relief, he doesn't see anyone in the hallway this afternoon and is able to slip out of the main entrance unobserved. He stands on the uneven pavement to catch his breath.

Though it boasts unrivalled sea views, Ocean Heights is not quite the coastal paradise it claims to be. It is not one of the grand Georgian houses that line the seafront or the private squares, with bottle-bottom windows and tall arched doorways. Ocean Heights is reached via a tiny back street that smells of the rubbish from the giant metal bins belonging to one of Brighton's poshest hotels. Discarded bottles and cans line the alleyway: condoms and fag-ends and needles and polystyrene take-away trays, the detritus of urban humanity — Andy knows the road's rubbish well; it's on his work route. Few people walk this way, though it does provide a short cut to the shops on Western Road — those that do often wish they hadn't, for even if there is no one around there is a sinister ambience to the area, as if something bad has happened here, or as if something bad will.

Andy gags on the stench of urine and stale beer. At the bottom of the road the deafening noise of a road drill starts up — Andy's eyes ache from within. It seems to him that there is always someone drilling within earshot, regardless of the hour. He notices it most when he is trying to sleep. He thinks that maybe if the drilling ever stopped he too would cease to exist. He sighs deeply and walks away from Ocean Heights — around the workmen wearing yellow jackets and industrial ear muffs — and onto the traffic-heavy avenue of the Kings Road.

Down in the playground a mobile phone goes off; a jazz-funk ringtone. One of the mummies pulls a phone out of a giant leather handbag and starts chatting about her aromatherapy class — her toddler stuffs handfuls of wet sand into his mouth and chews thoughtfully. The child's eyes move upwards as a red kite floats brightly against a patch of blue sky. Behind him on the promenade, a pale man in a denim jacket and sunglasses grips the peppermint-coloured railings. Unknowingly, he taps his wedding ring against the metal and stares through the darkness of his Ray Bans into the playground below.

Three little girls in flouncy pink bikinis are chasing seagulls by the paddling pool, their spaghetti-strapped tops stick flatly to their twig-like bodies. They take it in turns to tiptoe as near as they can to the birds; turning before they are within pecking distance and splashing noisily back to the water's edge. The seagulls stand impassively, regarding them with steady ochre eyes. As the girls approach again, one of the gulls spreads out its wings, stopping them in their tracks, and steps off gracefully into flight. The girls grab at each other and scream shatteringly — a woman in dark glasses sitting at a nearby table lowers her head into her hands, as if trying to keep her brains in place after a night of too many Chardonnays. The man watches all of this from his elevated position and then his eyes rest on the fairy castle.

Oscar and Arabella are still fighting the dragon. Their burnished-gold heads bob in and out of Andy's sightline. He tries to focus once again on the black skeletal form of the Pier, imagining himself imprisoned in its bars like Hansel in the witch's childcage. He taps his wedding ring again — flat fingered — the metal makes a hollow sound, reverberating along the pipe. Oscar hears it and peers over the parapet, his strawberry blond hair haloed by a sudden flash of sunlight through the cloud. Andy smiles.

'Look!' says Oscar, 'A magician!'

Arabella stands on her tippy toes to see, hanging her skinny arms over the castle wall and resting her chin on the wood.

'He doesn't look much like a magician. He doesn't have enough hair *and* he's wearing jeans.'

'But he is one,' says Oscar, flicking his wrist at the man as if he were holding a Harry Potter wand. Andy taps again at the railing making the same strange sound. Oscar and Arabella look at each other and giggle, then duck down to hide in their wooden fortress. When Arabella peeks around the drawbridge a few moments later, after much consultation with her little brother, the magician has disappeared.

Oscar and Arabella's mother, Gill, realises she will have to get a move on if she's going to be in time to pick up her eldest child from school. Reluctantly, she packs up their bags, stuffing more than is humanly possible into the sagging net under Oscar's pushchair. He's getting a bit old for it now but Gill doesn't know how she'll manage when she doesn't have it to carry their stuff anymore. She chats to her friends as she packs, arranging to meet them again tomorrow — *if the weather's ok.* When she's ready to go she looks around the playground for the children; there's no sign of their soft red hair, her usual marker. Gill calls their names, scanning every inch of the fenced-in space. Her voice is perfectly calm but after calling them a few times a wave of panic begins to lap at her silver Birkenstocks.

'Can you see them?' she asks the mothers she is with. Dia and Louise, who have now stopped their chatter and are also scanning the playground, shake their heads slowly, as yet relatively unconcerned.

The western end of the playground is completely empty. There are no longer any children in the paddling pool — even the seagulls have abandoned it — the water ripples in the breeze. Only a couple of children are still playing in the sandpits that make up the middle area, industriously digging and patting at miniature castles. None of these children have the bright rosy hair the women want to see. The fairy castle is empty too, there's no sound of little footsteps on springy wood. Gill calls for her children again, loudly, crossly, the panic rising in her voice. All three women begin to physically search the playground, moving in different directions, repeatedly calling out the two names.

'Oscar! Arabella!'

They look under the castle and around the pirate ship. They walk around the empty paddling pool gazing out onto the pebbly horizon on the other side of the fence. They peer around the back of the toilet and refreshment huts.

'Oscar! Arabella!'

But Oscar and Arabella don't come.

The adrenalin trigger switches in Gill's brain causing her

heart to thunder against her chest, filling her head with rushing blood. Her stomach constricts, her pupils dilate and the downy hairs on her forearms rise up a fraction from her skin. A hundred terrible thoughts cross her mind, unwanted images flicker on the screen of her imagination. Tears well up in her eyes and her hands begin to tremble. One of the other mothers, who has been watching the drama unfold, asks what the children look like and joins the search.

'Where are they?' Gill says to Louise.

'Try not to panic,' she replies, rubbing Gill's arm sympathetically. 'They're probably on the beach. I'll go and have a look. '

She calls to her own children who are throwing sand at each other.

'Girls! Where did you last see Oscar and Arabella?'

'I dunno,' says one, while the other hits her square in the face with a wet sandball.

Gill is getting more frantic by the second — she has crossed the barrier all parents dread, into the territory of lost children. Her spray-tanned face is turning a sickly grey colour and she stands looking around feebly with unnaturally wide eyes. Dia and Louise make one last sweep of the playground, crawling on their hands and knees to look into the dungeons of the fairy castle.

'Oh God, oh God,' whispers Gill. In her mind she is moving on to the next step — to the idea of calling the police — and all that implies. She is shaken out of her trance by a sharp tug at the hem of her skirt. It is Orlando; Dia's four-year-old.

'Aunty Gill,' he says seriously, 'I think I can see Bella.'

Gill crouches and grabs him a little more roughly than necessary by his bony shoulders.

'Where Landy? Where?'

He points beyond the fence to the bucket and spade shop next to the café.

Bundles of neon rubber rings, inflatable dolphins and multi-coloured buckets of various sizes hang from the walls and overspill from the crates outside the shop front. In between an enormous plastic dinghy, complete with oars, and a bucket of flapping union jacks, Gill can see the wispy bodies of two children sitting opposite each other, sandy soled feet touching, straw-coloured heads bent forward in conference. Gill runs towards them, sandals clacking on the decking. Oscar and Arabella look up at her with huge innocent eyes, each has an ice cream cone, and the white foam runs stickily down their arms. Their mother scoops them up in a desperately thankful embrace; kissing their hair repeatedly, tears pouring down her cheeks. Arabella pushes her away first.

'Squishing my ice cream.'

'Want some?' says Oscar, sticking it in Gill's face. She takes a sideways lick and frowns.

'Where did you get it Oscar?'

'Mag-ic-ian. Mag-ic-ian bought for us.'

Gill takes her children home. She gives them extra cuddles at bedtime and a serious talking-to about the dangers of straying too far from their mother and taking sweets from strangers — even if they are magicians. She's still not sure if she should report it to the police. After all, it was only a man buying ice cream for two lost children — but something sits uneasily with her, perhaps the disquieting knowledge of a near miss.

Andy closes the door to his flat and steps over to the window. The playground is deserted now, its fairy castle locked up for the night. The early evening traffic snakes past the relic of the Pier, lights casting slow white squares against the walls of Andy's room. He thinks about the events of the afternoon — the way the children had approached him at the gate to the playground without him having to do anything. How trusting their faces had been as they asked him if he was a magician. He'd made a coin disappear, and then reappear, in the soft curls of hair behind the little boy's ear — a trick his father had taught him years ago. How easy it would have been to take them — to slip his hands in theirs and lead them into the dark sheltered hallway of Ocean Heights — how difficult it was for him not to have done so.

After he left the children, Andy sat for a couple of hours on the pebbles amidst the Pier's splintered pillars. He watched the waves roll against it, lifting and dropping long fronds of seaweed from their seabed anchor. He was comforted by the rhythmic sound of the tide. He thought about his mother — before she left him for the freak — and how she used to stroke his hair and sing softly to him when he woke terrified in the night. He lay back on the shingle and let himself breathe in and out with the rhythm of the waves.

Andy looks down to the street below, it's changing. Even the gulls have deserted it. It's no longer a place of sunshine and ice cream and children — the night people are beginning to emerge — he should try and get some sleep before he has to leave for work. He takes a piece of toilet paper from the bathroom and uses it to wipe away the sticky corpse of the wasp, and then he turns his back on the window.

PEBBLE-DASHED

They walk along the beach separately, a few steps out of pace with each other. She can hear the click of his camera as he photographs her against the sparkling sea; it makes music with the hot crunch of the sun-soaked pebbles under her feet and the wild sobbing of the gulls.

They're not speaking, but while she can hear his camera she knows he's still there. It will be alright because he hasn't stopped entirely, leaving her to walk on alone. It has to be alright, because in two days he'll be gone, and until then she needs to touch him as much as possible, so she can remember what his skin feels like. Between them they'll find a way to give in without losing face, so that they can get on with their last weekend together.

Next to the slowly turning carousel, Dia walks onto the steady concrete of the promenade. The diminishing organ music is overwhelmed by a radio pumped loudly through the speakers at a coffee bar festooned with Italian flags. It's The Clash, *Should I Stay or Should I Go?* — one of Alastair's favourites — she is acutely aware of the title's significance as she stops to buy him an espresso.

A dark young man, wearing cook's overalls and a jaunty white hat, leaps out of a bored trance when he sees her at the counter.

'Ciao Bella,' he says authentically.

Her eyes are drawn to the tiny silver crucifix hanging around his neck — it glints in the sun each time he breathes. He notices and grins at her. It's a good smile, just the right side of leery, naughty but not offensive.

'Hi — a double espresso and a cappuccino please. I like your hat.'

'Sorry Bella, but we only have black or white — is not London you know.'

He winks at her and turns to the coffee machine behind him.

'You having a good day?' he asks over his shoulder.

'Mmm,' she shakes her head. 'Boyfriend trouble.'

She looks over at Alastair who is kneeling on the beach looking for the perfect place to line up his camera. He looks long and beaky in this position, craning his neck and bending his shoulders like a wading bird.

The Barista leans back and looks at him too.

'That him?' he asks with an air of disbelief.

Dia laughs. 'He's not always like this, sometimes he's quite normal.'

The Clash give way to Bryan Adam's *Everything I Do* — Dia and the Barista groan. It's been number one for half the year — it's driving sane people crazy. It has a mercurial power, turning people into wide-eyed zombies, so that even if you hate it, you find yourself humming it on the bus. Dia knows that when she hears it in the future, Alastair's face will pop into her head.

The Barista hands her the coffees and points at Alastair.

'He crazy. You are beautiful — like Madonna. Maybe you should go out with me instead.'

Because of his accent she's not sure if he said Madonna or The Madonna. There's a big difference and at the age of twenty she really doesn't want to be either, to any man.

She looks back at Alastair to see if he's noticed she's being chatted up. He hasn't. Now he's lying on his front looking through the viewfinder, transformed from bird to stick-insect — a body of length more than anything else. He's appraising the pebbles as if he's considering eating them. His T-shirt has risen up his back exposing a line of smooth brown skin. She sighs heavily, wishing he would give her as much attention as he does the grey stones.

'What do I owe you?' she asks the Barista with his open face.

'On the house — and if he don't treat you right, you know where I am.'

He winks again — he really is quite gorgeous but there's nothing she can do.

She walks over to Alastair and places the caffeine peace offering in front of his lens just as he takes the shot.

'Damn it, Dia!'

He looks up at her angrily, for a moment she thinks he's going to say something really hurtful. She feels like she did when she was a little girl and she'd done something to upset her father.

'Do you have to be quite so — irritating?'

She stands over him waiting for him to give in, to see the ridiculousness of photographing pebbles, to laugh and take her hand, pull her down onto the stones and kiss her, forgetting for once about his bloody camera. But he just moves his coffee out of shot and clicks away, peering through the lens and caressing the image into a different focus with the fingers of his left hand. She stands like this for a few minutes, staring ahead to the silver horizon, and then she turns and walks away.

At the Pier she leans on the parapet to look down at him on the beach below. He is oblivious to her absence — she doesn't exist for him, her being there or not being there doesn't matter — there is only Alastair and his camera.

She pushes past the crowds on the promenade, couples entwined as they walk, women pushing prams, children with ice cream faces and candy-glutted eyes, several hen parties wearing feather halos and net wings over their clubbing clothes. They are all smiling, every one of them filled with sunshine happiness. She feels sick, and there's an actual pain in her heart — like a voodoo pin, twisted by Alastair from his point of indifference on the beach.

The crowds dwindle as she makes her way up the hill towards the B&B; soon she is completely alone on the wide trajectory of the street. An enormous seagull sits on the railings outside *The Bougainvillea Guesthouse*, its feathers as white as summer clouds and its jagged yellow beak too long for its body, the red dot on the underside like a single drop of blood. Dia stops and stares at it, looking it in the eye. Its eyes are so cold, so predatory — there's something wrong about yellow eyes, something inhuman. It doesn't flinch, just stares straight back at her, she is the interloper — it isn't going to look away first. She turns from it and rushes past the *hellos* of Mrs Thompson at the reception desk and up the stairs to their top-floor room.

The tears come as she unlocks the door. She crouches on the floor between the two single beds and sobs into her knees. All the way back she thought he might follow her, realise she'd gone and run after her begging for forgiveness. But there was only ever one set of footsteps echoing off the bleached house-fronts; a lonely sound she realised she would have to get used to. When he leaves on Sunday that will be it, he won't be coming back to her — no matter what he says now.

Alastair doesn't return to the B&B for hours. The pink flowers of the bedspreads slowly glow orange under the sinking sun. She cries for the whole time, the knees of her jeans are damp with tears. She hears the thud of his footsteps on the stairs and looks up to see him fling open the door. Her eyes are small and rabbit-like. He stares at her mascara-stained face with a look of genuine puzzlement, suspended in the doorway between the fight she knew he'd have planned and the urge to comfort her. Finally he speaks.

'Where did you go? I turned away for a minute and you'd gone. I've been up and down the sea-front looking for you all afternoon. I asked a guy at a coffee stall if he'd seen you and he called me an idiot.'

She lets out a cross between a laugh and a sob.

'Hey,' he says kneeling in front of her, 'I'm sorry —ok? We shouldn't fight — not this weekend. I'm sorry.'

He holds her like she might break and kisses her with soft lips.

'I love you,' she whispers. It's the first time either of them has said it and she thinks if she says it too loud he'll simply turn and run away.

He lifts her onto one of the beds and silently undresses her, covering each new exposure of skin with slow kisses. Her breasts are sore, pins and needles ripple through them under his touch — hormonal devilment even at this early stage. She is shocked by the mingling of pleasure and discomfort and arches her back, feeling the static starchiness of the bedspread under her shoulders.

How many couples have done the same thing in this room? She wonders. *The same thing — yet always different.*

'Is it safe?' he asks.

She shakes her head. *No it's not safe; it's never been safe, not with us.*

He uses a condom. She wishes she could tell him not to, to feel him totally again without separation. She wants to tell him there's no need — that pregnant women can't get pregnant — but that would mean telling him about the baby. He's always been so careful about it all, so desperate not to be caught out. He checks her pills, actually looks at the packet and if there's any doubt, it's condoms for a fortnight. She tries to remember, but sometimes in the reeling enormity of her love for him she simply forgets. Even so it's bad luck — a million-to-one chance, impossible odds for anything else. She knows he would stay for a while if she told him, but she wants him to stay out of need, not obligation. She's booked into the clinic the day after he's due to leave. If he's still around he can go with her — but he won't be, she knows that already. Whatever hopes she had for them this weekend were dashed as he lay on the pebbles with his camera, unaware that she had gone.

'I love you.' She cries it out this time, part of a climax so intense with emotion that tears pour down her cheeks at its end. 'Alastair!'

He looks down at her and his face shows that he doesn't know what to do.

'Dia. Stop.' His voice is husky with pity. She's sobbing again, her face crumpled with the knowledge that this could be the last time.

'Don't leave me — please.'

'Dia — don't.'

He holds her in his arms but he doesn't say he'll stay.

***

The day had started promisingly. He arrived at her door at eight, an hour early, carrying a rucksack packed so there was enough room for her clothes to nestle on top of his. She wasn't ready, her hair was a mess and she wore only sleep-creased cheeks and a scruffy nightshirt.

'You look beautiful' he said, with that glorious smile, moving her hair behind her ear to hold her face in his hands and kiss her.

Dia had wondered how the weekend would go — things had been difficult lately. She knew it was her fault. She'd found out she was pregnant two weeks before, the same day he'd told her about his upcoming travels — three months at least — around Croatia in a van with journalists, photographing atrocities. *An opportunity not to be missed. He'd be mad to turn it down. It could the making of his career.*

She didn't want his baby, not yet, but she wanted him with her. They'd been together for eight months, if he left her now for three months, or four or six, what would happen to them? She knew the answer — nothing. Nothing would happen to them because there wouldn't be a *them*.

It was a declaration of separation. He was going to a war zone to get away from her — the anarchy of Croatia in the summer of 1991 — no telephones, no postal service. No contact. A new conflict with ancient roots; new methods, old prejudices. Unpredictability. She worried about the escalating violence reported on the news, the fact that she wouldn't know he was safe, the risks he would take to get a picture.

She withdrew from him; the easiness of their last couple of months degenerated into snappy arguments and things left unsaid. She was tired all the time, and irritable, the slightest little thing and BOOM! Explosions of bitterness that he frowned through, when she really wanted him to shout at her, shake her, to react in some way that was as dramatic as she felt.

Then he'd said they should go away — spend the weekend together to sort things out, find out if...

If what? He didn't say; just smiled and played with her hair.

They got to Victoria in time for the first train out after rush hour. The station was cold and echoing; he held her close to keep her warm as the last of the commuters bustled around them. She went to buy trashy magazines she would never read, and because they both loved them, coffee and Maltesers for breakfast — he bought the tickets.

It was one of the old-fashioned trains, made up of private compartments with twist-handle doors. They walked to the front and took one for themselves — there weren't many other passengers but he stood with his back against the door to discourage anyone from thinking of joining them. They didn't speak, just beamed at each other, until the train snaked its way out from the darkness of the underpass and into the bright dust-flecked air of the London morning.

He sat beside her, stretching his legs in front of him, again curling her hair behind her ear — that habit of his that made her neck tingle at the lightness of his fingertips. He was kissing her lips as the ancient train squeaked its way passed the iconic Battersea Power Station, and he never once reached for his camera. He pulled her onto his knee, his hand on her thigh, kissing and kissing throughout the three languorous miles from Victoria to Clapham Junction.

The train brakes screeched like a wounded dinosaur, lurching so hard that she nearly fell from his knee; his tight embrace just enough to keep her off the floor. There was a clatter of doors, and then a young man in a suit pulled open the door to their carriage as he spoke over his shoulder to his colleague. They looked in at Alastair and Dia.

'Sorry mate,' said the first man, then he winked at Alastair and shut the door with a bang, moving onto the next carriage.

They looked at each other and Alastair laughed.

'Jesus,' said Dia, shaking her head.

'What?'

She got off his knee and arranged herself primly on the seat opposite. A whistle shrilled from the platform and the train rumbled off haltingly, as though it were stretching. She scraped the purple nail polish from her nail with her front teeth, annoyed by the conspiratorial wink between Alastair and Suit Boy. His bemused expression made the anger flare up suddenly from inside her, she grabbed a magazine from the seat and flicked through it hard, almost ripping the pages.

'Dia, what's up?' He phrased it in a sing-song, as if he were talking to a child, and she raged from within, wounding but not quite killing his smirk with her glare.

'Dia?'

She looked across at him, eyes like flares.

'Men are just so fucking sure of everything all the time.'

'What *are* you talking about?'

'That wink, that stupid *I know what you're up to* wink!'

She realised when she said it that she shouldn't be angry with him, that he hadn't actually done anything wrong, but it didn't matter. He was doing something wrong — he was leaving her when she needed him most. For the first time since he mentioned it, she saw the trip as it was undoubtedly intended — the last waltz — the break-up weekend. Maybe they should just get it over with and end it now before they even got there. She created an argument out of the dust-filled air of the musty carriage.

'I bet you winked at him too didn't you?'

He laughed and held up his hands. 'I did not. He was just being nice and leaving us to it.'

'Right — and did you really think we were going to do *it* on a busy train full of tourists?'

'Well I didn't mean *it* like that,' he said, looking around the empty carriage, 'but now you've put the idea into my head it could be fun. Someone might catch us.'

He whispered this last bit and raised his eyebrows theatrically, flashing her *the* smile. As always, it was as if he'd taken a pin to her balloon of rage and burst it with his easy charm. She opened her mouth to say something else but she knew he'd defeated her. She smiled helplessly and shifted herself back onto the seat beside him, laying her head on his chest to listen to the miraculous one-two beat of his heart.

They sat like this for a while, silently watching the suburbs pass by the window, real and reflected. Then he began to talk about his plans — how they would drive down Europe through Italy, and cross into Croatia via Slovenia. How much film should he take? Did she think he could find more there? Should he take his overcoat to sleep in? (The one he was wearing when she met him, thick black wool that he'd wrapped her up in, holding her close all winter long...) What did she think?

She sat up. 'I think its utter madness,' she said, speaking her mind for the first time since he'd told her.

He frowned.

'Well it is. They're throwing bombs and machine-gunning each other and you want to go and take pictures like it's a school project. Its nuts — *and* it's really patronising. Ordinary people are dying, women and children and fathers, it's really happening to them and you can go home whenever you want — they can't.'

'Which is why I want to go — to make it matter.'

'You are so full of yourself — it matters already!'

He looked away from her, 'You know what I mean.'

'You know what I think? I think you're going because you don't want to be with me anymore.' Her voice cracked slightly, and she felt hot as the odour of the old carpet-covered seat overwhelmed her senses.

'Now who's full of themselves? — if I didn't want you anymore I'd just tell you.'

Alastair's parents lived in Hove, had done all their lives. He'd told her about his childhood growing up there by the sea, the lanky kid with the camera, encouraged in his hobby by a doting father. She'd wanted to know all about him, she lay in bed with him cocooned against the crisp winter mornings and listened to his life story. Everything revolved around his camera — his first photo, winning his first competition, the picture of a seagull attacking a tourist printed in the local paper when he was just thirteen. He talked about how the light was different by the sea, how over time his eye had become attuned to it, how it made him view things from a different perspective, to realise that emotion could be conveyed by light.

She'd met his parents in London; they were nice people — though his Dad seemed a little bitter, and his Mum a little too eager to please, as she fussed over Alastair and his Dad and eyed Dia suspiciously from the kitchen, tea towel at the ready. She wondered if all couples turned out like them in the end — together, but at the same time, apart.

She thought he might suggest they visit them this weekend, spend static hours in their terrace house near, though not quite on, the seafront. But Alastair had said that this weekend was about them and booked a B&B in Kemptown for Friday night.

It was after 12 by the time they walked up Devonshire Place to *The Bougainvillea Guesthouse*. They hadn't said much since the train, the sun shimmered above their heads and it was hot — very hot. Sweat clung to her skin. A balm like Vaseline collected at her armpits. She fanned herself with the magazine she'd pretended to read on the train rather than talk to him as he took photographs out of the window. He insisted he knew where Devonshire Place was, being a local boy. In truth he'd barely been back in five years, had lived at the other end of town and had no idea how to get there. They wandered up and down the labyrinthine hills above the sea, getting hotter and more pissed off with every wrong turn.

'I know where it is,' he kept repeating against her silence, as she lingered a few paces behind. The sun radiated in the cloudless blue, seagulls drifted like vultures on the plain, cutting the pavement with sharp-shadowed wings. She was ready to give up and sit on the baked flagstones until a taxi came by, when he turned excitedly, pointing to a tall Georgian house a few metres up the road.

'Here it is — I told you I knew where it was!'

Mrs Thompson, the owner of *The Bougainvillea*, had the most extraordinarily coloured hair, a sort of pinkie-brown — like decayed rose petals. The smell of the whole place matched it, a stale pomander reek coupled with a fresh squirt of floral air-freshener and the strong odour of *Mr Sheen*. Her face gave the impression of being almost entirely pink; covered with thick foundation, blusher, lipstick and heavy-powdered eye shadow under extravagant spider-leg lashes. Her makeup was so ghastly, Dia wondered if she had once been a cabaret singer, who was still waiting for one last curtain call.

She felt sick again and couldn't stop herself from gagging. Covering her mouth with one hand, she steadied herself by clutching the reception desk and almost melted onto the hideously patterned carpet as Alastair turned on the charm for Mrs Thompson. He registered under the name of Mr and Mrs Smith and chuckled to himself as he followed the rose-coloured woman upstairs to their room on the uppermost floor.

The room was tiny. It must have been the attic once; the roof sloped to an abrupt point so that Alastair could only stand upright in line with the door. There were two single beds enrobed in nylon bedspreads, and a rickety chest of drawers harking all the way from the 60s. The window in the roof was surprisingly large, it looked original, and the sun cast its chequerboard shadow starkly across the two beds. There were plastic flowers in a vase on a wooden chair below it. The room smelled both damp and dry at the same time, as the heat warmed the man-made fibres, and the plaster under the wallpaper oozed a hundred years of exposure to the sea.

Mrs Thompson explained that the bathroom was down the first flight of stairs at the end of the corridor and that breakfast was served between 7 and 9. Alastair gave her his full attention as Dia kicked off her shoes and lay on one of the beds. When the landlady finally left, he flung himself backwards onto the other bed and whistled.

'What do you make of her? Incredible. I mean it's so realistic. Do you think she's post-surgery?'

'What are you talking about?'

'She's a man — don't tell me you didn't notice?'

'Oh she is not — it's only bad makeup. She's just an old lady.'

He turned to her and propped his head up on his elbow; the bed creaking under his body.

'Sometimes you are so naive. Our Mrs Thompson is a bonafide Mrs Madrigal. Why do you think she's got that scarf round her neck?'

'It's just a bow — she probably thinks it's pretty.'

He shook his head, smiling with superior knowledge. 'It's to cover up her Adam's apple.'

He'd started to annoy her again, inanely chattering on. She sighed and stood up, walked to the window and stood on her tip-toes to look out. She could hear him scrambling on the bed like a puppy, rummaging in his rucksack.

'Want one?' he said.

She looked over her shoulder at him. He was holding out a packet of Marlboro, his mouth was down-turned as if he was knowingly mimicking her sadness.

'I've given up.'

'Since when?'

'Since about three weeks ago — haven't you noticed?'

He shook his head.

She turned back to the window. 'Don't smoke it in here, the room's too small.'

***

It is raining in the morning. Dia wakes early; still tired, slightly nauseous. Alastair's arm twitches under her neck; his breathing is rhythmic in his deep untroubled sleep. The rosy pinkness of the room in the sun has been replaced, under the grey rain-smeared light of the new day, by a tainted salmon colour. It's windy too, a vicious seaside gale that rattles the sloping Georgian window like an unwanted guest. The drops prattle on the pane below the blind they didn't have time to close the night before.

She feels despondent — another day closer to the day he will go. She wriggles into him, absorbing his warmth through her skin.

A little while later they go down to breakfast, he's held her hand since he woke up, letting it go only to dress and go to the bathroom. He's holding it now as they walk into the breakfast room. The other guests look up when they come in; a uniformly beige old couple and a family with a smiling baby and a sulking toddler.

Dia is embarrassed, she wonders if they heard — the slamming doors and hours of sobbing, the noise of their love-making, the shouting out of his name. From their faces she can tell that they did; the old man grins at her and says 'good morning' as his wife becomes suddenly fascinated by the checks on the tablecloth. The young husband leans forward and whispers something to his wife, who tells him to 'stop it' but laughs anyway.

Alastair helps himself to a mini pack of Cornflakes and crunches obliviously. She sips tea so strong it has a coating, and tries to keep her eyes from the absurdly ugly china dogs on the Welsh dresser. The Full English arrives, piping hot on willow-pattern plates, and Alastair wheedles another piece of toast out of Mrs Thompson 'for the wife'.

Dia takes a bite of fried egg; it's beautifully cooked, fresh and yellow and just runny enough. It tastes delicious. She tries to swallow it but she can't, her throat is too dry; it sticks there and won't budge. Acid rises from her stomach. She flushes and breathes through her nose, then runs from the room knocking her chair over as she goes.

He finds her in the downstairs loo. He's worried but there's no need, she felt better as soon as she threw up, now all she wants to do is eat. She assures him it's just a bug and suggests he go for a walk while she has a lie down. He's reluctant to leave her. He's attentive and sweet but she feels as though she won't be able to breathe if he's with her, so she presses him into going, saying she needs to sleep. He admits he'd like to take some pictures of the Pier in the rain.

She lies on the unmade bed in the tiny darkened room, eating Maltesers and listening to the raindrops on the window. She thinks of him out there under the open skies, picturing him clambering on benches or lying on the slick wood of the deserted Pier to capture his vision — that elusive combination of light and form that few people ever see. She realises that it would always be like this, she only borrows him between photographs. He's never really been hers. There is only ever Alastair and his camera.

***

The train back to London is full; there's been a points failure and only half the trains are running. It's a modern carriage with strip lights, automatic doors and electronic announcements; it smells of plastic and evaporating rain.

They don't get a seat and stand pressed together among the other passengers, her arms hooked around his neck.

'What was your name again?' he asks as the train lurches out of the station. He catches the eye of the middle-aged woman standing next to them reading *Hello*.

'She just came over and put her arms around me,' he says. 'That's the trouble with young women today — no standards.'

The woman smiles at them and goes back to the soft furnishings in Joanna Lumley's Chelsea home.

Dia looks up at Alastair, photographing his face with her eyes to hold in her memory when he's no longer there. Her lashes close softly over the image. She knows that eventually it will fade; one day the colour of his eyes will escape her, then his features will shade into black and white, next patches will appear that she can't fill in, until all that is left is the remembrance of his fingertips.

He smiles *the* smile and pushes a strand of damp hair behind her ear.

'I do love you, you know,' he says. 'No matter what happens.'

BURNING FEATHERS

Between the ages of 14 and 17 Barney was a total stoner. He blundered around in an oblivious fog of wonder. He viewed the world about him in hyper-real detail, point by point. He would spend hours at a time watching ants crawl through grass. He would take in each specific detail: the differing colour of the blades as the sunlight hit them, their lengths and widths, the way they bent and inter-linked, the fresh chlorophyll smell as the leaves bruised under his touch, the coal dark earth showing through the gaps, and the slight shift of the invisible insect world underneath. Then there were the ants themselves; the intricacies of their wriggling legs, their tiny bulbous heads and bodies, the jointed symmetry of their feelers as they plotted their way through the forest of the lawn, twisting one way, then another.

On an unseasonably warm day late in March, Barney was engaged in this very pastime. He'd skipped school and gone to his favourite city park to relax and smoke. Feeling particularly mellow, he knelt green stains into his jeans and then, in a parody of prayer, lay his palms flat on the grass and placed his cheek between them to get as close as possible to the mini-world of his latest preoccupation. He heard the rush and roar of the insect traffic on the herbaceous spaghetti beneath his ear, and smiled in wonder at the incomprehensible enormity of it all.

'Wow.' He breathed. 'Wow!'

Two girls sitting a few feet away, eating sandwiches out of plastic triangles, looked at each other and giggled. Barney turned his head to look, and seeing that they were about his age and that one of them was righteously beautiful, he jumped onto his heels in one fluid and athletic spring. He stood over them framed by the hazy afternoon sun, brushing the grass from his jeans. 'Ladies,' he said, blowing his fringe out of his eyes. They shifted their legs on the school cardigans they were using as cushions and smiled encouragingly up at him, sandwiches suspended between lap and lip.

Barney heard the sharp bark of a dog behind him and shivered involuntarily. He knew whose it was without looking. He'd been waiting for this moment for weeks now, knowing it would come but pretending it wouldn't. Maybe it wasn't Cassie. Maybe it was just an ordinary fluffy dog chasing a ball.

He looked behind him. The white pit-bull was racing across the flat of the green at breakneck speed, her ears aerodynamically pinned back; her lips bared, exposing rows of pointed teeth and a foaming, lolling tongue. He could see her owner, Bulldog, standing next to the swings in the kid's playground, staring at him with ferocious intensity.

He took one last look at the girls, shrugged his shoulders in regret for an afternoon that might have been, and ran as fast as possible, with undone laces and a foggy head, across the grass towards the Lewes Road.

Cassie caught him in seconds. He felt her teeth sink into the flesh of his calf and he cried out in pain. The dog shook her head violently from side to side as if his leg were a rabbit. Barney hopped on the spot, swearing and crying. He tried to pull away, but Cassie clamped her jaws tighter, making slathering noises with the frenzy of a wild beast. A warm trickle of blood ran down the skin of his calf and into his trainers. Barney felt woozy, he lost his footing and stumbled backwards, falling flat with whirling arms, his other leg twisted over the dog's back. Cassie's teeth clenched like a hunter's trap.

Bulldog arrived a minute later, puffed from the exertion of a 100-yard dash.

'What ya run for?' he said between breaths. 'I only wanna talk.' He yanked Cassie's studded collar. 'Drop Cass — Drop!'

The dog immediately loosened her jaws and sloped off in search of the nearest tree.

'She was just playing — she would only really hurt ya if I tole her to.'

Bulldog held out his hand to pull Barney up. Barney took it, but when he limped to his feet, Bulldog didn't loosen his grip; in fact he squeezed harder and harder until Barney thought that the little bones under his flesh might pop. Bulldog pulled Barney close, looked up into his eyes, and whispered the words that freeze-dried his soul.

'YOU OWE ME.'

Barney had started working for Bulldog when he was 15. One of the kids Barney knew from the beach recruited him. Bulldog wanted to sell dope to posh kids — they were reliable and had a never-ending supply of ready cash. But he couldn't just walk into the private schools of Brighton and hand out bags of grass; he needed someone on the inside — and that was where Barney came in. The kid told him he could make wads of cash and take as much smoke as he wanted.

Barney wasn't entirely convinced; he'd heard the stories about Bulldog from the kids on the beach. He'd heard that Bulldog had a complete set of gold teeth. He'd heard that his teeth had been knocked out, bare-knuckle fighting at a secret club underneath the railway arches. He'd heard that Bulldog had killed the man who did it — with his fists.

He saw him walk past once — a squat scary-looking man who totally matched his name. He had no neck to speak of, but what he did have was hung with thick gold chains, there was more gold on his fingers and wrists, and a light fuzz of red hair covered his head like a tennis ball. He walked with a swagger, as if he owned the beach.

Still, the promise of cash and free dope allayed Barney's fears, and he agreed to meet with the man who was to become his mentor.

The kid gave Barney a crumpled post-it note and told him to go to the address on it the next day at 2pm. Barney watched the boy skate away along the promenade and then looked down at the paper in his hand.

BEACH HUT 323

Just before 2pm the next day, Barney walked along the Hove seafront. The sun blazed in the cloudless blue and the surf-kites swooped brightly overhead. Barney's heart quickened as he counted down the numbers on the beach huts — 318, 319, 320. His eyes had been drawn to Bulldog's beach hut for some time without him realising it. It was one of the older ones, in a set of five, slightly bigger than the others and made out of brick. The doors had been re-hinged so that they opened outwards — breaking a golden rule of beach hut tenancy — they were smartly painted in a post-box red and held open by several terracotta pots of trailing white geraniums. Bulldog sat on a striped deck-chair, a mug of tea in his hand and an ugly looking pit-bull snoozing at his feet. He looked up as Barney approached, taking off his mirrored sunglasses and squinting against the light.

'You Barney?' he asked. Barney nodded. Bulldog smiled widely and leapt to his feet to shake Barney's hand. 'Sit, sit,' he said, opening up another deckchair that had been propped up against the door. He kicked the dog to one side with an expensive trainer. It snuffled off into the cool interior of the hut. 'You wanna drink? Tea — Coke?' He spoke with a soft, faintly West-Indian accent, though nothing about his physical appearance suggested he was anything other than Bulldog British.

'Yeah — Coke would be good.' Barney sat on the deckchair while Bulldog ducked into the hut and pulled a can of Coke out of a mini-fridge that sat on a shelf at the back. Frank Sinatra sang sleepily from an iPod inside. *Frank Sinatra! Like his Nan played at Sunday tea.*

'You like Sinatra?' said Bulldog.

Barney shrugged. 'Dunno — my Nan does.'

'Oh man — he's quality. You ever see *The Godfather*?'

Barney shook his head.

'It's a great film — gangstas and that. There a guy in it — a singer — Johnnie Fontane. He needs to get outta this contract and the Godfather's son explains to his girlfriend how he does it.' Bulldog's accent changed into a New York twang, perfectly impersonating Al Pacino. 'My father made him an offer he couldn't refuse. Luca Brasi held a gun to his head, and my father assured him that either his brains or his signature would be on the contract.' He held his fingers in the shape of a gun, and pressed them to his own temple, his face covered in an open grin that showed the glinting gold of his teeth. 'That singer was based on Frank Sinatra — no word of a lie. I'll give ya a copy of the film.' He jumped to his feet again and rummaged around in a box behind the beach hut door, emerging with a DVD and a couple of Sinatra CDs, 'for yer Nan'.

By the end of the afternoon Barney had agreed to work for Bulldog. He could keep 10% of whatever he made, and take all the dope he needed for personal use — within reason.

Things went brilliantly for Barney for nearly two years. He made a ton of money very quickly. The kids at school couldn't get enough of the stuff and he became very popular. Bulldog's swagger rubbed off on Barney by association — he was the cool kid in town, known to everybody who mattered. He had more girlfriends than he could keep up with. He could buy whatever he wanted, clothes, shoes, booze, music, the latest skate gear. He was very happy. Bulldog was happy. The kids in school were happy. The only people who weren't happy were Barney's parents, who didn't understand why, when they were paying such exorbitant school fees, their darling boy's grades had plummeted like a rock in the ocean. They sat him down a couple of times to talk to him but Barney just shrugged and said he'd try harder. Besides, they had their own problems, and the unlikely prospect of them both being away from work at the same time meant that such interviews were mercifully few and far between.

Barney met Bulldog once a month at the beach hut to conduct business. He looked forward to these visits. He liked Bulldog, he liked listening to him talk about films and music — classics he called them; *Scarface*, *True Romance*, *Taxi Driver*, *Point Break*. He played Barney old records on a tinny stereo at the back of the hut — his beloved Sinatra of course, but also *The Who* and *The Beach Boys*, *Love* and *The Lively Ones* and scratchy ancient reggae that filled the hut with a broken sound which made conversation unnecessary. It seemed to Barney that Bulldog was nothing like he was made out to be, he liked things you wouldn't expect him to like — flowers and herbal tea and unfashionable music. He would sit for hours outside Beach Hut 323 and listen to this fascinating man hold forth on the ways of the world.

Only once did Barney see something that made him feel uneasy. He turned up for his monthly meeting with Bulldog a half hour early. He had a sure thing with the older sister of one of his friends and he didn't want to be late. The beach hut doors were firmly shut, but the padlock wasn't closed on the outside so he assumed Bulldog was in. Barney knocked on the door, lightly at first but then, when there was no answer, more insistently.

'What?' The door snapped open and Bulldog stood there dressed only in his underwear and tattoos. 'Barney! You're a bit early. 'Am busy — fuck off for a bit an come back later.' He gestured behind him with his head. Barney looked through the door. A young black girl was sitting on the tiny bare floor space holding a towel around her. She was very beautiful with skin like chocolate ice cream and huge rum-coloured eyes. She looked younger than Barney, little more than a child, and her pretty eyes were filled with fear. Bulldog grinned and shut the door.

It unnerved Barney, threw him off a bit, seeing Bulldog, who couldn't be much younger than his stepfather, in the beach hut with a girl younger than himself. It seemed wrong, and it played on his mind as he walked up the promenade to meet his friends. After an hour of skating and drinking and smoking, he'd shoved it to the back of his mind; by the time he was in his new girlfriend's bed he'd forgotten it altogether.

After a while Barney was so permanently stoned that he started to forget things. Important things, like dates and exams and his mother's birthday. Then one day Barney forgot the price of an eighth. One of his customers came up to him at morning break, and for some reason, Barney had no idea how much to charge him so he just plucked a figure out of the narcotic mist of his brain, a figure which was about twice as much as it should have been. The kid didn't even flinch; he simply paid up without question. Barney realised his mistake by the time the kid left the common room, but when the next client came to see him Barney charged the same amount. Then Barney had an idea. What if he carried on selling at the new price and kept the difference for himself? His clients wouldn't care — it was their parents' money anyway — and Bulldog need never know. It was a win-win situation.

And it did turn out that way for about six months. During which time Barney's consumption of Bulldog's dope began to exceed what was reasonable — by a long way.

One Saturday in early March one of the kids from Barney's school, who was supposed to be studying for his mock exams, looked out of his bedroom window and decided that he should be at the beach. He hurried down the stairs and was out of the door before his parents knew he was gone — better not to have the conversation about opportunities and responsibilities again. He met up with some of his friends at the volley-ball courts, hung out on the pebbles, skated up and down a bit, and bought an ice cream from The Pump Room.

At one point in the afternoon, he felt in his pockets for his little metal tin with the Russian army insignia and realised that in his haste to leave the house, he'd left it under his mattress. He asked around a bit and was directed to another of Bulldog's boys who was dealing next to the skate park. He watched him for a bit and then approached him to buy. When the boy told him the price he said, 'Cool! Barney charges twice that!'

Bulldog walked Barney across the grass towards the Pavilion; his arm firmly around his shoulder and neck so that Barney had to stoop as he walked. His leg hurt like hell and he stumbled along, dragging it behind him. At the edge of the green, Bulldog released his grip and stood looking Barney in the face for a full minute without speaking. Time slowed to an agonising crawl. Eventually it was too much for Barney; nauseous with fear and the pain in his leg, he spoke first. He didn't recognise the voice that came from his lips, it sounded like a child's.

'Wwww-what are you going to do Bulldog?'

'How much do you think you owe me Barney?' Bulldog's voice was calm and throughout the exchange that was about to take place it never wavered.

'I'm ssorry. I just overcharged once and then it all took off I couldn't stop it.'

Bulldog stopped walking and released his hold on Barney's shoulder slightly. Barney's leg pulsed and he took in several deep breaths.

'Barney, how much do you think you owe me?'

'I I I don't know.'

Bulldog smiled. 'A lot, right?'

Barney nodded, he was crying now, snot and dirt stained his cheeks.

'So in answer to your original question Barney, I'm not gonna do anyting — you are.'

Barney shook like he had an affliction.

Bulldog let go of his shoulder and stood opposite him taking his face in his hands and holding it steady so Barney had to look into his eyes.

'Meet me at the Marina at 8 tomorrow morning — I need you to help me with sum ting.'

With that Bulldog turned and walked away. He stopped at the

edge of the park where Cassie caught up with him and clipped the lead onto her collar; he looked back at Barney, who was just beginning to breathe again. 'Barney,' he shouted. 'Don't be late!'

Barney was at the Marina by 6, just to be sure. He hadn't slept the night before; nothing had calmed him. He'd smoked until his throat was raw and his eyes were dried out and red hot. He sat on his bed twitching with anxiety as the dawn broke through his curtains and the birds began their song. Normally he'd spend hours listening to the birds, to their kaleidoscope of notes, but today he couldn't concentrate. His heart raced as the seconds replaced each other loudly on his alarm clock. He left the house quietly, just after 5, hoping to calm himself by walking to his destiny. His mother stirred and turned over in the cloaked semi-darkness of her room as the front door clicked shut.

The Marina was deserted. Barney made his way to the bench opposite the floating Chinese restaurant and tried to breathe. The walk had been hell; with each step agony vibrated through the ripped flesh of his leg. He'd dragged himself to A&E the day before, given a false name and address, and spent most of the afternoon waiting to see a doctor as his blood seeped through his trainers and pooled onto the floor under his chair. The nurse checked him out and said he needed stitches. There were 12 in the end. They tried to get him to talk — to file a complaint — but he said as little as possible, only that he'd been attacked by a dog in the park and that it had run off. They gave him painkillers and Diazepam and sent him on his way. He managed to get into his room without seeing his mum and stayed there until morning. She knocked and asked if he wanted any food but he shouted back that he was tired and just wanted to sleep. She was working anyway — always working.

The walk to the Marina normally took twenty minutes but today it had taken an hour. He'd finished the painkillers hours ago and under his dressing he could feel each stitch spiking the skin as though they'd zipped up his flesh. He hurt everywhere but most of all behind his eyes, where two boreholes wormed their way into his brain, radiating in all directions. He sat down and gripped the cold wood of the bench for support and stared at the tatty restaurant in front of him. He'd never been in it; he thought it was a weird idea, eating dinner bobbing about on a boat. He visualised prawn balls rolling about on white tablecloths while diners clicked at them with their chopsticks.

Isn't there a story about Hell being a banquet eaten with enormous unwieldy chopsticks? Of seeing or smelling delicious food but being unable to get it in your mouth?

He started to think about hell and hunger and over-long chopsticks, picturing contorted faces and straining necks as starving people tried to manoeuvre morsels into their mouths. A raven, slimy and dark, landed with a thud on the deck of the boat. It slurped something fleshy from underneath the golden dragon's nose and lifted its head, gulping its prize in a lump down its thick feathery throat. The raven didn't have chopsticks; it just did what it had to do to feed itself.

Why don't the damned just use their hands? thought Barney — then he caught sight of the two men on the dock at the other side of the Marina and trembled violently, involuntarily working his jaw from side to side so his teeth grated inside his pressed mouth.

A man with a briefcase was standing on the boardwalk looking at Bulldog who was sitting in a small fishing boat with Cassie sticking her head over the side. The thing that struck Barney about the man was how white his shirt cuffs were as they stuck out from under the dark navy pinstripe of his suit. As he spoke to Bulldog he put down the briefcase and gestured with his hands exposing an unwieldy gold watch at his left wrist. Though he couldn't see his face, Barney knew that up close it was clean-shaven and that he smelled of expensive aftershave. An aura of wealth hung around him and Barney felt a new terror in his belly. Compared to this man Bulldog was a lesser evil. He looked ridiculous next to him in his disguise of thick black overcoat and yellow baseball cap, either an unbelievably ill-conceived smokescreen or a deliberate challenge to eyewitnesses. *Do you remember seeing a man in a bright yellow baseball cap?*

Bulldog smiled and nodded like an idiot. The man in the suit took a large envelope out of his briefcase and handed it to Bulldog who stuffed it inside his coat. The man walked away and disappeared into the darkness under the arches. Throughout the whole exchange Barney never got to see his face.

Barney walked unsteadily along the boardwalk until he was level with Bulldog's boat. Bulldog looked up and a grin spread across his face.

'Come on down Barney Morgan, your time is up!' Bulldog shouted, clearly amused by the way Barney looked. Barney didn't think it was funny; his heart somersaulted as he clumped down the wooden steps to the jetty.

'Get in.'

Barney stood still and looked around to see if there were any witnesses.

'Get in! I'm not gonna throw ya overboard if that's what's on ya mind.'

Bulldog held out his hand — it was the same iron grip as in the park the day before. Once Barney was in the boat he pushed him down roughly by his shoulder.

'Sit there an' don't say any ting.'

Bulldog untied the boat and lifted the wooden plank connecting it to the jetty, dropping it heavily, missing Barney's toes by a fraction. Barney jumped in his seat and started to shiver again. Bulldog sucked air over his teeth and stepped into the tiny open cabin to flick on the engine and steer *The Mermaid* out of her berth. He spun the wooden wheel like a pirate about to take to the high seas and whistled as he went — *Wild Thing* — all he needed was a tricorn hat and a parrot. Barney huddled in the boat as they buzzed out of the harbour. He felt decidedly under-dressed in his surf shorts and sweatshirt, and wrapped his arms around his body to protect himself against the biting wind.

Once clear of the Marina, Bulldog broke full into song, theatrically projecting his voice so that it resonated above the wind. Watching Barney over his shoulder from time to time, with steely eyes and a wide golden grin, he looked crazed, dangerous, and Barney couldn't take his eyes off him.

'What you lookin' at?' he said catching Barney's stare.

Barney took the hint and forced himself to look elsewhere. Cassie sat in the puddle of water that sloshed at the bottom of the boat and licked her bum, her fat little leg raised to one side. Then she bit at the skin with her pointy front teeth, ending the life of whatever parasite had the misfortune to pick her as its home. Next to her, under the seat beside a small cardboard box, was something that looked remarkably like a gun and next to that was a green plastic petrol can. Barney felt sick; his stomach heaved and he puked up the chocolate Weetos he'd had at 4am over the side of the boat. Bulldog laughed.

They didn't see any other boats on their journey, only huge commercial ships way out in the distance. It took twenty minutes to reach their destination. They swung past the static rides on Brighton Pier. Barney looked up at them hanging above the Pier — sleeping mechanical giants waiting to be woken into roaring action and hurl screaming tourists around like rag dolls. *The Mermaid* bobbed steadily down the coastline until they were almost level with the West Pier. Bulldog stopped singing, slowed the motor and steered her underneath the edge of the soot-coloured landmark. He tethered her to one of the struts, then unfurled a rope ladder and threw it up so it caught on the outer walkway. He pulled at it to make sure it was firmly wedged then tossed the petrol can at Barney.

'Got matches?'

Barney held the can that had landed in his lap.

'Huh?'

'Got. Any. Matches?'

'Yeah.'

'Go on then — get up there.' Bulldog pointed to the ladder.

'Bulldog, what am I supposed to be doing?' he asked quietly.

'Get up the ladder, climb into the ballroom, shake the paraffin on the floor, drop a match an' come back down.'

Barney looked at Bulldog in astonishment.

'You're crazy — I can't climb up there! I can't just chuck a match on petrol, it'll explode.'

Bulldog wiped his nose on his sleeve.

'Paraffin — burns slowly. An' yes Barney you can — 'cos you owe me an' this is how you pay.'

He slapped Barney gently on the cheek and pointed up.

'You'll be able to climb in through one of the broken windows — go on, fuck off! I might still be here when you come out.'

Barney didn't see what else he could do. He stood unsteadily, hooking the small Billy-can under the thumb of his left hand. The boat veered from side to side as he reached for the ladder. It swung back and forth while he climbed, his stomach rolled as if he were a baby flying on a swing. The skin on the curve of his thumb serrated under the seam of the can as it rocked on every heave upward. When he reached the top, Barney flung his arms forward onto the outer ledge, sending the can skipping across the platform, and bent his body at the waist so his top half lay flat on the birdshit-covered wood. Then he shuffled sideways, pulling his legs over as he went. Lying with his cheek on the dirty balcony, he smelled dried salt and damp wood — the odour of decay. After a few minutes lying still like an insect clamped to a twig, listening to the birds crying overhead, Bulldog shouted up at him.

'Barney! Get on with it!'

Barney jumped, springing to his feet in fear, almost losing his footing and plunging over the edge. He grabbed the rail to steady himself, watching dust filter down from under his feet into the soupy sea below.

'THIS IS CRAZY,' he whispered and climbed over the railings. Rust particles rubbed off on his hands and clothes as he dislodged paint that hadn't been touched for thirty years. He found the paraffin and shoved it under the waistband of his shorts. He stood facing the back of the concert hall, looking for a way in. The walls were crumbling, the whitewash paint now a mixture of ochre and grey, streaked with seagull shit in various states of freshness. The ornate carvings around the windows and roof looked powdery, like old icing. Barney reached out and touched the head of one of the serpents, he expected it to rub away but it was hard and cold and it remained intact. Most of the large windows were missing, there was glass and splintered wood everywhere.

Barney's stepfather, Alastair, had taken a set of photographs inside the derelict Pier just before it was closed to the public forever, sometime between the occupation of the squatters and the birds. He remembered going to see them in an art gallery in town; he was about 11 years old. They were huge black and white pictures of birds and windows and jagged metal; Barney thought they were rubbish.

He peered through the nearest broken window. Inside, the concert hall was huge and surprisingly bright, its walls still painted in shining fondant green. The wind rushed through the open spaces with a ghostly howl, swirling dust around the circle of the dance floor. The floor itself was relatively clear with just an occasional lump of plaster that had fallen from the ceiling. It looked carpeted, a spongy Axminster in swamp green and black, dotted here and there with little white tufts that were periodically dislodged and flicked around the room by the inconstant breeze. Barney realised with disgust that the *carpet* was actually layer upon layer of bird shit and that the white tufts were feathers. It didn't smell but the thought of a carpet of shit made him retch, and he spat clear acidic fluid from his gut onto the floor where it soaked into the excrement.

The huge domed roof was bare, wood beams exposed under umbrella spokes that met at the top around a giant square skylight that cast its reflective shadow on the floor like a phantom swimming pool. A makeshift walkway ran across the middle of the room, complete with hardwood bannisters; it must have been constructed by the restoration team — to preserve the floor when the work began on it — before the birds took sole possession. The curved windows watched him from all around the room like the half-closed eyes of a sea monster.

Barney lifted one leg through the window, careful not to rest on the spikes of broken glass embedded in the pitted wood. A cloud of dust fell from the rafters as he pulled his other foot inside. Two pigeons dropped in surprise from their rooftop perch with a spectral flapping of wings, before resettling on one of the beams like a pair of lovers.

Barney could hear the thump of his heart so loudly it felt like someone else's. His wide eyes scanned the room; a shredded net curtain blew into it, its translucent fingers slowly lifting heavenward. *Miss Havisham,* thought Barney.

'I gotta be losing it — I'm remembering stuff from school.'

His whispered words echoed around the hall with the wind. He gasped.

'Chill Barney,' he said, and counted backwards from 10. He was suddenly overcome by the cold, his teeth chattering in the dampness.

He unscrewed the top of the Billy-can; it squeaked in the quiet and fell to the floor with a ping. The spicy fumes of the fuel inside pricked Barney's nostrils — he liked the smell and took it in deeply. He sighed and looked again at the room he was about to destroy; the serpents and lions stared at him from above the door frames and windows.

'Sorry,' he said, and flicked the paraffin in tear-like drops across the floor and onto the wooden walkway.

When it was all gone he pulled a book of matches out of his pocket and looked down at it.

The Pelirocco — a hotel in town — *funny, never been there, must be Alastair's.*

There were 11 matches inside, only one had been used. Barney ripped one off and struck it against the pink strip on the back — it flashed into life, the flame fizzing an inch from his fingertips. He took a deep breath and threw it on the floor — it went out instantly.

'Shit.'

He took another — this time it went out before it even hit the floor.

'Shit. Shit. Shit.'

By the sixth attempt the flint strip had worn away to white, only a few streaks of colour visible along its edge. Barney struck futilely at the card, but the pink nipple of the match was soaked in his sweat and it bent over greasily under his touch.

'Shit. Shit. Shit.'

The two pigeons flapped down from the ceiling and flew out through an empty window.

'Where ya been?' asked Bulldog as Barney neared the bottom of the ladder.

'It wouldn't light — it's too wet in there — the matches kept going out.' His voice wavered as he fought back tears.

The boat wobbled when his feet landed on it. Bulldog laughed and slapped him on the back. He bent under the seat and pulled out the gun. He straightened up and pushed something into it. Barney hunched over and folded his arms around his head. The flare whizzed past his ear, tickling the skin on his arm. It popped as it went through the floor of the Pier into the concert hall. Bulldog repeated the process again — the second flare brought down some floor boards, they hit the ironwork below before splashing into the sea.

Then it was quiet.

Barney peered around his arm. Bulldog was grinning like a kid at Christmas.

'Oh Man! Your FACE!' He slapped Barney on the back again. 'Sit down and let's get outta here.'

Barney's mind raced. Images real and imagined reeled across it — he saw the ballroom, still, haunted by the shadows of a million tourists. He saw himself destroying it, the matches lighting, the paraffin catching on the wood and the feathers. He saw himself shot by Bulldog and cast over the side of the boat into the alchemic potion of the waves below. He sat in silence as the sea spray cooled his burning cheeks, his eyes heavy with visions of his own death.

Was he free now, or did he still owe?

At the Marina they were out of the boat in seconds. Bulldog marched Barney up the steps along the boardwalk and across the road into Asda's car park. It was just after 9, there were quite a few people about now, lines of cars sidled past them. They must have looked odd; a tall trembling boy, a short solid man in a floor-length black coat, and a wet waddling pit-bull.

Bulldog stopped at the far end of the parking lot. He cupped Barney's face in his hands.

'What ya do with the can?'

Barney didn't answer but his eyes widened in terror.

'No worries — even if they find it there won't be any prints. You did good.'

'Is that it? Are we quits?'

'That's it — we're quits. I never want to see your beautiful face again.'

Barney shuddered with relief. Then Bulldog kissed him full on the lips. His mouth was cold and tasted of salt. It lasted longer than a kiss between men should but it wasn't sexual — this was a kiss of power bestowed by an emperor on his slave. When he pulled away Bulldog's face was close, his hands still held Barney's cheeks.

'Just one more ting.' Bulldog paused. 'Dead men don't speak.'

That was it — simple enough. Cassie squatted on Barney's trainers but it didn't matter, they were already wet — the golden trickle had reached them by the time Bulldog had uttered the word *speak*.

'Cassie!' said Bulldog, yanking her lead. 'Manners baby girl.'

Cassie gagged and snuffled through her nose. Bulldog winked at Barney and swaggered off into the cavernous dark of the subway.

TAXI!

Summer ended a month ago. In Britain summer ends in the first week of September — on the day schools reopen — but someone should tell the weather. The sun beats down onto the dusty road, turning the tarmac to toffee and holding petrol fumes in the air as cars slither northward to the train station.

The inside of Graham's taxi is sticky with the heat. However many cardboard pine trees he hangs from his rear view mirror, his taxi always smells of old people's clothes, that odd mingling of sweat and citrus and smoke without fire. He often wonders where the smell of smoke comes from; even he can't have a cigarette in his own cab so the stale tobacco smell is a mystery. He ponders on it a while, leans his elbow on the window, and waits for the line of cabs to edge along the concourse. It's 11:30 on Tuesday morning and business is slow. There aren't many tourists about and even when the London train arrives it only brings a handful of businessmen and the odd back-packer.

After half an hour Graham is third in line. He looks at the missed customers as they get into the taxis in front of him — a woman in a navy blue suit carrying a briefcase, black hair scraped back into a ponytail. She looks stuck up, as though she thinks she's better than everyone else. *Nice arse though*, he thinks as she bends over to speak to the cab driver. She turns and glances down the row of cabs before getting in as if she's heard his thoughts. It wouldn't surprise him if she had — *women are so bloody clever.*

Next in line is a couple with a mountain of suitcases. The white-haired woman is wearing a purple wool coat and ankle boots, *she must be expecting snow.* Her bald-headed husband helps her into the car, takes off his brown raincoat and folds it neatly, handing it to her through the open window, then he and the driver load the luggage into the boot; one, two, three, four, five, no six suitcases — £2.50 and they haven't even set off yet — *I'll probably get a student who'll do a runner.* The driver shuts the old man in next to his wife and speeds off the concourse with screeching tyres.

There is no one else in the queue so Graham turns off his engine and twiddles with the radio, the traffic report tells of delays and roadworks north, east and west, *there would probably be roadworks south as well if the council could get their machines into the sea.* A young man with a rucksack walks towards the pick-up point; he looks confused and stares at the list of fares as if it's written in a foreign language. He's tall and tanned, in his early twenties — *rich enough to be bumming around Europe instead of getting a job. Lazy bastard.* Graham had his own garage by the time he was 22. He could have fun with this one, take him the scenic route, play the dodgy taxi driver role that tourists expect. He enjoys the little game, shocking the customers so they have a story to tell over dinner. He doesn't do it with all of them, only the ones that — in his opinion — ask for it. He has this friend, Kevin, his parents grew up in Walsall but he tells his fares he's an exiled Iranian artist who can't go back because he'll be thrown in jail for his political views — the locals, especially, love that one — he's very popular, Kevin from

Walsall. Americans are Graham's favourite — *you can tell them anything.* He once told a couple from Texas that Oscar Wilde was buried under the cricket ground. 'Golly,' said the wife, 'I thought that was in Dublin.' *Everyone's at it. I can take surfer boy all around the houses; he won't have a clue where he is and with a rucksack that big he couldn't do a runner if he wanted to. It looks like he's carrying a second person around with him. Maybe he is, maybe he's smuggling his friend the dwarf around in it so they only have to buy one ticket.* He practices the patter in his head. *You got a dwarf in there mate? You're not allowed to call them dwarfs anymore are you? Might offend Snow White.*

The door to the cab slams shut.

'Hove please — take the coast road — I need to think.'

Graham looks over his shoulder but she's sitting directly behind him so he can't see her very well. His eyes move to the rear view mirror and he can see her face framed in the middle. She's young with white-blond hair hanging long and straight to her shoulders, bright blue eyes and pink lips, perfect honey-coloured skin covered with a sprinkling of freckles rather than makeup. He gives a little two-note cough. *That's more like it.*

'No problem darlin' — coast road to Hove.'

He winks at her in the mirror and starts the engine. He'll be nice to this one; she looks a bit like Ellen.

As he pulls out of the station he almost runs over a man with dark hair holding hands with a little boy. The boy looks at Graham though the front window, recognition crosses his face and a huge smile covers it. He jumps up and down waving his free hand excitedly at Graham and tugging at the man with his other hand. The man leans down to see what all the fuss is about. The child points at Graham in the taxi, David stares straight at him — their eyes hold each other for a moment — then he shakes his head and drags Adam away across the road.

***

David, Adam's real father. Ellen said he was the man who held the universe in his hands and smashed it to pieces. By chance, by the sheer fluke of needing to go to the toilet at precisely ten past eight in the morning and of being in the hallway, and so, nearest to the telephone when it rang, David brought Adam back to her. From the moment he came back into the room and passed on the news that Adam was safe, me and Ellen were over. We all hugged each other, out of relief I suppose, and I kissed Ellen on the lips but she was distant, more distant than when Adam was missing and she'd clung to my arm until it was numb.

It was three months before she dumped me but I knew it was coming from the moment they found Adam. David was around more and more. I would come home between shifts and find the three of them sitting at the kitchen table laughing and chatting. It would go quiet when I walked in, I wasn't one of the family — I was a stranger in my own home. David always left quickly, kissing Adam on the forehead and squeezing Ellen's hand, gazing into her eyes as if I wasn't even there.

She said it was because of Adam — that after everything that had happened he needed his Dad around, that David was better now, no danger to himself, or anyone else. We both knew that wasn't all, she wanted him around too. They'd talk about things I didn't understand, poetry and art and poncey films I've never seen. He looked better too; lost weight, had a haircut, always clean-shaved, new clothes. When David first came to the flat to pick up Adam I couldn't believe she'd married him; he was like a wino, dirty, smelly, never said a word. Near the end, I would catch Ellen looking at him out of the corner of her eye, the way she'd looked at me in the beginning.

He was happy too, instead of standing about like a druggie

61

when he collected Adam, he chatted away to me like I was his best buddy. He talked about cricket and football, he was funny — I have to admit I liked the bloke. One day, just before the end, I sat at the kitchen table with him while Ellen got Adam ready for his appointment with the child counsellor. I tried to warn him off, tell him that he shouldn't make out he was cured if he wasn't, that in the end it would be worse for Ellen and Adam if he cracked up again.

'But I won't Graham,' he said. He believed it too. 'I can't explain it — it's like since Adam was born I've been waiting for the worst to happen, eaten up by dread,' he said, 'not able to think about anything else. But since Adam came back it feels like the worst happened and we got through it — so now there's nothing to fear. It feels good you know — I haven't been on any meds for over six weeks.'

Then there was the crap about the ghost — some sleep-deprived vision he'd had working nights at the museum — a woman in black. I know about seeing things at night — you get it all the time driving a cab — giant rabbits, phantom cars with no drivers, I even saw a walking fish once — it's not real, just the mind playing tricks, lack of sleep, boredom, whatever. In one of his counselling sessions Adam said a woman in black had looked after him when the pervert wasn't there, that she had sung him to sleep and made him feel less afraid. Another time he drew a picture of roses. David also said his ghost was carrying roses. But the poor kid had been drugged by Watson; he was as confused as his father. He would have thought he'd seen the tooth fairy if someone told him he had. But David told Ellen a ghost watched over Adam and she fell for it.

The police said it was nonsense but she wouldn't have it, she liked the idea of a ghost nanny. We argued — I told her it was all shit and not good for Adam. She told me to mind my own *business, that Adam wasn't mine. It hurt you know — I'd been that kid's father for five years, since she first stepped into the cab. I've been thinking about it a lot — I think she blamed me. Without me she'd have kept an eye on him more that day on the beach. She never said, but she thought it was my fault, you could see it in her eyes.*

A few weeks after the ghost argument I came home and found her on her own in the flat, boxes and suitcases piled up in the hall. She tried to say it was because of Adam, that he needed stability, a normal family set-up. It made me angry and I told her to be honest — it didn't have anything to do with Adam, she was a bitch who'd strung me along until David was better. There was a lot of shouting; then she said it.

'I never wanted you. I just didn't want him and you were about as far away from him as I could get — stupid and common. Not like David at all.'

I hit her — hard — across the face. Her lip bled. I'm not proud of it; I'm not the sort of bloke who hits women. Never saw her again. She left without saying another word, didn't even look at me, collected her things when she knew I was out and posted the key through the letterbox. Five years of my life gone.

I miss the kid though; she never even let me say goodbye. He was a good kid, even after everything that happened. Adam was like a little ball of sunshine.

***

The girl in the mirror looks like Ellen. Younger obviously but her eyes are the same. He keeps sneaking a peek at her in the rear view. His mind's not really on the traffic and since seeing Adam on the crossing his heart feels as if it's trying to jump from his throat like a shout. She's very pretty — classy. If he weren't a taxi driver he'd never meet women like her, women like her and Ellen. She doesn't want to talk — he knows that because she told him she needed to think — but she sounds like Ellen and he wants to hear her voice. Maybe if he hears her voice it'll stop him shaking.

***

There are too many people about and it's too hot. Katie can't imagine walking down to the bus, let alone sitting on one all the way to her Aunt's house. All those people crowding her, staring, as if they can tell. This surfer type is too out of it to read the fares sign; if she waits for him to take the first taxi she could still be here at dinner time. She skirts behind him and gets into the back while he's still staring at the board.

'Hove please — take the coast road — I need to think.'

She hopes the driver will realise this means she doesn't want to talk. She looks at him in the mirror; he looks harmless enough, young, soft eyes. She's met some interesting people driving taxis. They get bad press.

'No problem darlin'.'

She hates young men that call her *darlin'*, it's ok if it's someone old, but anyone under forty and it sounds like they want to be on Eastenders. She supposes she can forgive a taxi driver.

He pulls the cab to a halt at the crossing near the exit. There's a little boy waving at him. He's cute, a big smile on his face, enormous brown eyes and curly hair. The man with him looks smiley too, then he looks in the cab and his face changes.

She can't see the taxi driver's face in the mirror, just the crinkle of his ear sticking out through the hair hanging over his collar.

'That kid's waving at you,' she says, 'do you know him?'

He flashes his eyes to her in the rear view. They don't look soft anymore.

'No. It's just a stupid kid.'

They snail along past the crossing and down the road to the sea. The traffic stops every few seconds, there seem to be a hundred buses on the streets, their chrome mirrors shining in the sunbeams as they stop in pairs on the road ahead.

She wanted silence but now she's in the cab, so close to the driver, she wishes he'd say something. The silence unnerves her. She realises she doesn't need to think, far from it — she needs not to think. She catches him looking at her in the mirror. *Say something.* She smiles, and he smiles back.

'Whatcha do then darlin'?'

'I'm a student.'

'Thought so — it's the outfit that gives it away, only a student would wear something like that at this time of the morning.' His eyes have smiles again. *His eyes are sort of sexy.*

She looks away from his eyes and down at herself; just before she left the house she threw on a silk rainbow-print maxi-dress, taking care to wrap a matching scarf around her neck to hide the lump.

'Do you like it?' she says. 'It's from Oxfam, but I think it's Ferreti or something. I love that about this town — you can get designer in charity shops for 10 quid.'

The cab is at a standstill at the lights and he taps a little tune out on his steering wheel and winks at her in the mirror.

Beeeeep! 'Get a move on, the lights changed an hour ago!'

He is shouting out of the window. She's surprised by the violence in his voice; an instant flick of a switch from Cheeky Chappie to Mr Angry. *I wonder if he's like this at home with his wife and kids. Pass the sauce darlin' — No! I meant the BROWN SAUCE!!!*

Katie smiles to herself. He catches it and raises his eyebrows in a question.

'So what you studying then?'

'Architecture.'

'Architecture? What do you do with that then?'

'Well, you study buildings and then you try to design your own.'

'Try! I hope you do more than that darlin' — bet it's costing your parents a fortune.'

God he's a bit familiar isn't he — we only just met. She frowns at him but he's overtaking and doesn't see.

'What's your favourite building then?' he says, returning his attention to her.

'Favourite building?' She's surprised by the question. 'No one ever asked me that before.'

'Really? No offence but if I was teaching architecture to someone that's the first thing I'd ask.'

She nods in agreement with the logic of this statement and tries to think of a building he'll know.

'In Brighton?'

'Yeah ok.'

'Well The Pavilion is the obvious choice.'

'Now I knew you were gonna say that — everybody does. I don't see it myself.'

'Don't you like it?'

'Well it's ok, brings in the tourists and that but it looks like a bloody wedding cake to me. It's a bit poncey innit? — a bit — Indian.'

Oh God, he's one of those taxi drivers.

'You think the Pavilion is poncey and Indian?'

'Not that I'm racist mind — but all that Christmas tree stuff on the outside — it doesn't really fit in England does it? Have you been inside? Looks like a strip club.'

So he's not a racist but he thinks that Indian doesn't fit in England — hasn't he heard what the nation's favourite dish is? Chicken Tikka Masala — that's what — we had a big discussion about it in class, what makes us British. Bet he eats it all the time.

She doesn't answer just chews her nail and looks out of the window at the sea shimmering at the bottom of the hill like liquid gemstones. Her fingertips move under her scarf to the lump on her neck. It's been there for nearly a month, hard under the skin. It started off small but you can see it now, a curve below her ear that shouldn't be there. She's scared, it's how her sister's started and now she's on her second set of chemo. She hasn't told anybody. She rowed with her boyfriend last night because he thinks she doesn't want him to touch her. *I'm just tired — that's all.*

She can't tell her mum; she's got enough to worry about with Diane, the endless hours at the hospital and then afterwards when everybody is so helpless. She doesn't want it to be her, the needles and chemicals and puking, losing her hair, parading about in a ridiculous wig with yellow skin, hoping no one will know.

The thing is, even if they treat it, when your time's up it's up. Look at Jade — all that money and fame but no one could save her could they? — Dead at 28.

Today she thought she'd visit her Auntie Karen — not to tell her — well maybe to tell her, or maybe just to be near to someone in the family — to someone like her mum. Katie's mind flits from one thing to another, it's been like this for weeks, she can't hold any thought for long without it being replaced by another — it's exhausting.

I hope her creepy ex isn't there, she thinks, *he's always hanging around these days. He was always really grumpy when we visited Karen when we were little; lately he's got that slimy look about him like he's mentally undressing me. Last time I stayed and he was there,*

67

I lay awake all night and left at 7 in the morning so I wouldn't have to see him, that's when there was all that weird stuff going on by the Lagoon. Two men with what looked like a body in a sheet by the overflow pipe. It was in the paper a couple of days later how they'd found the paedo in there. Shit — if Jerry's there I'm not staying.

'Are you bird-watching or what mate? Look at this joker staring at seagulls — red man darlin', means DON'T WALK!'

'You're very angry aren't you?'

'Sorry?'

'You seem like a very angry person — are you always like that or is it just today?'

'What were you studying again?'

'Architecture.'

'Thought that's what you said, but then you sounded like a shrink and I've had enough of that to last a lifetime.'

His tone is harder as if she's offended him. The next question comes out of her mouth before she can stop herself.

'You've been to a psychiatrist?'

'What me?' He points two fingers at his chest in an exasperated gesture, then his eyes move to the mirror and he softens his voice again. 'No darlin' — I just mean I've had enough of all that psychobabble mumbo jumbo — my ex she couldn't get enough of it, astrology, ghosts and all that shit.' The switch flicks again. 'C'mon, you could fit a tank through there!'

Jesus — it's like being on a rollercoaster. This guy's unhinged. There's something odd with the kid he ignored at the station. Maybe he's a paedo too. Shit. An unhinged racist paedo cabby — I always know how to pick 'em.

The West Pier stands blackly ahead of them, contrasting with the brightness of the sky and the sea, and the angel-white feathers of the birds swirling around its maze of iron.

He changes the subject, waving his hand towards the Pier, but his voice is still teetering on the edge of violence.

'Take this monstrosity — why they can't just pull the bloody thing down I'll never know — makes the place look like a rubbish tip.'

He's just crossed the line. She files people she meets into two categories — those who love the West Pier and those who don't, the latter aren't worth knowing.

'I think it's beautiful,' says Katie gazing at it, 'In fact I've changed my mind. IT is my favourite building.'

'It doesn't count — it's not a building anymore.'

Just then the lights change; a man with a tiny pink poodle on a gold lead and the tightest shorts imaginable decides to run across the road in front of the cab.

'Out of the way Dorothy!' He shouts out of the window raising his body from the seat, it's the loudest and most violent voice yet. Muscle Mary flicks him the V's and carries hurriedly on his way. Mr Angry settles himself back into the comfort of his seat. He looks in the mirror again and says, in a quiet voice that's even more unnerving than his loud one, 'That's the trouble with this town — too many tourists. I don't mean the ones that come for a week in August — I'm talking about the ones that stay. Foreigners and gays — take up too much room.'

That's it — this guy is a prize moron.

'Well I'm sure some of the gay people that live here were born here.' But he's off on a roll as if he's not really talking to her — just thinking out loud. *What next? Women? Taxes? Teachers? Students? At least the traffic's moving now, we've gone further in the last few seconds than in the last twenty minutes.*

His voice scatters on, 'not that I mind poofs either — make a lot of money out of them on Friday and Saturday nights, their money's as good as anybody's — can do what they like in their own homes, so long as they don't ram it down my throat.'

She can't help laughing at him.

'I don't think there's much danger of that,' she says.

He flashes her a look in the rear view mirror. He's not happy at having the piss taken out of him — she doesn't need a second warning.

'Stop here.'

He pulls across the inside lane in front of a line of cars, which blast him with their horns, and mounts the cycle lane, almost knocking down one cyclist and pulling another to a sharp halt. There's shouting and hand gestures. She waits, purse open.

'£8.95'

'Jesus.'

She thrusts him a tenner and he puts it into the leather bag on the passenger seat. *No change then.* She gets out without saying goodbye and slams the door. The cab pulls off before she's moved away, horns fire at it as it barges angrily into an opportunity between the cars.

Jesus, they're all the same, educated women. No idea about anything. Treat me like shit and expect me just to take it. She was just like Ellen that one, Ellen before I met her, when she was with him. We could've been a family. They'd have been happy with me, her and Adam, this thing with David won't work out — then she'll be stuck.

Katie thinks about walking the rest of the way to Hove but remembering the last time she was there, and what she saw at the Lagoon, she decides against it. She'd been a bit freaked out by it — the two men by the pipe — it looked odd. As she walked into town she'd tried to dismiss it but for some reason she hadn't been able to get it out of her mind — endless 'what ifs' had rolled over in it — various scenarios of murders and gangsters and kidnappings. She'd found a phone box and called the police — anonymously. She saw it in the paper the next day and her heart nearly stopped. The report said it had been a known paedophile and that he had a child imprisoned in a box under his bed. They even mentioned her — *a tip-off from a mystery girl the police are anxious to contact.* She never went to the police. She never told anyone what she'd seen — those two men looked scary, one with white dreads and the other almost totally covered in a big coat and yellow baseball cap. She couldn't be sure they hadn't seen her. She kept up with the story in the paper but when it all died down she forgot about it. Until today, and suddenly she can't face the Lagoon again. Even though it happened months ago — the taxi driver and his reaction to the kid at the station have made her nervous.

Katie breathes salt air into her lungs and turns to walk back into town. At the top of the next set of steps to the beach she can see a woman looking at her. She's wearing odd clothes, a full crepe skirt and a white lace collar, her hair is old fashioned too. She looks like she's going to a fancy dress funeral. People are just walking past her, no one gives her a second look, but then that's not unusual in this town — anything goes — that's what she likes about it. The woman's face is white, like it's never seen the sun. She's holding a pink rose. Suddenly a skateboarder skates right through her as if she isn't even there. It happens so quickly, a flash of tiny wheels and the swing of the boy's arms as he skates along the pavement. He doesn't think anything has happened; he's just a boy skating. He looks Katie in the face as he goes past; the way she is looking at him — her mouth open as if she's had a shock — it holds his attention and he turns his head as he moves away wondering if he knows her. When she looks back to the top of the steps the woman is gone.

She crosses the space where the woman stood. It doesn't feel any different; she half expected it to be colder. *What the hell was that — a ghost from the past? Course not — must be lack of sleep or stress or something. Didn't Mr Angry say something about a ghost?*

Her arms are trembling from her elbows down. As she walks down the steps to the beach she focuses on the dying Pier. The tide is in and the sun on the water makes it look as though the pier is floating above the sea, wholly disconnected from reality. Katie finds herself wondering what it would have been like to be alive a hundred years ago when the Pier had just been built. The turn of the century — on the edge of the future. She imagines she is there, surrounded by men and women taking the sea air in their Victorian finery, she sees the bobbing parasols and the horse-drawn coaches, a string quartet at the bandstand and children peddling swan boats around a boating lake. It would have been nice to be alive then. This future — the one that actually happened — is full of littered beaches and drunken stag parties, road rage and angry taxi drivers, stolen children and bodies in storm drains — and tiny hard lumps under the skin that have to be hidden.

At beach level she pulls out her mobile phone, 'Hi Helen — I've had the morning from hell — will you come and get drunk with me?'

She walks along the promenade in the midday sun towards the bars facing out to the blank sea.

CORNFLAKES

'Bloody cat!' I hiss. I slam the phone back on its stand. 'C'mon Izzy — we've got to go and get Tom again.'

I lift my daughter and carry her to the buggy. She realises just as I'm about to put her in. 'Na!' she shouts, thrashing her head exaggeratedly from side to side and twisting her back, 'Na! Na! Na!' She lifts her little chin as high as it will go. I force her tummy down with my knee and clip her in — she wails like a Valkyrie.

Outside we are engulfed in horizontal drops of freezing rain. My hair rises instantly in a shaggy red halo, I'm so glad I spent Izzy's nap time with the straighteners. Izzy's rain cover is ripped from the bottom of her buggy by the poltergeist wind, and thrown up and inside out over my head. I frantically pull it away from my face, and smooth it over Izzy with both hands and my upper body, securing it with wet fingers. We are not even down the path yet.

'BLOODY BLOODY CAT!'

'BAGGA GAT!' says Izzy, looking at me with narrowed eyes and a defiant mouth, 'BAGGA BAGGA GAT!'

We head against the wind towards Miller's Road. This cat is nothing but trouble — I have to rescue him daily.

So far he's been to the private school across the dual carriageway (when I collected him from there, I was ushered into the principal's office to find him curled on a leather armchair), the football stadium, two branches of Tesco and an enormous house on Dyke Road (where he was being pampered to death by a young man without a shirt. I wanted to stay there myself!)

Every phone call starts the same way. 'Hello — do you have a cat called Tom?' Each time he is a little bit farther away than the last — I don't know what he's looking for, but he's been doing it since he was three months old, so it can't just be sex. With Tom there's some primeval instinct to wander — some need to do his own thing. He's the original free spirit. This time he's about a mile away; he followed some foreign students home from the pub the night before, ate a tin of tuna and slept in their cycle-basket.

Tom blinks his amber eyes in slow motion. It's like he's not really looking at me so much as trying to hypnotise me. He sits perfectly still — front paws together like white ballet shoes, the thick grey tiger-stripe of his tail snaked around them. His left whiskers shudder and he mews plaintively. I carry on loading the dishwasher. He mews again and leaps onto the worktop, pacing a figure of eight, tail raised, lychee-bollocks in full view. He rubs his face against my neck as I bend to put a coffee mug in the rack — *Me-ow!*

I sweep my arm across the surface at his ankle level, knocking him onto the floor, 'I just fed you Tom. Out of it.'

He lands on his pink pads and makes for the door, then checks one last time, *Me-ow?* Sensing that I'm not giving in, he opens his face in a sharp-toothed yawn and noses his way out of the cat-flap, showing off the tell-tale bald patches on the inside of his back legs. Go on Tom! Make kittens while the moon shines — soon, when the vet has finished with you, you'll be half the cat you are today.

'We can't call him that!' you laughed.

'Why not? Nobody calls their cat Tom. It's classic yet knowing — postmodern.'

You raised your eyebrows in a way that made you look both patronising and childish at the same time, 'Postmodern cat-naming. How very Brighton.'

You turned to face the window and uncorked a bottle of wine with a satisfying pop.

You poured me a glass of the red stuff, then raised your glass in salute, 'Tom it is then.'

I pride myself on my cat-naming. Our first — a Persian tomcat with tangerine fuzz for fur — I called Zuma (as in catZuma) because he was the colour of autumn fruit. He arrived the day after my father's funeral, the same day I found out I was pregnant with our third child — we'd forgotten he was coming until our friend brought him to the door. He stole our hearts with clever blue eyes that were too big for his tiny face and his vicious little claws. Zuma started to sneeze after about three weeks, we took him to the vets for antibiotics regularly over the next five months — and then one day he fell down in the hall like a lump of lead, unable to move his back legs. They tried everything, but after a week his milky third eyelids were permanently closed over the summer blue, and we let the vet end his pain.

It was Valentine's Day. I sat opposite you in the candle light of our kitchen table, unable to eat my romantic dinner, and sobbed inconsolably — the loss of my father finally hitting me after months of ignoring it in favour of the new soul in my belly.

Our second cat I called Mia. Mia Cat — nervy, jumpy, wild. Grey and black stripes framing Cleopatra eyes — she pranced like a dancer. She stayed just six months. A taxi ran her over the night before Izzy's first birthday party. The driver rang us from just outside the front door, rubbing the blood off the tag on her velvet collar so he could read the number. He was a nice man — I remember he had soft eyes.

We kept her in a box in the garden shed all the next day as the house filled with friends and relatives celebrating our child's anniversary. There were few tears this time — as though the whole family accepted death as a possibility, even the children shrugged it off, content with the new DVD given in lieu of their pet. I cried — still emotional about Dad with every little mortal brush.

Over the next year I managed to kill two other cats — both trying to dodge lorries on the main road behind the house — as well as two clown fish and an angel fish, a Mcleay's stick insect, that I threw out with its sticks, and a rabbit, which was dragged from its hutch in the middle of the night and sacrificed on the lawn for the kids to see when they opened their curtains at dawn.

'It'll be a fox,' said my friend Gill, 'they're always getting our chickens. Paul tries to shoot them but he always misses. God,' she laughed watching Izzy scratch her head vigorously, 'Louise the pet terminator. It seems the only animal you can't kill is nits.'

Then came Tom. Tom with his silky white chest and his peppercorn fur. Tom is Mia's half-brother — two litters later — I was comforted by the family connection. He's more affectionate than the others — when he's home. He purrs like an engine on your lap, twists and curls and stretches, more like a lover than a pet (on those long and languid Sundays before children, when all there was to do was read the papers and lie on the sofa together.) Then he goes — and he's gone for days and all the worry of rejection and loss floods in. Will he come home? Or will this be the time he leaves forever, bored by the constraints of our little family, by the constant tail-pulling and the humiliation of his bird-alert bell. Then he comes back, and purrs again — as if he'll never leave.

'We'll have to get him done,' you said with a frown, 'it's probably why he's wandering so far — looking for girls.'

I couldn't help but laugh at you — you looked so serious.

'Maybe we could get you done at the same time.' I said, and was treated to a look of such wide-eyed horror I laughed again. 'It's not as bad as childbirth you know, you're in and out in an afternoon — sit on a bag of frozen peas for a bit and we're done.'

'We?' you said.

'Yes. *We*. You know, like when you said *we're doing fine* as I was pushing Izzy out.'

You looked incredulous, as if it had never been mentioned before, and changed the subject.

The truth is after several sexually stagnant years, when children were all that was important — the making of them, the carrying, birthing, feeding, then the making of them again — after years of this, we are actually beginning to enjoy it again. Sex for the sake of sex, rather than any other purpose. It's different, but different is good isn't it?

I don't know how we got it back. For over a year, after Izzy was born, we hardly did it at all. It felt like we'd replaced it with arguing. I seethed and shouted with resentment at being the one at home with the children, the one who was fat and tired and never allowed to do anything by myself — not even go to the bloody toilet for God's sake.

You went to work on the train and talked about grown-up things with grown-ups, went out for drinks and away on business trips to glamorous cities. I made Play-Doh ducks and folded washing. Sometimes the only adults I talked to were shopkeepers. I ate too much chocolate and drank too much wine. By the time you came home at night I was ready to fight and you were too tired not to.

Saturday mornings were the worst. The kids had football and ballet at 9am — all I wanted to do was sleep, but both of us had to be up and out catering to our children's social lives. It was always a rush — lost kits and tutus, milk to be made up and snacks packed, kids to drag away from the TV. Your brain never seemed to be in childcare mode, naturally you wanted to play with your children rather than do anything practical. Running late, with a house that looked as though it had been ransacked, I always ended up shouting at you. You tried to ignore me, but that made it worse — I felt ignored enough already. I'd up the stakes, get personal, swear at you, and then you'd break. Often we'd carry on arguing until the car reached its destination. We still had passion — it was just the wrong sort.

In a rare moment of daytime solitude I sat in the armchair with Tom curled on my lap. Above his purrs we watched Fern Brittan seemingly shrink before our eyes as she introduced a portly middle-aged couple who hadn't had sex in a year. They were told to make a video diary for a week, during which time they had to lie naked together every night and tickle each other with a long pink feather. Then they mentioned their ages, they were both younger than me.

Jesus, I thought, *I don't want to have to resort to feather sex therapy.*

When you got home that night, late and slightly pissed, I rushed at you. We did it on the stairs: fast, frenzied, fabulous.

Today we are late for school because I am standing across the road under a conker tree shaking a box of Go-Cat. Tom is stuck; he is clinging to a branch making a noise like a siren. The tree belongs to the grumpy man with the dog who can never look you in the eye. I need to get Tom down but I don't want to ring his doorbell and ask for help. Freddie and Libs think it's hilarious, and are literally rolling with laughter. Izzy points at Tom and shouts.

'BAGGA GAT. BAGGA BAGGA GAT!'

Other people on their way to school stop to help, calling his name and clicking their fingers. Very soon there's an assortment of around 10 neighbours underneath the tree, all late for wherever they were going. Eventually the chef from the café comes over with a ladder and grabs Tom by the collar. On his way down, my fluffy pet swipes with an open paw and escapes into the path of an oncoming car. The crowd gasp — but by some miracle Tom manages to weave between the tyres and bounds away like a leopard.

Last night we went to see Leonard Cohen at the Brighton Centre. We watched an old man in a trilby sing about lost loves on a stage that seemed too enormous for his shambling, age-shrunken stature. *I remember you well in the Chelsea Hotel.* In an audience markedly older than we were, I found myself crying — tears pulled from my eyes by the longing of a man on the downslide to death. *You got away didn't you babe?* I don't even like Chelsea Hotel much, it's not one of my favourites — too self-congratulatory for me, too *we're better than everybody else* — but his voice resonated with the regretful passing of his years, and my heart broke.

The woman next to me cried too, she must have been twenty years older than me, and as we smiled at each other I wondered what my life would be like in twenty years — when youth is long gone.

This morning when you reached for me, and we rolled into each other, it felt so vital. It had been so long since we tried this in the morning. I miss the mornings; having the time to stay in bed, to slumber and kiss and consume tea and toast, to make love in the 6x6 room of our bed. We bought a king-size because it was important to us, because it needed to be big enough to match the time spent in it. Then the time spent in it was less and less, these days we are lucky if it's six hours in every twenty-four. Rumour has it that Margaret Thatcher only needed four hours of sleep — but who would aspire to be like Milk Snatcher? Not me, I need at least eight. Just six hours in an enormous bed, head resting on three fluffy pillows, leaves no time to make love.

I remember coming home to this bed after having Izzy. Leaving her to sleep new-born sleep in her Auntie's arms downstairs, I sank into this cloud mattress and floated on the breeze, the freshly-laundered jasmine sheets covering my senses for a whole heavenly hour.

As I lay on top of you in the darkness of our duvet, nuzzling your neck, making you moan, I thought I heard myself years ago.

'What are you doing?' I said sweetly. I didn't understand the question so I ignored myself — then it came again, more insistent, through the goose-down walls.

'What are you doing Mummy?'

You moved me gently onto the bed with your hands on my hips and peered over the covers, 'Hello Libby.' You giggled, and I did too, burying my face in your shoulder as our daughter asked again, 'What were you doing?'

'Just playing,' you said. I laughed and showed the flush of my face over the duvet.

'You look all red Mummy.' She looked so tight-lipped and unbelieving we both giggled again.

'Did you sleep alright Libs?' you managed to ask. Then Izzy tottered in, holding her floppy white rabbit by the paw, closely followed by Freddie.

'What's going on?' he asked, still foggy with sleep.

'We must remember to shut the door at night,' you said, as if that would make any difference. I smiled as you ushered them out of the room.

'I can see your willy!' Libby sang, skipping thunderously away down the stairs.

If our daughter recalls this particular primal scene at some point in her future, I hope she at least remembers that Mummy was on top. Tom leapt onto the bed and curled his frozen *out-all-night* body into the warm gap left by you.

In Waitrose I put a family pack of cornflakes in the trolley. Izzy's face is smeared with chocolate and snot; she smiles brownly and yabbers in her own language. Behind her the green and red cockerel winks at me.

I remember a packet of cornflakes we bought together years ago with scraped-together grant money, because it was cheap and would last us all week. I remember when we were back in your house, me pulling open the box with purple-lacquered fingernails, then ripping at the bag inside — it wouldn't open so you bit it and tore it with your teeth. We poured ourselves two enormous bowlfuls, splashing on shining white milk, and sprinkling lumpy Silver Spoon over the top. We carried them upstairs to your room and ate them sitting on the mattress on the floor that served as your bed. The orange flakes crunched with freshness, sugar crystals grinding against tooth enamel, spoons clattering on the mismatched bowls — then there was milk on the sheets, and our feast was discarded in favour of a more important need.

In the dairy aisle at Waitrose I want you suddenly. I feel your hands on my breasts, your tongue entwined in mine, my legs wrap around your thighs. No one notices — they are more interested in the ginger-haired soap star pushing her trolley round the aisles. We move against the fridges, swaying with kisses, purposeful in our longing, students again, with all the abandon of youth. The orange juice cartons wobble on the shelves as you lower me to the floor, your fingers move into my jeans, I…

Oh!

The milk carton I've been holding slips from my fingers, heavy as lead and lubricated with condensation. It falls slowly to the floor and bounces off the metal rim of the fridge, splintering like a splatter-movie victim, milk pours from the wound onto the shiny grey lino.

'Uh-oh!' says Izzy, clapping her hands in delight. I step back from the milky pool, whiteness soaks into the dark blue suede of my boots. I start to giggle, quietly at first, but then with less control. Two men in grey overalls, one young, one old, rush over to the crime scene — falling to their knees and dabbing at my mess with wads of blue tissue paper.

I can't stop laughing. I stand over them giggling like a teenage chav. The old one looks annoyed and breathes heavily through his nose, keeping his eyes on floor. The younger one, tanned with bleached surfer's curls escaping from under his hat, looks up and smirks along with me. His badge reads NED — it's a good name for a surfer.

'You shouldn't be here Ned,' I say to him, 'You should be out on the waves.'

His eyes widen and he looks away. I laugh even more. People are looking now. I wish I had a white hoody, like the wispy girl browsing the magazine stand. I would pull the toggles tightly, hide my face in the snowy frame of the hood, and carry on giggling — all the way back to my youth.

Across town Tom wakes in the afternoon sun. He opens his eyes wide — ancient eyes that tell of the limits of evolution. He stretches, first his front paws then his back ones, a little shiver runs up his tail. He yawns and wonders if he should go outside. He thinks better of it, walks around the cushion a few times and then settles back down — to dream of the days when he roamed freely around the world and stayed out all night.

ROSES AND BIRDSONG

The viciousness of the attack stunned her as much as the physicality of it. She'd known she was in trouble the moment she opened the door to him. Finley Barker was wound like a spring when he pushed past her into the hall, glaring at her wordlessly, wild eyes reddened with fury. May closed the door softly and followed him into the living room. He was standing near the kitchen door, eyes darting around the room, as if he expected to suddenly discover their hiding place — his unfaithful wife and May's unfaithful husband. He opened and closed the fingers of his right hand repeatedly making a fist — May noticed the marks left by his fingernails in the flesh of his palm as he did so. Tiny beads of sweat collected on his pencil-thin moustache He couldn't look her in the eye. May wondered what she could do to appease him — after all they were both victims in this sorry little situation. She plumped for the British solution to everything, 'I'll make you a cup of tea.'

She edged around him through the beaded curtain into the kitchen. She took her time about making the tea, hoping he would be less volatile when she returned — she spooned the leaves from the caddy, letting the kettle boil on as it whistled shrilly, then poured the scalding water into the pot and stirred it. She heard the clock strike two and Finley Barker cough dryly in the other room. May realised that she'd have to face him, to go over her heartbreak with him so that he could go over his. She poured the tea into two mugs, added milk and sugar, stirred, and tapped the spoon against the china. He was pacing as she came back into the room. He took one of the steaming mugs of tea without looking at her and gulped at it — it must have burned his mouth because he let out a roar and threw the rest of it at her. She flinched as the blistering liquid soaked through the sleeve of her jumper onto her left arm — then her right forearm snapped as Finley Barker was upon her, jerking her down to the floor, smashing her body and head with kicks and punches. May tried to shield herself, to curl herself up like a baby, protecting her unborn child by pulling her knees to her chin, but Barker kicked her six times in the back, each one a little harder than the last, and instinct forced her to unfurl — to stop him damaging her spine. She lay supine on the carpet and for a moment he stood unmoving above her. She blinked up at him — he had transformed into another kind of being, a thing of rage and primordial evil, his face twisted with malevolence, the face of vengeance and distilled hatred.

In those seconds of silence — as she witnessed Finley Barker's true self — May decided not to fight it, to let herself go limp. Barker held his clenched fist high above his head — it was covered in blood, May's mingled with his own. As it hovered, opalescent drops like red tears dripped down from it — for a moment they were the only movement in a room quiet with an electric stillness. Then the drops of blood landed on May's geranium-patterned skirt, and Finley Barker's fist came down. Everything after this was darkness.

May woke in a greenish half-light. She was cold, her fingers and toes iced and numb — for the first moments of emerging consciousness it was the only thing she was aware of. Then came the pain. Every part of her ached — pins and needles — on the verge of an excruciating cramp throughout her body. She tried to move her head but a sharp spasm ripped across her scalp, blinding her with an intense light. She lay still again — aware of a cold dampness in her hair and on her neck, she realised her skirt was soaked with it underneath her body. As slowly as she could she lifted her left hand, index finger first, letting it draw up the rest of her arm from the elbow — again she felt agony so intense that she all but blacked out, and dropped her hand back down to the carpet. Black ghosts clouded her vision — she saw roses, vivid red roses, with perfect drops of dew in the crevices of their petals, and tarmac-black thorns on brittle stalks. May blinked — a tear dropped from her right eye, salt sending a grazing sting to her cheek.

Lying there, coherence beginning to claw its way back, May tried to work out if the imperfect light in the room was cast by the rising or setting sun. Her brain flickered into reason — if the light was coming from the setting sun she had only been out for a few hours, if, as she was beginning to suspect, it was dawn, she had been unconscious for the whole night — around sixteen hours.

She couldn't shake the roses from her mind. Tea roses — but tea roses aren't red, tea roses are pink, like the ones in her wedding bouquet. Their fragrance had been musky sweet, and their shiny petals had matched the embroidered silk circles on her gown. The smell of tea moved into May's consciousness, spilled tea, cold tea, a smell like no other — cold wet tea on damp wool. She remembered him throwing the tea at her, and wondered if it would have had time to chill so deeply after a couple of hours. Another smell came to her bloodied nostrils, a metallic smell — it reminded her of marmite — the red and white label flashed, too vividly, across her mind. Red and white and black — thick black sticky goo. May was suddenly aware of her blood loss. Her stillness was helping her mind to clear (if I have been unconscious for sixteen hours I will need to get help, or I will bleed to death). She looked towards the window without moving her head, just the ball of her left eye — the only one still open, her right eye was sealed shut, smothered by a bulbous eyelid — even this small movement causing pain to rip around the eye socket and cheekbone. She lay there, listening to her wheezing breath, trying to figure out if she really needed to put herself through the trauma of moving or if she could sleep, just a little longer, to ease the pain. Then she heard it — a sound so clear and beautiful she thought she'd imagined it — a single constant note, high-pitched, otherworldly. Others followed it, a melodious warble, a flickering scale of perfect chirps and whistles, building note for note into a crescendo of harmonious non-human voices. The dawn chorus.

May had never heard anything so shatteringly beautiful — she'd listened to it the day before, sitting at the table in the chill, brought downstairs by a bad dream, Jack's blue-white envelope unopened in front of her. She'd listened to it but she hadn't heard it. Twenty-four hours later, knowing she was lucky to be hearing it again, she was lifted into action by the birdsong. The notes acted as a mattress for her body, she imagined herself carried on them across the room like Snow White in her sleeping death. In reality she pulled herself across the carpet, using mainly her left arm and her buttocks for leverage. Every roach-like drag was agony; she had to rest for a moment between each halting lurch to refill her lungs with painful breaths — the clock ticked loudly, reminding her of every second lost. The scratchiness of the carpet on the underside of her legs was eventually replaced with the cold smooth wood of the hall's parquet floor. It was easier on the wood — she moved more fluidly — though she quickly realised with panic that this was because her blood was creating a slide to ease her way. She found the front door with the top of her head, pain prickling her matted hair as it rested on the draught excluder — from this position she heard another whistle above those of the birds. May's eyes searched for something to make a noise with — she felt to the side with her left hand, and found the brass owl doorstop her mother had given to her one Christmas. May grabbed at it and managed to bash it against the door, just as the milkman clinked down two bottles of gold top. His whistling ceased.

'Help,' breathed May. Then, with all that was left of her disappearing strength, she smashed the owl against the door a second time.

'HELP!'

May's injuries were horrific. The ambulance sirened its way through the hushed, pre-rush-hour streets to the County Hospital. There, May was rattled along hollow corridors, looking at the blindingly bright strip lights above — until she came to a halt, and was given oblivion in the scratch of a needle.

They kept her heavily sedated for two days. The weeping roses bloomed behind the curtain of her swollen eyelids — roses so deeply red as to be almost purple, petal upon petal furled into gigantic pom-pom heads, scent-heavy and bent over by their own weight. The petals fell to the disinfected floor, until all that was left were thorny black stems bearing dried tracing-paper leaves.

'May? May?'

A slight slap on the back of her hand, and a rub on her arm.

'May? I need you to wake up now.'

A sound came from her first — a dry nasal rasp — made by a throat so devoid of moisture it was as though it had been sealed entirely. May felt the cup pressed to her lips, and sucked in water, coughing as it struggled down her throat. She tried to open her eyes — it was difficult, the lashes were glued bottom to top. The instinct to rub them with her fingertips was thwarted by her arms being tightly tucked down, under starch-heavy sheets. She prised her eyelids apart, blinking sorely in the light, and focussed on the serene face watching her from under a white lace nurse's cap. The face smiled, and spoke in an Irish lilt that reminded May of her mother.

'That's it May. Have some more, slowly now, slowly. Now just lie back and get your bearings, try to stay calm. I'm Nurse O'Reilly. I'll stay here with you.'

May turned her head to look at her surroundings and winced with pain — it took a moment for her vision to clear. The drapes, blue and white striped, were drawn fully around the bed. There was a dusty angle poise lamp and a plastic jug of water on the bedside table, and a vase containing half a dozen long-stem roses stood between them — fleshy pink petals beginning to turn brown, several already tumbled and curling on the table top. May frowned.

'Who are the flowers from?'

'One of the other patients got a big bouquet and thought you might like to see them when you woke up. That was a nice gesture now wasn't it?'

'Peachy.'

The young nurse ignored the bitterness in May's voice and carried on talking in her brisk upbeat manner.

'Now May, do you think you're ready to try sitting up. We

need to get your lungs working properly. You've still the pain relief so it shouldn't hurt too much.'

It hurt like hell. It took two nurses to pull and heave her up against a stack of pillows, until she was half-sitting, her back uncomfortably taut against the strapping that had been wound, round and around, beneath her borrowed hospital nightdress. One arm was in plaster from just above the elbow, and the other housed a drip, wadded to her skin with a lump of cotton wool and sticking plaster — whatever it was feeding her, it barely touched the pain that tingled in her legs and ribs and stabbed brutally at her groin and stomach.

'Now, said Nurse O'Reilly, 'how about a nice cup of sweet tea?'

They didn't tell her about the baby for another two days. May knew already. She'd known when she'd woken, battered and bloodied, on the freezing living-room floor. She'd known when most of the doctors and nurses avoided her eyes, and when sweet Nurse O'Reilly gently soaped the dried blood and iodine from the wound on her empty swollen belly. She'd known because of the pain under the dressing, the fresh stab of a knife twisting, this way, then that, whenever she lay flat — worse than this had been the little hollow it cut into — no longer brimming with new life, it was now a nothing-cup filled with blood.

A female doctor came and told her, while Nurse O'Reilly — Glenda — sat and held her hand. (They'd tried their best, but in the end there was nothing they could do...) May couldn't even cry anymore, her body had rejected tears to spare her the salt sting that followed them onto the raw flesh of her cheeks. She became suddenly fearful of what might have happened after she'd blacked out.

'Doctor, did he...'

She couldn't bring herself to ask directly.

'No,' said the doctor, 'there's no evidence to suggest he did that.'

May lay back on the pillow and closed her eyes, hoping to shut it all out. She cursed them all — Jack and Lily for their duplicity and betrayal. She cursed herself, for being so bound up in her own happiness she didn't see Jack's unhappiness. She cursed herself again, for not telling him about the baby sooner — for wanting to wait for the perfect moment that never came. (*Would it have made a difference? Would it have made him stay?*) The person she cursed most of all was Finley Barker. May cursed the day he was born, and the day Jack met him and his stupid, pouting, feather-headed wife. One thought replaced all others in her head, revolving round and around in that first week of recovery, repeated ad nauseam, so that at those times between sleep and wakefulness, she wasn't sure if she was saying it out loud or not.

I wish Finley Barker was dead.
I wish Finley Barker was dead.
I wish Finley Barker was dead.

A week after May was found, two policemen came to visit her. She had given a brief statement, to a sympathetic WPC, as soon as she'd been able. These two were different. They arrived on the ward with authoritative steps — it was the sound of their feet that caught May's attention. She saw them stop at the nurse's station, and then look towards her as the duty nurse pointed the way. They walked slowly down the ward — one smiling, one grim-faced, both dressed in dark suits and raincoats, shoes shining blackly on the sunlit lino. The older one had kind eyes and greying hair growing in tufts around his ears. He spoke softly, and put his trilby down on the counterpane so he could take her hand as he sat on the edge of the bed.

'Good afternoon May. I'm Inspector Finch, and this is Sergeant Watson.'

The younger man stood at the foot of the bed, hands resting on its bottom rail. He wore black-rimmed spectacles, had short red hair and a pencil moustache like Finley Barker's — he looked harsh, lips thin, pale eyes narrowed. May didn't like him but it was into his eyes she looked as Finch told her the news.

Finley Barker had been found dead under the Palace Pier. He'd been missing since he'd attacked her, and it appeared he had taken his own life.

'How?' asked May.

Finch sighed and looked at the floor.

'He shot himself with an old German pistol,' said Watson, his voice as hard as his face, clipped and nasal — almost a bark.

'In the head?' asked May.

Watson nodded and mimed the action — sticking two fingers up to the roof of his mouth and jerking his head back as he pulled the imaginary trigger. Finch glared at him and clicked his tongue.

'He was in Germany at the end of the war,' said May. 'When did he do it?'

'We're not sure,' said Finch.

Watson was more forthcoming.

'Must have been a couple of days ago at least, judging by the clotting of the blood and the stiffness of the body. He was found slumped against one of the middle pillars, about a hundred yards down the beach. The tide had covered his legs to the knees with silt and seaweed, and one of his shoes was missing.'

Finch glared at Watson again and patted May's hand. She looked at his hangdog face.

'Who found him?'

'A man walking his dog. We don't suspect anyone else was

involved in the death.'

'We did try to find your husband,' said Watson, 'to see if he could shed some light on the matter. But he took the night ferry to Calais last Thursday with Mr Barker's wife, so he couldn't have been involved. They seem to have disappeared after arriving in France. They could be anywhere by now.'

May pictured Jack and Lily sitting by an aquamarine swimming pool in the sun, drinking cocktails with little paper umbrellas in them — laughing.

Watson continued.

'As Mr Barker's wife is his next of kin, we need to locate her and inform her of his death — I don't suppose you have any idea where they might have gone?'

'No.'

'Are you sure?'

'Yes.'

'We read your husband's letter — and Mrs Barker's. There's no mention of a destination.'

Don't try to find us, the letter had read. *You won't be able to, so there's no point trying.*

'It does appear that your husband and Mrs Barker were intent on starting a new life together. They may be in touch regarding a divorce, or they may try to get married without one. That's bigamy, so we'd probably find a record of them if that was the case.'

Finch looked angrily at his subordinate in rank.

'Watson! Really.' He turned back to May.

'Unfortunately,' he said, still patting her hand, 'as Barker's dead, the case is pretty much closed. There's not really anything else we can do.' His eyes were blue — the kind you would like a father to have.

'I understand,' said May.

Finch let go of her hand and stood to leave.

She turned to the foot of the bed, to see Watson follow the form of Nurse O'Reilly with his eyes as she carried a covered bedpan along the ward.

'Mr Watson?'

'Mmm?' He frowned and looked May in the face.

'Barker. Did he suffer?'

Watson's eyes and lips narrowed.

'No Ma'am. Death would have been instant.'

'Then he's won hasn't he?'

'He's dead,' said Finch. 'I'm not sure I would call that winning.'

May fiddled with the tiny silver crucifix on a chain around her neck and then closed her fingers over it, hiding it in her palm.

'Yes he's dead. But on his own terms — he's denied me any involvement in his punishment, hasn't he? He's taken everything from me — even that.'

Finch stared at her.

'I'm sorry,' he said, and May could tell from his voice that he really was. But it didn't help her one little bit.

May was suddenly tired. She turned her face to the wall and closed her eyes. She heard the two men move back from the bed.

'Poor cow,' muttered Watson when he was only a few paces away.

'Shut up Watson,' said Finch through gritted teeth.

After another two weeks May left the clinical safety of the hospital, on two crutches, with an enormous brown paper bag filled to the top with boxes of pills. Never having had a single visitor, save for the two policemen, the nurses asked her if they

94

could call anyone to take her home. May told them there was no one. She realised as she was saying it that it was the truth — she was totally alone. There was no one.

Her father had died when she was tiny; her mother never remarried and so May had no siblings. She'd been happy with this as a child, as the only recipient of all her mother's love, but then, as an adult, it fell to May to care for her mother through a long terminal illness and she'd longed for a sister to share the burden.

May met Jack a month after her mother's funeral. She was leaving the solicitor's office near the train station after the reading of the will, still dressed in mourners' black despite the heat of the August sun — Jack had literally run into her. He was late for his shift at the station, driving a train full of day-trippers from Brighton to London and back again — the force of him knocking May off her feet had broken the heel of her shoe. Later Jack would say that it was actually he who had been knocked off his feet — by her pale, sad beauty. He didn't turn up for work that day — instead he took May to a café and bought her a cup of tea, then took her broken shoe to the cobbler's. When he returned, he'd knelt at her feet, and lightly held her ankle in his hand as he eased her bare foot into the newly mended shoe. They were married within six months. Jack became May's life.

She stood on the doorstep of the house on Argyll Street, an ordinary red-brick terrace with a black and white mosaic path. This was her house — it was the only thing she had left. She had lived in it all her life, first with her parents, then just her mother — then with Jack. It was her home, the one place in the world she should feel safe. But as the taxi pulled away down the tree-lined street, May couldn't quite bring herself to turn the key she'd just slotted into the lock. She stood propped on her crutches, suspended between outdoors and in, afraid to go any further. Since Finley Barker had come to call, the month had changed from September to October — there was a distinctly colder edge to the air that the orange afternoon sun couldn't quite banish. The house looked the same as it had three weeks ago — from the outside at least — white lace curtains barred the windows, reflecting the glowing sky on the glass. May looked at her hand as it held the key. Her fingers trembled, but the grazes and bruises were almost healed, their vivid brightness replaced by the browns and yellows of autumn. She turned the key and gave the door a little shove with the mound of her hand. It didn't budge so she pushed again, harder, and the door swung open propelling her painfully forward into the hall. She steadied herself by leaning her shoulder against the door, then taking a deep breath, carried on through into the living room.

May walked into a cathedral silence — broken only by the steady ticking of the clock on the fireplace. The October chill had seeped in through the walls, its moisture permeating the air, curtains and carpet giving off that pre-damp smell — amazing how just three weeks without people can bring a home to the brink of mortality. To her relief the room looked as it had before Finley Barker's visit; one of the neighbours must have come in and cleaned up when the police had finished their work. She didn't know who it was but this small act of kindness moved her immensely. She hobbled over to the armchair, dislodging fine dust on every surface she touched. She lowered herself into the chair. It had been Jack's chair — he'd filled it with his bulk when he came home from his shift on the trains, kicking off his great black boots one at a time, onto the floor, and stretching out his long overall-covered legs, watching her as she busied herself making him tea. When she brought it to him he would grab her waist and swing her, laughing, over the chair arm and onto his knee for the first kiss of the evening. It was her chair now — Jack didn't want it anymore.

May watched the room grow dark — shadows climbing upward along the walls as the hours passed, like fingers of loneliness reaching out to her. At dusk she made her way slowly upstairs, leaving one crutch hooked around the bottom banister. In her room she lay down on top of the shiny bedspread that covered the double bed, her coat still buttoned to the neck. She slept.

She woke early the next morning and went downstairs in the blue darkness. The kitchen was cold; an early frost brought icy tentacles to the edges of the window. As she stood at the sink filling the kettle, May noticed the brightening glow of dawn over the garden wall and then heard the shrill melodies of the birds. A robin stood on the yard gate, tail raised, head cocked, bright black eyes gleaming, singing its welcome to the rising sun.

May turned from him and sat down at the kitchen table. She picked up the biscuit barrel, it was blue and gold with a hand-painted picture of the royal wedding — Jack had bought it for her when they were on their honeymoon, three days and nights in Hastings. She pulled open the lid with her grazed fingers and peered inside. There were a few biscuits at the bottom — Coffee Morning — Lily had brought them round the last time she came to visit. They'd listened to Buddy Holly and done each other's hair, dunked the biscuits in hot sweet coffee, coating them in milk skin. They'd flicked through movie magazines and gossiped about the barmaid at the Crown and her affair with the man from the Pru.

May put her hand into the barrel and crumbed the soft biscuits into pieces, then she opened the back door and threw their remains out into the yard. The birds sang.

A FIELD OF MUD

'Mummy! Mummy! We saw Graham — he was in his taxi! Wasn't he Daddy?'

I look at David to see if he's ok, he's looking at me to see if I am. Our eyes are wide, he nods solemnly.

'Did you speak to him?'

'No, he was in the taxi at the train station, we crossed the road in front of him. He saw us but that was all.'

Adam has opened the fridge and is looking for a snack.

'Can I have a Club?' He looks at David. 'Why didn't we speak to him Daddy?'

Do you believe in love at first sight? I do. It's happened to me twice — once it was me who fell in love and the second time it was someone who fell in love with me. Both times it changed my life; I'm not sure if either time it was for the better but it moved things on. Isn't that what life is?

David.
I fell in love with David in a field of mud.

My father is a professor of Earth Sciences at Oxford University; my mother was an adulterer. She left us when I was

13 for one of my father's colleagues. She didn't even say goodbye. One Friday she packed me off to school as usual with an argument about lip gloss and skirt length.

'Just go, will you,' she said and then closed the door on me. She wasn't there when I got home. The house was silent and I remember it being excessively tidy, polished within an inch of its life, every surface gleaming in the afternoon light. She never came back.

I became the one who cleaned. There was no one else to look after my father and he needed terribly to be looked after. His mind was in the world of the past and there was no room in it for the practicalities of life. I didn't mind doing it; he was like a sad old teddy bear, the stuffing knocked out of him by my mother's betrayal. I looked after him for eight years before I met David. I met David because I was looking after him and then David became the one I looked after.

I was a rebellious teenager, though there wasn't anything to rebel against as far as Daddy was concerned, he pretty much let me do what I wanted. I rebelled against her in her absence, drugs, drink, piercings, a tattoo and boys, lots of boys. I was the village bike. I don't think Daddy even noticed; I was like a dutiful housewife at home, though sometimes I stayed out all night. Daddy never mentioned it. The rest of the village noticed, especially the mothers — especially the mothers of sons. One day as I was leaving the local Post Office I heard a woman say, 'Just like her mother.'

By the time I was 18 I was burned out on the teen rebellion. I didn't know what to do with myself. I'd done well in my exams but I didn't want to go on to study anymore. I didn't want to be like her — too clever for anyone's good - so I took a job at the University library, Daddy put in a good word for me. I stamped books and drafted fine letters and spent hours shelving, replacing the lyrical poets at P269 or Goethe at G2089. I read a lot of them too, just for the hell of it. Daddy was more concerned with old bones than dead poets but he was happy that his daughter was educating herself.

I first saw David in the library; he says he doesn't remember it. I watched him from my place behind the desk, he was trying to photocopy something and he couldn't work the machine, the paper either jammed or too many copies came out. He had his back to me, he was tall but he stooped over the copier tapping the buttons like they were on a typewriter. He stopped and straightened up, running his hand through his hair — soft brown curls interleaved with long delicate fingers. He sighed and tapped the buttons again, the machine whirred and the paper jammed. He growled at it, a marvellously basic sound, and then gave it a swift kick with his boot. I went over and cleared the paper-feeder without speaking to him. He stood to one side muttering to himself. When I'd finished and folded the mangled paper I looked up into his face. 'Thank you,' he said but he was looking at me without seeing. I saw him, and I found the love of my life in the hazelnut colour of a pair of impatient and indifferent eyes.

I thought he might be one of Daddy's students from the books he was copying, yellowing pages with pictures of the Dorset cliffs and fossil finds. I asked Daddy about him at dinner, doing my best to describe him without sounding too keen. He looked at me with a wry expression.

'You mean David,' he said, pouring me a glass of wine, 'quiet, but unbelievably clever. Why the interest?'

'No reason, he was rather rude in the library today — kicked one of the photocopiers.'

'Really? Seems very gentle to me — it must have been the photocopier's fault.'

I looked for him everyday after that but he never came back. A few weeks later Daddy went on the annual dig in Dorset. I knew David would be there; it took me a week to pluck up the courage to ring Daddy and ask if I could join them for a few days. I booked the time off work and spent hours packing — just the right sort of casual for digging up bones, with a touch of glamour.

He wasn't with the others when I first got there; he'd wandered off on his own looking for something unfindable in the mud. I'd scanned the assembled nerds and been bitterly disappointed — maybe I was wrong, maybe he hadn't come on the trip after all. Then he was there, striding across the mud to the beach, like Mr Darcy with the dawn, and I felt the warmth of him spread across my face in a smile. His eyes flashed over me, and then he looked away.

This was the pattern of the next few days. I spent most of the time looking at him and once in a while he'd look at me and then he'd frown and look away. *He hates me*, I thought, and pined at night in my bunk bed — an ugly girl with greasy hair snoring underneath me — when it should have been him underneath me, or on top, or any way he wanted.

Then came the last night of the trip with its dull social evening — the now-or-never moment. He avoided my gaze all night, brooding in a corner, holding a plastic cup of beer in his beautiful hands. I stared at the white of his fingernails and the dirt trapped underneath, and tried to make small talk with the drunken scientists without thinking of those fingers touching my bare skin. The plastic-tasting gin and tonic I swigged for courage had dried in my mouth, so I wove my way toward where he was sitting, but he picked up a packet of cigarettes from the table-top and headed for the door.

'Lend me a cigarette,' I said to one of the students.

'You don't smoke,' he said.

'I do now.'

He smiled and handed me one from his pack.

'He's a lucky bastard,' he shouted after me as I went through the door.

The night air was cool as I stepped into it, but my face flushed when David looked at me and threw his half-smoked cigarette to the floor with a sigh. He hates me, I thought again.

'Do you have a light?'

He looked me in the eyes as I drew the flame from the lighter and I knew when he did that he felt the same way. The light reflected between us seemed to be more than had flared from the tiny flame, and his pupils shrank in the glow, then widened in the dark. I cupped my hand over his to light my cigarette and held it there for a while when it was lit. He was so beautiful — to actually be touching his hand filled me with hope.

I remember every detail of that night. I can see it all, smell it, feel it on my skin. We talked for hours in the chilled air, the skin on my arms tingling in the breeze. He was shy at first, barely answering my questions but then he loosened up, began to offer information before he was asked. We shared his cigarettes, the feel of his lips still on the filter as I took it in my mouth. The stars were bright in the sky and he knew all their names. He stood behind me to point out The Plough and Taurus, and the feel of his body separated by a hair's breadth from my own made it hard for me to breathe. I turned my face to his and kissed the side of his mouth, then moved round to face him and kissed his lips. Our first kiss — I floated with the stars above our heads, no longer with my feet on the ground.

David.

We walked in the moonlight across the fields of half-grown wheat and stopped under an oak tree. The world was grey, desaturated by a silver light that made touch the most vivid of the five senses. I remember the wind through the leaves as we made love on a mattress of spongy grass. He told me he'd not had many lovers, that there hadn't been anyone for over a year. It had been that long for me too, rebellion against my mother had run its course and I'd decided long before to do what she couldn't and keep my knickers on. He was so full of longing, but he was slow and tender till the end, when he gave into his passion. His intensity made me realise I'd never really been intimate with anyone before, and that despite all the others, David was the first.

We walked back over the silent fields to the sleeping youth hostel and found an empty room, curling naked on the bare single mattress of a bottom bunk. At dawn he reached for me again and in the stark white daylight I knew I would be his forever.

David went mad. Literally, heart-breakingly mad. Our first night together produced a child, a boy called Adam. When you're young you don't think you can get pregnant from one night, and by the time I realised, we'd slept in each other's arms for six weeks. It felt right to me. He kissed me when I told him.

'I can get rid of it if you don't feel right about it. It's you I want, not a baby.'

'Marry me.'

'What?'

'I love you — marry me. We can be a family.'

David couldn't cope with creation. He crumbled, like the bones he worked on, from the moment Adam was born. I lost him when I gained our child. Adam was premature and it was a close thing for a while. When he pulled through and started his little life out of hospital, David cracked like an egg.

At first he simply stopped speaking. I mean he'd grunt the odd word in response to a direct question, but he sat silently over dinner and in front of the television. Then he lost the power of touch, he refused to pick up Adam or hold my hand. The delicious sensation of his skin on mine became nothing but a memory.

I thought it was me; that despite what he'd said I'd trapped him and he didn't really want a wife and baby so now he was pretending we didn't exist. Then there were the nights I'd find him crying, curled up on the living room floor sobbing, unable to say what was wrong, pulling away from my embrace and locking himself in the bathroom. On those nights I was sure he'd kill himself, throw back paracetamol behind the locked door and wait until it was too late to be saved. I'd bang on the door in a frenzy but he'd just tell me to go away. It was practically the only thing he said for a year.

'Go away!'

I booked him appointments with the doctor but he never went.

He really went crazy just before Adam's first birthday. He was working at The Natural History Museum in London and instead of preserving the bones entrusted to him one day he took a hammer to them and smashed them to dust. They called me at home to tell me he'd been taken into hospital. They wanted my help to commit him — it was either that or a charge of criminal damage.

He was away for a year but when he came back he still wasn't there. David had gone — there was someone else in his place, a functioning human being, but not David. Not the David who had walked with me tenderly in the moonlight.

We tried to start over, moved to the coast, Daddy calling in a favour to get him a job at a local museum. I stuck it out for a year. I couldn't stand it any longer — I just wanted him to touch me but he couldn't even look at me. Every day was a repetition of the moment we met. One morning as he left for work I leant in to kiss him on the cheek and he pushed me away. Those hands I loved so much pushed me away.

When he'd gone I packed a suitcase and a bag of toys and called a cab. The taxi-driver helped me with my luggage — his name was Graham.

I didn't love Graham. He loved me.

I sat in the back of Graham's cab with Adam sleeping on my knee, unable to stop the tears.

'Where to darlin'?'

'I don't know yet — a hotel, I suppose, a cheap hotel.'

He drove.

'Are you leaving him?' he asked.

I told him everything as he drove, and then he stopped in a parking space on the seafront and listened some more as the waves rushed against the stones. When there was nothing else to say we looked at each other in the rear view mirror.

'It's not your fault,' he said. 'Sometimes people just can't take it. My Dad was the same — killed himself, when I was little.'

It was the first time anyone had said it wasn't my fault.

He took us to lunch. He was nice. He was talking — he even touched my hand.

Graham visited us every day at the hotel for a week and then on the seventh day he offered me his spare room — no strings, I'd be his lodger, he didn't expect anything more.

I couldn't see David, it was cruel I know but I simply couldn't do it. Seeing David would have killed me. That's why I didn't go back to Daddy; I didn't want David to find us. He didn't want us anyway; he made little attempt to track us down. He wrote one letter to Daddy asking to see Adam but that was it. I said I'd think about it.

Things were starting to get better; I got a part-time job in a tea room when Adam was at nursery so I could at least pay Graham some rent. He was good with Adam; he really played with him, lying on the floor for hours building Lego towns and train sets, reading to him. He was like a real father.

He was a perfect gentleman too, never once made a move on me, although I knew he wanted to. One evening he came home early because business was slow.

'You look beautiful in that dress,' he said.

Something in his eyes as he said it made me take it off and stand in front of him in my underwear and shoes. He opened his mouth to say something but I crossed the floor to him and put his arms around me. He was warm. It felt good to be touched, to feel the flesh and blood of a man against my own. I didn't think about David, just the male body beside me. He was strong but he whimpered when he came, shivering on top of me with a look of disbelief in his eyes. From that day on we pretended to be a family.

It was easy, uncomplicated. Graham didn't think too much and that's what I liked about him, he just did what he had to do for a reasonable life. Daddy hated him, thought he wasn't good enough for his little girl, and urged me to see David. Eventually I did let David see Adam. Graham had made me stronger and I could see him without wanting him back. He looked terrible, he'd stopped looking after himself, he had red eyes from lack of sleep and he smelled ill, as if his medication were oozing from his pores. He still barely spoke. He got better after a while, cleaned himself up a bit but words had left him. Adam said he didn't talk to him much when they were out either, but that he liked going because he got fish and chips, and his Dad worked with dinosaurs.

Graham couldn't believe we were married.

'Well, he's changed a lot — he wasn't like that when I first met him.' I felt annoyed with myself for remembering how he was.

'We should get married,' said Graham. 'You should divorce him and marry me.'

We were on the beach when he said that — an hour later Adam was stolen.

Until it happens to you, you can't imagine the hell of losing a child — of not knowing where he is or who has him — it's like the repeated lash of a whip across your back. There was no trace of him, no clues, no witnesses, he simply disappeared, and Graham and I had been too busy looking into each other's eyes, planning a future, to notice where he'd gone. The police try to say it's not your fault but it is. The coast guard searched the sea for two days in case he'd been swept away — and then when he wasn't found we began to think that drowning was the least scary possibility. We huddled together in Graham's flat for five days — David sat in the armchair, I clung to Graham's arm on the sofa. The thing I remember most of those five days was the rhythmic sound of the cricket commentary. It was on all day and all night, runs scored and wickets lost as I lay on the bed with my eyes open, unable to sleep for a second — the way David had felt for years.

At ten past eight on Friday morning David answered the phone. Your heart almost bursts when the phone rings, the two possibilities pump into it from your brain — safety or death, heaven or hell? The room stopped. I gripped Graham's arm so tightly it bruised under my fingernails. The policewoman stood beside David ready to take the phone from him and begin the actions necessary for bereavement. David's grey, tight-lipped hello disappeared into the glow of a sun-coloured smile, and in that moment I realised they were both safe — Adam and David — both of them would come back.

I'm sorry Graham, I really am. You were a good man, and when you hit me because I was leaving you, I knew it was my fault. The thing is I never loved you. The only man I've ever wanted is David. David who I fell in love with in a field of mud.

TOMBSTONE

Ned gets off the bus at the clock tower. The clock reads 10am, still quite early but the streets are already rammed. Tourists in bad shorts wander about with fold-out maps. He hears some fat Americans arguing about which way the sea is. *Just look behind you, you morons.* The tide shimmers in the sunlight at the bottom of the hill.

He waits at the lights and notices a group of girls, a couple of years younger than him, on the other side of the road. They stare at him and whisper to each other behind cupped palms. When the lights change they pass halfway across the road.

'Ladies,' says Ned with a smile and a nod. The girls smile back at him red-faced and giggle, when they have all reached the other sides of the road, both parties look over their shoulders. *Chicks love it when you call them ladies* — his friend Barney taught him that.

Ned is used to this kind of attention. He is 17 years old and well over 6 feet tall, he has shoulder-length wavy hair, bleached gold by the combination of sun and sea salt, and as he spends most of his time on the waves, he has the toned body of an athlete. Ned rarely moves his eyes up from the floor, he is used to shielding them from the reflection of light on water, and he keeps them partially closed most of the time. His eyelashes are long — almost white in colour — perfectly framing his eyes, which are an unusually pale blue. When he does look up — usually into the eyes of a girl intrigued by his elusive personality — the effect of their blueness is devastating. Ned is only just learning to use this to its full advantage, but he's learning fast. The only woman not taken in by Ned's heavy-lidded ocularity is Mrs Parks, his boss at the supermarket.

'Look up Ned!' she tells him. 'The customers want to see your eyes.'

***

Ned was not always so physically blessed. He was an unhappy adolescent, geeky with a slight stutter, and by the age of twelve, an abundant covering of angry acne. He spent his first few teenage years lacking the confidence to bring himself to even say much. He'd been a bright and clever child whose hand was permanently raised in class with enthusiasm for knowledge. The kids at school started to lash out at him; unnerved by his cleverness they picked on him. There was one kid in particular, Derek Jones. After the familial comfort of junior school, Ned found himself in a seemingly huge secondary school on a hill near the A27. It was a typical school in many ways, a dilapidated three-storey building from the 1970s, with peeling paint and damp patches on the ceilings, even on the ground floor. The playground was sufficiently large for the teacher on duty to miss everything that went on in it.

Ned's two best friends from junior school had been sent to a school nearer to where they lived, and for reasons known only to the city council, Ned had missed out. He was in the unenviable position of walking to the end of his road with his friends, then saying goodbye as they walked on and he waited at the bus stop for the bus out of town. He spent his first day at his new school on the fringes of a group of boys he knew vaguely, but who largely ignored him because he was just a bit too uncoordinated to play football. He leaned against the goal posts as the other boys played, a thick lump in his chest and a tight line where his confident smile used to be. On his second day he was late for maths because a football knocked him down and sent the contents of his bag scattering across the playground as the bell rang. His trousers ripped at the knee and his belongings fell on the dusty tarmac. A trickle of blood ran down his shin from a graze on his knee the size of a 50-pence piece. He looked at it through the hole in his trousers, a jagged circle of red and grit. When he managed to get up and shove his things into his bag the playground was empty. He ran through empty, unfamiliar corridors looking for the maths room, his feet slapping loudly on the tiles like peas in a maraca. He finally recognised a boy from class through the window of a door he'd already passed. Sweaty and tearful, he felt like he was hours late, but in fact it was only five minutes. He pushed open the door and stood against it as thirty faces turned from the teacher towards him. The only seat left was next to Derek Jones, and the teacher dispatched him to it with a slap on the back of his head. Jones made a point of moving his chair to the edge of the desk. There was a test — a multiple choice — to see what they knew. It was easy, Ned had it finished in twenty minutes, he put his pen down and glanced at Derek's paper — Derek was still on the first question.

Derek was stupid and not particularly popular but he was a brilliant comedian, and the next day when Ned walked into the form room, Derek stood on the desk, mimicked Ned's unconfident shuffle and sang in a loud operatic voice:

'NNNNNNned thhththe NNNNNNnerd.'

Ned went red and the other kids laughed and that was it. From then on, every time Ned put up his hand to ask a question, Derek and his cronies sang the song. Even when Derek wasn't there, other kids sang the song, and in the playground, kids he didn't know sang the song. In the end, Ned stopped answering questions, he just sat at the back of the classroom and prayed no one would notice him.

It wasn't the best school in town and the teachers chose to ignore his persecution. The only person who ever said anything to the other kids was Mr Watson, the games teacher. Even though Ned was rubbish at games and needed to suck deeply on his asthma inhaler if he did anything more strenuous than walking, Mr Watson was never anything but kind to him. When someone pushed him or slapped his buttocks with wet towels after showers, Mr Watson gave the offender a swift slap on the back of the head and crouched down to Ned's level to ask if he was ok. It wasn't much, but it was the only human kindness on offer in a world where kids accepted nothing but football-playing conformity and perfect skin.

His Mum was no help, she still treated him like a baby, hugging him in public and trying to hold his hand all the time; he couldn't tell her what was happening because he was frightened she would start walking him to the school gates and give the bullies further ammunition. He tried to tell his Dad once but he was busy in his workshop, lathing wood in a storm of whirrs and wood shavings. He said something about the bullies being the real victims, that it was them who felt inferior to him so really it was them he should feel sorry for.

'You'll be alright son,' he said. 'Keep your head down and they'll move onto someone else soon, it's the way it works.'

'Ok,' muttered Ned. 'Don't tell Mum.'

Ned didn't feel sorry for his bullies, from what he could see they weren't the victims, he was. He never tried to talk to his Dad about it again.

One Monday afternoon Mr Watson left the school for good. The kids saw the police car first. It pulled into the staff car park while they were in algebra. There was the usual scrum to the classroom window, until they were ordered back to their desks with threats of detention and missed playtime. Ned remained at his desk the whole time but as he was next to the window, he could turn his head and furtively glance out of the window whilst pretending to be engrossed in sympathetic equations. Ned saw Mr Watson being walked to the car by two men in pale raincoats, one on either side of him. He was holding his arms in a funny position and when they reached the car they turned him round and eased him into the back seat, one of the men holding his hand over the back of Mr Watson's head so he wouldn't bump it on the doorframe. His face was so pale it was almost green, shockingly contrasted from the usual ruddy cheeks of games lessons. Ned thought Mr Watson saw him too, it seemed that his eyes focussed on him inside the maths room, but when he thought about it later he realised that it would have been impossible to see through the window from that position in the car park. It was then that Ned saw the handcuffs, a mere glint in the car park's rare carpet of sun. Ned didn't see anymore, he'd not heard the question he was asked by Ms Edwards, and was jolted out of the moment by a hardback book dropped from a great height onto his desk by the enraged teacher.

After Mr Watson left, Ned withdrew completely. He became a small grey thing, hunched over with his chin tucked into his chest, a curtain of lank mousy hair covering most of his face. Derek Jones left school too. Without Derek the bullies had no focus, they continued half-heartedly for a couple of weeks but in the end Ned's Dad had been right. After a while, the other kids didn't even notice him enough to bully him — to them Ned had all but disappeared.

Ned's Mum and Dad were consumed with worry. What had happened to their bright and happy child? His Dad felt guilty about the bullying, but Ned told him it had stopped so he pushed it to the back of his mind. He told himself he'd bring it up at the next parents' evening, but when that came around, they were met by teachers who had no idea who their son was. One after another they read his grades from the forms in front of them and agreed that they weren't good. Ned's Mum wondered about Mr Watson — had Ned been involved somehow? Had Mr Watson harmed their son too? She'd twirled an embroidered handkerchief in her hands as her husband drove them home in silence; neither of them wanting to say what they were thinking.

When they got home she'd gone into Ned's room to ask him about it. The room was dark; he'd pulled the curtains shut against the sun. She noticed that he'd covered his mirror with a tablecloth he must have taken out of the laundry for that specific purpose. The room smelled sour. It reminded her of the milk smell that had pervaded the house when she'd been breast-feeding him, all those years before. It wasn't right. It smelled too raw somehow — too desperate. Ned was curled on his bed under a grey and black camouflage duvet. She had trouble seeing him.

He'd gone mad when she asked him about Mr Watson. He'd leapt at her from his bed arms raised, hands like cat claws, and shrieked and pushed her, swiping at her with his skinny white fists.

'G-get Out! G-get Out!! GET OUT!!!'

His father had wrestled him to the floor and lay on top of him as he wriggled and raged for a full ten minutes, before finally lying still and whimpering like a frightened animal.

They went to the doctor the next day. Ned was diagnosed with severe depression and signed off from school. The doctor prescribed counselling and anti-depressants, antibiotics for his acne and recommended some form of physical exercise, preferably outdoors.

It took the better part of a year to get Ned to go out at all. He was 15 years old.

***

Ned waits at the entrance to the shopping centre. Tribe central. Hundreds of kids gather in little groups, dressed to fit in. Some sit on the low wall outside the bookshop drinking Big Gulp coke out of plastic cups; others just sprawl on the floor surrounded by carrier bags from the clothes shops inside. There's an abundance of black and piercings and feet that seem too big for bodies. Ordinary shoppers have to step over them to get inside. There's a hum of voices and muffled music played straight into ears through iPod headphones. A group of Japanese girls chatter excitedly next to H&M, hair in high pigtails dyed pink and purple, they are wearing tutus over thick stripy tights and stack heels with silver buckles. Ned leans his head to one side to look at their legs from a different angle.

A hand grabs his shoulder. It's Barney.

'Not bad — be better without the tights!'

The girls sense they are being talked about and turn to see Ned and Barney, heads cocked, looking at them. They giggle and wiggle their tutus.

'You ready?' asks Barney with raised eyebrows. Ned nods, and they amble along the pavement towards the backstreet down to the beach.

115

'Byeee!' the girls shout after them.

They walk past a newspaper vendor selling stories about a lost child.

Once on the beach Ned and Barney discard their flip flops and T-shirts. They wrap them in their towels and weigh them down with stones. It's extremely low tide and there is a layer of sand a metre wide between the pebbles and the sea. It feels soft and muddy underfoot, oozing through their toes as they pad over it.

Parts of the Pier stick up out of the sand as if they'd crash-landed from the heavens. The Pier reminds Ned of a skeletal flying saucer, stuck for millennia in the sediment, newly dredged up for the modern age. Its two domed roofs were not made to cover ballrooms and amusement arcades but to spin through space, piloted by creatures from another world. Ned read a lot of science fiction novels when he was a kid, in his unmanageable crossover from child to teenager. Friendless in his bedroom, he escaped on warp drives to Arcadian galaxies to meet robot women and blue two-headed space captains. He's still got a stack of them under his bed, with yellowing pages and tattered covers.

The sea is warm; it's had ten days of unbroken August sunshine to heat up. Barney and Ned run into it to overcome the initial chill of the English surf. When it's deep enough they plunge in, feeling the sting of salt on their faces and the marine stickiness in their hair. They swim quickly out to sea. The water is unusually clear today; when they are just past the tide–line they can see the bottom as clearly as if it were the Mediterranean.

Ned gulps in a lungful of air and dives down into the muffled silence of the world below. Barney joins him a second later. There's not actually that much down there; the sand is surprisingly pale, covered with a few brown shells and groups of blue and white pebbles, clumps of feathery seaweed blow in the current. A crab scuttles curiously past, eyes literally on stalks. There's a shoe: half-buried. Ned picks it up; it's an old fashioned brogue, the sort his Dad wears to work. Ned looks at its frayed laces then drops it back down to its resting place.

The remains of the Pier are more interesting; covered in slimy green foliage, thousands of mussels cling to them in strings, swaying blackly like exotic seeds. Barney grabs a clump and pulls — it's stuck fast, entwined in the metal and rust. He gives it a decisive tug and it comes away sharply, flipping him backwards, and slipping from his grasp to float softly to the sand below.

A minute later they kick back up to the surface, taking salty air into their lungs, swimming in and out of the rusting girders of the Pier, lying on their backs to gaze up at the underside of the bare frame. Hundreds of sea birds perch on the ironwork above them. Huge white herring gulls stretch their wings, and huddle together against the breeze. Primitive-looking cormorants, glossily black like they've been coated in oil, stretch their necks and pick at their feathers with long beaks. Then there are the pigeons. Ned hadn't expected pigeons. Pigeons are city birds, scavenging in bins and pecking at leftovers from picnics and café tables. There are as many pigeons on the Pier as there are sea birds. Their noisy cooing fills the air, mixing with the caws of the gulls and the barks of the cormorants and the constant hypnotic swish of the sea.

A duo of jet-skis zoom in a race between the two portions of the Pier, the drivers shouting encouragement and insult to each other in equal measure. The wave they create rushes at Ned and Barney, pushing them swiftly upwards and sideways. Ned's head thumps against the nearest metal strut.

'OW!' he says rubbing it with one hand, losing his balance and going under unexpectedly. He flaps his arms and treads water to right himself again.

'Mind the giant metal girders!' laughs Barney, flicking water at his friend. 'Shall we go up?'

Ned nods, and then frowns, his courage suddenly leaving him. 'Do you think we should? I mean, it might be too dangerous, there's a lot of sharp metal out here.'

'You can't back out on me now. It's not much higher than the donut and it's really calm — we'll clear the struts no problem. Jonesy did it last week — said it was awesome. C'mon it'll be wild! Think what everyone will say tonight at The Shack.' Then, sensing that Ned still isn't convinced, he adds. 'Eleanor will be impressed.'

Ned nods again enthusiastically, a smile breaking his frown. 'OK then. Let's go!'

Ned and Barney swim to the sea-bound edge of the Pier, take a leg each and begin to climb up. They haven't worn their rubber-soled surf shoes, not realising the difficulty they would have gripping onto the surface. The metal is slippery with green slime and bladder wrack, barnacles as sharp as glass stick to its rusted coating, scraping their hands and feet as they scale it.

After twenty feet or so, sea creatures give way to bare metal for a relatively easy climb to the top. The breeze has picked up into a sharp wind. It chills Ned's torso, goose bumps cover his arms and his shorts stick coldly to his legs. Icy drops trickle down his neck from his hair, which has lost its yellow brightness in favour of a mousy dampness. He looks over at Barney and they both grin, adrenaline pumps through their bodies, their hearts thump in their throats.

Barney gets to the top first. He crouches on the charred

platform and gives Ned a hand up. They stand next to each other for a minute looking out to the sea in silence. Barney sits down with his legs over the ledge, and curls his arms around a fire-damaged pillar.

'Next stop France,' he says. He seems troubled, the grin has gone and he stares straight ahead as if he's looking for something on the horizon. Ned perches next to him on the black edge of what was once the promenade. It's a long way down — into the waves.

'You OK? We don't have to — if you don't want to.'

Barney shrugs. 'Last time I was here was the day it burned down.'

Ned looks over at him but Barney is still staring at the waves.

'You're losing it! We were here yesterday. We paddled around the Pier and then lit a bonnie on the beach. That lifeguard came an' told us off.'

Barney turns and looks at Ned. 'No. I mean here. Right here — on this bit.'

'What? You climbed the Pier the day it burned down? I thought it went on through the night. Wasn't it still hot?'

Ned is confused. He looks at Barney for some clue as to what he is on about, and then the look on Barney's face gives it away.

'Shit. You're saying you did it. Aren't you? That's what you mean isn't it? You did it.'

Barney nods sadly. 'Well, not just me — but I helped.' And he tells Ned the whole story, or at least as much of it as he remembers. Some of it's still a bit hazy, but as he sits on the burnt-out shell of The West Pier it's becoming clearer by the minute.

***

Ned isn't sure what Barney wants him to say. He's listened to a story so far removed from the Barney he knows, that he's not even sure if his friend hasn't made it all up. Gangsters and drug dealers and arsonists — the Barney he knows is so straight he wouldn't even drink a beer. The Barney he knows only gets a buzz from the waves, yet all this happened just two years ago. Barney hasn't said a word for a few minutes; he just stares out to sea, slowly swinging his legs. His face is bright in the sun, his eyes are all but closed and he seems to be on the point of a smile. He turns and looks at Ned.

'Shocked huh?'

Ned shakes his head. 'I just don't know what to say.'

'You don't need to say anything. I just wanted to tell someone. I didn't even tell my Mum, though she sorted me out — after. You are one of the only three people on the planet who know how the West Pier burned.'

Ned grins. 'Cool.'

Barney jumps to his feet. 'Shall we?'

Ned joins him; he's not scared anymore. Now he can't wait.

'Who's gonna go first?'

'Why don't we both go together?'

'On three?'

'On three.'

'One. Two. Three!'

Ned jumps — arms and legs whirling — crying out in a mix of fear and freedom. Somehow he remembers to straighten his legs, lock his ankles together and hold his arms to his sides — *like a tombstone* — like he'd done before at the Donut.

Something's wrong this time. He must have left it too late to straighten up. He hits the surface with winding force. A sudden pain racks his neck and back. He gasps for the air that has been knocked out of him but takes in water instead. It rushes down his throat and up his nostrils, even into his eardrums, which feel as if they are bursting from within. He's still plummeting downwards at great speed. His feet hit the bottom, but they don't just hit sand — there's something buried underneath it, harder than sand, something hidden by men, something built to last.

Ned's bones shatter from his ankles to his pelvis as they bumper-car into each other.

He feels a moment of consciousness in the pain, seeing the underwater world in beautiful clarity — the swaying snakes of seaweed, the shiny white sand, silvery sunlight flickering through the swirling waters.

It's so beautiful! he thinks, lost for a moment in its simplicity. Then his instinct for survival takes over. He's not yet ready to leave a world of such wonders. He's got things to do: places to go, girls to kiss, oceans to swim.

He tries to kick up off the bottom, but it feels as if there are hands holding his legs at the ankles, keeping his feet anchored in the sand. There's no sign of Barney.

Chicken-shit! he thinks and smiles. Black shadows are forming on the edge of his vision, gradually taking up more and more space, like a slowly closing camera shutter.

It's then that he sees her face. As pale as the moonlight, bow lips tinged rosebud fresh; her unblinking eyes are the most dazzling green he has ever seen, a shining red storm of waving hair swirls around her face and shoulders. She takes his breath away. Her body is as white as her face, so white it's almost blue. She is naked below her hair; he can see the small mound of her breasts topped with cherry nipples and the slight outward curve of her belly. She is smiling at him, her eyes darting in the ripples of the current. She reaches out and takes his face in her hands, her long and slender fingers as cold as ice on his cheeks. She pulls him to her, his feet finally lifting off the seabed, and their lips meet in a kiss. The coldness of her mouth is electric. It stirs something in him he has never known, something he could never know — up there, with the sun. He opens his mouth to kiss her back.

The last bubble of air from Ned's lungs floats slowly upwards, meandering in the pull of the tide to join the sunlit air above the water. It breaks unnoticed on the leg of the Pier — lost amongst the hundreds of other bubbles created by the fish and the seaweed and the shifting of the sands — just below the bough where Barney still sits, swinging his legs, waiting for Ned to resurface.

DENTISTRY

The pain was like being kicked in the face by an enraged donkey. Giuseppe hadn't slept at all that night. He wasn't sure where he'd been or where the time had gone, he had flashes of various bars, and then one of the clubs on the seafront. He'd finally climbed under the covers at around 5am. At first he couldn't sleep because the pills hadn't worn off yet; then he couldn't sleep because they had. He lay on his back sucking air in through his teeth, making a whistling noise, saliva swooshing around his angry molar. After about an hour of niggling away at his tooth with tongue and spit, like a child unable to leave a scab alone, it began to throb with a laser-like intensity. He groaned and held his jaw with a cupped palm, unsuccessfully feeling for the packet of paracetamol he was sure was on his bedside table.

Giuseppe could smell cigarettes on his fingers and the faint, artificial tang of amyl nitrate — bile rose in his throat. He looked through watery eyes at the green neon numbers on his alarm clock — 6am. He whimpered, and pushed his swollen face into the pillow.

At 10, Giuseppe staggered from his room in search of pain relief. The tender nerves of his tooth radiated across the whole right side of his face, tendrils of agony ice-picked their way from his ear to his chin and up into his eye socket. He held his jaw, and made a soft keening sound with his throat to express his distress without disturbing the tooth. Karen looked up from where she was standing by the kitchen sink.

'Jeezus!' she laughed. 'You look like shit.'

'Thanks Kags. What happened?'

She handed him a mug of coffee and a packet of paracetamol. 'You wanted to go for a drink — to take the pain away — so we went to *The Feathers*, Byron was in there and that scary Bulldog guy. After about ten vodkas you felt much better and decided you wanted to go clubbing. I went home — that's all I know.'

He pulled out a chair and sat down at the table. His hands shook as he gulped down the hot coffee and squinted at the clock on the wall. 'Shit — I've the dentist in half an hour! Why'd you let me do it?'

Karen wagged a finger at him. 'Old and ugly enough to look after yourself Giz. Which dentist you going to?'

He shrugged, knowing what she would think. 'The orange one off Western Road.'

Karen raised her famous eyebrow, the one that betrayed all her emotions. 'Typical — the only dentists in town entirely staffed by beautiful young Australian men.'

It was true; they were all gorgeous, far too bouncy and sunny for the backstreets of Brighton. They didn't belong under grey skies and freezing rain but Giuseppe was glad they were there; as a total 'dentophobe' it was the only way he could get through.

'I don't know what you mean.' He smiled weakly. 'Some of the nurses are Polish *and* female. Besides, Daniel is from New Zealand.'

'Wow,' she said. 'Didn't know they had dentists in New Zealand. Didn't think they'd evolved that far.'

Giuseppe laughed and then cried out as his face was ripped apart by shattering pain. Karen placed an arm tenderly around his shoulder. 'Oh babes. It'll soon be over — Daniel will make it all better.' She winked. 'Gonna see Jerry, do you want a lift?'

Karen stopped the car under an orange sign with perky white lettering and a smile motif — *BRIGHT SMILES!*

'Cheesy,' she said as she helped him out of the car like a maiden aunt. She hugged him briefly — something in her eyes was sad again; he'd seen that look before.

Giuseppe sighed. 'Say hi to Jerky for me.'

She got back in the car. 'I'll let that slide,' she said 'seeing as you're in pain.' Then she drove away, sticking her tongue out at him as she went.

Giuseppe loved Karen. He'd known her for seven years. When she'd split from Jerry she needed to rent out her spare room and a mutual friend had recommended him. He'd gone round to see the room and, forgetting he was coming, she'd opened the door in a red kimono and a green face pack, with Dolly Parton blaring from the stereo. He'd fallen for her instantly. He loved her wiry beauty, the tell-all eyebrows, the Bette Midler nose, badly dyed hair and the slightly crazy way she dressed. She wore flowery blouses with leather, and Ugg boots with sundresses — she'd once gone out wrapped in the bathroom curtain because she had *nothing else to wear*. He loved her loud nasal accent, and the way she used it to say exactly what she thought, and then cried foul if anyone did the same to her. Karen was the female love of his life — best friend, fag-hag, dancing partner and drug buddy; she was arrogant and sensitive, gorgeous and damaged — hell to live with, but never, ever, boring.

Giuseppe hated Karen's ex, Jerry, nearly as much as he loved her. He hated what he'd done to her. In the years between the split and the divorce, Giuseppe had wiped away Karen's tears, got royally pissed with her more times than he could count, even stuck pins in a voodoo doll with Jerry's hair in its belly — but every time Jerry came back on the scene, Karen welcomed him with open arms. After the divorce Jerry seemed to be around even more, the proverbial bad penny. She'd let him into her bed whenever he wanted; she said it didn't mean anything, but Giuseppe knew it did. He hated the way she waited around for any little crumb of affection Jerry saw fit to throw at her. They weren't even well suited. Jerry was so buttoned up and intense, whereas Karen, well Karen was simply effervescent.

'Why do you hate him so much?' she'd asked once. They were sitting together on the sofa, watching *Desperate Housewives* and drinking cheap Merlot.

Giuseppe lied, 'Because he made promises to you he didn't keep.'

'You're one to talk.'

'Gay men don't make promises the same way as straight men do.'

'You sure about that? Don't think Gary would agree.'

'I'm not married to Gary. I never said I'd be faithful to him in front of our friends — or God.'

She smiled. 'Sometimes Giuseppe Vincenzo you are such a…' She searched for the right word. 'A Catholic!'

But it wasn't true, Giuseppe didn't hate Jerry because he'd broken his promises to Karen — Giuseppe hated Jerry because he was in love with him. He knew that if Jerry asked him to, he would fall into bed with him, with no thought of Karen.

He couldn't help it; it was that damned Scottish accent, and all the dark moodiness and the way he acted as though Giuseppe wasn't even in the room most of the time. Most of all it was his smile. On the rare occasions Giuseppe said something Jerry thought was funny, he would break into the brightest and most delicious smile. It transformed his face. Karen had told him once that Jerry's smile had the same effect on her; it was why she couldn't let him go. Being on the receiving end of Jerry's smile made you feel special — that you could be the cause of something so wonderful.

Of course nothing would ever happen between them, so Giuseppe contented himself with the opposite emotion to love.

Standing on the pavement outside *BRIGHT SMILES!* he was worried by Karen's expression — he hoped it didn't mean that Jerry would be round again. He didn't know if he could cope with another bout of bedroom noise, and Jerry swaggering about the flat looking pleased with himself. This time he might have to move out, at least until it all came crashing down again. These conflicts spun around Giuseppe's brain, mingling with the pain, as he mounted the stone steps for his appointment with a tooth extractor.

BRIGHT SMILES! had such a bright and jolly reception area that it instilled a sense of unease in its clients the moment they walked through the door. Everything was orange, from the gigantic comfy sofas to the Perspex coffee table, from the reception desk to the receptionist's skin. Giuseppe was not cheered by the tangerine sunniness that surrounded him — it just made him think that they had something to hide. And he knew exactly what it was, because as soon as he walked in and smelled the antiseptic pong of professional mouthwash and heard the whirr of a drill from behind closed doors, he was transported back to the worst experience of his childhood.

When Giuseppe was twelve he found himself standing in front of a wicket on the long flat green of the school cricket ground.

Opposite him stood Martin Thornton. Thorny was in the same year as Giuseppe but he was altogether different. He was 13 already but looked 16, he was tall with burnished skin, as yet unblemished, and sleek blond hair that hung down over the collar of his cricket whites. The sun shone behind Martin Thornton, casting an aura around him. He looked like an angel in the Renaissance paintings they were studying in art history. Giuseppe had recently begun to think he was different from the other boys in school, and watching Martin Thornton standing 22 yards away from him, scowling magnificently, he realised for the first time that he thought boys could be beautiful — in the same way that his mother was.

The young Giuseppe gulped and limply gripped the smooth handle of his cricket bat. Thorny moved back from the wicket and narrowed his eyes, as if he knew what Giuseppe was thinking. He ran forward, flinging the ball with an exaggerated over-arm — it spun with such terrifying speed towards Giuseppe's head, that he'd already given up and dropped the bat as it smashed with bone-crushing violence into his mouth. Giuseppe tasted blood, and a bizarre mix of milk and cabbage. Then, as his top lip swelled until it blocked his nostrils, he felt the tiny shards of enamel on his tongue and saw the red poster-paint rivulets run down his whites. He heard the pad of footsteps running towards him as he hit the green, falling flat on his side like a dead tree in a forest.

There was a cricket-ball-shaped hole in Giuseppe's mouth. His top and bottom lips ballooned outwards to reveal four jagged white stumps on his lower gum and two completely absent incisors on the top.

The hospital dentist told them he couldn't do anything until Giuseppe's mouth had fully healed — three to four weeks at least. After that there would be months of treatment — the bottom teeth would need to be filed down and capped, the top set would require a bridge. Giuseppe would need to wear a false plate while he was having the treatment. His mother fussed and sobbed like a proper Italian mamma, as if she had been born in Bologna rather than Basildon. Giuseppe nearly died of shame right there in the consultant's office.

When he went back to school, the other kids treated him with even more disdain than they previously had. Even Shirley and Vanessa, the only ones he'd thought of as friends, kept a polite distance. It was as if the whole school thought they might catch some dreaded tooth-loosening disease if they got too near to him.

Martin Thornton looked at him once in the dinner queue, while Giuseppe waited in line for his soup and milkshake. He frowned in disgust and whispered to his sidekick Jeff, who looked at Giuseppe as if he were a bad smell.

You did this to me, you dick! How about an apology? Giuseppe looked away, towards the fat dinner-lady sweating under her hat. She mopped her forehead with her fingers, then picked up a ladle with the same hand and tipped watery soup into his bowl.

On his first day of treatment, Giuseppe woke in a state of terror. The feeling worsened as the morning progressed. By the time he was sitting in the drab waiting room watching the strip lights flicker, he was ready to run out of the door and spend the rest of his life toothless.

Looks are overrated anyway. He reasoned. *Take Martin Thornton.*

They called his name, and a smiling nurse led him and his Mum to a large white room containing several aluminium sinks, two enormous theatre lights and a long black chair, reclined to almost flat. It was so bright in there it made his remaining teeth ache.

He stood in the doorway as his mother walked in, and felt his hands involuntarily grip the frame, preventing him from going any further. The nurse was talking and pointing to things, but Giuseppe's mind didn't understand her, he felt faint and sick and swore he could feel the heat from the theatre lamps burn the skin on his face. His mother turned to look at him and her eyes widened as she realised her son had slipped into a state of total, and potentially embarrassing, panic. She peeled his fingers off the doorframe and spoke to him in her soothing Mama voice as she walked him towards the chair.

He was fairly pliant until his body touched the squeaky black leather, then his fear overcame him and all rationality vanished. As he remembers it now, Giuseppe thinks he tried to run — all he knows is that he was held down, a needle was brandished, and a foul-smelling black mask was pushed over his nose and mouth. Giuseppe tried not to breathe, but eventually he had no choice — the odour of concentrated Fisherman's Friends filled his nostrils, and within seconds the black outline of the mask had covered his eyes, and then he fell into a pit of nothing.

In the all-encompassing orangeness of *BRIGHT SMILES!* Giuseppe flicked through a three-month-old copy of *Elle Decoration*, and wondered why there wasn't a newer issue to read. He looked at his watch; Daniel was already over-running by twenty minutes. He rubbed his palms on the legs of his jeans in an attempt to rid them of sweat; he realised how awful he must look — hung-over and dirty and anxious. A woman in Prada, whose child was banging a dinosaur on the curve of the fish tank, smiled at him with a mixture of pity and amusement.

'Don't do that Oscar dear,' she said glancing up at him from a wallet-covered copy of Vogue.

The child looked at her with a defiant stare and carried on smashing T-Rex's head against the tank now shouting 'BANG!' with every thud.

'Don't do that!' said the receptionist in a harsh Eastern European accent. She held up a finger, showing a long pointed fingernail, and the child jumped in fright, running to his mother to wipe his nose on her £500 skirt.

'Sorry,' she mouthed.

Two other women, dressed at similar expense, sat smugly grateful that it wasn't their children being told off.

Giuseppe got up and went over to the fish tank. It took up the middle portion of the waiting room; a seamless wave of Perspex. It was thin, no more than six inches across — the fish had no choice but to swim along in motorway lanes as there wasn't room for random shoaling. There were clown fish of course, to keep in with the colour scheme, but there were also a few zebra fish and hundreds of tiny shimmering blues. Giuseppe crouched on his heels to take a closer look; he marvelled at how unrestful they were, darting around, crashing into each other, head-butting the side of the tank. Dribbles of miniscule bubbles rose from their mouths to the inch of air between the slimy surface water and the orange plastic lid. The floor of the tank was covered with jagged orange and white stones; a hallucinogenic simulacrum of a real seabed. Seaweed, so threadbare it looked more like a flash of colour than an actual plant, wafted in the wake of a school of danios.

A painted mermaid sat on an oversized boot just level with Giuseppe's line of sight; she was elongated by the glass, ice white, with a green iridescent tail and flowing ruby hair. Giuseppe stared at her face, it looked faintly demonic — the eyes a little too green and angular, lips too red and bowed eyebrows like giant ticks — she was creepy, a childhood fantasy gone very wrong. She put him more on edge than he was already.

He saw the baseball-boot-clad feet walk across the artificial seabed, and heard the collective sigh from the three women sitting behind him — Daniel was in reception.

Giuseppe stood unsteadily to find Daniel peering over the tank at him with an amused look on his handsome face.

'Hi Giz — you ready?'

Giuseppe nodded, his voice failing him. He realised he had pins and needles in his legs from crouching and couldn't move them right at that moment. He looked over his shoulder at the women following Daniel's retreating form as he strode out of sight. When he was gone they all looked at Giuseppe, as if to say *Go on! Then it'll be our turn.* Giuseppe tip-toed out of the room.

'So Giz — did ya take your sedative?' asked Daniel, as Giuseppe was settled into the squeaky leather chair by the nurse.

'Shit — I forgot.'

'No worries — so long as you promise not to bite me!'

Not sure I can do that. You look even better than I remember. You surf don't you?

Daniel leaned his face over Giuseppe's, the bottom half now covered by a surgical mask, leaving only his heavy-lashed eyes to look at. 'Open up!'

The nurse slotted an orange visor over Giuseppe's eyes and he opened wide, settling himself down for an hour of root-filling and tooth-pulling.

The Lidocaine stopped the pain in Giuseppe's jaw but it didn't touch the all-encompassing headache above his eyes. The whirr of the drill was at such a pitch it sounded like a siren spinning on a toy ambulance or a police car, maybe one patrolling Barbie's neighbourhood. Giuseppe had collected Barbies since he was seven; he had over a hundred. He closed his eyes to block out the light and tried to imagine what Barbie's town would look like. Brrr brrr brrr — went the drill, resonating off the enamel on his tooth, sending his head spinning, as if he had bitten down on it and couldn't let go. He opened his eyes and saw, though his tangerine-tinted glasses, the flash of a tiny ice pick on the end of a pliable metallic arm.

There's no way that can go inside my tooth! No way is the root that deep. Stick that in the cavity and it'll come out my arse!

But in this terrifying world of Barbie sirens, Ken was an ice-pick-wielding dentist with perfect teeth, who saw fit to stick his weapon of choice down the hole in Giuseppe's tooth as far as it would go, excruciatingly wiggling it from side to side before pulling it out by degrees, cleaning it off, and going back in even deeper than before.

'Uggg, uggg, URGGG!' *What the hell happened to the Lidocaine?*

'Sorry,' said Daniel. 'Did that hurt?' His voice was sympathetic, but Giuseppe could tell from his eyes that underneath his mask he was smiling. He looked like he was welding; his face was now covered in a giant orange plastic shield.

What the hell is he expecting to happen? Has somebody's face actually exploded during surgery?

Giuseppe gripped the arms of the chair until his wrists hurt. He knew he should close his eyes again but he couldn't even blink; his eyes were as dry as his mouth. The nurse swept Barbie's suction tube over his gums. Daniel held up another syringe and squirted a tiny jet of liquid into the air; then plunged it into the dark hole of Giuseppe's mouth with jolly eyes.

You love your work don't you? You sick bastard.

Giuseppe's tongue swelled. He managed to close his eyes again as a new sabre rattled in his jaw, prodding and pulling at the root.

'All done with the digging,' said Daniel.

Giuseppe opened his eyes, 'Fyun ee yol?' he said. Daniel pulled two soggy wads of cotton-wool from inside Giuseppe's cheeks, he swallowed. 'Find any oil?' Daniel and the nurse looked at each other over their masks and shook their heads. They knew that Giuseppe's pathetic attempts at jokey bravado did nothing but betray the fact that he was scared shitless. Daniel said something to the nurse Giuseppe didn't understand and then disappeared from view. Giuseppe could feel his heart go into overdrive.

'Rinse,' said Daniel, handing him a plastic cup of bright blue liquid. It did nothing to wet the desert in Giuseppe's mouth and he spat it dryly into the sink — or Barbie's Jacuzzi as he now thought of it. There was a crash of glass and metal behind the chair and Daniel looked over. 'Clumsy cow,' he said.

There's a lot of eye contact going on here — are they at it? I bet she wants to even if they're not.

Giuseppe realised he'd never seen the nurse without her mask.

I bet she's really ugly underneath it — her eyes are definitely her best feature.

The nurse passed a container over Giuseppe's head and Daniel picked putty off it with a mini-scythe, then stuck it in Giuseppe's mouth and pushed down on it with a thickly gloved finger. Daniel counted as he did this, 1-20, with elephants in-between, all the while looking over the back of the chair to where the nurse was standing.

I'm starting to feel like a spare part here — do they want me to go?

Daniel released the pressure and clicked his fingers at his partner in torture — she handed him a small stun gun that sparked when he tested it.

'I'm just gonna seal the plastic filling with this baby. It'll smell like burning but don't be alarmed — you're not on fire.'

Giuseppe looked into Daniel's huge brown eyes.

That's what you think.

There was a pssst sound, and an acrid smell, as a puff of Aladdin smoke rose from Giuseppe's mouth.

Don't be alarmed!

His jaw really ached, it had been open too long and too wide and they were still only half-done. He felt very sorry for himself and lifted his goggles to rub his eyes with his fingertips.

Another syringe swung into view. It was so close to his eyeball the needle looked like a metal girder. He pulled the tangerine-dream goggles back over his eyes, thankful for the protection. There was stabbing pain in the crook of his jaw and then another underneath the tooth; his tongue thickened like a flannel.

'So!' said Daniel. 'Just relax and let that take effect and then we'll get that tooth out. You can close your mouth.'

I could if my tongue wasn't the size of an elephant's testicle.

'Be back in a few minutes.' He nodded to the nurse and they both left the room.

Giuseppe looked around his holding cell, uncomfortable in his isolation and in the anticipation of the pain yet to come. There was a poster for a laser wrinkle treatment showing a group of beautiful twenty-somethings who probably didn't know what a wrinkle was. Next to this was a horrific diagram of the cross-section of a tooth, each layer represented by a different pastel colour, but ending with the bright scarlet of the nerves. The local radio station played from a tiny DAB radio on the window sill. Bad disco and loud adverts for taxi firms and pound-shops, tuned in and out with white noise from the movement of the city.

Daniel and the nurse had been gone for about fifteen minutes.

What can they be up to? Coffee — or wild semi-clothed sex in the store cupboard, surrounded by dental moulds and false teeth, taking full advantage of the free-flowing drugs?

135

Giuseppe smiled at the thought of it, but his chin had grown to Bruce Forsythe proportions and it hurt to show pleasure. His head thumped and sweat gathered around his visor.

'OK!' Daniel breezed into the room. He looked disappointingly undishevelled. The nurse followed — mascara still perfect. Daniel dragged the stool over the floor and perched on the edge.

'Open up. Is your mouth nice and numb?'

Giuseppe nodded. *Why do they do that? Get you to open your mouth and then ask you a question?*

Pliers! Daniel had pliers — not toy Ken and Barbie pliers either, these were massive serrated-edge things. Giuseppe's hands grabbed at the chair and he pushed his back flat against it. Daniel wielded the pliers like a gun-slinger, passing them from left hand to right — then they disappeared into Giuseppe's mouth. He didn't feel pain as such, just the clamp of the instrument around his tooth and a hard decisive pressure — the kind you want to be over quickly because it's far too intrusive. Both Daniel's hands were in Giuseppe's mouth, his nose was filled with the smell of rubber gloves and he could feel the rough starch of Daniel's overall resting on his upper lip.

Daniel's face was very close; he was frowning with concentration and looking deep into Giuseppe's mouth. He wiggled the pliers repeatedly from side to side for what must have been a full two minutes. Two minutes isn't long when you're dancing to a favourite song or watching a sunset, but having a piece of you forcibly pulled from your body for two minutes feels like an eternity. Giuseppe wriggled as much as his tooth — his hands were dripping with sweat, his breath came in tiny little pants, and he felt as though he could have keeled over at any moment had he not been so totally wired.

'Try and keep still,' said Daniel, blowing at his fringe in frustration, 'Damn, thing, won't, budge.'

There was a surge of pressure deep inside Giuseppe's jaw and a deafening internal crack.

'Shit!'

Giuseppe's blood pressure soared, tiny light spots passed before his eyes, as if he'd been looking at the sun without sunglasses. Daniel pulled out — the pliers were empty.

'Sorry mate — tooth's shattered. Won't come out in one go. I'm gonna have to cut down into the gum and dig out the roots. I'll take about a half hour — and I'll need to stitch it.'

Giuseppe felt his eyes bulge as he took in the full horror of what was being said. *Cut. Dig. Stitch!* This was the reason he hadn't been to the dentist for 15 years — it wasn't the expense, it was cut-dig-stitch. His skin turned green, and he gulped back puke as it pushed its way up his throat.

'Don't worry. I'll give you loads more drugs. It won't hurt — much — but I'll have to tug at it quite a bit.'

Under any other circumstances that statement would have had a wholly positive effect on Giuseppe, but even though it was uttered by a man as beautiful as Daniel, it brought actual tears to his eyes. The nurse patted his hand as though he were five years old.

Daniel jabbed at him with another syringe. It was hard to imagine his mouth getting any bigger, he already felt like one of the fish trapped in the tank in reception, blowing bubbles at Satan's mermaid. He licked his lips but he couldn't feel them. The nurse sucked again with Barbie's hose.

'I'll just go ask my boss to take my next patient.' With that Daniel was gone. Giuseppe whined.

'I know,' said the nurse patting his hand again. 'It'll be fine. Daniel's a good dentist.'

Good! He better be fanbloodytastic.

'OK! Let's do it!' And Daniel was back in there, digging away with his hands, scraping and tugging. Pulling and pulling and pulling. This must have gone on for at least ten minutes. Sweat pooled in Giuseppe's armpits and at the crease of his buttocks, his breath came in quick bursts and little drops of moisture trickled from his nose onto the latex of Daniel's gloves. Every so often Daniel lifted out the pliers and dropped a tiny piece of white tooth onto the silver tray at Giuseppe's chin.

'Right,' said Daniel, mopping at his brow with his sleeve, 'that's the top done. I'll just make an incision and cut out the root.'

Giuseppe whimpered like a frightened dog. The nurse carried on stroking his hand, as Daniel produced a Ken and Barbie saw. There was more pushing and tugging in his mouth. Then Daniel yanked so hard at the root that he did a wheelie on his chair. Giuseppe saw the root on the end of the pliers; a bloodied maggot — he was sure he saw it wriggle. Daniel dropped it onto the tray. Giuseppe wailed with relief as Daniel shoved cotton wool into his mouth.

Daniel blew a dark, sweat-laden curl of hair out of his eyes.

'OK! Now for the other root.'

What? Other root!! Fuck me Daniel. I can't take any more!

Daniel's hands filled Giuseppe's mouth again. He gripped onto whatever was left of the root with the pliers and tugged. Nothing. He pulled and pulled. Nothing. Sweat ran along the deep furrowed lines on his forehead; he really was trying with all his strength. Giuseppe hadn't blinked for five minutes, his whole body felt raw, as if he had been skinned.

The door opened and the pressure was released. A tall grey-haired man with piercing blue eyes looked at Giuseppe and the blood on his bib and then at Daniel.

'Can I have a word?' he said.

Daniel threw the pliers down with a clang and went over to the door. The nurse looked at Giuseppe with real pity in her made-up eyes. He couldn't catch all of the conversation in the doorway but he heard the words: *Ages. Blood. Five minutes* and *Ambulance.* Daniel was all hushed tones and reassuring nods.

'It'll be fine,' he said. 'I can do it.'

The door closed and he went back over to Giuseppe and looked deep into his eyes.

'It'll be ok. Don't sweat it.' He lifted the pliers with a pianist flourish and went back in.

Daniel was in a curious position, leaning sideways over Giuseppe's head with one knee on the reclining chair. His face was as close as it was possible to be without touching. He pushed down hard with one set of fingers and pulled back even harder on the pliers with the other hand. Then, without warning, he put his knee on Giuseppe's chest. At that moment Jerry's face flashed over Daniel's. Giuseppe blinked in disbelief but he could still see it — that wonderful heart-stopping smile. He felt the familiar ache in his groin and widened his eyes as his penis began to swell unstoppably.

Oh God No! Not now!

He tried to concentrate on his tooth, shifted on his buttocks and pulled at the seam of his jeans, but it was no use; Jerry's face was in his mind, he could smell the sweat of Daniel's exertion, and now he had a full-on erection, massively straining against his zipper like the monster out of *Alien.*

Stop it. Stop it. Stop it.

The nurse saw him lifting his bottom from the chair and looked down; she raised her eyebrows and glanced at Daniel, then at Giuseppe, then back at his crotch.

Daniel's knee pressed harder against Giuseppe's chest. He pulled back with all his strength, grunting with the effort. Giuseppe lifted his hips from his seat and arched his back, rising to meet Daniel as he pushed him down with his knee.

'Uuurrrghh. UURRGHH!'

Daniel flew backwards across the room sending the stool and lamp spinning with him. The remainder of Giuseppe's tooth hit the wall with a pulpy splat. He leant forward and threw up in Barbie's Jacuzzi, his hard-on melting away into sponge. The nurse rushed over to him with handfuls of paper towels. All three of them stared at each other. Kylie chirped on the radio.

Daniel crouched at Giuseppe's side. 'You okay?'

Giuseppe nodded but his hands shook as he wiped blood and sick from his completely numb chin. Daniel grinned.

'Jesus — that was extreme. I need a drink!' He stood up and passed Giuseppe a cup of the blue stuff. Unsure if he should spit or swallow, Giuseppe sat, limply holding the cup in his hand. Daniel noticed the blocked sink, 'You can rinse in the sink behind you,' he said. 'Then I'll stitch you up — I'll be gentle, promise.'

Giuseppe got up from the chair to go to the sink but his legs gave way at the knees. Daniel caught him. His hands were strong and as he hauled him back onto the chair, Giuseppe noticed that his smile was much nicer than Jerry's.

'Just sit there and get your breath back,' he said, lightly rubbing him on the shoulder.

Daniel and the nurse left him alone. Through the closed door he heard Daniel let out a huge '*Whoop!*' and both of them laugh — post-traumatic laughter.

The Polish receptionist eyed Giuseppe with a curious expression, somewhere between a smile and utter disgust. The nurse had obviously filled her in already.

'£365,' she said flatly.

Giuseppe's legs nearly buckled again. 'Jesus.'

'Yes. That's the bit that really hurts.'

He looked at her in disbelief, and she pointlessly shuffled a pile of forms so she wouldn't have to look him in the eye.

'I'll call you a taxi.'

As he sat in the back of the cab, clutching his pack of cotton wool pads, Giuseppe realised that he had become Daniel's dinner party story. *The patient who got an erection whilst having an extraction.* He realised he had become his own dinner party story and anticipated the look on Karen's face when he told her. He pushed his tongue against the numb fleshiness of his gum, and vowed never to see a dentist again — at least not professionally.

ANGEL

Keith looks at her as she comes into the staff room.

'Jesus, what happened this time?'

She frowns and it hurts. She thought she'd covered it up better but he saw it straightaway, even under the artificial light of the windowless room. She touches her cheek lightly under the eye.

'It's nothing — I fell.'

'Off what — the Palace Pier?'

She pours herself a coffee and stirs in Sweet'n'Low and Coffee Mate from the jars next to the sink; creamy flecks cling to the surface, refusing to dissolve. She can feel him watching her and explains herself to the coffee.

'I tripped down the garden step and fell with my face against the washing-line prop. You know how clumsy I am — came down the step really heavily, dropped clean washing everywhere, had to redo it all.'

She takes one of the plastic seats opposite him at the low coffee table and cups her Nescafe, warming her hands with the mug.

'You know,' she witters on, avoiding his eyes, 'I have a recurring dream about falling off the Pier — jumping actually.

I climb over the railings at the end and then I just leap off. It's quite nice then, like I'm a bird flying, all I can see is the sea and I'm going really fast. I don't want to stop, I like it — the flying — but the bit before — when I have to jump — that's terrifying.'

She looks at him when she says *terrifying* and realises he has been looking at her cheek the whole time and probably hasn't heard a word she's said.

'You have to leave him you know.'

'Keith — don't.'

'You have to — I'm frightened for you.'

'Andy,' she says, as if that word will explain everything.

'That's another reason — do you think it's good for a child to see his mother beaten up by his father?'

'He doesn't see it Keith, it's always after he's asleep.'

'He knows chérie, he knows.'

Glenda looks Keith right in the eyes, her chin held high, the bruise angry under the institutionalised light.

'He wouldn't let me take Andy and I can't leave him.'

Keith frowns, then looks away and pulls a leaflet from his smock pocket. He lays it flat on the table in front of Glenda — she looks at it briefly. She recognises the blue and white house motif and the roses growing along the margin. *The Pierpoint Women's Refuge — Safety In Numbers.* Keith must've given her twenty of these by now.

'Or you can stay with me for a while — until you sort yourself out.'

He looks down at his hands. He's never offered this before; her eye must look really bad this time. She'll have to go and put some more makeup on it before her shift.

'Thanks Keith, but really now there's no need — I fell down the garden step that's all.'

She couldn't move in with Keith — Sidney would kill him.

She's late by the time she's reapplied the camouflage. Her heart beats quicker as she walks past Sister's office on her way into B Ward, but the door's not open and it looks like there's no one in. She's a few lighter paces down the corridor when the door opens and Sister Blake shouts after her.

'Nurse Watson — a word please.'

Glenda Watson has been clumsy now for five years — since just after Andy was born. First she kept tripping over the pram wheels. It was a Silver Cross and the wheels were so big — and hidden under the back of the carriage — she was always misjudging where to put her feet, and her shins were often black and blue under her stockings. Then, because she was so tired she'd fallen asleep when she was ironing and had accidentally ironed her right arm — despite being right-handed — you could clearly see the keel shape where the hot metal had glided over her skin.

As Andy grew up he'd accidentally smacked his mother's nose with his toys on several occasions — so hard that it broke a couple of times. A unique combination of her leaning towards him as he swung a tractor or a cricket bat through the air resulted in a series of bruises and scrapes across her face. Poor kid — it wasn't his fault — he's stronger than he looks.

'What did the dragon want?' asks Keith in the sluice room, as they are both emptying bedpans into the huge metal sanitizer. The room fills with steam, visually and audibly, as Glenda closes the lid. Her chin shudders but she fights back the tears and rubs her forehead with the back of her hand, her makeup streaks away under her touch.

'She said I should take some time off.'

'What?'

'Until the bruise goes down — said I would frighten the patients, that I looked worse than they did.'

'Bitch,' says Keith, 'she can't do that.'

Glenda sighs. 'She's right though, I do look a sight.'

The tears wobble free. He holds out his arms.

'Come here.'

He holds her, shocked by how tiny she is; a little bird in a starched uniform.

She snuffles into his chest for a moment then pulls away. He kisses her forehead.

'Sidney will do his nut.'

'I'll have a word with her.'

Sidney Watson wasn't always a wife-beater. She met him on the ward only a few weeks into her training, September 1953, nearly ten years ago. He'd been to interview a victim of GBH. She saw him by the woman's bed, tall and straight with an air of confidence about him. He came back to the ward a few minutes after leaving it, striding up to the nurse's station where she was sitting.

'Did you forget something?' she asked.

He smiled, lopsided, so his left cheek rose more than his right.

'Yes — I forgot to ask you for a date.'

She smiled back. He was so sure of himself, so full of chat and determination, smart in his work clothes and so clean, he almost shone. She was 19 and she was speechless.

'I'm a police officer,' he said. 'The only answer we ever really want to hear is yes.'

So on Friday night Glenda O'Reilly found herself at the Regent watching *Genevieve* with Sidney Watson. When she walked into the lobby he was already there holding a red rose and a small box of peppermint creams. He bought the tickets and they made their way into the auditorium. He talked about the film, and how he'd been on duty when they'd filmed it near the Palace Pier, how he'd met the stars, shook hands with Kenneth Moore and Kay Kendal.

'She's beautiful,' he said as he steered her gently into one of the plush red seats about halfway down, 'but not as beautiful as you.'

Glenda blushed, at once thankful and disappointed that it wasn't the back row.

He talked easily to her until the lights went down and a man behind them hushed him loudly. He looked at her and waggled his finger and they both laughed. His arm rested lightly on the back of her chair and at some point during the film, perhaps after he'd offered her a peppermint cream, he moved it so his hand touched her knee and he left it there. The heat from his hand increased as the film rolled, a pulsating warmth that was almost too hot to bear. She forced herself not to move away. No man had touched her knee before. The farm boys back home didn't count. As far as Glenda was concerned they were dirty and stupid and she'd never liked a single one. Besides, to them she was the school swot, always looking in books, always top of the class. That's how she got away — trained her brain so she could come to nursing college. This man sitting next to her in the dark and flickering light with his hand on her knee was precisely that — a man. He must be at least 25, sophisticated and relaxed; no stammering lines, no obvious pretensions. Sidney Watson moved through the world with purpose, she could tell that right away. He'd met Kenneth Moore for God's sake — shaken his hand like an equal. She knew she would let him kiss her when he took her back to the nurse's home and the thought of it thrilled her. Her knee burned under his fingers and though she was watching the film she didn't really know what was happening in it, the only thought in her mind was his touch. When the film finished and he moved his hand away, her knee felt desolately cold, as if a miniature blizzard raged in that part of her body and nowhere else.

After the handover at the end of the shift, Keith waits till the nurses have left Sister Blake's office. He smiles at Glenda as she leaves and squeezes her hand, then he closes the door and turns to face Sister Blake. She stops writing her report when she hears the door close, aware that he is there, and places her pen on the table and regards him with steady eyes.

'I know what you're going to say but I really do think she needs to take some time off. She's a mess, her mind's not on the job and she looks terrible. It's not good for the patients and they are my only priority.'

'What about your duty to your nurses — isn't that a priority?'

'Are you questioning the way I run my ward Nurse DeAngeli?'

'Of course not — it's just — it's not easy for her, at home I mean.'

Sister Blake's expression softens.

'I am well aware of her home situation. I have tried to help her countless times, as I know you have, but really Nurse Watson is the only one who can help herself. I thought perhaps this might bring things to a head, that time off might help her reach the right conclusion.'

'Sister Blake, what if all it does is enrage her husband? You don't know what you've sent her home to. He likes the idea of her working, her being a nurse fits into his image as a pillar of the community — he won't be happy at having it taken away from him.'

'I gave her a leaflet for the women's refuge — the rest is up to her. I have had dealings with Mr Watson in the past Nurse DeAngeli, treated a victim of his over-zealous policing — he is a dangerous man. I would advise you to leave well alone.'

'She's my friend — I can't just leave her. Who knows how it will end. What if one day he actually kills her?'

Sister Blake sighs and picks up the file in front of her — the conversation is at an end.

'Tell her she can come back to work in two days, when the bruising isn't as obvious.'

'If there isn't any more.'

She looks at him for a moment then picks up her pen and begins scribbling on the notes. When he gets to the door she presses another warning on him.

'Nurse DeAngeli,' her tone reminds him of his mother, 'be careful.'

After the film, Sidney took Glenda to a pub down a little side road in Montpelier. She'd never been to a pub alone with a man before. He held open the door to the snug and she walked into a dark little room that smelled of dust and beer and furniture polish. He steered her to a rickety table in the corner, pulling the velvet stool out for her to sit on. The only other inhabitants were a middle-aged couple who hadn't taken their coats off, despite the warm September evening, and who both had shiny red noses. They sat side-by-side not speaking, but Glenda could feel their eyes on her as Sidney asked her what she would like to drink. She didn't know what to order, but saw an advertisement for Babysham above the bar with a happy-looking deer winking at her and decided on that. Sidney looked over his shoulder at her from the bar and smiled. Her heart beat loudly and she turned a beer mat in her fingers, tearing the edge with her nails.

'Cheers,' he said placing her drink on the table in front of her. 'Here's to you.'

She took a sip; she was surprised by the bubbles and giggled as they tickled her nose.

'You have a beautiful nose,' said Sidney. 'Just then when you laughed — it wrinkled up — beautiful.'

He leant forward and turning his head to the side, kissed her nose lightly and then moved down for the briefest touch of her lips. The snug was silent but for the murmurs of the customers in the main bar and the clinking of glasses. Glenda wondered if she would ever breathe again.

'C'mon — let's get out of here,' said Sidney standing and holding out his hand. She hesitated for a moment — then took it, allowing herself to be led away past the silent red-nosed couple who followed her exit with their eyes.

Sidney took her to his flat on the seafront, not far from the pub. She followed him up two flights of wide marble stairs and though a large door with frosted glass panels. He held it open for her and she walked into a cavernous hall which led off into three rooms. Sidney closed the door and flicked on the light. The hall was bright white with a mosaic floor, to the right was the lounge; she could see the pearl drop lights on the Pier through the window. In front of her was a closed door which she presumed was the bathroom. She glanced quickly to the left and saw through the open door the dark shape of a bed with a white sheet turned down over a bedspread.

Sidney came up behind her; she heard the rustle of the air as he took off his jacket and walked across the hall. His hands held her shoulders and then he lifted her hair up with his fingers and kissed her softly where the cool air touched her neck. She closed her eyes and he turned her to him, pressing his lips on hers, gently at first then forcefully. She could feel his body against her, the iron curve of him pushing into her belly, his tongue forcing her mouth open as his hands tightened around her arms. She was a nurse, she understood the biology but this feeling was in her body not her mind. This feeling was different; this was unknown, at once pleasurable and terrifying. She was totally bewildered. She pushed him away and they stood breathlessly looking at each other in the still hallway. He wiped his mouth with his hand.

'I'm sorry,' he said, 'it's just, you make me crazy. I know that after tonight I won't be able to think about anything else but you.'

He held his hands up as if he were approaching a frightened animal and crossed the small space between them in two slow steps. He leant down and whispered again into her ear, 'you make me crazy'. He purred and stroked her back into his arms and then he carried her through his bedroom door and laid her down on his bed.

Glenda found herself in Sidney's bed most nights. She didn't always make it back to the nurses' home by lights out and after a couple of months she was called into matron's office and severely reprimanded. She was sobbing when Sidney opened his door to her, and rushed into his arms, spluttering the details of the official warning she'd been given: one more count and she was out. Sidney was unmoved, hardness crossed his face and his eyelid flickered as he listened.

'Stupid cow,' he said wiping her eyes with a handkerchief. Glenda wasn't sure if he meant the matron or her, and for a moment, she was sure he was going to finish it — that he was done with her. Then he smiled. 'You don't have to go back there, you can move in here — until the wedding. I was thinking March.'

'Oh Sidney!'

She flung her arms around him and covered his face with kisses.

'I take it that's a yes,' he laughed; and she felt herself melt under his kiss until she couldn't tell where her lips ended and his began.

And so the lovely Nurse O'Reilly became Mrs Sidney Watson.

There is no sign of Glenda in the staff room or the corridors. She must've gone already. Keith grabs his coat and rushes out to the car park — maybe he can catch her before she gets to the bus stop, tell her it's only two days. It's raining heavily; a low cloud fills the air with grey mist. He turns his collar up against the squall and catches sight of Sidney Watson across the car park. He's standing against the door of his green and white Ford Zodiac despite the driving rain, looking at his wrist-watch. He does it three times in quick succession; each time water drips from the sleeve of his raincoat. There's no sign of Glenda. Keith sighs and pulling his coat around himself tramps through the puddles towards Sidney.

When Sidney sees him he straightens up and folds his arms.

'Keith,' he says, with a nod.

'Sidney.'

Water drips from Keith's hair into his eyes and he flicks it to one side by jerking his head so he doesn't have to take his hands out of his pockets.

'I was looking for Glenda but she must still be inside.'

Sidney narrows his eyes.

'Must be. Thought I'd surprise her by picking her up but she's late.'

'She's probably covering up her eye.'

Sidney frowns then says with a light laugh, 'Yeah, terrible isn't it? She's a silly mare, always tripping over things, fell down the garden step this time.'

Keith doesn't know what possesses him; he just comes straight out with it looking Sidney directly in the eyes.

'You and I both know that isn't what happened.'

Sidney's eyes widen and Keith thinks his hand may have clawed into a fist but he holds his stare so he can't be sure.

'What did you say?'

'She didn't fall down the garden step. Andy didn't hit her with his toy tractor and she didn't fall asleep while she was ironing.'

Sidney steps towards him.

'I don't think I like what you're saying.'

He seethes the words through almost closed lips and moves to grab Keith's collar. Glenda's hand rests on his left sleeve.

'He's not saying anything — are you Keith?'

Keith and Sidney glare at each other, this is between them now. They stand in their little triangle buffeted by the wind and the rain.

'Keith?' says Glenda softly.

He looks at her. Her eyes are terrified, not for herself he realises, but for him. She's used to standing between Sidney and the weak. He's making it worse.

'No,' he says, 'I'm not saying anything.'

'Come on Sidney,' she says quietly and gently lowers his arms with her hand and strokes raindrops from his face. He looks at her trance-like, his head on one side.

'Come on, take me home. We'll get Andy from Mrs Atkins — have chips for tea.'

He lets her turn him and gets into the car. She closes his door and briefly shakes her head at Keith as she walks round to the passenger side. She shuts herself in next to Sidney under the thunderous applause of the rain and looks at her hands as he starts the engine and drives away into the fallen cloud.

Keith had only spent time with Sidney Watson once. He and Glenda never came to any of the work functions. She'd have a quick coffee after her shift but any farewell parties or birthdays were out of the question. She said she didn't like to leave Andy with a babysitter at night and Sidney was always working late. Glenda said that it would be different if she had family nearby, but her parents lived in Ireland, and Sidney didn't see his parents anymore.

Then came Imelda's wedding, another Irish girl who was a nurse on the ward. She was marrying a policeman and both Glenda and Sidney were invited. So Glenda left Andy with their neighbour Mrs Atkins for the day, and she and Sidney joined a party made up of fifty guests, from the hospital and the police station, for a reception at the Royal Albion Hotel.

At the time of the wedding, Keith hadn't known Glenda long, but they got on immediately, making the trials of the ward a little easier for each other with a helping of black humour. Glenda's clumsiness was yet to reach noticeable levels (just the occasional bruise) and it could easily be explained away by random accidents. The question of Keith's sexual preferences never came up but he assumed she knew he was queer. She smiled when he stared a bit too long at some of the doctors and once or twice had winked knowingly at him. There was never any awkwardness between them, and they were so close and intimate during their breaks that sometimes the staff would nudge each other and mutter some gossip about them under their breath. Glenda would giggle and link her arm though his and then they would whisper about the gossips.

He met Sidney at the church. In the chilled quiet he saw a tallish man with short russet-coloured hair and a pale face. Well dressed, slim build, but nothing special. He'd done well to get Glenda, thought Keith, but then he saw her face as Sidney steered her by her elbow down the aisle and along a pew several rows in front. She looked so different from the Glenda he knew, like a little girl on her first day of school, pale with the fear that she would do something wrong.

After the ceremony she introduced Sidney to Keith. He was nice enough, but Keith thought he saw a smirk as they shook hands, as if Sidney knew something about him that Keith didn't want him to know. They all sat together at the reception with Imelda's cousin Cee, and a young constable called Chris; a blind date arranged for her by the groom. It was light-hearted and Sidney entertained them with stories about the drunks the police dealt with on Saturday nights. He was attentive to Glenda; Keith could tell he loved her. He began to think maybe his first impression had been wrong. A noticeably bored Cee made a break for freedom from Chris by going to sit with the bride, promising she'd be back in a minute. They watched her go and Sidney smirked, telling the clueless Chris not to worry — *Keith will look after you* — as he drained his glass of wine. Glenda laid her hand on Sidney's arm and said, 'Go easy — it's still early.'

He put down his glass and refilled it to the top from the bottle on the table, a couple of drops splashed purple on the white tablecloth, then he whispered something in Glenda's ear that made the colour leave her face. They looked at each other and then he turned to Cee's abandoned date.

'Here Chris, dance with the wife will you — get her off my back.'

Chris jumped to attention, eager to please, and held out his hand to Mrs Watson. Glenda hesitated, looking from Sidney to Keith and back again. But Sidney's demeanour changed in an instant and he said softly.

'Go on love — you know I hate dancing — and you should always dance at a wedding.'

She looked quickly at Keith, then allowed Chris to walk her to the floor and push her around to an off-key version of Moon River.

Keith felt odd, being inside the Albion Hotel in a curtained room at three in the afternoon. Something wasn't quite right. They'd tried to create a night-time atmosphere, but every so often one of the kids playing chase around the hall would lift up one of the heavy curtains, sending in a shaft of sunlight sprinkled with dust. Keith looked up at the huge net of balloons above the dance floor and not knowing what to say to Sidney, ventured, 'I wonder if that's for show or if at some point the whole lot will come tumbling down?'

Sidney lit up a Rothman's and leant back in his chair blowing yellow smoke through the air. He flicked ash onto the floor and looked steadily at Keith.

'So, Glenda tells me you're a fruit.'

Keith almost choked on his wine.

'Sorry?' he said knotting his brow.

'Fruit, queer, fudge-packer, whatever you want to call it.' He took another drag of his cigarette and exhaled deeply, blowing smoke in Keith's direction. 'One of Danny La Rue's boys aren't you?'

Keith was suddenly aware of Sidney's job. Had he heard some gossip about him and Glenda? Was he trying to make sure Keith had no desire for his wife, or was he trying to make an easy arrest? Keith sensed he'd have to be careful about what he said.

'I'm not a transvestite if that's what you mean?'

'Same difference. You're a poof though, right?'

Keith didn't answer, he scanned the dance floor for Glenda but she was way over on the other side, swirlingly avoiding Chris's two left feet and chatting to Imelda.

'You fancy men?'

Keith didn't answer — just blinked.

Sidney laughed and held up his hands — that instantaneous

switch in mood again — no wonder Glenda was edgy. It struck Keith that you could never be sure what way to take Sidney Watson.

'It's ok — I'm pulling your leg. I'm off-duty. I just want to know who my wife's hanging about with, that's all.'

Keith nodded. 'Yes, I prefer men.'

'What I'm curious about,' said Sidney replacing his smile with a measured stare, 'is what you actually do? I mean do you get down on all fours when you take it up the arse — like a dog?'

The strains of Moon River receded and Glenda and Chris appeared back at the table, red-faced and smiling. As Glenda looked at Keith her smile wobbled and then she sat down next to Sidney.

'Everything alright?' she asked.

Sidney patted her arm, 'Fine Beautiful, just getting to know your friend here a bit better.'

Keith smiled briefly at Glenda then stared straight ahead at the stage. The MC began a countdown from ten and when the crowd reached zero, a rope was tugged, the net fell away and a thousand coloured balloons glided delicately to the floor.

Glenda hasn't been back at work in two days. After a week Sister Blake tells Keith that she's handed in her notice and won't be coming back at all. He tries ringing her but no one ever answers — it just rings and rings. He holds on for ten minutes, then puts down the phone and tries again. Still no one answers. He thinks about going to her house but realises he has no idea where she lives. He asks Imelda but she doesn't know either. What next — the police station? Follow Sidney home just to make sure she's alright? Then comes the postcard — care of the ward — *I'm sorry I left you without saying goodbye. Andy is ill. I'm fine. I miss you all terribly and hope to see you again soon.*

Glenda.

She's not fine — he can tell. He manages to get her address from the admin office by flirting with the secretary, even taking her out to lunch for heaven's sake. Glenda will laugh at that one when he tells her. He goes to her house on his day off; making sure the Zodiac isn't parked outside. He rings the doorbell, his heart in his mouth as he sees a figure moving behind the frosted glass, but when the door opens it's not Sidney, or Glenda. The woman tells him they've moved — she has a forwarding address and writes it down for him. It's out of town in a village near Devil's Dyke; he has to walk miles from the bus stop.

When he gets there the house is silent. There are roses growing on a trellis around the door and Andy's bike is upturned in the front garden. Keith knocks. There doesn't seem to be anyone in, but he has the feeling Glenda is inside — hiding. He writes a note on the back of the forwarding address.

Was passing and thought I'd pop in. Keep in touch — Keith.

He posts the folded paper in the letter box, peering through as it hits the mat, sure that in a few minutes Glenda will pick it up.

He sits on the wall at the bus stop reading a newspaper he's bought at the village store. He has nearly an hour before the bus comes but he doesn't mind, the sun warms his face, the air smells sweet and the bees buzz in the cornflowers around his feet. He feels satisfaction that he has let Glenda know he is there if she needs him. He becomes so lost in a story about a haunting at Wilson's Museum that he doesn't notice the Ford Zodiac glide past him with Sidney Watson at the wheel.

The gift of parenthood didn't come easily. Sidney said they should try straightaway; that he wanted a son. Money wasn't a problem — he'd done well at work and was fast-tracking up the ranks. They moved into a house, decorated the spare room as a nursery and planted vegetables in the back garden, but by the time the carrots were ready, there was still no sign of a baby. They enthusiastically tried to create one, but each month Glenda felt the rumbling leaden pain in her stomach and then the blood would come, telling her she'd failed.

After a while the tiny explosions that erupted in Glenda's body whenever Sidney reached for her dwindled, she began to think only of the failure. Soon she just lay there beneath him as he worked, barely able to move.

'What's wrong love?' he'd ask. And she would cry and say, 'it's never going to happen.' And Sidney wouldn't answer.

Sidney began to stay out after work, to come home smelling of whisky and perfume. *He had to go out with the lads it was part of the job, being popular was one of the reasons he was doing so well.* At first he felt the need to offer these explanations though she never asked for them — in her mind she didn't deserve one. Soon, when Sidney staggered home after midnight, covered in the scent of another woman and an ocean of alcohol, there were no more explanations. There was only silence between them. Glenda just lay on her back with her legs open and thought how everything would be alright if only she could give him a baby.

Five years after they were married, when all hope of a baby was gone, Glenda was chopping vegetables to make a stew for Sidney's dinner. She knew he probably wouldn't be home to eat it but she made it anyway just in case. If he came home and there was no dinner he'd go straight out again. As she cut the end off a carrot she caught her finger with the knife blade and a drop of blood, thick and so red it was almost black, trickled onto the pitted wood of the chopping board. She dropped the knife and ran to the calendar and then she smiled, not noticing the drops from her finger staining the white cotton of her skirt.

Sidney was delighted — truly delighted. He really tried to be normal again. For the six remaining months of her pregnancy he treated her like a queen, flowers and foot-rubs and early nights and breakfast in bed. No more staggering home late at night stinking of booze, no more women — just the two of them and their future.

Andy was born at Mrs Atkins' house. He was three weeks early. Glenda didn't realise she was in labour, thinking she had indigestion from the dinner Sidney cooked the night before. She only just managed to get next door before the pain overwhelmed her and Andy was born on her neighbour's kitchen floor half an hour later.

When she lay on the couch in Mrs Atkins' living room, Glenda looked down at the tiny sticky baby snuggled to her breast, at his perfect little head and thatch of russet hair and knew that he was the only thing in the world that mattered to her. She folded her arms around him like an angel's wings and whispered into his silken forehead, 'I will be yours forever,' just as Sidney walked through the door.

She shut him out. She knew that much — that it was all her fault. She'd catch him watching her and Andy and be annoyed that he was there. When he picked the boy up she was on edge, fussing around until he put him down or gave him back to her. She froze when he touched her. If Andy was asleep and Sidney stroked her arm or kissed her neck she'd pull away saying they might wake the baby. Sidney told her it was time they moved the cot out of their room and into the nursery, but Glenda wouldn't have it — not yet.

Sidney began to sleep on the couch so he wasn't disturbed by Andy's cries. Sometimes, when he popped into the bedroom in the morning to say goodbye, Glenda would pretend to be asleep. Soon Sidney began to work late again and when he came home Glenda would detect a slight whisky smell covered up with mints. By the time Andy was eight months old Sidney was back to his old routine, coming home after midnight barely able to stand. He rarely went upstairs but when he did and Glenda let him climb on top of her she could smell the other women on him. It was never the same perfume and it was always mixed with the smell of sex.

After a while Keith begins to forget about Glenda. She's still there at the back of his mind but he can't do anything about her. If she needs him she'll find him. Besides, he's in training. He's doing a sponsored swim for the hospital charity, Pier to Pier and back again. The secretary roped him into it, said it was the least he could do after leading her on, and he couldn't argue with her logic. Keith loves to swim in the sea and he loves it all the more because it means he gets to spend time with Darren, a young doctor who is also doing the race. A young doctor who has a lot in common with Keith and looks incredible in a pair of swimming trunks. They've become very close and Keith is immeasurably happy, he finds himself grinning all day long.

He swims most days, usually after his shift. Sometimes with Darren, before they have dinner together; sometimes alone. Today he's alone. Today he is fast. He powers through the scant waves in the reflecting sun. The chill of the water disappears after the first few strokes, and as he reaches the end of the Pier and turns west he is as fluid as the sea itself, a part of it, unstoppable. He swims back to shore, full of vigour, running over the crippling beach stones as if they're feathers. The sun toasts his body after the bracing brine, it glows through his muscles, there's no other warmth like it. His skin is oily from the sea salt and his hair is matted at the neck, a slink of seaweed is caught in a curl.

He makes his way to the communal shower near the outdoor pool — it's nothing more than a rusted steel pipe, perforated head and swinging chain. He waits in line for a mother and infant to rinse themselves under the water — smiling as they vacate — and steps under the cup. He pulls the chain, the pipe splutters and a freezing stream cascades over his head. He breathes in sharply then quickly becoming used to the temperature, closes his eyes and sways beneath the spray, coating his shoulders, rubbing his hair. The sounds of the pool come muffled to his ears, joyous screams, splashes, footsteps on tiles. He pulls the front of his trunks slightly away from his waist to slosh out his privates, water drips down his legs and trickles around his pubic hair. He replaces his waist band and hears seagulls cawing across the sky. The water runs down his flickering eyelids — then it stops. Abruptly. Like a broken chain of thought.

Keith opens his eyes, puzzled. The air is bright — it takes a moment to focus. He notices the silver buttons first, then, as the water clears from his eyelashes, he can make out the shape of a blue police uniform. He blinks. The policeman is young, a face like a baby, he thinks he recognises him but they all look the same, don't they?

'Excuse me sir,' he says, 'but we've had a complaint.'

Keith shakes the remainder of the water from his hair.

'A complaint?'

'Yes — it's a bit delicate really — a man said he saw you exposing yourself a moment ago. Called us over as we were walking past.'

It is then that Keith sees the other policeman, a few feet away talking to a middle-aged man in a dirty raincoat and trilby. He's pissed, swaying on the spot, pointing blindly in Keith's direction. Other people are staring, sunbathers sit up on their towels, kids stop running along the side of the pool, whole familial generations hover open-mouthed over their ice creams.

'Don't be ridiculous,' laughs Keith. 'That man is obviously drunk — he can hardly stand up.'

The policeman is stony-faced.

'He said you pulled down your swimming trunks sir.'

'Oh, for goodness sake. I did this,' he demonstrates, 'to clean out the seaweed — that's all.'

Keith hears a gasp nearby and looks over at a middle-aged lady in a straw hat staring at him goggle-eyed.

The policeman looks around. Keith can see that he's weighing things up. He realises that he's in the right and that this officer of the law has nothing on him, only the testimony of an old drunk and a sexually frustrated woman.

'C'mon,' he says coaxingly, 'do you really have nothing better to do?'

It's the wrong thing to say.

The policeman's inclination to relent is engulfed by a steely resolve.

'You'll have to accompany me to the station sir,' he says. He turns and calls over his fellow officer.

'We're taking him in.'

Keith moves to walk away towards the changing rooms.

'Can I at least get a towel?' he asks.

The next few seconds are a blur. There's a flash of metal and then Keith finds himself with his hands cuffed behind his back. He struggles to get free, twisting between the hands of the two policemen which are now firmly clasped around both his arms. His shoulder aches from its strained position and his wet skin feels cold in the breeze. They walk him up the steps silently ignoring his protests. Four boys are hanging over the peppermint-coloured banisters, bare sandy feet hooked on the bottom rail. They all stare at Keith as he is escorted upstairs; his feet leave dark footprints on the concrete which fade to nothing by the time he reaches the top. They walk him along the pavement in the direction of the West Pier, he feels incredibly naked, amazing what a difference a set of steps makes. Everyone up here is fully dressed — jackets and hats prevail — even under the July sun. Everyone stops and stares; Keith can feel his face burning.

He sees the police car a little way off. That's where they're going — odd that it's here, so close, when they're just beat coppers. As they draw level with it he glances across the road; in front of the Wanderin Café he sees a green and white Ford Zodiac. There's a man leaning on the driver's side door, sunglasses covering his eyes, tie loose, smoking a cigarette. He takes off his shades and looks over at them. Sidney.

Keith thinks about calling out his name. He'd be able to sort this out. He's his wife's friend after all, despite their differences, and in the end Keith had left them to it, minded his own business. Then he sees the nod to the policeman on his left and Keith remembers his name — Chris, Cee's unwanted date. Then he knows. He knows that at the station he'll be charged; that there'll be a witness, maybe two, a court case, a guilty verdict, a sacking. He knows that the only job he ever wanted will be taken away from him. He knows he will never see Glenda again. But most of all he knows without a doubt that Sidney Watson is behind it all.

He shakes his head and almost laughs at the absurdity of it. Is it enough? He's sure it is — they'll make something up, bring in a rent boy, exaggerate innocence into depravity. It will be his word against theirs and all the time Sidney will be there in the background pulling the strings. He could do time, he could lose Darren. He's going to need a good lawyer.

He looks at Sidney one last time as Constable Chris ducks him into the back of the police car, and he knows that tonight as this man is laying his fists into Glenda, he'll punctuate each blow with a word. THAT'S. WHAT. YOU. GET. FOR. CROSS-ING. SID-NEY. WAT-SON.

THE EDITOR

The door to the café crashes open, blasting the fireside warmth with a brutal gust of wind. Jerry looks up to see her struggling through the door — dragging her carrier-bag-laden pushchair with one hand and a snot-nosed toddler by the other. Her hair is windswept, rain stains her pale raincoat in leopard patches and there's mud on her boots. Jerry loves these boots — he has watched her walk in them many times — they are deep blue suede, overlaid with butterfly bows, and the heels are just a little bit too high for everyday comfort. They are not the sort of boots you'd expect a woman with three young children to wear, yet Jerry thinks of them as much a part of her body as the ankles they cover. His heart beats like a drum. He is the only other customer in the café, and he wonders if this monumental noise in his chest is loud enough for her to hear.

As she tries to get inside, Jerry knows he should go and help her. He knows he should get up from his seat, hold open the door, pull the pushchair into the café and set it next to a table, whisk the toddler up in his arms and place her on an empty chair with a smile and a wink. Jerry knows he should do all this (with a measure of charm and small talk) but all he can do is stare open-mouthed, teaspoon in hand.

She glares at him as the waitress helps her to a table and takes her order. Jerry closes his mouth and looks away in shame. He wanted to help her, but when he saw her eyes his legs wouldn't move.

Jerry's coffee goes cold as he pretends to work at his laptop. He watches her furtively over the top of the blank screen. She's taken off her coat and hung it on the back of her chair to dry in the heat of the fire. Her body is slender in her clothes — her chest falls and rises as she gets her breath back. She tries to get herself in order, buttoning her cardigan and smoothing her hair with her hands — there are rogue curls and waves where the rain has soaked in, and there's a smudge of mascara under each eye. Jerry is finding it difficult to function — he purses his lips tightly together so that his mouth won't fall open.

Louis Armstrong toots and growls from the stereo. The waitress brings her order (black coffee for her, the children have smoothies and enormous chocolate brownies covered in snowstorm icing sugar). Jerry feels sorry for the older child — the one that must be at school — who's missing out on all this. There is laughter and hand-clapping, chocolate smeared on tender lips — and her smile — her smile as she watches her children.

The older girl holds out her brownie for her mother to try, and as she leans in and nibbles at the corner, the child pushes it into her face, laughing, covering her mother's cheek with sugar and goo. Jerry's stomach and heart flutter simultaneously. He stumbles to his feet and bulks behind the child's chair to the till, thrusting a five-pound note at the waitress. As he waits for his change he glances over his shoulder at the object of his obsession — but she isn't looking at him — she is lovingly wiping chocolate from her daughter's face. A moment later Jerry is outside in the icy rain, leaving his still blank laptop behind him on the café table.

These unnerving encounters are a daily event for Jerry — since she moved into the house across the street. She was pregnant then, full and soft; her face flushed as she struggled to carry boxes in from the van — her husband cross with her for doing too much. Jerry watched them for a few minutes through his window (a welcome distraction from the badly written novel he was working on).

It wasn't love at first sight. As he watched them argue mildly on the pavement below, he didn't feel the way he does now, but he wishes he'd gone over to help them. If he'd introduced himself then, and carried a few boxes for them, maybe they would be friends now (maybe he wouldn't be so in love with her or, maybe, she would be in love with him too). It's too late now, that particular window of opportunity has passed — now they are destined to be strangers who live on the same street. This doesn't stop her being the most important person in Jerry's life — more important than Karen, his ex-wife, or the handful of close friends he's known since college or the authors whose books he edits to perfection. This woman he doesn't know is the only person he actually cares to see. Only his dog, Gatsby, matters as much.

Jerry knows exactly when it happened — when he started hoping he would catch sight of her on his journeys to the café or the shops. It was a couple of weeks after she'd moved in. He remembers watching her one morning, the sleep still crusting his eyes, as she kissed her husband goodbye. She waved him off from the doorstep, still enfolded in her dressing gown and slippers, then suddenly ran down the gravel path and stooped to pick something up by the gate. When she straightened up again Jerry could see it was a tiny stripy kitten. She held it aloft and rubbed its nose with her own, then rested it on her baby-bump and kissed its pom-pom fur. In that moment Jerry felt like a marionette — his arms and legs suspended on invisible strings, controlled by unseen hands. Since that day Jerry has spent more and more of his time looking out of his window, waiting for her to go out or come home. He calls her Beauty because he doesn't know her name.

Jerry is not a shy man. Although his work is by nature solitary, he enjoys the social aspects of it — the lunches and launches. Jerry's not been unsuccessful with women either, tall and dark with a soft Scottish accent — he has perfected the art of making them feel special and used it to his own advantage. Jerry's marriage ended because he was serially unfaithful. He and his wife, Karen, split fairly amicably — even though he'd slept his way through most of the women at the publishing house where they both worked. Karen is still in his life, they even tried to get back together a few times. Of course it was disastrous, Jerry never wanted Karen to the exclusion of all others and she knew it. He made her look like a fool and she's never totally forgiven him for it, though neither of them can quite let go.

For the last few years Jerry has felt a growing sense of dissatisfaction. The whisky bottles he puts out for recycling have increased in number whilst the women who helped him drink them have dwindled. He used to be the sort of man who would meet a woman in a bar, take her home a couple of hours later in a taxi and then kiss her goodbye the next morning with the promise of a call he'd never make. He never had a relationship after Karen, but he can't even muster the enthusiasm for a biologically necessary assignation anymore. These days he'd rather be at home, within easy reach of his window, waiting for Beauty. He knows that the lack of Beauty in his life was the cause of his dissatisfaction and he doesn't want her to see him with other women.

If Jerry hears footsteps in the street below, he rushes to his window and peers through the blinds — if it's not her his heart sinks, if it is, it soars with the seagulls that patter on her rooftop. He watches her as she walks up the path to her door, usually followed by her cat, he can divine her moods by the way she swings her keys. Her door is green with leaded glass panels. He watched her paint it. She was barefoot, dressed in splattered overalls that stretched over her bump, a scarf tied around her hair, her toenails painted a post-box red. When she was finished, she stepped back to view her handiwork, stretching, and rubbing the base of her spine with her fingertips, then she realised she'd painted it with the door shut. She must have left her keys inside because she put her hand to her mouth and laughed. She patted down her overalls and looked around her, putting the green-heavy brush on the garden wall.

I'll go down there, thought Jerry, *I'll go down there and I'll rescue her!*

He rushed downstairs, sliding over the last three steps, and pulled on his trainers and fleece. He grabbed his keys and skipped out of the door. Jerry looked across the road, but there was no one in her garden; in the seconds it had taken him to get outside she had disappeared. *The café?* He'd set one foot down on the road, ready to cross between two tightly parked cars, when he saw her swing the MPV out in front of him, mobile phone cradled at her chin, as she sped away from him down the street. Jerry crossed the road and picked up the paintbrush. He took it into his house and cleaned it carefully with white spirit, the green paint staining the skin round his fingernails, then he put it back for her where she'd left it on her garden wall.

Jerry's dog, Gatsby, came to him by accident, just after his divorce from Karen. There's a little private road at the back of

Jerry's house. It leads bumpily down the hill; the locals use it as a shortcut to the main route into town. Jerry's office window overlooks it, and quite often he watches its to-ings and fro-ings when he needs a break from work. It is steep and littered with potholes and rocks, but the residents refuse to club together and tarmac it once a year. Cyclists come off their bikes on it, careening into the bushes at the bottom; children skid and trip on the rocks hidden in the grassy banks down its side; cars dip and shake when they hit its unevenness with too much speed. Jerry enjoys watching their misfortunes, and as yet no one has been seriously hurt.

He'd heard the barking all morning, and looked out of the window several times. Whenever anyone went down the road, in a car, on a bike, on foot, a large dog would run after them snapping and barking wildly. It had been comical at first, especially as the pedestrians and cyclists tried to shake the beast off by speeding up, but now it was getting on Jerry's nerves and he couldn't concentrate on his work. He decided to go down and see if the dog had a tag on its collar, so he could phone the owner. He took some bacon from the fridge and made his way onto the road through the back gate.

Once on the grassy edge, Jerry crouched and held out the bacon for the dog. It stood like a statue, head down, sniffing, obviously ravenous but unwilling to come near. It was a liver-grey Weimaraner, still a puppy and in a pitiful state, filthy, with blood caked around its collar and shoulders. Jerry spoke softly to it.

'It's alright boy, I won't hurt you.'

It didn't move but raised its eyes to him and cocked its head to one side. Jerry threw the bacon at its feet and somehow managed to grab it while it was gobbling at the meat. It let him carry it home — too exhausted to protest. He shut it in the kitchen, and was about to phone the RSPCA to come and take it away, when he changed his mind and called a vet instead.

Jerry called him Gatsby, after Fitzgerald's self-made prince —
his favourite book. It took Jerry the best part of a year to gain
his trust. At first the dog would cower silently whenever he tried
to pat it, shrinking on its haunches, eyes lowered. On the advice
of the vet, Jerry patiently allowed the dog to come to him in its
own time, while he fed and walked it, holding out treats on his
flattened hand. Then one day Gatsby took a treat, licking it off
Jerry's palm with his warm pink tongue, before slinking away to
his basket. Now Gatsby is Jerry's best friend — his family, his
child — Karen hates him, maybe she sees him as her
replacement.

They used to argue a lot — Beauty and her husband.
Especially in the months after the baby was born — Saturday
and Sunday mornings mainly, but also in the mid-evenings
when he got home from his daily commute. In the mornings
Jerry would hear them through the fog of his sleep. She did most
of the shouting. They would be up and out at some unearthly
hour, when most of the other residents were still wrapped in
their curtained rooms. She didn't care about the neighbours, she
would be shouting as they walked to the car, her voice strained
with frustration — a barrage of rhetorical questions: *Did he
think he worked harder than she did? Did he think it was easy
bringing up three children virtually unaided? Why did everything
have to be about him all the time? Why couldn't he do the one
thing she had asked him to do?* She would pepper her sentences
with swearwords, with fucks and fucking, shits and buggers.
Jerry liked the way she swore. It excited him — it made her into
something more than a mother. He liked the way she didn't care
who heard, not even her children — as if the passion of her
anger was too ardent for her to control. When she told her
husband to FUCK OFF!, she spat it with such vehemence that

she denied the word any sexual connotation — yet as Jerry lay on his bed with his eyes closed, he breathed in the word as something whispered in an entirely different context, and the skin on his earlobes bristled, as if she, and not just her voice, were really in the room with him.

After a few loud minutes of constant provocation her husband would crack and snap back at her, then one of the kids would start to cry, the car doors would slam and the space outside Jerry's window would be quiet again.

Jerry had never thought about having children, even when he was married to Karen the subject had never come up. They weren't that kind of couple — or so he thought. He saw his friends look at their children, with pure love shining on their faces, and he would pity their lack of freedom. Now, as he lay in his room listening to her argue with her husband, he knew that if she came to his door, with all three children in tow, he would wordlessly take her in and exchange all his freedom for the life of husband to her and father to them. She could shout at him as much as she needed to.

They hardly argue at all these days. On Saturday mornings they breeze to their car and buckle in their children with idyllic synchronicity. He holds her hand, squeezes her waist, and kisses her hair. They smile and look into each other's eyes. They are happy and Jerry is miserable. He tortures himself by thinking of what might have brought about this change — of how they rediscovered they were in love.

A few weeks ago Jerry tethered Gatsby outside the post office as he went in to pick up a manuscript. He could hear the dog barking madly outside while he waited in the queue. *What now?* he thought — an old woman in front of him paid for her stamps in pennies.

As Jerry left, he saw her, standing a few feet away from Gatsby, cradling her hissing, wriggling cat to her chest. The cat often followed her up the street, it must have seen Gatsby and freaked. Gatsby strained on his lead, yelping and paddling in the air with his front paws. Unable to push her buggy and carry the cat at the same time, she stood frozen, glaring at Gatsby and whispering to the cat. Jerry didn't know what to do. He needed to get Gatsby away, but he also wanted to speak to her — to end the torment of never having exchanged a single word with her. Once again he found himself incapable of doing anything. There was an interminable moment of inaction, as they all stood together on the pavement in a frozen tableau. Annoyed with himself Jerry frowned, and immediately wished he hadn't, as she assumed it was intended for her.

'Move your dog please,' she said. Her voice was clipped and rude, conveying her need in the shortest sentence possible — it punched him in the gut and he felt as though he might actually cry.

'I'm sorry,' he gruffed, red-faced with his head down. He unhooked Gatsby's lead and dragged the dog away across the street.

Karen is sitting opposite Jerry in the café, facing the window, as he reads through an unusually brilliant but problematic novel she's working on.

'She's new,' she says. 'Pretty. Great boots! You didn't tell me you had new neighbours.'

He turns to look, although he knows who it is already — she's standing at the post box talking to one of the neighbours, sunlight shining on her hair. When he looks back at Karen she laughs.

'My God Jerry!' she says, her eyebrow as arched as her tone, 'You've gone a very peculiar shade of red.'

'I have not,' he says, trying to keep his eyes fixed firmly on the manuscript in front of him.

She smirks, 'Have so! What's up? Has Jerry got a little teenage crush?' She looks out of the window again. 'A bit *mummy* for you isn't she? What's her name?'

'I have absolutely no idea,' mutters Jerry. He points to the manuscript, 'I like this bit — when Mia sees Joshua Bones in the graveyard.'

Later Jerry watches Karen leave from his bedroom window. She's parked opposite his house and as she's getting into her car, the green door opens and Beauty comes out pushing her pram. Karen stops and holds the gate open for her; they stand for a minute chatting, all smiles and hand gestures, with that instant camaraderie that women find so natural. Karen points at Jerry's window and they both look up — he stands back sharply against the wall. He is suddenly furious. *What the hell did Karen say to her? She has no business talking to her about him.* Why can she never leave things alone?

The text comes as he is eating his M&S lasagne that evening.

NAME'S LOUISE — SAYS SHE DOESN'T
KNOW YOU AT ALL L XX :(

It is a particularly cold November morning and the road behind Jerry's house is more dangerous than ever. There is frost on the grass and invisible ice on what's left of the road's surface. Jerry's up and about earlier than usual today, his whole body tingles with the electricity of life. He stands at the foot of the road waiting for Gatsby to finish peeing, looks at the lights of the city rise on the hills above them. He is smiling — finally he knows her name.

He hears the car hit the pothole with a metal bang, then skid on the ice, brakes screeching. Jerry turns just in time to see her behind the wheel, her mobile phone still in her hand, a look of pure terror on her face. He is thrown up into the air by the impact and lands with a thud on the white-glazed grass. A stray triangle of thick black tarmac knocked up from the road's surface makes its opposite impression in the back of Jerry's skull. His vision blurs.

When it clears again, Louise is kneeling at his side holding his hand, stroking it with trembling fingers. Gatsby has rested his head on her knee and is whimpering softly.

'Please be alright,' she says, 'Oh God, please be alright!'

There are tears in her eyes. Jerry smiles at her; his warmest smile, it fills his face with sunshine. He gestures for her to come nearer. She brings her face up close to his, her hair brushes his cheek. She smells sweet, of heavy-scented flowers and coconut — a tropical island smell. He looks into her eyes; they are the colour of an endless summer sky. Jerry's voice is weak but perfectly calm.

'I just wanted to tell you,' he says, 'you are the most beautiful woman I have ever seen. I — love you.'

Louise breaks down. She is so close he can feel her warm breath on his cheek. Jerry breathes it into himself, in one short, tight, little gasp. The breath he expels is long and laboured — his last.

TARGETS

Whitsun bank holiday, 1964. Miriam stands in the cool of the living room at Number 43 St Leonard's Avenue. The picnic is packed and she's just finished applying her makeup. She fiddles with her hair in the mirror over the fireplace, smoothing the curls to perfection, then she looks at her face, pulling the flesh of her cheeks up behind her ears with the slight bag of her jowls, to try and make it look like it did twenty years ago. She can only manage to correct one slack at a time and decides to spend the day with her chin raised so the skin sags less. Where did it go — all the elasticity?

There is no sign of the rest of the family; they're all upstairs getting ready. Stanley has been waiting nearly an hour to get into the bathroom for a shave. Ava got in first — at 15, she spends more time in the steam-filled room than anyone else. Miriam heard the doors slam earlier and realises that Stanley missed his spot and Frankie is now in there beautifying himself. Frankie is nearly as bad as his sister, the amount of time and money the boy spends on his appearance is unbelievable. She can hear Stanley pacing up and down the hallway, every so often the footsteps stop and he bangs on the door, 'C'mon son, it's nearly 11.'

Miriam lights another cigarette and decides to get in the holiday mood by playing some music. She opens the record box on the sideboard and flicks through the 45's inside. She's looking for one in particular — *Anyone Who Had A Heart* by Cilla Black — Stanley bought it for her for their wedding anniversary. Twenty years last week. It had been a special night, she'd made his favourite — roast chicken and all the trimmings — Stanley had come home all la-dee-da with flowers and a bottle of wine. When dinner was through he'd given her the record and they'd danced around the furniture in each other's arms with the kids sniggering from the stairs. Then Stanley had shooed them away and shut the living room door and they'd fooled around on the sofa. She smiled at the thought of it, behaving like a couple of kids at their age.

She can't find Cilla; she's sure she put her back in the box. Maybe Stanley's moved it — or one of the kids — though they wouldn't normally be caught dead with such a thing. Old-fogie music — that's what Frankie calls it. She puts out her Consulate in the ashtray and kneels down to look for it in the other record box in the sideboard. She's bent over; her head entirely consumed by the cupboard, heady with the smell of damp felt and Christmas liqueurs, when Stanley comes downstairs. He stands in the doorway looking at his wife's bottom; her summer skirt has ballooned around it accentuating its roundness in a pretty smattering of rosebuds.

Stanley never tires of his wife's arse, even after twenty years he grabs it as often as he can. Time may have thickened it and dropped it slightly but it's still a wondrous thing. It started off pert you see. It was the first thing he saw of the future Mrs Morgan as she tottered around the race course at a Bank Holiday meet, it was wrapped in a tight tweed skirt and it wiggled as she walked arm-in-arm with her girlfriends. She looked like a race horse from behind, long and thin with a marvellous arse. Then she turned around and he saw her face and he knew he was lost.

There was a war on and people wanted to have fun. It was easy to talk to girls then, especially if you were young and in uniform, and Stanley was in the fortunate position of being 21 and a sailor. He and his friend Mack helped the girls place their bets and they watched the race together. As Miriam's horse took the lead she jumped up and down near the white rail and hooked her arm into his. He tried not to look at her breasts jiggle under her cream silk blouse but it was almost impossible. When her horse won she was so excited, she threw her arms around him and kissed him on the cheek, missing his mouth by a mere fraction. By the end of the afternoon he was in love, and after he'd taken his time kissing her goodbye on her doorstep he knew that she was the one. They were married within six months — you don't hang around in wartime, not when you've found a girl with a body like Betty Grable's.

Miriam was still gorgeous in Stanley's eyes, not even Doreen from the travel office — his one lapse in twenty years — came anywhere near. When he held Doreen's younger, but less perfect arse in his hands, he wondered what the hell he was doing. Had it just been because it was a thing men did after ten years of marriage? A rite of passage — like your first cigarette? Miriam's time had been taken up with the kids but even so he felt bad, ashamed that he'd stooped so low for something he didn't really want. It made him feel less rather than more of a man. The affair didn't last long and he never felt the need again.

Miriam looked better than ever now, she was thin and toned and although her hair came from a bottle, rather than being its former natural gold, it still shone in the sunlight. Whenever he asked her how she kept so fit she'd tell him it was walking in high heels, but it was more than that, she watched what she ate and made the effort to stay pretty for him. He loved her for it, for not letting herself go and for making him the envy of his friends.

As he stands in the doorway eyeing his wife, Stanley wishes they could pack the kids off somewhere, lock the doors and spend the Bank Holiday in bed like they used to when they were first married. They probably could — Frankie and Ava were old enough to find something to do for themselves — but it was the Bank Holiday, and that was time you spent with your family.

'Now that is a pretty picture,' says Stanley, his head cocked to one side.

Miriam looks over her shoulder and smiles.

'Have you seen Cilla Black? I can't find it anywhere — could've sworn I put it in the record box.'

Stanley shakes his head and Miriam sticks her face back in the cupboard to have another look. She spots half a black circle underneath the wooden crate they use for their 33's. She pulls at it, lifting the box so it won't scratch any more than it has already. She shuffles backwards on her knees, pulling the record into the light. It's scratched to bits; the middle isn't there, just an empty gape about an inch across.

'Look at this,' she says standing and handing the record to Stanley.

'Oh what a shame — it must've fallen down the back — I'll get you another one love.'

Miriam looks hurt; she scrunches up the left side of her mouth as she always does when she doesn't agree with something.

'I don't think it was an accident — look here, the middle's gone — and it wasn't one of those press-out ones either.'

Stanley examines the record closely. The sunlight hits the

black, sending bright patches across the grooves. The middle is crudely gouged as if it has been attacked, a frayed circle of jags and serrations.

'You're right you know — looks like someone's deliberately cut out the middle, gone at it with a penknife or something.'

They both look at each other.

'FRANKIE!' they shout in unison.

Frankie was in his bedroom brushing his hair into a flat fringe on his forehead. He'd just greased his eyebrows and made a little nick in one of them with his razor to break the natural line, only a fraction but just enough. He pulled on his jacket and straightened his tie-pin, then pulled down his shirt cuffs so the matching cufflinks showed at his wrists. They were Italian, like his socks, and they'd cost him a month's wages. He did up the single button on his hound's-tooth jacket and smoothed his hair again. He whistled as he worked — The In-crowd — and weaved from side to side, checking every angle in the mirror.

'You look good, man. Sweet!'

He'd be buggered if he was going to waste all this on a family picnic, with his Mum and Dad and Ava and the Joneses and their ugly brat of a daughter! The kid, who was 14, spent her whole time staring at him and baring her metal-covered teeth. Frankie was nearly 17 and he was working, so he should be able to do what he wanted. That was the deal, he'd forfeited Art College for a year on his father's insistence to save up his money and prove he wasn't afraid of work. Dad got him a job in the bank. He paid rent now — so he should be able to come and go as he pleased. He'd wait until they were about to leave, then go downstairs and tell them to count him out — he had made prior arrangements.

He wouldn't let on that the 'prior arrangements' were meeting a bunch of mates on the seafront and hurling rocks at rockers.

Rocks at rockers — he liked that — had a ring to it. He was meeting the lads at noon and it was after 11 now.

His bedroom door creaked open.

'Talking to yourself again?'

It was Ava; she leant against the door-jam with one foot resting on it, inspecting her scarlet nails and chewing gum. Her hair was combed back into an enormous beehive and she wore ultra-tight clam-diggers, a halter-neck sweater and more makeup than Danny La Rue — applied in much the same style.

'What do you look like?' smirked Frankie, still patting down his hair.

'What do I look like? — pot/kettle!'

'Are those mum's shoes? They're never gonna go for it you know, you'll be sent upstairs to wash and put on that little flowery dress they got you at Christmas.'

'Do all girls have awful brothers — your trousers are tighter than mine — hoping to pull a poof?'

They both laughed at that one. They got on well despite their differences; banding together to fight off the embarrassment of having to live with Mum and Dad. Besides, Ava loved Frankie's friends — a house full of boys two years older than her — what could be better?

'You trying to get out of it?'

He nodded, still working the mirror.

'You won't — besides, you can't leave me to spend the day with dippy Dora and her braces.'

'You're not selling it to me sis.'

'*FRANKIE!*'

'Uh-oh — whatcha do now?'

Frankie runs down the stairs as fast as his pointed boots will allow. Ava follows behind. In the living room Miriam is standing against the back of the sofa with her arms folded, Stanley next to her holding the record.

Frankie ducks through the door, all arms and legs. He can tell by their faces he's in trouble.

'Do you know anything about this?'

Frankie shrugs and looks at the floor.

'Oh Frankie love, how could you? You know what it means to me,' says Miriam.

'Sorry Mum I needed to play something Kevin leant me; it came without a middle so I took yours.'

Miriam's voice softens. 'You could've used one of the press-out ones.'

'I know I didn't think, just grabbed the first one I found.'

'You selfish little bastard,' says Stanley. 'You can buy her another one — use some of that money you waste on making yourself look beautiful.'

There had been tension between father and son since the argument about art school. Frankie wanted to be a photographer. He was good too — had a real eye for it. But Stanley thought he should stay on and get some proper qualifications. Proper qualifications were a waste of time was what Frankie thought; instead he agreed to work at the bank where his Dad was assistant manager, just for a year. He thought he could win his Dad over and earn some money at the same time, and in a way he did; what he hadn't considered was the mind-numbing monotony of being a general dogsbody in a national bank. He wanted to be out and about with his camera and instead he was behind closed blinds under neon lights listening to typewriters tap out the seconds of his life. He began to resent the man who'd put him there, and these days he sought out arguments with his father at every opportunity, and Stanley, more like his son than he would ever have imagined himself to be, always took the bait.

So, in the living room at St Leonard's Avenue, Frankie sees the window he can climb through to get out of a family Bank Holiday. He narrows his eyes and gives his father an insolent look.

'I'm not wasting my money on that fucking crap,' he says.

Miriam takes a deep breath, Ava 'woo-hoos' from her place in the doorway and Stanley steps towards his son.

'What did you say?'

'You heard. I said it was fucking crap.'

Stanley goes to slap his son but Frankie grabs his hand — there's a tussle that seems to last for hours, though in reality it's over in a matter of seconds. Cilla Black falls to the floor and cracks in two under Frankie's boots. Stanley applies all his strength to the struggle and shoves Frankie back against the wall, his arm across his chest. He holds back his fury but when he speaks, he spits the words violently in his son's face.

'You think you're pretty smart, don't you? I'll tell you something boy — you're nothing, you've done nothing special and you probably never will.'

Frankie struggles like a steer, trying to avoid his father's eyes, then he lifts his knee into a sharp point under Stanley's bollocks. Stanley drops his arms between his legs and crumples to the floor. Frankie sees his mother's face — disbelieving — and after a moment's hesitation turns, pushing Ava out of the way and stopping only to grab his camera from the hall table — then he is off so fast out of the family home he leaves the front door swinging on its hinges.

Kenneth Jones pulled his Humber into the empty space in front of 43 St Leonard's Avenue just as Frankie ran out like a robber towards the sea. He watched the boy's feet and legs, elongated by the slap of his pointy boots, propel him swiftly along the pavement. He looked at his wife Cheryl and raised his prematurely bushy eyebrows.

'All's well in the house of Stan then,' he said. 'Another carefree family day out. Honestly — I don't know why they don't just let the boy get on with his own life.'

'None of your business Ken,' said his wife. 'Keep out of it.'

She glanced over her shoulder into the back of the car at Dora, who looked like she'd just been punched in the mouth as she watched Frankie disappear at the end of the road.

The Joneses and Morgans went way back. Ken and Stanley had lived on the same street when they were little, sat next to each other in school, joined up together, picked up girls together and though they were apart during the war, had kept in touch and slipped back into an easy friendship when it was all over.

The Joneses walked through the open door of Stanley's house to find him crouched on the floor struggling to get his breath back, Miriam at his side rubbing his back.

'Jesus,' said Ken, 'what happened this time?'

Ava took great delight in telling the tale.

'Frankie's in for it this time — said fuck and kneed Dad in the bollocks.'

'Ava!'

Dora giggled.

'I'm only saying what Frankie did — you can't tell me off for reporting news.'

Stanley got to his feet, 'Knees like javelins that boy,' he said rubbing his crotch.

Ken couldn't help smiling and slapped his friend on the back.

'You're getting old mate, time was you would've seen it coming.'

'Talking of the news,' said Cheryl, 'there's supposed to be trouble today. Mods and rockers coming down from London; gearing up for a big fight. There's police everywhere.'

Miriam looked at her husband in alarm.

'You don't think that's where he's gone do you?'

The men looked at each other.

'Ava — is that where Frankie's going?'

She shrugged, 'I dunno — he's my brother he never tells me anything.'

Miriam laid her hand on Stanley's arm.

'Can we go and look for him? I don't want him to get hurt — he's only 16. Couldn't we just drive along the front and see if he's there?'

The girls hoped the answer would be yes — the adults no. Everybody looked at Stanley.

So it was decided, they'd spend the first part of their Bank Holiday driving along the front looking for Frankie among thousands of other teenagers and the usual influx of weekend tourists.

Frankie runs full pelt for about a mile. He likes to run — he's always been good at it — it was the one sport he enjoyed at school. He had the advantage of extra-long legs and when it came to sprinting he always won — he was pretty good at middle-distance too — it used to drive the sporty kids crazy; the big rugby players simply couldn't catch him. The sports teacher tried to persuade him to join the football team but Frankie didn't want to, he wasn't a team player, he preferred to be on his own with the wind at his back and the crowd far behind him. He won athletics trophies — and the quiet respect of the sporties — but he hasn't run since he left school, and today sprinting along the pavement away from the family home, he is really beginning to enjoy himself.

Kevin is there already, standing on the corner wearing a new pork-pie hat and smoking a cigarette.

Frankie is running so fast he can't put his brakes on in time and skids past his friend, slipping on the soles of his boots.

'Whoa — where's the fire?'

They slap hands in greeting and Frankie sits on the wall next to his friend.

'Had a fight with my Dad,' he explains breathlessly, 'kneed him in the balls and ran all the way here.'

His friend shakes his head with a smile.

'You're bonkers. They'll kill you when you get home.'

'Don't care — they wanted me to go for some stupid picnic on the Downs — no way was I missing this. Where's Sparky?'

'Had to go to his Nan's in Worthing! Well gutted.'

Kevin rummages in his Parka pocket then pulls out his closed fist. When he opens it, his palm is full of little blue pills.

'Want some?'

'You star!'

'Oi you!'

The boys jump and Kevin drops his stash on the pavement. It's the bellhop, dressed in an elaborate red and gold uniform. They recognise him from town, though he doesn't usually wear a monkey suit. He bends down at their feet and picks up the pills, then sticks two in his mouth before handing the rest to Kevin.

'Manager's told me to move you along — don't want riff-raff spooking the toffs.'

Kevin and Frankie look over the bellhop's shoulder and see a man in a suit glaring at them from the hotel steps.

'Do me a favour an' piss off.'

'Andrew — tell them if they don't leave I'll call over those policemen.'

The manager's clipped accent echoes across the steps and Frankie and Kevin's eyes move across the road to a large unmarked van with two policemen sitting inside. Kevin stands up from his place on the wall and throws his cigarette to the floor.

'Have fun for me will ya?' says the bellhop. 'I'll be watching from here.'

They walk away towards the Palace Pier as another police van skids round the corner and blasts its siren into action. The van parked opposite the hotel turns in a screech of brakes and chases it up the road.

'Follow that cab!' says Kevin and they run laughing towards the action.

By the time the Morgans and Joneses set off in their cars along the front, the roads were full of traffic. They made slow progress, stopping and starting as the brake lights of the car in front flashed palely in the sun. Ava decided to ride with the Joneses — Dippy Dora was a more attractive prospect than her father with his anger and her mother with her repetitive concerns. Her mother would be wondering out loud if Frankie was ok; if Stanley had been too hard on him; if he'd get into trouble without her there to look after him. Her mother had always loved Frankie more, she worshipped the ground he walked on, he got away with murder and their Mum always seemed to think it was funny. When Ava got into trouble — no matter how minor — it was never funny; her mother gave her the silent treatment for days, even if it was something trivial like borrowing her perfume or coming home from school an hour late. Her Mum didn't realise she was doing it, but Frankie knew; he took advantage of it and sometimes Ava wished she too could have a younger brother or sister to take the flack for her. Today Ava's 'little sister' would be Dora. So she wordlessly got in the back of Ken's car next to the love-struck 14-year-old and ignored her parents' attempts to wave her into theirs.

Ava and Dora looked at each other excitedly as the roaring of engines filled their ears and first a line of gleaming black motorcycles skidded in and out of the traffic, and then a cluster of buzzing scooters followed in insect-like pursuit. The air filled with the smell of gasoline. Dora clapped her hands together when the mods weaved past, fidgeting in her seat like a five-year-old at the circus.

'Keep a look out for Frankie,' said her father from the driver's seat. He turned to his wife, 'Waste of bloody time — we should just go have our picnic and leave him to it.'

Cheryl looked out of the window at the passing crowds. So many young people — she couldn't remember being that young.

Frankie's flying now and it's not just the pills; adrenaline throbs around his body, his eyes are wide with excitement. He and Kevin and a few hundred others run in relays up and down the roads adjacent to the front. There's a smell in the air that reminds him of gunpowder on bonfire night, the crowds chant and horses' hooves clatter alongside human feet on the cobbled streets. Someone throws a brick through a shop window and there's a huge cheer from the mob. Then it feels as though they're being pushed together, everyone is squeezed into a smaller and smaller space and they can't help but shuffle backwards. Frankie can see rows of white helmets bobbing up ahead, the flaring snouts of the horses behind them and the dark looming figures of police riders pulling the reins to twist the horses and the crowd in the direction they want it to go. A girl next to him, dressed in a short white suit, loses her footing in the push and stumbles to the ground, she cries out in pain as the bloke in front stomps on her arm with his Chelsea boot. Frankie pulls her to her feet. She smiles at him, breathless, fear and excitement in her eyes.

'You ok?' he asks.

She nods and all the fear is gone. They both look down at the black comic-book footprint on her white sleeve and laugh.

'Wild,' says Frankie.

Then they're off, pushed back again towards the beach, down the tiny lanes of jewellery shops and out onto the wide open road at the front. They spill onto the pavement — half the crowd forced down the steps to the beach, the others breaking for freedom eastward towards the Pier. Frankie is one of the lucky ones; he escapes the cattle drive and runs in a zigzag along the front across the roundabout and over the other side of the Pier, to where there are fewer crowds and fewer police.

They're not in separate tribes anymore — mods and rockers merge into one — either joined by fists and boots or by the amble out of danger. He stands on the Aquarium sun terrace and lifts his camera to his face, clicking like it's a pop-gun, hoping to get the feel of it, the sheer thrill of being alive. Four or five rockers pull a mod from his scooter by the railings. It's a beauty — peppermint-green and covered in mirrors that gleam in the pale sun as the rockers kick its owner away and rock it from side to side. Frankie can see the caption under his photograph in the paper. **Rockers Rocking**. He likes that. They haul her up between them onto the railings, then pitch her over the top to crash onto the pebbles below. There's a collective gasp, the mod sits and cries into his hands and the rest of the crowd run forward to look at the damage on the beach. His Lambretta lies wheels up on the stones, fender bent and mirrors broken into a thousand years of bad luck. The rockers laugh and jump the fifteen feet to the scooter to steal her broken mirrors as mementos. They are pursued by several outraged mods and a new skirmish breaks out on the stones below, fists flying and rocks stuffed in socks for weapons. The beach is littered with discarded shoes. Frankie leans over the railings and takes pictures, he doesn't want to fight; besides his socks are Italian — there's no way he's throwing them around the beach.

The Morgans and Joneses had to drive around the one-way system because the coast road was blocked; they managed to find an illegal space to park on the other side of the Pier. Everyone got out of the cars to look for Frankie, only they didn't know where to start because all they could see were the rear-ends of police horses and clusters of white fists and bobbing heads. The roar was incredible. Dora jumped onto the bonnet of her father's car to get a better view, Ava joined her, they held hands and watched the tussles and punches and the wielding of truncheons. The police looked as if they were enjoying it as much as the kids. Dora felt a tightening at her crotch and her heart beat like a fist in her chest. That night, when all the fuss had died down and the house was asleep, she'd touch herself under her pyjamas and think about this noise, and the smell of excitement in the air and imagine Frankie in the middle of it all — the coolest boy alive.

Miriam and Cheryl stood with their backs to the trouble at the beach looking for Frankie amongst the stragglers wandering away from the Pier.

'He's a good boy really,' said Miriam. 'He wouldn't do anything spiteful. Probably just came along to have a look and take some pictures.'

Cheryl didn't say anything, just picked at her nail. In her eyes Frankie was a spoiled brat who led his mother a merry dance. Miriam knew she thought this, they'd argued about it before and she didn't want to hear her opinion now, not while Frankie was out there somewhere, doing lord knows what. She changed the subject.

'Guess who came into the Co-Op the other day?'

'Who?'

'Jack Milligan.'

'No! Did you speak to him?'

'Oh yes. He came up bold as brass and asked where May was.'

'Oh good God Miriam — what did you say?'

'Well what could I say? Told him everything — and that we'd not heard anything of her for years. Told him we missed her, and do you know what he said then? Said he did too.'

'No! Oh Miriam, what did you say then?'

'Told him he should've kept his trousers zipped.'

Just then two youths ran across the road and landed in a ball of kicks and punches at their feet — one of them accidentally hitting Miriam on the shin.

'Oi!' she cried out and Cheryl beat at them with her handbag. Ken grabbed the leather jacket of the one on top and pulled him to his feet, then smacked him on the back of the head.

'Fuck off Mister,' the boy said.

Ken smacked him again. 'Have some respect you little bastard. Now apologise to the lady.'

The mod giggled, not realising that Stanley had squared up behind him, almost double his size with his puffed-out chest.

The two youths looked at the older men, then at each other, and realising they were outgunned, looked down and whispered the word sorry.

Ken pulled the boy's jacket again.

'Didn't quite hear that,' he said.

'Sorry Miss.'

Ken loosened his grip and the pair ran off down the road and disappeared into the crowd.

'Were we like that Stan, when we were young?'

'Course not — we had a proper war — we didn't have to play at it. Think I managed to get the better of you a couple of times though.'

'In your dreams,' laughed Ken and pulled his friend down into a playful headlock.

'God — you are so embarrassing,' said Ava jumping down from the car and getting into the back seat to hide from her parents. Ken let Stanley go and they moved towards their respective cars with boyish grins on their faces. As Miriam and Ken crossed each other's paths he placed his hand lightly on her arm.

'You sure you're ok?' he asked softly and his eyes lingered on hers just a fraction longer than they should have before she smiled and nodded to reassure him.

At the sun terrace, Frankie is busy taking photographs, there's a crash as a deckchair hits the wooden bench and splinters into pieces, then another goes and finally the glass in the shelter shatters onto the floor as the result of a large stone being hurled through it. Frankie gets it all on film. He's pumped — jumping around the scene on his long athletic legs, crouching and clicking, laughing with excitement, his fringe wet with sweat from the exertion. He's having a ball. He gets a perfect snap of a rocker swinging a deckchair high above his head and just as the shutter comes down, a hand grabs at his jacket and he's hauled up with such force that the wool rips at the seam.

He's dragged kicking across the pavement to a police van and thrown in the back. As the doors are slammed shut and the siren wails, he catches sight of his father and Ken Jones standing by their cars, watching the van speed away towards the town's centre.

The Town Hall — built in 1830 — an impressive pillar-fronted building, painted cold white. The police cells in its basement have housed many vicious criminals — child-poisoner Christiana Edmunds, Trunk Murderer Toni Mancini, cop-killer John Lawrence — and today, a few hundred excitable teenagers.

Frankie is scared now; he's bundled through huge double doors into the large reception hall. The staircase rises in front of him to the first floor, then curls away into two separate staircases. He looks up and sees a spiral of brass banisters and landings and staircases stretching up over three more floors. The marble floor echoes with the tramp of booted feet and electric gas lamps flicker as bodies cross their paths. His throat is dry and his eyes are wide. He's never been in here before and he's in awe of its majesty.

It's all he'll see of majesty today, because they're not going upstairs to the town offices or the mayor's chambers. He's being pulled away by the arm and marched down a tiny dark staircase hidden on the side of the hall.

'C'mon Stan. He's only 16 — they're not allowed to take him away. Are they?' Miriam's voice quivered.

Stanley didn't answer her question. 'They'll have taken him to the Town Hall. This traffic's unbelievable. It'll be quicker on foot. Stay in the car, I'll go get him.'

He turned off the engine without moving from the parking space and squeezed his wife's arm.

'It'll be nothing, won't it — Frankie wouldn't have done anything wrong would he?'

Her husband looked at her with reproach in his eyes; her years of spoiling Frankie had finally borne fruit. Miriam started to cry.

'Stay here,' he said again and got out of the car, leaving her alone with her tears.

The overhead lamp swings as they tramp down the stairs. The sound of their footsteps becomes more muffled with every step. The walls are close, painted a dingy yellow with darkened plaster showing under paint that has chipped and flaked away. At the bottom of the stairs they turn down a long corridor, even darker than the staircase; to the right are two doors, each set back from the tunnel by three concrete steps. The doors are made of iron, prison doors with bolts and peep-hole windows. A policeman stands outside one and a policewoman outside the other, they wearily survey the latest mob shuffle past; dampened shouts come from behind the doors, echoing around the corridor like the cries of the damned.

At the end of the corridor they turn left down more steps then on into a large room teeming with policemen in various grades of uniform. A group with rolled up shirt-sleeves sits at a table in the corner, playing cards for matches; cigarette smoke drifts up and hangs around naked light bulbs near the ceiling. The men look up at the rag tag line of hooligans; they don't disguise their amusement. One of them is in plain clothes; white shirt, thin-striped tie loose at his neck, his hair red and slick with Brylcream, his pencil-moustache as thin as his lips. He looks at Frankie as if he knows him, gives him a terrifying little smile, then takes a cigarette from behind his ear and lights it with a gleaming Zippo. Throughout all this he never moves his eyes from Frankie's face. Frankie feels cold and uncomfortable, he's glad he's not alone with this man.

There's a tall broad desk in front of the door with a black telephone and two wire trays sitting on it. The desk sergeant points at Frankie, 'You,' he says tiredly and motions for him to come forward. The other boys are led to a bench along the wall where they sit silently, mod next to rocker, entirely deflated.

'Name?'

'Frankie. Francis Albert Morgan.'

'Birthday?'

'November 11th.'

'Year?'

Frankie's forgotten and doesn't answer for a moment. While he's thinking, the man with the pencil-moustache has moved from his seat at the poker table and is now standing at his side.

'Year?'

'1948.'

'Sixteen?'

Frankie nods, trying not to look sideways at the man next to him.

'You're a minor then. Where can we contact your parents?'

'Look, am I being charged with anything? I was only taking photographs. I didn't do anything.' His voice shakes — all he can think about is how mad his Dad is going to be.

'Empty your pockets.'

Frankie fishes around in his trouser pockets, there's nothing in them but a stick of gum and his house keys, the roll of film he finished earlier is in his jacket and he doesn't want to give it up, luckily Kevin has all the pills.

'Camera.'

'Sorry?'

The sergeant gestures with his hand. 'Give me your camera.'

'I'd rather keep it.'

'Give me the camera.'

Frankie reluctantly removes it from his neck and places it carefully on the counter, giving it a little stroke as he does so.

'Be careful with it won't you.'

'Sign here,' says the sergeant handing him an almost empty biro.

As he's signing, the moustache-man picks up the camera; he

turns it in his hands running his fingers over the leather casing and the smooth metal of the lens.

'She's a beauty,' he says, his voice is quiet — a barely audible reptilian hiss. 'Olympus is it?'

Frankie nods.

The man holds it up to his face and takes a picture of Frankie.

'Get some good pictures today did you?'

Frankie starts to relax a little — maybe the man isn't as nasty as he looks.

'I think so.'

'Pity,' says the man with a smile and opens the back of the camera, pulling out the film in a long swirling snake and holding it up to the light. Then he throws the camera and its intestinal celluloid onto the desk.

'I'll take him up.'

The sergeant looks worried. 'Behave yourself Sidney.'

Sidney smiles. 'Of course — he'll be safe with me. C'mon Ace.'

He grips Frankie's elbow and steers him to the door. Frankie looks back at the now seemingly benevolent desk sergeant but he's bent over the desk scribbling in the notebook in front of him.

The man doesn't speak as he walks Frankie up the stairs and along the corridor, he stays a step behind and Frankie can feel his eyes boring into his back. The policeman at the cell door nods at Sidney and jangles keys from his belt, stiffly turning one in the huge gaping lock. The door creaks open onto a corridor on the other side. Sidney shoves Frankie over the threshold. On the left is a row of metal doors like the one he has just walked through. The noise is enormous, cheers and laughter from behind the doors and a sound like a cup banging on a drainpipe. There's another uniformed sergeant sitting on a chair reading the Sunday Mirror, he smiles when they walk in, folds the paper and places it on the floor.

'Got another one for you,' says Sidney. Frankie can tell he's smirking even though he's behind him.

The sergeant stands and walks toward the second door in the row.

'Not that one,' says Sidney, 'this one.'

'You sure?'

'He'll be okay — you're right outside.'

The sergeant nods and smiles, then unlocks the nearest door and pushes it open. The cell is tiny, about 8 feet by 10, with a small dirty window high on the far wall. Crammed inside are a sea of rockers standing shoulder to shoulder in every inch of space, they cheer when they see Frankie.

'Brought us a girl?' says the one nearest the door.

'In you go,' laughs Sidney and pushes Frankie in, so that he has to steady himself by grabbing the arm of one of the rockers.

'Hey! Hands off the jacket.'

The sergeant pulls the door shut and it closes with a heavy metal clang, the key squeaks in the lock and Frankie is alone with the enemy.

'Has he been charged with anything?' asks Stanley.

The sergeant shakes his head.

'Is he going to be?'

'No, I shouldn't think so. We could charge him with affray but to be honest it's probably not worth the paperwork. If you vouch for him we can just caution him and send him home.'

He picks up the telephone and dials a short number. Stanley can hear it ringing at the other end and somewhere along the corridor.

'Take a seat.'

Stanley sits on the bench between a girl in a white jacket and a young man with long blonde hair, lipstick and a flowery scarf around his neck; both of them edge away from Stanley as if he had the plague.

The hands on the clock move at a slug's pace. Stanley leans forward and looks at his own hands, with every passing second he's getting angrier. He's spent his precious Bank Holiday chasing around after his son and now he's collecting him from a police station. Wait till he gets him home — he'll wipe the smile off that face. There's a clatter of footsteps on the stairs leading into the hollow room and Stanley looks up to see Frankie in the doorway. He looks shattered, his face is grey and tear-stained, his hair sticks to it in sweaty strands. Frankie looks like he did when he was a little boy and frightened, like the time the neighbour's dog chased him up the road from school and chewed on his trousers just as he got to the front door. Stanley's anger melts in pity.

Frankie sees his Dad and hesitates in the doorway, then he's pushed harshly from behind and falls heavily on the floor crying out as his arm hits the tiles. Stanley leaps up and runs over to his son, helping him to his feet.

'You alright son?' he asks gently.

Frankie nods but tears come to his eyes. He looks at Sidney.

'He put me in a room full of rockers,' he whimpers, 'and he broke my camera.'

Stanley turns to face the man who has tormented his son, he sticks out his chest, a trick he learned in the navy twenty years ago and never forgot. He's taller and broader and Sidney Watson, who'd been so scary to Frankie minutes before, seems to shrink before his eyes. His father looms over Watson looking him straight in the eye, bigger in stature and in character, and as Frankie watches, he regains some of the childish awe he'd felt for his father growing up.

'Did he indeed?' says Stanley holding Watson with his gaze, 'I'm sure it was an accident — wasn't it? Obviously he'll pay for any damages.'

The room is silent, the poker players are suspended mid-hand, the industry of the other officers has paused and the bench of teenagers all stare at the two oldies squaring up against each other. Watson blinks, his eyes crossing for a fraction of a second, and he nods slowly.

'I'll see you out.'

'No need,' says Stanley. He turns to the desk sergeant. 'Give the boy his camera.'

It feels good to be outside. With every step up from the bowels of the cells, a little weight is lifted from Frankie's shoulders. Now, as he stands on the town square breathing in fresh air, a smile spreads over his lips.

'Don't know about you,' says his father, 'but I need a cigarette.'

Frankie nods and they cross the quiet of the square to a bench surrounded by pigeons picking crumbs off the floor.

'Out of it!' says Stanley and kicks at them with his foot.

Frankie laughs. 'You're pretty cool you know — for an old bloke.'

Stanley sits down next to his son and offers him a cigarette. This is the first time he's ever done this, before now Frankie had pretended he didn't smoke. He takes one from the pack. Stanley pats his pockets for a lighter but quickly realises he's left it in the car. Frankie reaches into his jacket for his then smiles. He pulls out a lighter and the roll of film he'd hidden there earlier, holding it up for his father to see.

They sit together on the bench silently sucking on their cigarettes, watching the smoke rise into the air with the seagulls that soar higher and higher in the white open skies.

SNIP

Drew falls through the train doors just as they beep shut. A group of lads enveloped in a thick odour of lager, laugh and jeer at him, 'Enjoy your trip mate!'

He staggers to his feet, leaning his hand open-palmed against the carriage partition, and moving it up in grades until he's standing. He swings the *Boots* plastic bag he nearly left on the tube into a more comfortable position over his briefcase, then pushes his way past the lads and down the aisle to wait for a seat. The train is packed; he's hoping someone will get off at Clapham Junction or at least by Croydon. He might be able to hang on till Croydon. His throat is sore and he can taste that last whisky sticking to where the back of his mouth joins his nose. His head feels heavy against his arm as it hangs from the monkey pole. The train lurches out of the station into an eternity of darkness and Drew's stomach rolls with it — more like he's on a boat than a train.

Drew is asleep by Clapham Junction but nobody gets up. At East Croydon he is shoved awake by a fat sweaty man with a stained shirt on his way to the door. In a sudden moment of clarity, Drew steps over the feet of three souls and drops himself onto the seat warmed by the fat man's buttocks. He rests his elbow on his knee and cups his hand under his chin, staring bleary-eyed at the girl sitting opposite with her eyes closed. Even with his late-night blurred vision he can see she's unbelievably beautiful, elegantly poised with clear caramel skin and foot-long eyelashes. Her slender hands rest on her knees and she doesn't shift position with the movement of the train, just sways slightly on the axis of her spine. He guesses she's about twenty — *I could be her dad* — God he feels old.

Drew looks away from her and fumbles in the plastic bag on his lap. He pulls out a box of depilatory cream, leaving the enormous pack of frozen peas he and Daniel bought to mush, on the warmth of his thighs. Drew yawns and rubs his eyes so they are clear enough to read the instructions:

VEET — SENSITIVE SKIN
In-shower Hair Removal Cream
Aloe Vera & Vitamin E
With Moisture Complex

The box is pale blue with a lush graphic of the aloe plant dripping with dew, and a pink symbol that looks like a cross between a teardrop and a DNA strand — mightily appropriate given the circumstances. Drew turns it over; the back is printed in blocks of dense cobalt instructions.

PRECAUTIONS

The text is small and Drew squints to clear the alcohol that's pooling in his eyeballs.

Designed for use on legs, arms, underarms and bikini-line but NOT suitable for use on ANY other parts of the body.

No mention of bollocks here; must've bought the wrong stuff. They didn't have anything specific in the vast array available at Boots. He and Daniel had studied the shelves, half pissed, between pubs. They'd stood and giggled picking up each pack and reading the promises, ogling at the headless bodies subtly rendered in pastel shades. But there was nothing to fit the remit.

There's a definite gap in the market there — must remember to bring it up at work. Could be mileage in it — a MALE depilatory cream. What would it be called? It wouldn't just appeal to poor unfortunate vasectomy victims like myself; our gay friend Gary insists on being totally devoid of hair, he once declined an invitation to Sunday lunch because of an appointment with a back, sack, and crack wax. Mind you he's pushing fifty, so he needs all the help he can get and I think the pain involved is part of the appeal. Still, there are probably wussy gay men that like to be hair-free without the masochism. What could it be called? The heterosexual version that is. HE-mac? Smooth Operator? No, wait — Bald Eagle!

Drew chuckles to himself, his head wobbling as he does. *What about a gay-themed product? Take That! You could combine it with a sparkling body cream and call it Take That & Party!*

Drew imagines hiring the band for the campaign — though they are getting on a bit so they'd have to use body doubles for the chest shots. Barlow could write a song for it.

He laughs out loud. He hasn't noticed the train empty and now it's just him and the girl sharing the carriage. She sucks on a strand of straight black hair and rolls her eyes, but it seems she can't be bothered to move to another seat.

God she's beautiful — like a long tall latte. What must I look like? A drunk, nearly-old man, wearing whisky aftershave and chuckling to himself over a packet of depilatory cream. God I'm pathetic.

He looks back down at the packet in his hand and tries to concentrate on the instructions as the train lumbers on into the night.

5 Steps to BEAUTIFULLY TOUCHABLY SOFT SKIN
MIN 5 MINS — MAX 10 MINS

Drew doesn't think his skin will be *beautifully touchably soft* anytime soon. If this train doesn't get a move on he'll barely have time to leave it on for 5 MINS MIN before he has to go and have his bollocks skewered, or whatever it is they do — he wasn't listening when the doctor explained it; he was too busy concentrating on his breathing.

There are five blue diagrams of a woman's legs under a shower. *It all looks incredibly easy — on beautifully shaped legs. What about on half-buried sagging bollocks? They don't tell you how to sponge the cream off every millimetre of them, do they? Which position you have to get into to check there's none left on for longer than 10 MINS MAX!! Obviously you have to use the softer coloured side of the sponge — the one designed for sensitive areas...*

Drew's mind is rambling now. He'd thought it had been a good idea, a quick drink after work. He'd been jumpy as a rabbit all day and then Daniel had phoned to say he was in town and insisted they have a drink - he thought it would calm his nerves. After an hour in the pub he'd found the Tamazepan the doctor had given him in the bottom of his briefcase, reduced to powder under the weight of work files on top of it. Daniel had taken the packet from his hands and emptied it into Drew's pint. It all went downhill from there. Drew remembers going to buy frozen peas at one point and has a vague recollection of a conversation Daniel had on his behalf, with a curvy chemist in the giant Boots store on Oxford Street, about which hair-remover would be the most effective. She'd looked at Drew pityingly, handed him the packet he now held in his hand and written down her phone number for Daniel.

The slow shift of the train and the rhythm of its wheels rock poor Drew off to sleep…

'Mister — wake up!'

Someone is tugging at the sleeve of Drew's jacket. He opens his eyes one at a time. His head feels like there's a Lilliputian army inside trying to dig their way out through the front of his skull with pick-axes.

'Jesus,' he groans.

He can barely keep his eyes open and strains to see under his half-closed lids. The train is in darkness but for the faint glow of a light somewhere outside. That's not right — the lights should be on in here. The girl is standing over him still pulling his sleeve; she is looking at him with wide frightened eyes that flash white in the dim light. It's unearthly quiet, clearly there's no one else on the train.

'Mister, have you got a mobile phone?'

'Wha?' He tries to make sense of where he is but his mind is heavy with the dark.

'A cell phone. Do you have a cell phone?'

She tugs his sleeve again to emphasise each word. He rubs his forehead with tobacco-tainted fingers; the smell of it surrounds him. *Why did I smoke? Bloody Daniel and his 'Go on, live a little,' nonsense — six pints, two whiskies and half a pack of Silk Cut later and he's stuck on a train in the dark with a psychotic teenager yanking at his arm. What time is it anyway?* He looks at his watch, 1.45, *Jesus, Louise is going to go mental (she wasn't happy with just a quick drink after work and that was nearly eight hours ago!) Shit, bloody Daniel — curse him and his*

28-year-old body and his no wife and kids — unfulfilled, that's Daniel (lucky bastard.)

'Mister — you with me? Do you have a mobile phone?'

'What? Oh — yes. Yes I've got a mobile phone.'

She holds out her hand. 'Can I use it?'

'Mmm — sure.' He pats down his pockets to find it. 'Do you know where we are?'

She sighs and rolls her eyes again. 'We fell asleep. We are at the end of the line.'

Her English is word perfect, in that way that only people who've had to make an effort to learn it have, she's foreign but he can't place her accent — probably someplace African.

'Ah-ha,' he says fishing the phone out of his inside pocket. He hands it to her and she sits down on the seat opposite. Drew remembers when mobile phones were as big as bricks — he had one in his first job, as a runner at an advertising agency — *at least then you could find them in your pockets, actually they didn't fit in your pocket, you just had to carry them around.*

His eyes are beginning to adjust to the dark and he watches her as she presses in the number. She's so young; her skin is perfect and her cheekbones lift like razors below the hugest eyes he's ever seen. She rubs her bottom lip over her top lip, exposing her tongue for the briefest moment. Her neck is long and Drew finds himself following the line of it down past her collarbone to the point where her small breasts curve into the neck of her white vest. Her breasts are unbelievably high on her chest. She's not wearing a bra but they defy gravity, nipples pointing upwards to the stars. He'd forgotten how far from the ground young women's breasts are. After three children and 38 years, Louise's nipples are down by her waist. *No, that's unfair, Louise still has a fantastic body — it's just not as fantastic as it used to be. Still, I'm not exactly Johnny Depp either…*

'Excuse me,' says the girl giving him a stern look. Drew realises he might actually be drooling.

'Sorry.' He coughs and presses his head against the window.

The Perspex is cold on his forehead — it eases his headache. He gazes at the world outside. They are not in the open — there are no fields or trees — they appear to be enclosed in some kind of shed. The wall is inches from the train window and made of huge grey bricks stretching forward and back as far as he can see. High up in front is the source of light — a football-sized white bulb — an interior streetlamp. *Maybe I'm dead, aren't you meant to go to the afterlife on a train these days, a sort of modernist river Styx? Maybe me and the girl died in a freak late-night slow-moving train crash and now we have to wait for the conductor.* He checks his inside pocket and finds his wallet, at least he'll be able to pay the excess.

The girl has finished her call, though she didn't speak to anyone or leave a message. He looks over at her; she shows no sign of giving him his phone back.

'They will call me back,' she says.

'Oh, ok.'

He stands unsteadily and weaves between seats to the other side of the carriage. When he bends to peer out of the window he over-balances and lands heavily on the seat banging his forehead on the window. He laughs then looks at the girl in the same way he looks at Louise when he knows he's done something wrong.

'Sorry,' he says again.

'You are very very drunk,' she says flatly.

'Yes. I am. I'm very very drunk.' He taps his nose and slurs exaggeratedly then chuckles.

She stares at him.

'Withnail & I.'

'Sorry?'

'Withnail & I — it's a film — one of the characters says *I'm vrry vrry drunk*. It's funny.'

She looks at him as though he were from another planet.

'Is it?'

'I guess you have to see it.'

His phone rings in her hand. The noise reverberates around the carriage; Drew closes his eyes and wonders why he let Freddie download the *Doctor Who* theme as his ringtone.

'Hello? Yeah — I fell asleep on the train and ended up at the end of the line with some drunk guy. No he is totally harmless — ok. Does it have to be him, can't you come? Ok. No like a big shed — Brighton train — yeah — bye baby.'

She clicks the phone shut but still keeps it in her hand. She smiles at Drew.

'So what cinema is this film on at?'

'Huh?'

'Nails and Eyes. What cinema is it on at?'

'Oh. Withnail & I. No it's an old film, came out in — let's see — about 1987. You probably weren't even born.' He realises with horror that this statement could be true, that when he was watching *Withnail & I* repeatedly and trying to play out as many scenes as possible, this girl sitting opposite him wasn't even in her mother's womb.

'When were you born?' he asks feebly.

'Don't know.'

'What do you mean — you don't know?'

'I mean I don't know. My grandmother brought me up. My mother died soon after I was born and I lived with an aunt for a while but she couldn't cope, so she sent me to live with my grandmother. My grandmother told me I was about three years old when I got to her, but she was just guessing, no one knew what day I was born — or what year.'

'Jesus.' Drew stares at her open-mouthed.

'I'm about 18 now so I had been born in 1987 — but I could have been two or three — I really don't know.'

'What did you mother die of?'

'AIDS.'

'Christ. Are you…? Ok?'

'I'm perfect. My Aunt had it too. She died a few years ago, just before I came here. She had a little money saved and my Grandmother added to it, saving a little each week so she could send me here to work at a good job in a factory.'

'Is that what you do now?'

'You ask a lot of questions.'

His phone rings again.

'Hello? No — wrong number.' She clicks it shut and it rings again almost immediately. Drew can hear Louise faintly at the other end.

'Look, he's not here.'

Drew throws his arms in the air. 'Great that's just great! My wife is gonna go nuts now. You could at least have let me talk to her.'

The girl shrugs, 'You want to get out don't you? I need to keep the line clear.'

The phone rings for a third time; he's heartily sick of the whoo-oo noise from the TARDIS.

'Yeah. Brighton train. No, a wall and a platform on the other side. Bye to you too.'

Still she keeps hold of his phone. Drew pulls a sulky face and rests his hands on his knees.

They don't talk for a while and he looks out of the nearest window. He can see an empty platform enclosed in an industrial looking shed, there are no signposts, only floodlights high up in the rooftop. It's like a train station from a dream. He wonders again if he might actually be dead.

'Why do you have hair-remover and the peas?'

Drew looks over at her; she has crossed her jean-clad legs and is kicking her foot up and down dangling a high-heeled shoe from her toes. She obviously no happier about being there than he is.

'I'm having a vasectomy tomorrow,' he looks at his watch, 'this morning.'

She nods seriously, 'A what?'

'A vasectomy. It's an operation to stop me fathering any more children.'

She laughs — a bit too loudly — then shock spreads over her face. 'Why would you want to do that?'

He rubs his face with his palm. 'Why indeed,' he says quietly to himself. 'Well, we have three children, my wife and I, and she was quite ill with the last one and we're nearly forty so we don't want anymore. It's the right thing to do.'

'You must love her very much.'

'Huh? Well it's quite minor — they don't cut it off or anything, just make a couple of tiny holes. You're the same afterwards.' He's almost convinced himself.

'Even so, no man I know would do that for a woman. It's a beautiful thing. This is why you are so drunk?'

He nods, humbled by her opinion of him. It had never occurred to him that he was doing it for love.

'So — the peas?'

'Well you're supposed to remove the hair the day before and the peas are for afterwards — to ease the swelling.'

She looks at the bag of peas on his lap; it's the size of an A3 envelope, the biggest money can buy.

'Do you think you bought a big enough pack?'

They both laugh, at the absurdity of a cushion of peas and of being stuck at the end of the line.

'What's your name?'

'Drew.'

'My name is Blossom.'

'Blossom?'

'Yes.'

Drew holds out his hand formally, 'Pleased to meet you Blossom.'

Just then there's a crash in the carriage behind, then the connecting door springs open and an extraordinarily scary-looking man thunders into the tranquillity. The man is like Blossom's antithesis, tall and thin but with a bulk to his chest and shoulders, he is dressed entirely in black. His skin shines luminous white and his dreadlocked hair is almost exactly the same colour. One of his eyes is opaque and the other is almost black; as he moves down the carriage he narrows them at Drew and curls his top lip, exposing a pointed gold tooth.

'Don't touch the goods unless you payin' for them,' he says in a thick West Indian accent.

'For God's sake Pingu I was just shaking hands.'

'Pingu?!' Drew sniggers.

'Sumfing funny?' The man spits the words at him.

Blossom widens her eyes at him as if to say don't mention the name. The carriage fizzes with potential violence; Drew's drunk but he's not stupid, he drops his smile and holds his hands up in surrender.

'I'm pissed — that's all. Ignore me.'

'I will if you're good,' sneers Pingu.

Drew and Blossom watch him storm down the carriage to the doors at the end, his black overcoat rustling against his legs as he goes, a gold bracelet sending light fairies disco-dancing across the ceiling. When he reaches the doors he pushes in the glass panel next to them with his elbow, then yanks down the lever inside. The doors make a depressed noise and open slightly in the middle. Pingu feeds his fingers between them and pulls them apart like he's working a chest expander. He looks back at Drew and Blossom, then strides towards them.

'Why couldn't U do tha?' he says to Drew. Then he grabs Blossom roughly under her arm and hauls her up, 'C'mon! Wasting ma time like dis — Bulldog waitin'.'

'Steady on,' says Drew standing so he's at Pingu's eye level. He puts his hand softly on Pingu's sleeve. Pingu looks down at it.

'Oh no,' mutters Blossom.

Drew feels the blow to his stomach first and then as he's crouching on the floor cradling it, his head is thrown back from the side and suddenly he's on his back with his legs bent under him being held up by his shirt collar and punched in the face, over and over. He can hear the sound of his head hitting the chair behind him as though it's someone else's and can feel moisture on his cheeks — spit, sweat, blood, tears — he doesn't know which. He's aware of the pain — sharp and infrequent — a Morse code of smashes. He hears Blossom's voice in the distance, calm, dripping with honey.

'Leave him alone — he's having a bad day. Come on Peter, Bulldog's waiting.'

Then the frenzy stops as abruptly as it started and Drew feels the swish of an overcoat brush his face and the sound of Blossom's high heels as they disappear into the night.

He shuffles backwards and rests his back against the paltry cushion of the seat base. He is alone in the carriage. *Was that the conductor? Why didn't he take me to the after-life?* He hauls himself up onto the seat with both hands then winces as he stands, a dull ache permeates his stomach and down into his groin. He breathes quickly but he slowly realises he's not that badly hurt, it wasn't a full-on attack just a show of power. He's aware it could be much worse — might have been, had Blossom not saved him. His breath slows but he's still shaking as he makes his way to the open door. Just as he's about to step out, he turns and hurries back to the seat, grabs his briefcase and the *Boots* bag and hugs it to his chest like it's the most important thing in the world, then walks back to the door and down onto the platform.

He looks anxiously down left and right but there's no sign of Pingu or Blossom. *Thank Christ for that.* He can't remember much of the last few minutes and wonders if he was robbed as well as beaten — he pushes his hands into the pockets of his jacket and trousers one at a time, wallet, house keys, work-pass — *Shit my phone. She's still got my fucking phone* — *all those pictures of Lou and the kids* — *gone. Louise and the kids.*

He looks right; the shed ends in a huge open-mouthed gape, train tracks running out of it into the distance. He can see the high embankment wall to the left and the twinkling lights of the city to the right. There are no trains, no people, no birds, just endless bricks and train tracks and dark swaying bushes. He sees the flash of a cat's eyes on the track some way off, and the shadowy shape of its stalking body as it makes its way up the hill. It freezes and its eyes turn — shining jewel-green in the moonlight, assessing the threat level — then sensing Drew's totally harmless, the cat turns and disappears across the tracks and into the black-leaved bushes beyond.

Drew walks to the end of the platform and jumps down onto the ballast at the edge of the tracks. Cold air stings his face and he hears the wind shift the branches of the trees at the top of the wall. There's a white sign with a silhouette of a man walking into a bolt of lightning — *DANGER ELECTRIFIED RAIL. Now, which track is electrified* — *is it the middle or the far, or the nearest?* He decides to do his utmost to avoid all the tracks, though given his luck tonight he'll probably trip up and fall on all three. He sets off towards what he assumes is the direction of Preston Park.

'Oi you!' A man's voice rings out in the hollow of the holding shed. Drew looks round to see the swinging light of a torch and a bulky dark figure running along the platform. He doesn't need telling twice and runs as fast as he can along the gravel, dropping the Veet through a tear in his carrier bag; this time he doesn't go back for it.

Preston Park station is only about a mile away and in minutes he can see its three floodlit platforms. The embankment wall slopes downwards to a manageable height and is tacked with yet more *DANGER!* signs. *There's so much danger in the world already, walking over electrified tracks at three in the morning is just foolhardy.* He steps exaggeratedly over each of the dull metal lines, glancing left and right as if he's crossing the road. *You never know when the milk train will come through — do they still have milk trains?* It doesn't come, and he reaches the other side of the tracks without further damage to his person.

The end of the line AND the other side of the tracks in the same night — now that's impressive.

When the wall is just above shoulder height, Drew throws his briefcase and the ripped carrier bag over the top of it and shimmies up the bricks. As he lifts his leg over the pointed metal of the railings he hears the sickening rip of fabric and feels a waft of cold air tickle the back of his thigh. *That'll be the suit then — could anything else go wrong tonight?*

On the street outside the station, the world is suspended silently in an orange streetlamp glow. He's about to cross the road to the steps that will take him up to the street above and home, when he realises that if he is to explain this whole mess to his wife, he might have to lie a bit. In his ever-sobering state he decides on a straightforward mugging rather than being stuck on an empty train with a woman — two teenage boys beating him up and taking his phone — but why wouldn't they take his wallet? He decides to throw his wallet into the bin at the station gate. He looks through it first, breaking his credit cards in half before throwing them away, saving the photographs and the letter from his mother she wrote just before she died, thanking them for having a third grandchild in her lifetime. There are two tickets to see Jarvis Cocker at the Dome in two weeks' time — a vasectomy present — Louise's idea of a joke, *Cocker, get it?* He didn't think it was funny — can't stand him anyway — they were more for her than him, one of those presents you give yourself under the pretence of giving to others. He rips them up into satisfying pieces and chucks them in the smelly cauldron of the bin. *Jarvis Tosser.*

He turns to cross, and is diagonally halfway when a huge fox slopes into the road in front of him. It stands and stares at him, its front legs are long and straight, the colour of its body matches the amber in the air. It lifts its nose and takes in his scent keeping its eyes on him the whole time. It's not afraid. It's not going to run away. At this time of night the street belongs to foxes, not advertising executives. They stand unmoving for a moment like Wild West gunslingers. The animal stretches its white throat and lets out an otherworldly bark — a banshee wail of intent. *That's it, enough is enough.* Drew runs at it shouting, a Viking battle cry, arms whirling, briefcase swinging blackly in one hand and the plastic bag in the other; suddenly the bag rips completely and Drew's A3 pack of soggy peas flies through the air skidding to a halt at the fox's paws, splitting on impact, tiny green balls exploding on the tarmac. Drew stops. The fox sniffs at the packet, eats a few of the peas, then turns slowly and walks disgustedly up the hill. Drew thinks it might even have shaken its head.

He almost cries when he sees the white beacon light shining above his front door. Lou must've left it on for him. He has his key in the lock, thinking he might be able to sneak in unnoticed if he's really quiet, when she opens the door arms crossed. She takes one look at his face and raises her hand to her mouth in horror.

'Shit Drew — what have you done?'

She helps him into the hall and eases his jacket off.

'You look awful — what happened?'

He had almost forgotten about his face but now he's thankful for it, at least he's getting Lou's sympathetic voice and not an ear-bashing.

'I fell asleep on the train,' he stammers, 'ended up in a siding. Then two guys woke me up — teenagers — I didn't want to give them my phone — it's got all those pictures on it of the kids — they hit me.'

'When was this? I rang you over an hour ago and a girl answered?'

He nods, 'about two hours ago. They took my phone and wallet and ran off. I must've passed out. When I woke up there was no one else on the train. I walked home along the tracks.'

He's crying now and snuffles into Louise's dressing gown.

'I'm so sorry,' he whimpers, 'I shouldn't have gone out with Daniel — you know what he's like.'

'Should we call the police? I mean you've been mugged — we should call the police.'

'No!' he tightens his grip around her waist. 'No. I just want to forget it,' he sobs into her breasts, 'oh Lou, I was so scared.'

'Ok — we'll get you to bed and see how you feel in the morning.'

He looks up at her face, she looks so beautiful, her night-time face in its raw state, no makeup, hair tied back, the face only he sees.

'I'm supposed to be having my vasectomy tomorrow.'

'Silly,' she says stroking his hair, 'there's plenty of time for that.'

He smiles sadly. *What a relief! Yes, there is plenty of time — in a couple of months, a year maybe.* She smiles back at him sympathetically.

'Your appointment's not till 12.30.'

THE WIFE OF JOSHUA BONES

BRITISH PHOTOGRAPHER
KILLED IN AFGHANISTAN

Press photographer Alastair Morgan was killed yesterday on assignment in Helmand Province Afghanistan.

Morgan, 45, was travelling with the US Marines when he was killed by a roadside bomb. He is the first British journalist to die in Afghanistan since 2001. A US Marine and Afghan soldier were also killed in the blast.

Morgan won numerous awards for his images of the world's war zones in the 80s and 90s. He covered the Balkans, the invasion of Iraq, the Chechen War and the Palestinian conflict for Time Magazine and was known for showing the impact of war on local people caught up in the conflicts.

Fellow photographer Ed Jackson said: 'There wasn't another photographer like Alastair Morgan, he was the best. He would stop at nothing to get the shot he wanted, to show the world how war affected real people — people like you and me. He used to scare the hell out me, pushing himself into the path of danger to show what it was really like to be there. He always came back with a smile and the best photograph. I guess today his luck ran out. He was my friend and I will miss him terribly and I am deeply saddened that we will never get to see the photographs he would have taken had he lived.'

Morgan moved away from war photography in the late 90s into celebrity portraiture for Vanity Fair and Vogue. He treated these subjects with the same honesty as those of his previous photographs and for some, exposed the ordinariness of celebrity. After battling drug and alcohol addiction, he married his psychiatrist Laura Rayburn in 2002, and left the world of glamour behind for a quieter life in his home town of Brighton. He had only recently returned to photo-journalism and was covering the current US surge into Southern Afghanistan for this newspaper.

He leaves behind his wife and their two children, his stepson Barney 19, and a daughter, Mila, 5.

'Meet me at the Pelirocco,' he said holding open the taxi door, 'I'll follow you in another cab. The room's booked in the name of Smith.' He giggled. 'I love doing that.'

As she sat down on the back seat he handed her the bag he'd been carrying when he arrived. It was from her favourite boutique.

'Wear this,' he said and smiled that smile. He shut the door and banged on the roof, the taxi sped away with her towards the sea-front.

The room was the epitome of 1950s charm with an edge of modern seediness thrown in, all leopard print and turquoise silk. She opened the large white bag and lifted out the parcels wrapped in turquoise tissue paper and lavender ribbon. He'd remembered she liked the shop though she'd only mentioned it once. She ripped at the paper revealing a set of exquisite underwear, lilac lace with bright pink ribbon, beautifully made but explicit in its purpose. There was a shoe box at the bottom of the bag — she flung off the lid — red high heels.

'Oh for God's sake,' she said out loud. But her heart beat a little faster at the image he had of her, and she began to undress. When she was done she looked at herself in the mirror, sucking in her stomach and turning round to check out her rear. She did her makeup; heavier than usual, a thick line over each eye, and scarlet lipstick. She brushed her hair — then mussed it up again. She took a baby wipe from her bag and rubbed the lipstick off, re-applying a barely-there gloss.

She looked at her watch, thinking he must be here by now, signing in downstairs. She arranged herself on the chaise lounge, hoping she looked more movie star than desperate housewife. After a few minutes she picked up the hotel magazine, flicking through it but not taking any of it in.

He was late now; it had been an hour since they parted. Where was he?

She found the minibar and drank a small bottle of acrid wine from one of the two shrink-wrapped plastic glasses. Flicking on the TV she went over to the bed and lay back on it, propped against the Pucci pillows and the brass bedstead. She slipped her wrist into the handcuffs hanging from the brass bar above her head, the perfect touch to the burlesque feel of the room. She clicked them shut just as Neighbours came on the television. Her right hand hung there suspended as she watched it, grateful in spite of herself for the vacuous distraction. When the twenty TV minutes were up she wriggled her wrist, trying to free it from its prison. She realised with growing trepidation that these weren't fake handcuffs, that she needed a key to unlock them and that she should probably have located it before putting them on. Now she was stuck in her underwear clamped to a bed, with no sign of him and a fast approaching school pick-up time.

She shuffled to one side of the bed and pulled open the drawer of the side table with her free hand — nothing. 'Shit' she said and almost laughed. Then she shuffled over to the other side and opened that drawer — nothing. Now she was beginning to get agitated, she was sweating and nervous, almost forgetting about him altogether. She lay still for a moment wondering what to do and then thought of the concierge Giuseppe and the words he'd said to her, 'If there's anything you need during your stay just call.' She picked up the Bakelite phone next to the bed and dialled reception. Thankfully it was Giuseppe who answered.

'Er... Hi,' she said, 'it's a bit embarrassing — could you come up. Let yourself in — I can't get to the door.'

She laughed at this last bit, replacing the receiver on its heavy handset.

He was there double-quick, knocking first with jangling keys, then peering round the door. She held up the arm attached to the bed. He laughed.

'You silly thing,' he said, coming over to the bed.

His face was so kind she almost cried. He walked over to the dresser by the door and took a small set of keys from the drawer, then sat next to her on the bed and unlocked them wordlessly.

'Thank you,' she said dryly, rubbing her wrist.

'Don't worry — it happens a lot. Most people can't resist.' He touched her arm.

'Is my husband here yet?'

'He is actually,' he said playing with the keys, 'he checked in a while ago, then met some guy in a suit and went to the bar.'

She let out an involuntary sound, like a punched pillow. Giuseppe gave her a sympathetic smile.

'If you ask me your 'husband' is an idiot.'

She laughed sadly. 'It has been said before.'

Giuseppe got up. 'I'll leave you to it,' he said squeezing her shoulder.

'You look very beautiful.'

He smiled warmly and left her alone.

She'd waited nearly two hours and he was downstairs in the bar — he didn't even drink anymore. What was he doing? Was it all a huge joke? She was upset and confused and now she had to go and pick up the kids.

She had one arm in her blouse when the door crashed open.

'Thank God — you're still here. I'm sorry, so sorry. I'm sorry.'

He held up his hands in supplication, closed the door and stood with his back to it. He looked flustered,

red-faced and sweating, but she was angry. She'd
waited a ridiculously long time — and now he knew she
had waited, that she would wait for him. It made her
feel even more humiliated. Her furious glare stopped
his apologies and he really looked at her for the
first time since he'd come into the room, his eyes
moving slowly over her body as if they were breathing
her in.

'You look — incredible,' he said quietly.

'I'm going. I'll be late picking up the kids.' She
pulled on the other arm of her blouse.

'I'm sorry ok? I bumped into a friend in the lobby,
used to work with Nora actually. I had to pretend I
was here to take photographs. He insisted on getting
a drink.'

'And you just couldn't say no.'

'He just kept prattling on. I couldn't get away.
In the end the guy at reception made up some story
about a meeting with the manager — remind me to tip
him.'

She buttoned up her blouse unevenly with shaking
fingers and turned away from him to redo it.

'What did you want me to do?' he asked, a desperate
edge creeping into his voice, ' say, 'sorry I've got
to go upstairs and meet my lover — don't tell Laura?''

'I'm not your lover.'

'Not yet.'

'I'm going.'

She kept herself from looking at him.

'Come back tomorrow. I'll keep the room for another
day. Meet me here in the morning.'

Anger scorched her insides — he was just the same
— so sure of himself, even after all this time.

'I can't do this,' she shook her head. 'I feel
foolish — like you're playing with me. I don't think
I want to see you again.'

'No! Don't say that.'

He actually fell to his knees at her feet. Wrapped
his arms around her legs and spoke into her belly. A
whisper, she felt its wet warmth on her skin, as hot
as the sunlight.

'I need this.' He looked up at her with tears in his eyes. 'I need you.'

He moved his hands up onto her behind, touching her lightly, almost imperceptibly.

'Stay.'

She looked down at him, at the face looking up at her, the face that had broken into her dreams, unwanted and yet desired. It was the same face, the one that her conscious mind had blurred over the years. It was greyer, fine lines crinkled at his eyes and lips, but there was still that unmistakably 'desperate' look she knew so well, the one that said he'd made a decision on what he wanted and nothing was going to stop him. For the second time in her life, what he wanted was her. Her breath came short and quiet; the air in the room stood still, even the clock seemed to suspend its ticking. She rolled through her mind the decision she'd thought she'd already made. Go now and forget he existed or stay, stay and love him, here in this room like she'd done in another seaside bedroom so many years before. It would be so easy to stay, to phone a friend and ask them to pick up the kids, to let herself fall back into the arms of the past. She looked away from his pleading eyes to the notice on the back of the door.

IN CASE OF FIRE ASSEMBLE AT MEETING POINT G.

Decision made. She pushed him away. 'Don't. I'm late. You've made me late.'

She dressed hurriedly; he stood against the door like a scolded child. As she went for the door handle he grabbed her arm and stared into her eyes.

'Don't leave me — please. I love you. I've loved you for fifteen years.'

* * *

The day that they met again was like the day that they parted. Rain lashed from the heavens, wind bashed its way along the coast, kicking over rubbish bins and hurling litter along the water-slicked roads. The beach was deserted — not a single soul on its salt-washed stones. Mia liked it best this way; she felt as though it meant it was all hers entirely. As she walked down the steps from the coast road, the wind took on a squalling strength, the surging air rushed at her nose and water drops clung to her face and hair, slowly seeping through her coat and down her back. Crossing the promenade she pulled the hood and zip of her cagoule down, shaking her hair free and taking the full elemental force of the sea. The smell of salt filled her nostrils.

I should have been a sailor, she thought, just me and the sea. All the time in the world to think.

The Pier stood stoically against the crash of the waves. As she approached it she heard a faint clanging sound, an otherworldly groaning. She decided to walk further down the beach among the derelict metal struts to the emptiness between the two broken halves. The sound grew as she paced towards it — the insistent clang of metal against metal. She stood in the ruins and looked out to the turbulent waves, the noise sounded like a thousand maritime bells crying out from their berths across the breach. It had no identifiable origin. She looked around hoping to discover its source, but there were no bells, nothing blowing against the Pier in the wind, nothing obviously crashing against it. Where was it coming from?

After a while she realised it was the Pier itself — each piece of it banging against the piece next to it, shoved along by the singing wind. It was a terrible desolate sound, full of melancholy. It reminded her of something a lover had said to her once; that nothing ever really touches anything, that there is always a molecule of separation inbetween, that there is simply no such thing as actual contact. A pessimistic theory — surely connection is the one thing everybody, everything, needs — she smiled at the memory of how untouchable he'd been and trudged across the stones away from the sobbing Pier.

The clanging lessened as the wind pushed it away from her but it was slowly replaced by a new sound. The echo of her footsteps on the pebbles gave her the impression that someone else was on the beach, a few paces behind, an invisible pursuer. This peculiar auditory illusion was so intense that she stopped and looked over her shoulder twice, despite knowing that she would see only the empty beach. Her unseen companion had unsettled her and she made her way, quickly now, towards the edge of the stones.

The footsteps ceased as soon as she walked onto the flat of the concrete; now she had only the increasing raindrops for company on the way up to the street. By the time she reached the sanctuary of her favourite café, the drops had become streams in a truly Biblical downpour — too much for anyone to be out in. Yet it exhilarated her — the drops on her skin made her feel alive. Even so, after the short walk from the beach, it was with some relief that she pushed open the heavy door and stepped into the wood and polish odour of the warm interior.

She often came here to write, and Mario, the owner's son, welcomed her warmly, asking her about her children and making small talk about the atrocious weather. She appeared to be the only customer and sat with her back to the window, taking out her notebook as Mario fired up the Gaggia. She stared at the blank page — something must come out of the walk on the beach — she played with words about rain, coffee and steam, but couldn't come up with anything satisfactory.

She heard the clicking before she saw him. At first she thought it was the Gaggia recovering from making her Americano, but then it went on too long and didn't slow. Constant, insistent, broken unevenly by a few seconds' pause here and there — the third unidentifiable sound of the day.

It was putting her off, distracting her from her task — so small a noise but like the roar of an avalanche to a writer with writer's block.

Then she saw him, sitting at the table facing her

at the back of the room.

She only glanced at him for a second not really looking at his face; still, there was something familiar about him, something ghostly. It was the camera in front of him that made the biggest impression on her, huge and grotesquely black, ridiculously large in an age of tiny digital machines — the unnecessary bulk of actual mechanics. Sitting on the table in front of him, its shutter whirring rhythmically, it seemed to be a part of him, as if he were taking pictures from his heart.

She wondered if he was photographing her or the window behind her, and glanced quickly back over her shoulder then at him again. His eyes moved over her face in the gloom and he smiled; that huge lop-sided smile she knew so well. He walked over to her, 'Mia,' he said softly.

'Johnnie?'

★★★

She didn't go back to Mario's; she didn't want to run the risk of him being there when she walked in again. It was Tuesday morning and as the mist rose from the frosted ground to shroud the Pavilion in perfect mystery, she felt a hand on her shoulder and looked up into familiar brown eyes staring at her over a curious half-smile.

'Johnnie.'

'Mia,' he crouched beside her his hand still resting on her shoulder, 'have you been avoiding me? I hoped I might see you at Mario's.'

She flushed at his words and the feel of his touch.

'I come here now.'

'The photographs I took of you in Mario's are marvellous — you must see them.'

He stood, 'Do you have time now? My studio is just round the corner.' He took her hand. 'C'mon it won't take long.'

'Well I…'

'I'll have you back in no time — I promise.'

So she found herself running through the city streets holding hands with a man who had once lived only in her memory.

His studio was a basement down some rickety iron steps, below a tiny gallery. He led her through the door into a large dark room that flashed into brightness as he flicked the light switch. The ceiling was low and the room uniformly white. There was high-tech photography equipment everywhere; about a hundred lenses piled on a shelf, a computer with a couple of screens, two enormous silver tables like morgue slabs, developing trays and lines of pegged-up photographs .

'Remember this?' he said pointing to a framed shot of a blurred coffee cup on a pebble beach.

She looked at him in surprise, 'Is that..?'

He nodded with the same amused smile on his face, 'Wait here, I'll find the pictures from Mario's.'

He rummaged in cupboards and drawers flinging handfuls of pictures aside onto the surfaces.

'Here,' he said laying a set of black and white prints on the morgue table.

She looked down at the pictures in front of her. Mario's had been restored to its 1950s glory, a Hollywood film set of smoky grey and white; she sat in the middle bathed in the light from the window, the word 'Refreshment' arched behind her on the glass. Her face was luminous, her wet hair stuck darkly to her cheek, and tiny droplets of water shining on her skin mirrored those on the window. If it were possible to capture thoughts in an image, Johnnie had done it with the look in her eyes. She'd never seen herself like that before, it was something you didn't get in a mirror, a vision of her mind, the complexity of self exposed on paper — as though Johnnie had photographed her soul.

He stood beside her, 'fabulous aren't they? I couldn't believe it when I saw them; I think they might be my best work.'

She looked up at him with tears in her eyes. He smiled and moved a strand of hair behind her ear, then he took her face in his hands and kissed her.

***

'My Dad was a mod.'

'Your Dad?'

She had only met Johnnie's father once, fifteen years ago. She tried to think of anything in the paunchy, bitter-looking man she remembered which suggested a fashion-conscious and passionate youth. She couldn't, so she didn't say anything else, just looked at the pristine target mural on the wall behind the bed. Johnnie nodded, solemnly stroking her arm with increasing diligence as if it were the most wondrous skin he had ever touched.

'You wouldn't think it to look at him, but he was a right little raver. He didn't set out to be a bank manager — he wanted to be a photographer but Granddad wouldn't let him. He took some good pictures in the 60s. I've still got them. He was at the Battle on the Beach, throwing deckchairs and stuff — got arrested and spent a night in the cells, had to pay for a broken window on a sun shelter near the Aquarium.'

'Your Dad? Your Dad, got arrested for affray?'

Johnnie kept working on her arm, softly, electrically; all her nerve endings seemed to follow his fingertips.

'Mum and Dad weren't as conventional as they looked. They ran off to Europe together when they were 18. He'd worked at the bank for a while hoping to save some money to go to art college but he met Mum and they just took off. Lived it up in Italy for a year until the money ran out, then got married and came home. Nobody could say anything — it was all official by the time they got back — but he got bullied into taking up his old job at the bank. After that it was just an ordinary life.' He frowned. 'At least they had that year together.'

'They had more than that Johnnie; they were married for forty years.'

'I suppose.'

She pulled her arm away from him, a bit too sharply, leaving his hand suspended over the space it had inhabited. He blinked at her questioningly.

'Sorry,' she said, 'I didn't like it — too intimate.'

He laughed.

'After what we just did? Stroking your arm is too intimate?'

She smiled — it did sound ludicrous but it was true, she felt as though her skin were a science project, his touch too probing, too powerful.

'I'll never understand you,' he said. 'I didn't then and I don't now. You used to drive me crazy. I never knew how to do the right thing.'

She wove herself into his arms, laying the back of her head on his chest.

'Shut up and tell me about your Dad.'

He laughed again and began running his fingers over her belly, feeling every contour in the same way he'd worked on her arm. She sighed and let herself go with it — no use trying to resist him. The feel of Johnnie's fingertips would be the thing she would remember on her death bed — the one thing on earth that had made the biggest impression on her. She pressed herself back against him. They would make love again soon, on this springy bed in a mod-themed room with the ghost of Johnnie's father watching them from the target on the wall.

***

Johnnie started to photograph her on their second coupling. He got up from the bed and wordlessly picked up his camera, clicking away at her as she lay under the crumpled sheet. She told him to stop and covered her face with her arm but this only dictated the style of the photographs.

Winter took hold with tenacious might — a year of vicious storms and floods, every day washed by incessant rain that seemed to be an extension of the sea. They met to take shelter from the rain together, always the same hotel but always a different room. The months passed in a water-logged light and Johnnie photographed her every time they met. She never saw

any of the photographs, and one day in March, when
the sun on the water made it clear that winter was
almost done, she noticed he didn't bring his camera
with him.

She worried that it meant it was the last time, but
she didn't mention it. Their love-making didn't feel
final, and when they left the hotel he suggested they
walk a while on the beach rather than part
straightaway. She was still worried as they crossed
the square and headed for the stones; but he opened
his coat and wrapped it around her as they walked,
like he had done when they were young, a gesture that
didn't speak of distance.

They walked past a man standing on the end of the
groyne, legs braced. He was literally throwing his
dog into the sea. It was a squat white dog with a
black patch on its face and enormous teeth. The man
picked it up, both arms circled around its four legs,
pitched backwards and then hurled the animal up and
seawards into the sky. The dog barked and ran through
the air, legs swimming, landing with an enormous
splash that sent sea spray up over the man; then it
disappeared beneath the waves. The man lent over the
edge of the groyne on his knees and fished in the
water, dragging the dog out by its collar. The beast
climbed awkwardly up the steep wall of the breaker,
barking and wagging its tail. The man wiped sea water
from his face, laughed deeply, then lifted the dog
again and on the count of three hurled it back into
the waves.

Mia and Johnnie looked at each other and smiled.

'Now there's something you don't see everyday.'

'Aren't you going to take a photograph?'

'Can't — no camera.'

'Tell me,' she said, 'until today, have you ever
been anywhere without your camera?'

He smiled and wrapped his arms around her waist as
she hooked hers behind his neck.

'Never.'

He kissed her on the lips, though both of them knew
such open affection was risky in a town as big but

also as small as this. Each day she spent with him made her care less about everyone else, so that at moments like this, it felt like there really wasn't anyone else on the beach but them.

'There's a conference, weekend after next, near Chichester. Three days in a country hotel. Will you come with me?'

He smiled that smile.

***

She ducks through the arch at the entrance to the church. She's taken a walk before dinner and spotted this little village church with its covering of ivy growing out of the stonework. The graveyard stretches out in front of her, it's large for such a small village, hundreds of years of tombstones standing in disorder on the undulated ground. She walks around seeking inspiration from the inscriptions on the lichen-covered stones. The sun dapples across the grass, casting shadows from the memorials onto the butter-coloured flowers. White butterfly souls visit the beds of their former bodies; she imagines she hears the voices of the dead whisper in the lightly shifting breeze. I once loved and was loved back. A frenzy of desire fuelled by nothing more than physical touch, the feel of fingertips on skin. The rushing voices build in the breeze to a crescendo of whispers, egged on by the buzzing of the insects and the rustling of the trees.

There's a huge stone — almost the biggest in the graveyard — lain over a memorial of mausoleum proportions. The writing doesn't fit with its stark stone page, too new, too 21st century, but it's the words that really resonate:

AMY, wife of JOSHUA BONES

She looks up; Johnnie is standing next to her, back from wherever he's been. He encircles her waist with his arms.

'Look at this,' she says. He rests his chin on her shoulder and looks at the stone. 'Odd don't you think? — that she's wholly defined by her husband — presumably 'Joshua' isn't dead yet or he'd be here too. As if she was nothing without him — as if her whole life was about who she was married to.'

'Maybe, or it could mean that it is so important to him that she was his wife that he could only put that on her memorial. Perhaps he couldn't conceive of having a life of any worth without her in it. When he dies and goes in with her, maybe he's asked them to put Joshua, Husband of Amy Bones. We'll have to come back in a few years and see.'

He is silent for a moment, tightens his hold on her, and then adds, 'I wouldn't mind being defined by the woman I loved.'

'Easy for you to say. You're already a success, you've achieved everything you wanted to — it doesn't really matter who you're married to.' She realises how this sounds and shakes her head. 'All I'm saying is that I think people should be remembered for themselves and not for who they were married to. Amy here could have been absolutely brilliant at something — making jam or playing poker, whatever — but the only thing you would know about her from this was that she was married to Joshua.'

'Maybe she was absolutely brilliant at being Joshua's wife.'

'Maybe she had hundreds of lovers, why should she just be remembered for what she meant to Joshua Bones?'

It's edging towards an argument; he tries to head it off. He turns her to him and pushes the hair back from her face.

'Maybe that's why he did it — to punish her for her infidelities! Besides in fifty years who's gonna care?'

'What does that mean? That it's only the present that matters? The past isn't important?'

She's angry with him again, the fifteen-year gulf between them rears across the churchyard; a tidal wave of resentment and missed days. She looks up at him.

231

'You made me think I was a goddess and then you dropped me like a stone on the beach.'

He winces and strokes her cheek with his fingertips.

'I came back for you, you know. Not three months later like I said — more like a year. I stood on the pavement across from your flat trying to pluck up the courage to ring your doorbell when the door opened and you came out with him. I stood and watched you for a while, hiding behind a tree — you were so happy, chatting about something, smiling a lot — he was so attentive to you steering you gently with his hand. The way you looked at him! It made me angry that you could be so happy with someone who wasn't me. At that moment I never loved you more, so I walked away, left you to it — to your easiness. We were never — could never — be like that'

She shakes him off — tears clouding her eyes with sunlit shadows — and kneels down next to Amy Bones. The ground is damp; she can feel water drops from the grass and the wetness of the mud beneath soak into the knees of her jeans. She runs her fingers over the carved words — The Wife of Joshua Bones — as Alastair stands silently a couple of feet behind her.

As they walked back to the hotel through the pollen-filled evening, they met a portly man coming along the path. He wore a pale linen suit and an open-necked blue shirt. He carried a panama hat in one hand and a bunch of pink roses tied with a silk ribbon in the other. As he drew level he smiled and said, 'Lovely spring evening isn't it?'

She knew who it was immediately and stopped to look back when she reached the gate. Joshua Bones knelt in the dirt at his wife's grave and placed the flowers on the stone he too would soon rest beneath.

They lie together under the moonlight that streams through the tall window, flickering shadows of leaves falling on their nakedness. A light breeze plays on her skin raising goosebumps even though the room is warm. She looks into his eyes as he props himself up on one elbow and runs his other hand over her stomach.

'Your body is so white,' he says in a whisper, 'it's beautiful.'

She laughs — he reminds her of his younger self with his serious and awestruck tone.

'It's stretched and scarred and worn,' she says with a smile.

'You're wrong — it's beautiful — it's a body of stories.'

He continues tracing his hand over her skin.

'Tell it another,' she whispers and closes her eyes.

It's almost noon when they wake. The early morning sunshine has been replaced by dark clouds and raindrops that race each other down the window. Her train is at 1 — they dress and pack quickly, barely speaking, she skirts around him to collect her things in the room that was the whole world the night before but is now too small. At one point as she walks past him, he takes her hand; she smiles at him briefly but can't look him in the eye so he lets her go. They leave the room, talk about who will pay and if they'll get to this station on time; it's all very polite and totally meaningless.

He pulls the car up outside the station and turns off the engine. Rain thunders against the windows and on the roof, wind flung from the branches of a row of chestnut trees that hang greenly around the car park. It's a pretty train station, one of those old-fashioned red brick ones with white wooden shutters and hanging baskets of bright flowers. The baskets rock in the wind and red petals fly across the black slicked tarmac. It seems like a fitting place to end it.

'I can't see you anymore,' she says simply.

He looks down at the steering wheel and says nothing.

'If I keep on seeing you, I'll have to leave them and I can't do that.'

233

'Yesterday when I told you about coming back for you and how I walked away because I couldn't be like you wanted me to be, I could be like that now. I love you like that now.'

Her voice falters, 'I love you too, that's why — that's why it has to stop. It'll be easier if I pretend we never met.'

'I can't do that — can you? Can you really do that?'

He puts his hand on her arm and she looks at him properly for the first time that day.

'I have to.'

She opens the car door and pulls her arm from his touch.

'Mia,' he says looking into her eyes, 'I can't live without you.'

She closes the door on his last words and walks across the car park to the ticket-office in a storm of petals and raindrops.

Later that day, a neatly dressed man with a camera walked through the gates of Brighton Pier. He moved purposefully, striding the length of the deserted promenade, his destination firmly in his mind. It being a weekday in grey mid-March there were no tourists; a man riding an industrial cleaner whirred past him and a lone angler cast out over the railings without noticing him. It took only a few minutes to get to the fairground at the end of the Pier. The big rides were being tested for the coming Easter holidays; they roared emptily on their giant clockwork cogs.

The man took a sharp right between the Turbo Blaster and the Waltzer. Most people miss this little alley — the only way to reach the furthest point of the Pier — which is hidden behind the attractions. He followed the route around; competing bass-heavy music played from each ride, fading in and out as he walked past them.

At the very end of the Pier he found a bench, it faces seawards; it has a little brass plaque on it with the words:

For Uncle Walter Who Loved the Sea

This is the last bench in Brighton. To the left of it are the rickety yellow stilts of the Mouse Trap. At the height of summer they rattle constantly under the weight of the mouse-shaped cars that whizz along to the screams of happy tourists. On this day they only shuddered slightly in the wind.

The man took off his coat. He needed to cool down. The breeze felt good on his back, gliding air beneath his shirt. He folded the coat carefully and laid it on Walter's bench.

In front of him stood the last set of black and white safety railings on the Pier; they had been freshly painted for the coming season. He wondered for a moment who had painted them, and if he should get a job like that -painting the city's railings. But he knew it wouldn't be enough for him and he stepped quickly over them, lifting his long legs so high he almost fell too soon and had to grab awkwardly backwards, hooking both hands under the top rail.

He steadied himself and stood with his heels on the three inches of wood at the end of the Pier, his toes sticking out over the sea. He looked straight out to the horizon — from this position he could see nothing of the city he would leave behind moments later, the city he was born in. There was only the stretch of the grey waters, rippled occasionally with gold from the new spring sunshine.

The gulls cried their frenzied song, as if in mourning for a man who was not yet dead. The man watched them sadly through long-lashed eyes and smiled — a thin-lipped defeated smile. He outstretched his arms and fell slowly forwards into salty oblivion.

One of the ticket-sellers — a fat brassy woman called Patricia — who occupied the booth nearest the end of the Pier, thought she heard a splash as she checked her ticket printer. It was a loud splash —

louder than the usual smack of the waves against the Pier's thick wooden legs.

Patricia locked her booth, out of habit rather than necessity, and made her way round to the back of the Pier — to the suicide point. She couldn't see or hear anything unusual. Then, just as she was about to turn away, she caught sight of a black bundle on the floor next to the bench. Picking it up she realised it was a folded overcoat. It was beautifully finished and made of the softest wool — cashmere, she supposed. She rubbed her face on it. Then she saw the camera, sitting on the bench, black and expensive; it was whirring automatically, taking pictures of the horizon in front of it.

Patricia pressed herself against the railings, and almost bent in half to look down at the sea fifty feet below. She couldn't see anyone floating in the water, dead or alive, waving or drowning. She clamped the barrier with white knuckles, stood on her tiptoes and then had a moment of panic when she felt as if she were tipping over. Patricia flung herself backwards and lay on her back on the damp wood of the Pier, breathing loudly through her nose with her eyes shut.

© Dia Clifton

STARLINGS

The call comes through at 2.31. Gary and his colleague Sara throw the remainder of their coffee out of the window and strap themselves in. The GP is in attendance — alerted by a district nurse — and there's a faint pulse still, but it doesn't look hopeful. The man is in his early 80s and he's not in good health, there's a history of high blood pressure and gangrene in his foot and he drinks to excess — every day. They switch on the siren and waa-waa out of their parking space and out onto the main road into town.

At 2:30 on a Friday afternoon the traffic is appalling. The schools have been back for just two days and hundreds of cars sit nose-to-tail with one female occupant, hoping to park illegally and pick up their children in the shortest time possible. It's unbearably hot, as humid as it gets in England and the pavements are full of people pushing prams and dragging tired toddlers towards their older siblings.

Jack lives beside an infant's school, built in the 60s over ground flattened by a leftover German bomb dropped on the flight back home to Hanover. It reduced four houses to rubble and dust. The woman who lived in Jack's house before him had a lucky escape. She was at the back in the kitchen washing up, when she remembered her sister had bought her some chocolate for her birthday. Chocolate was a precious thing in wartime, she ought to save it for Christmas but she couldn't get it out of her mind, it was her birthday present after all. She dried her hands on the tea-towel and walked into the living room to retrieve the treat from the dresser drawer. As she broke the slab into pieces with a satisfying clunk, the bomb whistled through the air and hit the house behind. She was knocked to her knees on the living room carpet. When she got up dazed and half-deaf from the ringing in her ears, her kitchen was gone; a mangled shell of bricks and broken glass, shattered porcelain and splintered wood.

'So chocolate saved my life,' she told Jack, when he came to view the house.

They looked out of the kitchen window at the workmen building the school.

'Do you have children?'

He shook his head. 'No,' he said, 'one day maybe.'

'Well the school will come in handy then.'

Jack remembers this conversation as if it were happening now. He can see the woman's face; the scarf she'd knotted around her hair and the smell of the scones she was baking in the oven. He sees her wring her hands on the rose-pattern apron around her waist as she places the kettle on the hob to make him tea. He sees this though he is far away and his eyes are closed. He sees it as clear as day, though his mind is black and the only real noise is the thud of his chest and a woman counting to four over and over as she pushes up and down on it. The counting takes him back to the army, to boots on a parade ground and a shouting drill-sergeant.

The ambulance swings left through the red traffic light, blasting its horn to warn the lady waiting to cross with her pram, and weaving around the line of cars that have stopped at the box junction. The lollypop lady at the top of the hill stares at it and waves the man with the dog back to the pavement as he starts to cross. They stand next to each other and watch it speed over the crest and down towards the school. A soot-black rain cloud looms behind them like a wall of misery against the blue.

The school traffic blocks the road up and down, and Gary has to manoeuvre between cars and up onto the pavement, to park between the white zigzag lines at the school gates. He runs out, a streak of green with his bag of life-saving equipment, leaving his door open and Sara to follow on after she's called in their arrival.

The old man's house is in a terrible state — broken steps and an overgrown garden lead to the front door. Untended cherry trees hang over the pavement in front of the house, casting clots of rotting cherries onto the road below. The garden itself is bordered by ramshackle bundles of thorny bushes and giant thistles; curling ivy and bindweed cover the garden in heavy tunnels of greenery. All this unfettered growth obscures the front of the house as if it's a fairytale castle, home to a wizard or a wicked troll. The children are scared of this house and rush past it on their way to school — it looks spooky in the summer, buried beneath the abundant leaves, and in winter, when the dark jags of thorny branches reflect on the dirty windows. Sometimes the children look up at the windows and catch sight of a figure behind the glass, then they run the last few yards to school, hearts beating like drums in their tight little chests until they are safely behind the classroom door.

It's cool under the leaves, and Gary would have welcomed the shade, were it not for the stink of catshit and the tacky white and green of bird droppings, sticking like abstract art to the once-red bricks on the path and crunching under his feet. He covers his nose with his hand to keep out the smell.

239

The door is wide open — its black paint, grey and cracked by years of sun and rain, showing decades of different colours underneath. The house smells even worse inside, it hits him in the face as he walks in, urine and shit and navy rum. It's cold inside and damp, Gary shivers as he tramps down the hall towards the sound of the doctor in the front room and the unbelievably loud ticking of a clock. His eyes move to the stairs in front of him; they veer up towards a window on the top landing — a window so covered in dust and cobwebs it looks like it's been buried.

He was in Sicily during the war. After his basic training at the hands of Sergeant Black, and months of mock landings in the Gulf of Aqaba, Jack was dispatched to Cassibile on Sicily's eastern coast. At the age of twenty he was running up a beach in skin-searing heat with a backpack, holding a rifle over his head, as men he'd shared the boat over with fell dead around him in the surf. He dodged the shells and the bullets and he ran — he remembers the running more than anything. It was exciting, the smell of salt from the sea mingled with cordite in the air, the challenge of staying alive and merely getting off a beach, without even having the chance to fight. He remembers the footprints on the sand, thousands of huge ridged boot shapes patterned on the flat softness of the ground — overlapping — one man's step over another, waiting for the sea to swallow them up.

There are so many cats in the room, curled on the soiled furniture, lying in the sliver of sun fighting its way through the ragged closed curtains. The room is filled with purrs and yawns and the occasional indifferent meow. There are bowls of rancid cat food everywhere. So this is what happens to them — the kitties on the homemade posters that line the lamp posts of suburban streets — not run-over or taken away in removal vans or chopped into Chinese takeaways — but banded together in the stinking house of a sick old man.

Gary nods at the doctor and kneels beside her to begin his work. The man's mouth is open and his eyes are closed, his shirt is stained and streaked with sick and sweat. His face is pitted and reddened; burst blood vessels have turned his nose a deep violet. The bottles he drinks everyday are lined up along the floor and thrown empty onto chairs, leftover drops of liquor have soaked into the cushions and give off the smell you only get in a dodgy pub or the house of an alcoholic. One of his trouser legs is rolled up, showing a scarlet swollen leg and a dirty bandage wound so tightly around his foot it cuts into the flesh. Yellowing puss has soaked into the filthy crepe, giving off the odour of rotten fruit.

'Jesus,' says Gary. 'Any output?'

The doctor nods breathlessly, 'There was a faint pulse when I got here — but I think he's gone.'

'How long?'

'Thirty minutes.'

'Want me to check?'

She stops CPR and moves aside. Her arms are shaking from her efforts and sweat beads on her forehead clouding her glasses around her nose.

There's no pulse, but as Gary lays his head on the old man's chest his ribcage shudders with an intake of breath. Gary and the doctor stare at each other.

'Christ — what the hell is he hanging on for?'

Gary lifts the patient's head and pushes an oxygen mask over it.

'Better get him out of here.'

Outside on the pavement, Sara stops parents trying to get to the school. They're not happy. Gary needs to get the stretcher out and into the ambulance so they'll just have to wait.

'Well how long is it going to be?'

'Can't we just nip through now, only Saskia's got ballet in ten minutes?'

'C'mon let us through, there's a traffic warden on the prowl.'

'Please,' says Sara, 'a man is seriously ill. We'll be bringing him out in a minute — it won't take long.'

Dia pushes her way to the front to where Louise and a couple of stay-at-home Dads are standing.

'Hi Lou, what's going on? The traffic's a nightmare.'

'It's that old wino bloke — you know the crazy one with the gammy foot. Collapsed — been there days by the sound of it. District nurse found him.'

'God! Imagine that, dying alone and nobody finding you for days.'

'He's not dead!'

'Not yet anyway,' says Drew.

'Oh Hi Drew, didn't see you there — Jesus what happened to your face?'

'Long story.'

'He got himself mugged on the train so he could get out of his vasectomy.'

Drew lets out a loud defeated sigh. The frostiness in the air between the couple is palpable, Dia looks inquiringly at Louise.

'I'll tell you later,' says her friend. 'Did you hear about Ellen?'

'I know — it's been nearly a week hasn't it? I can't imagine what she's going through. Remember when Gill lost the kids at the playground. I wonder if it has anything to do with that?'

Lou nods, 'Yeah, Gill went to the police the other day to tell them about it, thought it might help. The kids gave a description of the man who talked to them, but she's not heard anything else.'

'It's probably that bloke who looks after the playground.'

The women look at Drew who is rubbing his chin as if he's trying to figure something out.

'What makes you say that?'

'Well, he's always really grumpy like he doesn't like kids and I don't think you can trust anyone whose main job is to sweep up sand 24 hours a day. He's like an inferior Zen gardener — without the spiritual enlightenment. If it was my job, I'd hate kids too.'

Lou and Dia laugh, 'you do hate kids!'

'I do not,' he says grumpily, then looks at the derelict house. 'I wonder how long the council leaves it before they put the house up for auction.'

His wife looks at him in disbelief.

'Is that your idea of effectively changing the subject?'

'Well I mean — it's a fantastic house — I bet it would go for next to nothing. Needs a lot of work; but you could make a fortune out of it.'

Sara, Louise and Dia stare at him.

'Drew,' says his wife quietly, 'the man isn't even dead yet.'

'No, but they probably won't let him come back here to live on his own again. It's a beautiful house underneath it all — right next to school as well — might be worth getting in touch with the council to find out.'

'I apologise for my pig of a husband,' Louise says to Sara.

'What?' He says.

Just then Gary and the doctor come out with the stretcher bearing the old man. He's wrapped in a red blanket and the oxygen mask on his face makes him look like a pilot during the war. The stretcher rattles as it bobs down the steps and the man groans quietly. A hush descends over the assembled parents so that all that can be heard is the intermittent squeak from the wheels of the stretcher, and the happy twittering of the birds in the trees along the road.

The paramedics load their cargo into the back of the ambulance, Sara gets in the back; she stares at Drew and narrows her eyes then slams the door on him. Gary gets in the front and drives away haltingly against the bottleneck of cars, the siren blasting an ear-splitting farewell. The doctor shuts Jack's door and pushes it to making sure it's locked. She nods at the parents she knows as she walks past them to her car and then she too is gone.

The house stands silently, enshrined in its green eiderdown of foliage; the rain cloud eclipses the sun and sends a cooling breeze along the road.

'Great, now it's going to rain.'

'What the hell is the matter with you today Drew? – it's like those teenagers took your sensitivity along with your phone.'

Louise strides off towards the school without waiting for him.

The rumble of the ambulance takes Jack back to Sicily, to sitting on the back of a farm cart when the battle was won; dust thrown up in clouds by the wheels as the horse plodded forward on sun-powdered roads. In the villages there had been locals with white flags and broad smiles and women, pretty dark-eyed women, who'd welcomed the soldiers with comfort in the night for a bar of chocolate or a bag of coffee. It had been exciting, the most exciting time of his life and when he'd met Lily she'd reminded him of those girls and of the thrill of youth in wartime. His safe and comfortable life with May had held no such thrill - she did everything for him, and after a time, it had bored him to death.

Lily was different, she wanted things — she wanted him when he wasn't hers and she wanted a life out of the ordinary. She needed glamour and excitement and the unexpected. She'd married Finley to get away from home and then she saw in Jack a way to go further — to really go. They took off together with just enough money to get to France then worked their way down to Italy. They took whatever work they could and they loved it — the freedom, the excitement of a carefree, sexually ravenous existence. One big party. They settled in Naples, working in a hotel next to the aquamarine sea with the heady smell of flowers and the tide hanging in the air. He tended bar and Lily sang, between songs she sat on a stool at the bar and worked the customers. They were a hit with the regulars: the ex-movie star who thought she was Sophia Loren, the dipsomaniac priest who used them as confessors, and the ancient fake Count who sat by the bar all night and told Lily stories of the estate he owned in the Tuscan hills. 'Poor as a church mouse,' Lily whispered to Jack when the Count was out of earshot. After a while the Count began to give Lily presents, he asked Jack's permission, first telling him it was his dead wife's jewellery and saying he just wanted someone to take pleasure in it. 'Silly old sod,' said Lily, throwing the pieces into her jewellery box at the end of the night, 'nothing but glass and paste!'

Lily was beautiful and flirty and Jack was besotted with her, proud that she was his and that other men desired her. He spent eight years drugged by her and then, as she approached her thirtieth birthday, she grew distant and cold, shrinking from him when he touched her. One evening after the first half of the cabaret, she went outside for some air and never came back. She just left in the evening gown she was wearing and didn't even take her jewellery with her.

The Count had turned out to be authentic, as had his dead wife's jewels. Jack took the baubles to the pawn shop but they couldn't value them, so he went to a jeweller in the upmarket part of town. In a shop under a stone archway, a man who looked down the slant of his nose and told him that Lily's costume jewellery was worth thousands — that the diamonds emeralds and rubies were all genuine.

Jack wondered if Lily knew and had left it all for him out of guilt, but decided she couldn't have. Lily wasn't that kind of woman — she just moved on without petty considerations such as guilt; if she left her jewels behind it was because she didn't need them. Without Lily, Jack lost his job at the hotel. He carried on at the bar for a while, but the drink that had boosted his confidence and lightened his mood when Lily had been with him now turned on him. It stoked the anger that seethed within and, on one of the many nights he drank too much, he lashed out at the movie star, calling her a haggard old bag. He was told he wasn't needed anymore.

Jack took the money from the sale of the Count's jewels (no questions asked) and went home. Eight years had passed but in the back of his mind he had the idea that he would try to find May and somehow make amends. They were still married, she never tried to find him to ask for a divorce and he hoped this might have been because she still loved him. He tried to make some kind of sense of his life, of the decisions he'd made and the actions he'd taken, and on the long sea voyage back to England, he convinced himself that it was May he wanted, that he'd been a fool to reject the cosy family life only she could give him.

So the idea had been to find May and the life he had rejected; he would present her with a family home and try to persuade her to start again. She was in her 30s but she was still young enough to have kids. He decided that this was the key; May had longed for children. Whenever she saw a child her face lit up like a beacon and children sensed her need and were drawn to her too, even the tiniest baby cooed and smiled in her arms. Friends' babies, tots from the neighbourhood, they all found their way to May at some point for a biscuit or a cuddle. He remembered their home being overrun with the little cuckoos. Kids left him cold, they irritated him, and he'd just wanted them to go away, but now he'd changed his mind. He knew it would be difficult but he thought if he kept at her, romanced her, apologised as many times as was necessary, offered her what she had always wanted, that eventually he would win her over. She was his May and she had belonged to him since the day they met.

He went to the house on Argyll Street, assuming she still lived there, but the woman who answered the door wasn't May. Two young children ran up and down the stairs behind her shooting each other with pop guns, one dressed as a cowboy the other an Indian. Their mother told him they had no forwarding address for May, but she didn't think she had left the city, something May had said about waiting for her husband to come back from abroad. Those words had gladdened Jack's heart — May was waiting for him. She'd moved out of the house four years before; would she still be waiting four years later?

He redoubled his efforts to find her, went to the bakery where she used to work, checked the electoral register, and rang up doctors and hospitals, old friends, churches, anywhere there were people who might know her. Most of the people they used to know were gone, some said they didn't know where she was, Jack sensed hostility in them — as if they did know but weren't telling him.

He tried his best but he just couldn't find her. When he was almost ready to give up, he saw a woman he remembered from the past. Miriam. She was working in the Co-Op when he went in to buy his whisky. She looked uncomfortable when she saw him, and after a tense exchange of greetings, he asked her about May. He remembered her as being an outspoken woman, and she told it to him straight — the attack, the loss of his child, Barker's suicide, May's breakdown, how they'd carted her off to the looney bin. When she was released she'd disappeared, sold the house and was never heard of again. She missed her, Miriam, that's what she said; 'I miss her.'

'Me too,' said Jack.

'Well then, maybe you should've kept your trousers zipped.'

She'd said it loudly and he reddened, cold sweat collecting at his shirt collar as he felt the other customers staring at him.

After that he stopped looking for May, at least physically. It was too late; the past had been changed by what had happened. He was ashamed and he locked himself away in his empty family home and hid. He worked in soulless bars and pubs, drinking most of their profits until they asked him to move on. He created his own purgatory, years of self-pity in which nothing really happened except that he aged. When he was too old to work anymore, he made a career of drinking, repeatedly searching for May's love at the bottom of a whisky bottle and at the butt of a Rothman's Royal.

The ambulance blasts its way along the seafront. May hears the siren in her high-rise flat. She freezes halfway through making her afternoon cuppa and dries her hands slowly on a tea-towel. Though she's been too warm all day, the room feels suddenly cold. A shiver comes over her, the hairs on the skin of her back lift slightly and she wriggles to try and rid herself of the feeling that somebody is walking over her grave. She turns towards the window, and as she does, she sees Jack's photograph on the mantelpiece. She hesitates then says, 'It's alright now love.' She doesn't know why she says it — she hasn't talked to him in years. He smiles back at her in affirmation. May pulls her eyes from him and looks out of the window; her gaze is drawn to the ambulance which is stuck in the bundle of cars vying for space at the lights. Then its siren stops and it seems to hang there, suspended over the tarmac, as if it's just taken a breath.

He saw her once. He's sure of it. He didn't realise at the time, he shuffled across the road by the Clock tower and saw an old lady crossing from the other side. She caught his eye and he smiled but he was half-cut and wobbled unsteadily on his gammy leg and she didn't smile back. There had been something familiar about her, something that had warmed his heart, soft blue eyes in a lined face, bright white hair under a patterned chiffon headscarf. They both crossed to their opposite sides of the road but he looked over his shoulder at the woman's back as she stepped between the shoppers on the other side and disappeared.

He thought about that face all day but it wasn't until he was at home with the cats and the muddied clarity brought about by his whisky that he realised who it was. His brain hadn't connected the way May would look after forty years with the face he'd seen. To him May was still 25; though he'd prepared for her to look older, he'd probably stopped imagining her after 40 and a youthful 40 at that. In his drunken fog, with the cats prowling around his legs, he realised where he'd seen those eyes before. Sitting in a face with the edges rubbed away by time, they were still May's eyes. Your eyes never change, May used to say — from birth to death — *they remain the windows to your soul.*

'He's gone,' says Sara.
'Oh — ok.'

Gary switches off the siren and finds the track on the CD player. The *Flower Duet* from Lakmé. It was their little ritual. It started because an RTA died in the ambulance when *The Locomotion* was on the radio and Gary said it wasn't appropriate. Sara said she didn't want to listen to any of his screeching women but he could play the British Airways theme because she liked that. So Lakmé it was — and it was a fitting tribute to the countless souls whose last contact with humanity were Gary and Sara. Its mournful but uplifting strains fill the ambulance and Sara removes the oxygen mask and closes Jack's eyes with her fingertips.

'I think I'm going to ask Giz to marry me,' says Gary from the front. 'I know he won't be faithful, but that doesn't matter, so long as he's there at the end to hold my hand.'

'You can't marry someone just because you don't want to die alone,' says Sara. She's been holding Jack's hand since they got in the ambulance and she's still holding it now as the warmth starts to leave it.

'I know that — I love him too. I want to have a life with someone I love and then I want him to be there when I go — to die in love I suppose.'

'As good a reason as any,' says Sara. 'Do me a favour though — promise me you won't play this at the ceremony.'

There's one last call, at 8 o'clock, a birth. The child's small and a bit jaundiced and the mother fainted afterwards, so the midwife wants to get them checked out. The sun is low as Gary and Sara drive along the seafront; it bathes the sea in an orange glow, the sky is pink with puffs of silver clouds trailing diagonally behind the Piers. Huge undulating balls of black specks swarm the pale skies, moving back and forth like the wind.

'Look at the starlings,' says Sara, 'aren't they beautiful?'

'Amazing,' agrees Gary as they slow at the lights by The West Pier. The birds flock in the skies, the same colour as the disintegrating metal of the Pier's ribcage, they balloon around it in a slow ballet, not yet resting on its bars for the hours of darkness.

'I'm glad they're back. They went away for a while — do you remember? For a couple of years they just didn't turn up.'

'You know I do remember that, but at the time I didn't miss them at all — it's only now they're back that I remember them not being here,' says Sara.

'Did you know that close up they're not black at all?' says Gary. 'They're green and purple and navy blue and their feathers are tipped with tiny white dots, that's where the stars come in.'

'You learn something new every day. I never had you down as a birdwatcher.' She winks at Gary and looks out of the window at a man in extremely small hot pants walking a tiny dog along the pavement. 'Thought that was more your thing.'

'What, Muscle Mary? Hardly.'

The lights change and they slide away towards the new-born baby.

Upstairs in her flat, May watches the starlings flit around the Pier. She loves these birds in particular, probably because they're not here for long. They stay for a few weeks brightening the skies and then they're off to wherever they go to live their exciting foreign lives. Nightly she watches their dance from her window, she thinks it's the most beautiful thing she's ever seen and her heart is warmed by their beauty. After all the things that have happened to her — and all the things that should have happened to her but didn't — she is amazed that there are still such things in the world to make her smile.

As her gaze follows the dip and bail of the tiny birds from the land to the sea and back again, she notices the children's playground on the front below her window. It is empty, the gates are locked and the children have all gone; it is a blank canvas painted by the tangerine brush of the dying sun. It's the two sandpits that catch her eye, each has a pattern of swirls and lines traced over it, deep furrows circle around from one end to the next, creating dark lines out of shadows and bright hills out of orange light, the huge red triangle of the sun shade breaking into them, splintering the lines to create an abstract painting. It's as if someone has spent hours sculpting the sand with a loose-toothed comb to draw hollows for the light. May's smile widens, someone took the time to make these beautiful patterns and now the only ones who can see them are May and the birds, the passers-by on street level wouldn't know they were there, but the starlings would.

May stands at her window for another hour, until her knees are too sore to stand anymore. She watches the swirls on the sand and the boats out to sea, the clouds racing past the gas-lamp ball of the sun and the huge chrysanthemum swarms of the starlings, and for once she feels happy to be alive.

THE VAGINAS OF HURSTPIERPOINT

I have a little tale to tell if you will indulge me. It is a story of contrasts, of what is hidden beneath the surface of things. The now of the tale takes part in a little Sussex village. I have chosen to tell you about what happens there because I feel an affinity to this village, with its surface — and its underbelly. Things aren't quite what they seem. But for most of my life things have never been quite what they seem. This village is my present but it recalls my past. I want you to come along with me, and a couple of new friends, to spend some time out of town. Don't worry; we are going to a highly civilised place. And yet my current home has it secrets. You could even say that I am one of them. One of its... unexpected pleasures. But I am getting ahead of myself.

Imagine if you will, the sleepy village of Hurstpierpoint, 9.6 miles from the sordid metropolis of Brighton. It has recently been plunged into uncharacteristic disarray. Its residents pride themselves on their cosmopolitan attitudes, their *joie de vivre* and their love of the arts. A little bubble of creative tranquility nestled between the more conventional Hassocks and the down-at-heel Burgess Hill; it is the adopted home of many arty-types, tired of city life, who settle here in search of a less frenetic existence.

It's a pretty little place, clusters of streets branch off from the main artery of its beautifully old-fashioned high street. It has all the elements necessary for village life; a couple of decent pubs, a church, Indian and Chinese takeaways (but only one of each). Its gift and antique shops nestle behind newly washed Georgian windows. The beautifully ramshackle café only sells homemade organic cakes (an exclusivity reflected in its prices). It is the kind of place where the off-license is called a 'vintners'. This carefully manicured little village has everything you could possibly want, even and perhaps most importantly, easy access to the A23; so its inhabitants can high-tail it out of there at a moment's notice.

As with most villages, there is a particular equilibrium that has to be maintained for life to proceed at its leisurely pace. If things got a little off-kilter, if someone stepped out of line just a bit too far, who knew what would happen — anarchy could take hold, shattering the picture-postcard ambience and spreading terror among the villagers. There are several committees (Residents', Parish Council, and Neighbourhood-watch) always on hand to ensure this never happens. If someone builds an extension without observing the proper etiquette, it will soon be rectified by a phone call to the council. The same if you try to paint your house pink or park a camper-van outside it for too long, make a dividing wall a fraction too high, or smoke dope in the bus shelter with bored teenagers. Someone will be sure to set you right — in person or anonymously — they know who you are and they know where you live.

There is a lot of money in town, old and new, and with money comes responsibility. A duty to one's fellow man, to set them straight on anything that might be seen as out of line. Curtains twitch, the Mums huddle at the school gates. Everybody knows everybody's business because in a village that prides itself on its community spirit; nobody has any business minding their own business.

Sometimes things stay hidden. There's the mother of three with the coke habit, the loving family-man who works away a lot (invariably in Holland), the married friends who occasionally swap each other's spouses (and not always in the standard gender configuration). And then there is me, Arlene Thompson — respectable single lady of mature years, who moved here from Brighton after retiring from running a B&B in Kemptown.

***

Ten miles away in the big city, two young friends have a discussion about going out of town.

'C'mon Karen, please — for me?'

'No way — it's my idea of hell.'

'Please please please — it'll be fun, I promise. I'll buy all the drinks, it'll be over by 10 — 11 at the most — then we can come straight home.'

'Really Giz, I just want to stay home with a bottle of wine and a movie. Why don't you just tell him no?'

'I can't — I've been neglecting him lately and he's got the right hump. The last thing he said to me was 'don't forget Friday, Arlene's counting on us. I won't be happy if you let her down.''

Giz did a perfect impression of Gary, his older and much more sensible lover — a man who only liked classical music and drank wine for the taste rather than the inebriation. Karen laughed.

'C'mon please, besides you'll love Arlene, she's incredible.'

***

I am indeed an incredible woman. In fact it is incredible that I am a woman at all. When I was born close to midnight on April 23rd 1940, my parents called me Alan, on account of my having a penis and a scrotum. Bouncing baby Alan gurgled his way unknowingly through his infancy — a happy alert baby who loved to touch everything with his fat little hands. Alan was quickly self-aware. It was one of his earliest memories; he must have been about five. It wasn't an event but a feeling, a feeling of unease. It happened in the garden as he watched his mother dig up carrots in her shorts and huge straw hat with a ribbon on it. He can remember exactly what she wore and the exact line her legs took as they bent beneath her, he remembers the sun and the birdsong and the laconic buzz of the insects in the air. Then it all stopped. Time was suspended. And Alan looked down at his own little body. He didn't look at it as if it were a part of him, but as if he were outside looking in. From that moment on Alan would experience this feeling frequently, sometimes so intensely that he didn't know if his body was his own or belonged to someone else.

From a very early age Alan was irresistibly drawn to his mother's clothes. He didn't act on it for years, content to merely glimpse at the clothes lined up in rows in the wardrobe as he sat reading comics on his mother's bed, while the woman who was his constant companion busied herself in choosing what to wear. He'd glance at the full coloured skirts, hear the swish of the silk and the cotton and wish he could touch them, wish he could get into the wardrobe and close the door, bury himself in female material.

One day when he was about eight, his mother took him next door to sit with the old lady who lived there and who was suffering from a fever of some sort. Alan was bored and fidgety, he couldn't settle with his comics, so his mother told him to go home and wait for her there. It was his first chance to get at her clothes. He rushed into the house and up the stairs into his mother's bedroom. He flung open her wardrobe door and slipped on her enormous feather mules and silk dressing gown.

He stole her Avon — *Nectar* was her colour of choice — and with it he rouged his lips and cheeks, then secured his blond curls with jewelled bobby pins. He atomised a puff of Chanel at his wrists and neck. The perfume of it was delicious, for the first time in his life he smelled as he knew he should. He took his mother's pearls from her dresser and standing so he could look at himself in the full length mirror on the wardrobe door, he wound them around his neck, turning his head from side to side and rubbing the tiny white spheres between his fingers. He smiled a lipsticked smile and for a brief moment felt at ease. Anxiety was gone. It was as though he was floating on a still lake, warm water lapping over his weightless body, as the sun shone in a limitless sky and white birds soared in the heavens.

This was Alan's narcotic; and would be for many years to come. Like all drugs it wore off too easily, leaving only the memory of it, and the burning need for the next fix.

Alan began to dress in his mother's clothes at every opportunity — to try to recapture that feeling of the first time. In his mother's clothes he felt more like himself, but it was never quite the same as that first time. He noticed a male smell under the Chanel, felt the first dark hairs on his legs snag the silk of the kimono, realised that his body was straight down and not curved like his mother's. After a while he didn't even care if his mother saw him; he just ran up to her room after school for his daily high.

Alan's mother knew not to mention his activities to his father. She worried, but after much consultation with his grandmother and aunts, she decided to ignore his transvestism. However, as little Alan matured into youth and showed no signs of losing his passion for all things feminine, she began to indulge his obsession. She and her three sisters let him wear their jewellery and perfume. They asked his opinion of their clothes and makeup, practiced its application on him, even curled his hair with hot irons and hairspray. These after-school afternoons were a delight for Alan. Every day was a party crammed with gin and cigarettes and Cole Porter. He had no sister and his mother relished having a willing surrogate. His Aunts, who ranged in age from 19 to 28, found him utterly adorable. They hugged him constantly and he breathed in an intoxicating blend of warm female flesh, nylon and lipstick. Sometimes they'd let him have a sip of gin or a puff of a cigarette, and in return he'd sing for them, clicking his fingers and swaying along with the tinny notes of the bands on their shiny 45s.

Alan was in love with Auntie Pat in particular. She was the youngest, a rebellious beauty with hair like Marilyn Monroe, who always used a thin black cigarette-holder for her menthols. Her feet were only a little bigger than his own, and when he slipped his toes into her stilettos he was lifted higher than even the two-inch heels could physically manage. He glided with the movie stars.

Of course all this frivolity ended by 7, when Alan's father came home from work. The Aunts had gone, the movie magazines and records were tidied away, and Alan was washed and dressed in striped pyjamas, ready for bed and the next chapter of *Royal Flashman*.

Once, on the day of Auntie Pat's 21st birthday, the party went on for a bit too long. Too many G&Ts were consumed and it was still going way after 7, when Alan's father came home from his post-work pint. He walked into the living room to find his son dressed in his aunt's shoes and pearls, his face plastered in Max Factor, jitterbugging around the floorboards next to the rolled-up carpet.

Alan's dad went crazy. He threw his wife and her sisters out into the street in full view of the neighbours and slammed the front door. Alan was dragged upstairs, flung into the bathtub and unceremoniously scrubbed from head to foot with coal-tar soap.

Then, as he stood naked and shivering, crying bulbous tears, his father shaved his beloved blond curls with a less-than-sharp razor.

***

Back to our friends in town. She's giving in. She needs to give in.

After an hour of pleading and puppy-dog eyes, Karen relented on her plans for an early night.

'Ok, ok — but only so I can meet Arlene — and if it's unbearable I'm off.'

Giz whisked her up in his arms.

'Thank you. Thank you. You won't regret it.'

He smiled a self-satisfied smile. Karen knew what he was thinking. He wanted to get her out of the flat. Since they'd heard the news about Jerry she'd barely been out of the door. Her Friday and Saturday nights were spent in front of the telly with a bottle of wine — sometimes two.

***

The aunts stopped coming to the house but Mrs Thompson took Alan to his grandmother's to see her younger sisters, and the afternoons progressed in much the same way. Alan had learnt a valuable lesson from his father's reaction — men don't like girly boys and if you're girly you have to hide it from them. He learned that if he wanted to, he could still sing along to his favourite Doris Day songs, it was just that at home he had to do it behind his bedroom door and even then only in a whisper.

Alan knew at the age of 10 that he was only interested in girls. His father's disgust actually worked in his favour. He didn't want to provoke such a reaction from the boys at school so he kept his head down and eschewed all feminine affectation. He was largely left alone. The boys didn't seem to notice him. In later life he couldn't really remember much about the boys in his class, only that they liked getting muddy and playing football. Alan had no male friends but he loved the girls; Amelia and Caroline, Susan and Phyllis. He loved their softness and their prettiness and the tiny blossoming breasts that showed under their gymslips. He watched the girls as much as any other boy, more in fact, because the girls liked him and so he was around them more. He was never starved of affection from the girls. Like miniature versions of his Aunts, they let him join in their skipping games, play with their dolls, help them plait their hair. He loved the girls but not, he quickly realised, because he desired them. He loved girls because he wanted to be like them. He watched them and he took note of how they acted and what they said and he filed it all in his brain, next to the behaviour of his aunts.

Alan left home when he was 16. He felt bad about leaving his mother to her humdrum existence, but he had to get away from the suffocation of pretending everyday to be something he was not. He remembered her standing at the garden gate when he left, waving a lace-edged hanky as he walked away down the mile-long street. Every time he looked over his shoulder she and the family home shrank a little more until, as he reached the end of the road, they were nothing but a blur.

Alan moved in with Auntie Pat in London and worked with her in a ballroom near Charing Cross where he could wear makeup without anyone caring. He started to sing to earn money but sometimes, despite hours of practice, his voice would betray him and crack in falsetto when he least expected it.

One night Pat took him to a small club down a dirty backstreet in Soho. He watched a woman performing *Fever*, who sounded so remarkably like Peggy Lee that, were it not for a slight thickness of waist and neck, it could have been her. Enraptured, he moved towards the stage. The lights through the cigarette smoke covered the singer in a rosy glow and her black sequined dress shimmered as she swayed and lifted her gloved arms above her head. She was beautiful. Pat looked at Alan with a knowing smile and nudged his arm with her elbow.

'It's a man,' she said.

My career as a drag queen was born.

***

The Vagina Monologues. Not the obvious choice for the Village Players, but that is what they chose for the summer play. I must admit when I first proposed it I never thought they'd go for it, but boredom is a great mischief-maker. In a village more accustomed to Gilbert and Sullivan, the choice caused quite a stir. The locals were split between those in favour of trying something new and those very much against. Of the latter, few knew anything about the play, only that its title referred to a part of the female anatomy best kept hidden under a layer of M&S knickers, support tights and a tweed skirt. Some branded it 'filth'. At the meeting in which it was decided the production would go ahead, several members walked out.

Of course I voted for. I have been a member of the Players for several years since retiring to the village after my partner, Glenda, succumbed to cervical cancer and I could no longer bear to live in Brighton.

***

Glenda was my saviour. After years of numbing unhappiness, which served Alan well in his persona as *Arlene Cabaret Star*, I was finally recommended for gender reassignment surgery. Glenda was a psychiatric nurse at the unit I was referred to after my third suicide attempt. In fact I first met Glenda when I was neither one thing nor the other, but was living as a woman in preparation for my surgery in Casablanca. Glenda told me she was fascinated by the idea that you could be something other than the thing you are told you are. I soon found out why. Her husband was a pig, metaphorically and professionally. A respected police officer by day, at home Sidney Watson drank himself to oblivion and beat Glenda with gruesome regularity. She was stuck. She had a child, a boy called Andy and she didn't know how to get away.

Our friendship developed over held hands and dried tears in the hospital psychology department. It became precious to both of us. We found ourselves transcending our prescribed roles, each becoming patient and nurse to the other. Glenda accepted me for the person I was inside. She got me through my transformation, telling me over and over how special I was until I actually believed her. We were apart for two months when I had my surgery; I thought of her constantly. When I got back I told her I loved her. Maybe my change spurred a change in her. She said she was ready to leave Sidney; that with me by her side she could strike out against him. Together we hatched a plan.

Glenda had been saving money for years, hiding it under a loose floorboard in Andy's bedroom. Mother left me a considerable sum, bless her, and I had saved every penny I earned in cabaret to pay for my surgery. If we pooled our resources there was more than enough to run away to a new life and take little Andy with us.

We conspired for a year, meeting in secret at my flat. Our relationship was physical as well as emotional. Glenda loved me and this meant she could explore my new body sexually. I had never had a female lover but was nevertheless attracted to her soft roundness and the gentleness with which she caressed my implanted breasts and newly constructed genitals. Funny that it should be a woman and not a man who tried them out first. I warned her I would still want men, but Glenda didn't mind at all so long as I reserved love for her alone. After years of abuse, Glenda said she never wanted to see a penis again. She would rather be alone than trust a man.

When everything was ready, Glenda decided Andy and I should meet. I had a sick feeling in my stomach as I waited for Glenda and Andy at a seafront ice cream parlour we knew. I watched a young family at the table opposite — Mother, Father, Daughter. I remember the calm before the storm, the sun casting a strange shadow over the neon *Kermit the frog* printed on the child's T-shirt. Pink ice cream dripped onto her chest from her spoon. Her father squeezed her shoulder and her mother dabbed at the spots of ice cream with a serviette. They smiled at each other over the girl's head. Then the father caught me looking and frowned. I was used to this reaction. People don't know how to act when confronted with something as anomalous as me. A puzzled frown is the usual expression. I looked away, out of the window, squinting to catch sight of Glenda and Andy. There they were, a little way off, Glenda talking and smiling, Andy shuffling along with his head down and his hands in his pockets.

I knew from his face when they came in, the meeting would be a disaster. He was shakily silent as Glenda introduced us. He shrugged when asked what ice cream he wanted and stared at the table top while I went to the counter to buy him a Knickerbocker Glory. I set it down in front of him.

'Thanks,' he said without looking up or picking up the spoon. When Glenda told him about our secret plan he was shocked. He looked at his mother in disbelief, his mouth dropped open in his pale little face. I saw that the boy knew his mother was beaten, but I was not the saviour he had in mind. I was repulsive to him. His face contorted, and I could feel the spray of spittle as he screamed repeatedly that I was a freak and he would never live with me. He stood and backed away through the doors of the café, then ran as fast as he could along the seafront, a ribbon of lost childhood among the tourists.

Glenda was visibly shaken by Andy's reaction. She rushed after him, stopping only to assure me that she would find him before he got home and explain things to him in a way he would understand. I finished my tea, acutely aware of the stares and whispers of the other customers.

Glenda came to my flat three hours later. She looked dazed but thankfully there was no sign of a beating. She didn't catch up with Andy before he got home. She'd looked all along the seafront and with mounting panic had realised he would get there before her. She prayed Sidney was out but as she drove up to the house she saw his car and knew it was hopeless. She found Andy in his bedroom with his father and the ripped-up floorboard exposing her money and some letters from me.

Sidney didn't even hit her this time. He dragged her outside by her hair and made her watch him burn her money and letters in an oil drum in the back garden. Then he threw her out into the street with nothing, not even a photograph of Andy, and he told her that if she ever tried to contact his son again he would kill her. Glenda knew he meant it. He said it so quietly.

***

The theatre in Hurstpierpoint is an unimposing building. In fact, if you didn't know it was there, you could walk past the door on the high street and never guess what was inside.

Karen and Giz found a parking space with only minutes to spare before curtain up. Karen hooked her arm in Giz's and watched the theatre-goers edging into the auditorium.

They looked funkier than she expected; the women were fashionable with sleek dyed hair, geometric jewellery topping off neutral colours, and the odd flash of bright silk. The men wore linen and close-cropped hair and the sort of thick-rimmed glasses that betray a youth of prepschool trendiness.

Representatives from the local women's refuge were collecting tickets and taking donations in plastic buckets — all the profits from the performances were going straight to them.

'Would you like to buy a badge?' a hippyish woman asked Giz, as he handed over his ticket.

'Blimey! How did you make *them*?'

'We didn't,' she said with a look of puzzlement, pinning a small blue house to his shirt.

'I thought she said *vadge*,' he whispered to Karen as they made their way inside.

'Now *that* would be clever.'

It may have been too much for the fundraisers of the women's refuge to create mini-vaginas to pin on the lapels of the audience, but Arlene in her capacity as set designer had excelled. Giz and Karen stood open-mouthed at the top of the stairs leading into the small theatre. The hundred or so red velvet seats sloped down on a red carpet towards the stage, the walls and stage had been draped in reams of flowing silk in various shades of pink, ranging from almost white to the deepest fuchsia. They met in a point above the stage, creating a giant inverted V that without a doubt represented the soft folds of the vulva.

'Wow,' said Karen.

'I feel a bit uncomfortable,' whispered Giz, 'I've never been inside one before.'

'Sit down.' She steered him along the back row. Gary looked at them from his front-row seat and nodded in approval. As haunting piano notes filled the room and the lights dimmed, Karen caught sight of a woman sitting next to Gary, her head haloed in a candyfloss helmet of rose-coloured hair.

***

We didn't run away. We couldn't leave the city without Andy. Glenda believed Sidney when he said he'd kill her, so she didn't try to contact her boy. She watched him from a distance — on his way to school, at football practice, or in the park — stalking him like a PI.

Whenever she came back from these visits without any contact, her face would be rigid, as if she'd clenched her teeth all day and frozen the muscles into an unnatural state. It would take hours to relax her, to loosen the muscles into normalcy. Only I could do this. With warm baths and scented candles, cooing endearments, home-cooked meals and red wine. I poured tenderness over her until she was almost herself again. But each time her body retained a tiny part of its rigidity, a tightness that in time would overwhelm her.

We bought a B&B in Kemptown with the remainder of our money and settled into our life together. We loved each other and I told myself that was all that mattered.

Glenda tried to see Andy when Sidney died. She was so excited. She thought she could be Andy's mother again, that they could regain the lost years. But Andy was 19 and he didn't want anything to do with her. When she left, he had become his father's victim and for that, he could never forgive her. God only knows what he had to endure. It was his defence in court — *a childhood of unimaginable abuse*. Thank god Glenda wasn't alive to read that in the papers.

When she went to him on the morning of Sidney's funeral, Andy told her that in his eyes she was as dead as his father and that he didn't believe in ghosts.

Glenda was devastated. To be told by her own son that she didn't exist. Every fibre of her body tightened beyond rescue, and on that day, as she walked away from her only child, her disease set in. An anomalous cell inside her split and then divided again. And so it began.

I was all she had now and I vowed to be there for her. For the rest of our short time together we never spent a night apart, and when Glenda was admitted to the County General to die in a cloud of morphine, I simply refused to leave her side.

***

Karen thought the play was ok. The three women who performed in it did well, considering they were amateurs. Karen thought she recognised one of them, a woman with a subtle spray tan and a Tiffany necklace. She was prompted once by the director, to much heckling from her friends in the front row.

In the interval there was warm wine served in a tiny bar in the back room.

'You made it then,' said Gary to Giz with a chaste peck on the cheek.

'Of course — I always do what I say I will.'

Karen and Gary exchanged a glance and laughed.

'What?' said Giz. 'Are you two going to gang up on me again?'

And now here I am, standing next to Gary, waiting to be introduced to the face I haven't seen before. She's good this one — real star quality, the long red hair and the green eye shadow. What is she wearing? A green velvet dress; almost too much for the occasion but she can carry it off. Her face is pale and behind those anxious eyes there's a vulnerability I recognise — it's well hidden, but it's there nonetheless.

'Don't worry dear,' I said to poor little Giz. 'I'll look after you.'

His friend stared at me, her eyes wide. I know what I look like. I don't mind people staring anymore. I'm almost right but not quite — then again who is? I try to blend in, play the chic old lady — plain linen skirt, liberty-bow blouse, pearl-drop earrings and necklace, but I never go out without makeup and I never could resist a pair of false eyelashes. Obviously my hands are perfectly manicured, rosebud pink to match my perfume, but I know my hands are bigger than average, sausages for fingers and not chipolatas either. I could see her looking at them, she tried not to but she couldn't help it. I could tell that by the count of five she would look down at my feet. I was right.

'Massive aren't they dear? You can improve on many things but the hands and feet you're born with are the ones you have till you die.'

She blushed.

'I'm a 7 myself, so mine aren't exactly dainty.'

'I'm Arlene,' I said holding out my hand.

She took it. Cold hands — warm heart.

'This is Karen,' said Giz. 'She's always putting her size 7s in it.'

We chatted about the play and the 'wondrous' set design.

I told them about the fight we had just to get the play put on.

'There was a lot of opposition to it in the village you know — filth they said, degrading to women, using base words to describe the female anatomy. I'm probably the only one living here who realises just how precious a vagina is.'

'Tell them about the note Arlene,' prompted Gary.

'Ah yes — the note. It was pushed through my door about a week into rehearsals, like a proper blackmail note, written in letters cut out of the newspaper — the local freebie of all things — STOP THE PLAY — I KNOW WHAT YOU ARE.'

'Oh my god,' said Giz.

'I must admit I was a little shocked to get such a sordid thing out here. It seems someone in the village has been reading too much Agatha Christie.'

'What did you do?' asked Karen, really engaging with me for the first time.

'Well my dear, I framed it. I was flattered by the attention. Obviously it didn't make any difference to the show — I know what I am — I don't give a fuck if anyone else does as well.'

A couple of the more staid locals coughed uncomfortably at the word *fuck*, but Karen smiled, and oh my, what a smile.

The buzzer sounded five minutes to the second half and we downed our wine.

Something else happened in the theatre that night. Karen told me about it later, when she'd relaxed a little and let the past flood in.

On her way back from the loo, Karen came face to face with the woman who'd ruined her life. Louise, Jerry's neighbour, was waiting to use the toilet. She looked smaller than Karen remembered and more wrinkled around the eyes, but her hair still shone and the little turned-up nose was still perfect. Her smile dropped when she saw Karen. They hadn't seen each other since the funeral, and then Louise had hovered under the trees at some distance from the ceremony. Karen had only seen her as she bent to lay a rose on Jerry's coffin.

They stood together in the tiny ladies' room unsure of how to go on. After a moment Louise ventured a dry 'hello'.

Karen bit down on her tongue to force back tears and then she slapped Louise, hard, making a shockingly loud noise. She pushed passed her and out into the bar. There was no one else around — no one had seen — but as she took her place next to Giz she was shaking, her right hand burning from the impact.

'You ok?' he whispered.

'Fine.'

She stared at the empty stage.

As the music started, she noticed a seat in the front row was empty and even as the play began, nobody came back to claim it.

INTERLEWD

At 9.43 in the evening Major and Mrs. Phillips were walking their dog Ginger down the High Street for their nightly inspection of the recreation ground. Ginger, a little white westie with a terrible temper and a habit of weeing on anyone who gave him any attention, crouched on the pavement in the shadow of the theatre. As Major Phillips bent from his waist to pick up the steaming croissant of shit, his ears were assaulted by the muffled, yet undeniably clear, sound of one word shouted from within the building behind him.

Cunt.

The major straightened up on his walking stick and blinked at his wife who was frozen to the spot. They jumped in their Hush Puppies as they heard the word repeated, louder than the first time. And by the third and loudest CUNT they had turned on their heels and fled up the road as fast as their weathered feet could carry them.

Arlene had to bite her lip to stop herself laughing when she overheard the major talking about it at the grocer's.

'It was terrible, Mrs Thompson,' he said noticing her standing next to him by a pyramid of apples, 'Ginger hasn't been the same since.'

ARLENE ACT TWO

After the play I asked them back to my bungalow. My home is decorated like any old woman's home, with its random collection of ornaments and its unfathomable smell of oranges. But there are a few tell-tale signs of non-conformity; not many pensioners have framed posters from films like *Kiss of the Spider Woman* and *Dog Day Afternoon*, or a full set of signed Armistead Maupin books on the bookcase. In the hall Karen looked at the photographs taken from my days as a makeup artist, snaps of me with various theatre stars. She bent to look at one in particular.

'Is that Rudolph Nureyev?' she asked.

'Yes dear. Poor Rudi — he liked to party.'

She looked at me, unsure whether to believe me or not. You should always accept possible pasts in people you've just met. Especially the old; the old usually have at least half a century of possible pasts to offer. You should always keep an open mind — who knows what you might discover.

The rest of my home is covered in 1950s furniture; a chaise lounge and wicker chair, a Bakelite telephone and garlands of plastic flowers hanging over paintings of sparkling Mediterranean coastlines. The hideous china dogs that my mother left me growl at each other on the fire-surround and I have pictures of Elvis and Marilyn everywhere. I'm not sure why this should be; I wasn't particularly happy in the 50s. I mean it wasn't as crushingly awful as my childhood, but I still wasn't happy. I think it's the glamour — the 50s was all about glamour. Nobody was glamorous in the 70s, not even the beautiful, it was all so… synthetic. In the corner of the living room, I have a leather-upholstered cocktail bar with a pineapple ice-bucket. I rescued it from the skip when one of the clubs I used to work in closed down. It took a bit of work polishing it up. Karen's face lit up like a torch when she saw it — my kinda girl.

I set to work making pink gins while Giz chose the music from my vinyl collection. Karen picked up a bamboo-framed photograph from the sideboard. The photo has faded, taken on the green tinge of time-weathered images. It shows me some years ago — probably in my late 40s. I am smiling broadly; my arm is around a small dark woman. Our heads are close together like siblings at play. The woman has a naturally clear pixie face and big green eyes. She wears a huge smile. I remember the night it was taken, and in that instant we were immeasurably happy. Karen smiled to herself, a smile like Glenda's, and placed the photograph back on the sideboard.

Hello Dolly blasted through the speakers and feeling very sprightly, I sashayed into the room duetting perfectly with Barbara. This led to more Streisand. And after a while I was persuaded to change into a red-sequined evening gown and mime along in a recreation of my old act. I swung my feather boa and gestured diva-like with my arms. I could almost see the audiences from the clubs of my past, the applause, the laughter and tears. I could always bring an audience to tears — it was my thing. You weren't human if you didn't cry at an Arlene Thompson Show.

After several pink gins, *Memories* brought Gary to tears. He stood up to fling his arms around me and fell flat on his face onto the sheepskin rug, curling himself into a drunken sleep from which he could not be woken. I fetched my cashmere blanket from the bedroom and laid it gently over him.

'Ah look at him,' said Giz, 'the love of my life — after Martin Thornton that is.'

Karen laughed. 'Who on earth is Martin Thornton?'

'First love — captain of the cricket team, godlike — the straightest boy in school. He wanted me really but it would never have worked out.'

'What about you Karen?' I asked. 'Have you found the love of your life yet?'

Giz paused, mid-gulp as if I had asked a taboo question.

'I was sure I had,' she said avoiding my eyes, 'but it didn't work out either. My ex was a bit straight, you know, didn't like to party much.' She slugged back her gin and said bitterly — 'unless it was with other women. Unbelievably good in bed though — too good.'

I was intrigued. Was this why she had that subtle vulnerability?

'Do you still see him?'

She looked into her cocktail glass and twiddled the fake umbrella.

'No. He died. He was knocked down six months ago. He was in love with someone else anyway — the woman who ran him over.'

Not the answer I expected. I raised my eyebrows and then my glass.

'To absent lovers — wherever they may be.'

The three of us drank moist-eyed, then smiled in shared sadness.

They're going now, our new friends.

Karen and Giz loaded Gary into a taxi just after 3am. Karen ran back to me at my front door and encircled me in a wide hug.

'It was a pleasure to meet you Mrs Thompson.'

'You too dear,' I said, 'and don't worry — you're still young — he's out there somewhere.'

I waved the cab away.

Inside, the bungalow was as quiet as the grave. I changed from the sequins of the past into a nightie of the present. I put on the kimono I bought for Glenda in Capri, wrapping it around myself like a familiar pair of arms. It still smells of her even after all these years. I made a cup of Lady Grey and sat on the sofa letting the vapours rise up into my face. I read somewhere that steam opens the pores and rehydrates the skin. As I told Karen earlier, I need all the rehydration I can get, after a certain age *Clarins* just isn't enough.

Giz phoned the next day to tell me I had done Karen a world of good. He said she'd laughed to herself in the taxi on the way home and when he asked her why, she'd said, 'Jerry would have absolutely hated that evening. He was a bit of a prick really wasn't he?'

I have to agree, he did sound like a bit of a prick. Still we can't help who we love. I was lucky — eventually — nobody was more perfect than Glenda.

I'll see you soon, lovely Karen. Those of us who know the pain of a love lost should stick together. Perhaps you could help me pick the next production for the Village Players. I was thinking *Victor/Victoria*, or maybe *Spring Awakening?*

DALEKS

They appeared in stealth. It shouldn't have been a surprise to him, but initially he was mystified by them. First came the holes, marked out in 50-yard intervals — one big, one small, one big — running up and down both sides of the next street. Brinsley first saw them as he was walking his pug, Duckie, early one morning when the light was still green with the dawn. They hadn't been there the night before as the pair had taken their usual circuitous route to the recreation ground.

For a time there was no change — as if a geometrically-minded badger had worked its secret way along Reigate Road, pushing new doorways up through the pavement.

After a week or so the small holes were filled in, a tall metal trunk imprisoned inside. Then came the *daleks* themselves, each taking its place in the depths of the bigger holes, symmetrically stationed for the convenience of the city's drivers — so they didn't have to walk more than a few paces to buy a ticket.

Brinsley's heart sank as he turned the corner and saw the newly formed battalion of parking soldiers stand to attention down the length of the road. Their shining futuristic uniformity seemed at odds with the old-world charm of the ivy-clad Victorian terraces. Brinsley shuddered in the chill wind of change.

It'll be hell to park now — the street will be overrun by interlopers.

Not that Brinsley drove much anymore — not since Keith had died. These days the Triumph was almost permanently parked outside the front door. He took it for a spin to Sainsbury's on Friday mornings, but that was about it.

There had been a time when they'd driven the length and breadth of England together — roof down, the smell of sunlight on leather, and the mechanical whirr of the engine as they buzzed along the tall-hedged lanes in search of a pretty place to stay. Once or twice a year, they ferried her over to the continent and spent a week or two in whatever corner of sun-whitened Europe they fancied — *as free as the breeze.*

Before Keith had died — nearly ten years ago now — Brinsley had driven him to France *for a last holiday.* They'd sat at a café in Honfleur and watched the Triumph gleam red on the quayside, as clusters of locals touched her bonnet and whispered in awestruck tones about *la voiture anglaise.*

Say what you will about the French — they know a thing of beauty when they see it.

Keith had tried to drink his champagne, but it had burned his sickened chest and he'd left it to go flat in the evening sun.

These days Brinsley likes to walk. It keeps him fit and since his retirement, gives him something to do when everything else in the day is monotonous. These days, without Keith, he doesn't seem to have anywhere to go. Besides, it saves money on petrol and little Duckie must be walked so she doesn't turn to fat.

We wouldn't want that now precious would we? — No we wouldn't!

On the first Friday morning since the arrival of the *daleks*, Brinsley opens the car door for Duckie, and as she jumps into the passenger seat, a black Mercedes glides silently to a halt just behind them. Brinsley looks into the reflection on its front window. The passenger window winds down in a fluid swish and a man's voice shouts out in a new-world accent Brinsley can't place.

'You goin'?'

Brinsley peers at him. He's young, in a suit but with a T-shirt underneath, slightly receding black hair slicked back, his eyes hidden behind mirrored sunglasses.

'In a minute,' says Brinsley quietly.

'Only I've a train to hop.'

The cheek of it — he doesn't even live here!

Brinsley takes his time — slowly closing the passenger door, slowly walking around to the driver's side, settling himself into his seat, checking Duckie, pulling on his seat belt — like an old tortoise. He turns the key in the ignition and there is only a slight judder — she's often like this first thing in the morning — it takes her a while to get going. He turns it again and she jumps into life. As she's warming up it starts to rain — huge globular drops plonk onto the window — Brinsley turns on the wipers and they squeak across the glass. The man in the Mercedes blasts his horn — a loud shattering exclamation that sets off Duckie's bark and makes Brinsley's blood boil. He edges away from the kerb and down the road. Behind him the Mercedes fills the space he's left in a screech of brakes — leaving little room for the cars in front or behind to escape.

When he gets back from the shops there is not a single parking space to be had. The road is jammed with cars bumper to bumper. Brinsley can't imagine how they're all going to get out *without the aid of a tin-opener*. The rain is incessant. He has to park on the steep pot-holed lane at the end of his street and make two trips home with his shopping and then go back for

Duckie. Each time he passes the Mercedes, shiny and black, its windows screened in anti-glare grey.

It's still there as he takes Duckie for her lunchtime stroll. The pavements are slushy with wet leaves that stick to his boots as he walks. They turn the corner into Reigate Road. There are just two cars parked on its length, the rest of the kerbs are clear with only the silent *daleks* in attendance. A bored traffic warden tramps the flagstones.

'Excuse me,' says Brinsley when he draws level. 'I think there are some cars parked illegally in Tivoli Crescent.'

The traffic warden eyes him suspiciously, wondering if he's taking the piss.

'I don't think so mate,' he replies. 'Just been round there — didn't issue a single ticket.'

As he walks away the rain starts again.

Brinsley sees the Mercedes parked in various spaces along Tivoli Crescent throughout the week. In the mornings as he has his breakfast in front of the local news, he can hear the man outside his house talking loudly on his mobile phone.

'Hi Babe it's Daniel — look we've got to move forward on this, if it's a go it'll be worth a fortune.'

Or some such money-grubbing nonsense filled with over-familiarity. Who calls a work colleague Babe?

Brinsley's toast sticks in his throat and he feeds the honey-smeared crusts to Duckie.

On Friday morning he leaves the space outside his door, with no cars waiting to jump into it. The sun shines high in a bright blue sky. He does his shopping with a light step — *perhaps the parking madness is over.*

When he returns the Mercedes is once again parked in *his* space. Brinsley's face glows apple red as he drives past his own house to the nearest space at the end of the street. On his way up the hill he sees Doreen from two doors down and her hoody son come out of their flat.

'Can't even park outside your own home anymore, eh Brinsley? It's a nightmare — that's what — all commuters you know. No respect for people who actually live here.'

She licks at her fuchsia lips. Brinsley sighs and picks up Duckie, cradling her in the crook of his arm.

'It's that black Mercedes that's got my goat.' He tickles Duckie's slobbery chin. 'It's like he's deliberately persecuting me.'

Doreen's son widens his eyes, giving the impression that they are wholly made up of dilated pupils.

'You know what you wanna do to him,' he sniffs, 'superglue his locks — that'll teach him.'

Doreen slaps her offspring on the back of the hood.

'Don't be daft Derek — that would be criminal damage. He could get arrested.'

'Yeah, but if he was careful they wouldn't know who done it.'

Derek has been odd since he was a child, the sort of kid who sits on the pavement and throws stones at cats, but Brinsley thinks about Derek's words all day, and they don't leave his brain even as he settles down to sleep in his feather-down duvet with Duckie at his feet.

The man from the council has a disinterested nasally voice.

'Now let's see — Tivoli Crescent? Says here you voted against the permit scheme. I'm afraid we can't do anything if people are legally parked on an unmetered road.'

Brinsley had indeed voted against the permit scheme. He could ill afford the 150 quid a year for the privilege of parking outside his own home. He and Keith had savings but most of them had gone on healthcare — the exclusive London clinic that had served as Keith's home for his final days had chewed through their money like a piranha. The only end to the financial commitment had been death, and Keith had battled that for almost a year. Not that Brinsley begrudged him a penny of it. Keith died in luxury — two-inch deep carpets, chrome and glass and Sky TV and 5-star catering — it was some relief to Brinsley that in the end Keith had been as comfortable as it was possible to be.

Brinsley remembered the day Princess Diana came to visit. He'd walked the rail-thin and morphine-tripping Keith along the corridor to the day room, and there she was with the clinic's director. She had been luminous, and she took Keith's hand and smiled her coy smile with simple compassion. Keith thought she was his Aunt Dolly from Philadelphia.

'Oh Dolly!' he whispered. 'I always loved you the best.'

Diana had patted his hand and looked piteously at Brinsley.

She was dead a year later — Mercedes have a lot to answer for.

Brinsley looks out of his window — the sun is hidden behind a curtain of plump grey cloud. He takes one of the photograph albums of their roadtrips down from the bookcase. He opens the front cover and writes in fountain pen on the blank inside page:

'I swear by your memory I will keep the car safe and get rid of Mercedes Boy.'

On Friday, Brinsley prints fake parking tickets on orange cardboard and slips one under the windscreen wiper of the Mercedes. Later he finds it ripped up on the pavement.

The following Friday, Brinsley procures some traffic cones, abandoned by a team of cable-layers, and places them outside his house when he leaves. Mercedes Boy crushes them into the kerb as he parks.

The next Friday, Brinsley takes Derek's advice and buys Superglue at Sainsbury's. Back home he snaps off the lid and squeezes it into the locks of the Mercedes. That night he hears Mercedes Boy swearing outside his curtained window and half an hour later sees the blue neon lights of the pickup truck flash against the shadows on the ceiling.

A week later — Brinsley *accidentally* smashes the Mercedes passenger-side mirror with a spanner he bought on an impromptu stop at the hardware store. This time he can't resist — he's in the garden when Mercedes Boy comes up from the train. He sees the wing mirror and swears, violently kicking the nearest wheel.

'Oh dear,' says Brinsley, 'kids I expect.'

Mercedes Boy turns and glares at him and Brinsley tries to force down the sides of his mouth as they curl into an unbidden smile.

Today, Brinsley comes out of his house to find a police car in front of the Triumph, the Mercedes double parked, and a policeman and Mercedes Boy deep in conversation on the pavement.

At last — they've got him!

'That's him!' shouts his enemy, pointing at Brinsley. Doreen and Derek stand gaping at their garden gate.

'Excuse me sir,' says the policeman, walking over to Brinsley, 'I wonder if you wouldn't mind accompanying me to the station — just to answer a few questions.'

Brinsley stares in confusion as Duckie jumps all over the policeman's boots wagging her tail excitedly.

'Can you leave your dog with someone?' says the policeman not hiding his irritation.

Brinsley watches Doreen cuddle Duckie through the back window of the police car. She waves his baby's little paw up and down with her hand. As he is driven away down the street, he sees the black Mercedes slip unhindered into the empty parking space in front of the Triumph.

THE VICTORIAN WAY WITH DEATH

STRANGE HAPPENINGS
AT WILSON'S MUSEUM

Staff at Wilson's Museum of Birds and Natural Histories have reported burglar alarms going off at random since the installation of the new taxidermy exhibit — *The Victorian Way with Death*.

Police have been called to the museum on several occasions but remain mystified as to the cause of the disturbance.

The exhibit features a recreation of founder William Wilson's drawing room, complete with antique furniture found in the museum's stores, and a marble fire-place, thought to have been taken from Wilson's house on Dyke Road when it was demolished.

Jeremy Finn, the museum curator, states that he has no idea what is setting off the alarms, though he adds, 'it is probably the stuffed birds that constitute most of the museum's collection. Everybody knows that they come alive after dark and fly around the grand hall.'

Jeremy finished reading from the Argus and chuckled to himself.

Elizabeth rolled her eyes, 'Honestly Jeremy, we'll be overrun with even more nutters than usual!'

284

'Well, as if I have the time to answer stupid questions about the paranormal. We've still half the collection to catalogue.' He slurped noisily at his tea. 'Still, we need to find out what's causing it — can't have the police coming round every five minutes — and the neighbours are starting to lose patience. We must always keep the neighbours on our side.'

'Couldn't it just be Tut?' asked David, referring to the museum cat, so called because of the noise he made with his throat whenever he ate.

'Then why would it only just have happened? If it was Tut it would have started years ago. Besides, he can't get out of the inside door to the porch, and that must be where the problem is — there, or at the back.'

The two security guards, Kevin and Mark, exchanged glances.

At the back of the museum, behind the skeleton galleries, was a curious little room, accessible through a thin arched doorway. It was a surprise to visitors because it spread out further than they anticipated when they peered round the door. The room contained various curios at odds with the primarily scientific nature of the museum, including a lump of meteor rock, a tiny merman and a moth-eaten reconstruction of the dodo. The room had a spooky ambience to it; many a small child having skipped happily passed the cases of preserved creepy-crawlies and the stark white animal bones, simply stopped in their tracks at the doorway and refused to go any further.

'Yes we'll have to find out what's causing it — the alarms have been tested and there's nothing visible on the security cameras. I propose that we have someone here all night for a few weeks, just to see what we come up with.'

Jeremy looked pointedly at the security guards who both groaned.

'I'll do it,' said David.

Four pairs of eyes stared at him in surprise.

'I mean, I don't mind. I can work just as well at night as in the day — and I don't have a family anymore so I don't need to be at home.'

Elizabeth looked at the floor, and Jeremy scribbled on his notepad, suddenly taking minutes when he hadn't bothered before.

'Nice one,' said Kevin, unable to conceal his glee.

Jeremy looked up. 'Are you sure you'll be alright?' he said rubbing his chin.

'I'll be fine,' David replied his voice tinged with irritation. 'I'm not going to go crazy again if that's what's worrying you.'

'No no, of course not. In that case, David — thank you. Can you start tomorrow? Obviously we'll work out the hours so you don't do any more than you're paid for. Now — any other business?'

David was a Cambridge graduate in Earth Sciences. He'd left university with an MSc and a wife. He'd expected the former, but not the latter.

He met Ellen in his fifth year of study, doing field work on the Dorset coast. She was the daughter of one of his professors; she'd been at a loose end and had by happenstance come along to help with the final week of the dig. She'd been a popular addition to the little group of mostly male scientists, shaking them up a bit because she was female, under fifty and attractive. The first time David saw her — up to her knees in the chalky mud, the sun bouncing off her auburn curls, dirt smeared on her cheeks and the sea growling behind her — he knew he would never want another woman.

Hardly an experienced lover — with just two girlfriends in his 24 years — he avoided her all week out of shyness. But he couldn't help looking at her when he thought she couldn't see him, and once or twice their eyes met and she smiled. David's response was to look away with a frown.

On the last night of the dig she found him outside the youth hostel they were using as a base. He'd left the warm beer and awkward small talk of the farewell gathering to go outside and smoke a solitary cigarette under the stars. She'd asked him for a light and they'd chatted for a while about the constellations swirling above their heads. He showed her Orion and Sirius to the left then stood behind her and pointed out Taurus to the right. Their cheeks were a fraction apart and he could smell the scent of apple on her hair. She turned her face to him and found his lips with her own. He was surprised that she wanted to kiss him but was lost completely in her embrace.

'Come with me,' she said and led him down the driveway and out onto the fields away from the road — away from everything but themselves.

She told him she was pregnant five weeks later. He was shocked but genuinely happy. She offered to end it — to leave the beginnings of their child in a sterile room — but he wouldn't hear of it. David knew in his heart that this was the reason he was born, to love Ellen and to love their child.

They married quickly — one morning in August in the village she grew up in. A beautiful English church served as the venue, the bells rang out across the green and dandelion seeds floated as confetti on the breeze. David didn't know if he believed in God, but he promised before Him to love Ellen and to be faithful to her as long as he lived.

When he graduated, David got a job at the Natural History Museum in London. He followed in the footsteps of Owen and Huxley and Darwin into the grand vaulted hall and was immediately aware of his tremendous inadequacy. This feeling persisted through his first few months of service, as he chipped and brushed away at specimens in rocks shipped from South America. In his daydreams, he saw himself being carried around the museum in the jaws of T-Rex, shaken like a rag doll. Pleased with his progress, his superiors moved him on to work on the assembly and categorisation of the hollow bones of a dinosaur thought to prove the evolutionary link from reptile to bird.

Ellen had the baby, a boy, born underweight on March 29th. It was touch-and-go for a while — the child, wired to machines in a plastic tank, had underdeveloped lungs and struggled for each breath. David laboured to keep his feelings under control; in his heart he wanted to shout and tear at his hair, but his head told him to keep it together for Ellen. As he held his child's tiny fingers through the porthole of the incubator he shuddered at the fragility of human life. After several weeks his son named Adam, took his first breath on his own and two days later, much to their surprise, he was allowed home.

As Adam's body strengthened David's mind loosened. He couldn't sleep. He would fall exhausted into bed then lie for hours with his eyes wide open, sure that Adam would stop breathing. He cried a lot; silent tears that ran down his cheeks and melted onto his pillow unseen. He was afraid to make any noise; afraid he would wake Adam or Ellen and be responsible for needlessly unsettled hours. He was silent during the day too, he just didn't have anything to say — this was okay at work where concentration was paramount, but at home when Ellen cooed and fussed over Adam or they sat down to dinner and then to watch TV, David still didn't say a word.

Then one day at work he was left alone while his supervisor attended a budget meeting. David worked minutely away to free the bones from their sandstone prison. As he did, a trigger went off in his mind. He began to internally discuss the existence of God. He weighed up the evidence — for and against — guiding hand or random selection, benevolent provider or simply physical architecture, an afterlife or stony death. He came to the conclusion that whether there was or wasn't a Creator, the bones of the dinosaur in front of him held no significance at all. He saw the futility of everything; the big bang, the expansion of the universe, the coalescing of the galaxies, the solar system, the formation of the earth, the first spark of life and then the evolution of that life from bacteria to fish to reptile to these gigantic plant-eaters — all wiped out by one apocalyptic meteor — followed by the rush of modern history.

The bones before him meant nothing — less than nothing. They shouldn't even be here; without human intervention they'd still be stuck under a layer of mud, buried until the end of the world. Everything he was doing was meaningless — it could be buried or shattered in an instant. A human instant was a universal nanosecond or a billion years, unquantifiable, unknowable — maddening.

The synapses of his brain fizzed like carbonated water, and with a mixture of rage and fear he grabbed the tiny pick that lay on the table next to the bones. The point of it stuck into the leg bone with the first hit, so that David had to make an effort to pull it out; the bone cracked slightly as it squeaked free. David hit it again, then again and again — a frenzied attack of punctures and cracks that popped and crunched in the quiet of the sealed room. When all that was left were the fragments of fractured bones, David picked up a hammer and smashed at these with such ferocity that sweat ran into his eyes and his T-shirt was soaked under his lab coat. He stopped only when the lab door swished open and his supervisor stared at him in horror from the doorway. David stood, hammer raised, the little vein under his left eye pulsing beneath the transparency of his sleep-deprived skin. On the table before him, where the leg bone used to be, was a pile of rubble and dust.

Needless to say, David lost his job. His actions made the papers.

Mad Scientist Destroys Priceless Dino Bones!

Ironically, at the museum he became something bigger than himself, part of its mythology, to be talked about in hushed tones by the staff for decades to come.

He was committed for a while, housed in an institution with peeling paint and cabbage smells, sedated to the point where sleep was no longer necessary.

After months of talking, he was let out. He had no job, no future — no means of continuing.

Ellen's father came to his rescue, securing him the position at Wilson's Museum by taking responsibility for him and personally asking the curator, Jeremy Finn, for a favour. They had been friends for thirty years; Jeremy was Ellen's godfather. David had met him once before, at the wedding. At the time he'd thought him rather sad, with his brown socks and bad breath — someone not to turn out like — but when he made the trip South for the formal interview he was acutely aware that this man was to be his saviour. When David broached the subject of his breakdown, Jeremy sat in silence and listened.

'I'm cured now,' said David. 'I've letters from the doctors vouching for my sanity. I know you're taking a terrible risk, considering a lunatic like me but…'

He tried to finish the sentence — to let Jeremy know how grateful he was — but words failed him.

'Don't worry dear boy,' said Jeremy seeing his distress, 'none of us is perfect.'

David did okay at the museum, whilst not exactly thriving, he did at least maintain a semblance of normalcy. His symptoms persisted — lethargy, insomnia, impotence — he and Ellen co-existed rather than cohabited. Three months after they moved to Brighton, she left him for a taxi driver called Graham, who had probably never read a book in his life. She took Adam and denied David access. He didn't have the energy to fight.

The museum closed its doors to the public at 5 o'clock. Jeremy and Elizabeth usually stuck around for another hour or so, muddling away at something or other. On the evening of David's first nightwatch they seemed even more reluctant to leave — it was after 7 by the time he bolted the door from the inside, sealing himself in with the dead things.

He watched the news on the crackling portable TV beloved of the security guards, but since Ellen had left he never watched anything else on television, and so he turned it off at 8 o'clock. He ate his sandwiches and drank tea from his thermos flask. The crossword was done by 8.30, and then he didn't really have anything to do in the reception area. He could have got on with cataloguing the holdings in the back rooms, but he felt too tired to concentrate, besides, no one would know he hadn't.

He wandered over to the Victorian exhibit in the main hall. Jeremy had recreated a drawing room, complete with furniture, parlour palms and a marble fireplace he'd found in the storage room. On a desk in the corner he'd placed a half-finished stuffed squirrel that spewed straw from its insides, and had laid out taxidermy tools on a muslin wrap beside it. A gas lamp, converted to electricity, stood on a table next to a fake window cloaked in tasselled drapes.

David settled himself into the red velvet armchair, running his hands over the worn fabric of the arms and the intricately carved wood at their ends. He relaxed for the first time in months without the aid of medication. He breathed in and out to the *pfut pfut pfut* of the air-conditioning and was gently lulled to sleep.

He woke quickly, seized by a sudden panic, and sprang from the chair. The air was cold. The gas light flickered, and at the edge of the drawing room he saw, or rather, had the impression of, a swathe of material, a gown of some sort, the blackest shiniest satin, thick and heavy and wet, embroidered with roses in the same deep colour. It only lasted a second and he wasn't sure it had happened at all. When he turned to look at the door, the apparition had gone. He walked towards where it had been, then turned back and retrieved a torch from under the reception desk. He made a round of the dark and silent hall, the light of the torch catching unnervingly on the beaded eyes of the desiccated birds, the slow click of his shoes echoing off the newly polished lino. In the skeleton room, his nerves were assaulted anew as Tut leapt down from the suspended jaw bone of a whale with a mouse in his teeth, and tutted or gagged sickeningly as he pushed it down his throat.

Despite the excitement of the night before, David had fallen asleep, slumped in his chair at the reception desk, a line of dribble slinking from his half-open mouth. He didn't wake, even as Jeremy unlocked the front door, turned off the singing alarm and stood over him waiting for some sign of life. Jeremy coughed, then tapped his umbrella on the desk.

'David!' he said loudly.

David sat up in surprise and blinked at Jeremy. 'Um,' he said, then shook the confusion from his head and added, 'Good morning Jeremy,' with a sleepy grin.

'No nocturnal visitors I take it,' said Jeremy, walking away towards the staff room at the back of the museum, 'Do you want some tea? Yours looks like it's gone cold.'

David followed him past the cases of the eternally sleeping birds, yawning and stretching and trying to make sense of what he had seen during the night.

Once inside the kitchen, after a short chat about the weather and with a freshly brewed cup of tea in his hand, he asked Jeremy the question.

'Jeremy, was a woman involved in setting up the museum? I mean Wilson wasn't married was he? Was there someone else — a sister or something?'

Jeremy peered at him over his spectacles.

'You've seen her then? Our resident ghost.'

'What? There's a resident ghost? Funny how you didn't mention that at the meeting.'

'Oh yes — the *Lady in Black*. I've never seen her myself, but my predecessor swore he'd seen her several times.'

'What happened to him?'

Jeremy frowned. 'Well I'd like to say he lived out a peaceful retirement in the country, but actually he jumped in front of a train on his way home from his last day at work.'

David spluttered into his tea. 'You're joking, right?'

'Sorry dear boy, but no — that is what happened to him. Nothing to do with seeing the *Lady in Black* I'm sure — what's she like then?'

David scratched his head. He didn't know how to describe what he'd seen because he hadn't actually seen anything.

'Mmm — not sure really — just a sort of feeling I saw something, rather than actually seeing it, like a shadow, um, but a bit more than that — more solid. I know — it was like a cobweb, yes that's it — a cobweb.'

'A cobweb?'

Jeremy stared at him with the eyes of a sceptic on the brink of conversion.

'Well, if you want to find out about the setting up of the museum, take a look at the old box-files in the upstairs storage room, there are all sorts of documents and letters in there. Wilson himself died in 1894, he fell off a cliff in Lyme Regis trying to collect guillemot eggs. I suppose that's why he doesn't haunt the place himself — he didn't die here.'

'Is that really how he died?'

Jeremy smiled, lost in the reverie of his museum's history. 'Oh yes — brilliant way to go for a naturalist, don't you think? Out on the job — collecting,' he rubbed his hands together. 'I couldn't tell you who the lady was but if you go through the files you might find something. You could write a pamphlet on it — might help you stay awake.'

The following night, before the darkness set in, David made his way up to the storage room in search of the museum's original documents. The stairs at the back of the museum were a wooden spiral, unpolished and worm-eaten. They creaked underfoot and from some physical combination of weight and give, gave David the impression that someone else was walking up behind him. He stopped a couple of times to check he was alone, then hurried up the last few steps and flung open the storage room door, dislodging a flurry of dust.

He laughed to himself — a man of science frightened by a little echo on a staircase. Ghosts didn't exist, and even if they did, they were a naturally occurring phenomenon — a psychic photograph, a collective memory.

The light from the staircase shone weakly into the storage room as David felt around the wall for the light switch, and he pondered on the enormous shadow thrown across the dimly lit ceiling. Sharply defined and solid, the actual cobweb casting it was invisible to him. *Were cobwebs the only things on earth more substantial in shadow than as themselves?* It swung in the draught from the eaves, an ethereal circus trapeze high in the roof, joining another web, then parting again in the corner. Their dance made David sad; the shadows of discarded webs. Once intricate and purposeful — a unique and complex trap for prey — now they were a fragmented and useless cluster of threads, defined only by the way they blocked out light. David felt a familiar tightening in his throat and quickly flicked the old-fashioned light switch with his fingers, banishing arachnid shadows with the brightness of an uncovered bulb.

He found the files at the back of the room, under a layer of dust so thick it had become something solid that fell to the floor like a crust when he took down the first crate. The documents were housed in the cardboard tombs of lever files, decorated in a pattern particular to the 1930s — swirls of grey marl with maroon edging — he recognised it from the libraries of Cambridge and the storage rooms of *The Royal Geographical Society.*

On opening the first, David was certain that the papers inside had been dumped there eighty years ago and had not been looked at since. There was as much dust inside as out and a peculiarly comforting smell of decay, almost a fragrance. There was no inventory or note of explanation; on leafing through the first few documents he noted that they were roughly in date order, but that was all in the way of categorisation. After the initial exotic feel of looking at original documents from the Victorian age, the contents of the first box became boring; reams of purchase orders for the museum: glass cases, stationery, chemicals, sawdust — the means of preserving birds.

The second box was more interesting, containing letters of both a professional and personal nature written to and by William Wilson. One name cropped up again and again — Jonathan Westman Blake — Wilson's apprentice.

Blake was a few years younger than Wilson, born into a wealthy shipping family who ran a commercial fleet out of Southampton Docks. The Blakes had increased their already substantial fortune by importing luxury goods from India. Jonathan met William at Cambridge, both of them studying ornithology, Wilson a few years ahead. They embarked on their first field trips together in the Cambridge hills; there were beautifully illustrated diaries and letters between them discussing future plans.

On graduating, Blake took full advantage of the family business and he and Wilson set off by boat on a tour of Northern Europe and Russia, collecting specimens of birds and small mammals, even a bear, the stuffed remains of which were housed in the museum. Their diaries described the athletic feats involved in their pursuits — climbing, swimming, wading — they even had a gunboat made for shooting water birds from under the silent cover of reeds.

David saw the boat every day in the museum, pushed up against the wall of a corridor — a coffin-like structure with two oars and a large moveable gun with sights fixed to its centre. David had never thought how it might work, but here it was described in plans and diagrams — Wilson's precise instructions as to how it should be made.

There were photographs too, a whole box of them, thick and littered with white dots and scratches. Some were studio prints; like one of Wilson lying back in the gunboat with a painting of a riverbank as a backdrop and a stuffed duck — wings open in half-flight — near him on a cloth-covered table. David was struck by how young he looked, serious but handsome in profile. Another man stood behind the head of the boat, poised in motion, a huge net in his hand, dressed in whites with boots and a floppy linen hat, a scarf tied at his neck — Jonathan Westman Blake. He looked even younger than Wilson, clean-shaven, impossibly beautiful, a knowing smirk on his face. They were having fun, recreating their outdoor life inside the photographer's studio.

There were other photographs of them together, standing close but more formal, suit-clad, in front of a backdrop of a Mediterranean scene or a mountainside. Whatever the formality of the picture they always seemed on the edge of laughter. There was joy there, genuine happiness, an unbridled enthusiasm for life that David realised he had never possessed. These two men from a hundred years ago were more alive in two-dimensional flatness than he had ever felt.

There was a final image — a location shot — Blake and Wilson standing together in front of an oak tree, its leaves shimmering indistinctly in the background — too quick for the camera. They were dressed casually, the paraphernalia of exploration at their feet, Wilson's arm draped around Blake's neck, their heads close, huge grins on their faces. It reminded David of modern holiday snaps, people at their most relaxed and comfortable. It reminded him of the photographs of himself and Ellen on their honeymoon in Italy — before it all went wrong. *Of course!* A sudden realisation swept over him. *Wilson and Blake were lovers. Look at them — look at the intimacy and pleasure in each other's company.* He looked at the photographs again — in each one it now seemed obvious — Wilson and Blake were a couple.

David heard the faint slam of a door downstairs. He looked at his watch — 9am. He'd read all night without stopping for food or tea or sleep. There had been no visitation by the *Lady in Black* and no mention of her in the papers he had looked at. He was no closer to solving the mystery of the alarms, but he felt as though he had gained greater knowledge of the museum and the men who had created it than any other soul on earth.

297

David began to live for his nights at the museum. He glided through his days happier than he had been for months. He washed and fed himself, even slept soundly in the afternoons, then hurried off to work to immerse himself in the *Boy's Own* adventures of Wilson and Blake. Confining himself to the storage room, he had no further contact with the lady ghost.

Agatha came into his life at the end of the second week, first in the form of a letter, then a photograph — then in his imagination.

Rev. Jonathan Carmichael
Saint Paul's Church
Hove
13th July 1893

Dear William,
I believe I may have found a housekeeper for you. Her name is Mrs Agatha Turnbull. She is a most remarkable woman, the widow of an army captain killed in India. She has had the most tragic of lives, losing two babes to the cholera in the space of a month, yet she remains stoic and possessed of a lively mind and a genial nature.

At present, she is at a loss as to what she may do to earn a living. As is the plight of so many widows, her husband did not leave her sufficient means by which she might survive, and she needs to find work. She has asked me to aid her in this matter. Naturally, following the conversation on our last meeting, I thought of you.

Please consent to meet with her; I am sure you will find her most agreeable and conscientious.

Yours sincerely
Rev. Carmichael

The photograph, at the bottom of a file filled with household accounts and yet more purchase orders, raised the hairs on the back of David's neck. It was a picture of a woman, probably in her late 20s, pale, and thinner than was fashionable for the time. Her hair was jet black and parted at the centre, tied neatly, with ringlets at her cheeks, the bones of which jutted out as sharply as any on the models in Ellen's trashy magazines. Her eyes stared brightly into the distance and there was the merest hint of a smile on her lips, suggesting a liveliness cloaked under formality. It was not her features that gave David a shock but the dress she was wearing, the same colour as her hair, embroidered and shimmering, finished with delicate white lace — it was the dress he'd seen at the edge of sleep on his first night. Here before him was a photograph of *The Lady in Black*.

Throughout the night he found more and more pictures of Agatha, some formal of her alone and others, fewer, with Wilson and Blake. In his mind he imposed her face on the vision he had seen on the first night, merging the distinct and the indistinct into a new reality. He saw her walking through the museum, heard the swish of her skirts, felt the elegant movement of her slender arms. He found documents that suggested she was more than a housekeeper — that at some point she had taken a formal position in the museum. He imagined her in the company of Wilson and Blake, talking animatedly about the museum, laughing, planning — as what? Friend? Colleague? Servant?

Just before 7am David found a heavy dust-covered envelope. It was addressed to Agatha; he opened it and read Wilson's hurried script.

White Friar
Lyme Regis
June 21st 1894

My Dear Agatha,

I write in haste. We have just arrived; my cases are still in the hall standing where they were dropped. I could not wait; if I could I would have written to you in the coach on the way here. My mind is made up.

I am sure you know of what I speak. You must think me a fool to have taken so much time to realise what you have undoubtedly known all along — since the moment we first met. Forgive me Agatha — I am unused to romantic ways. I have been without a wife for so long I assumed there was no other way. And then yesterday — the touch of your hand, the scent of your hair, the warm press of your lips as they brushed my cheek. I am covered in the sense of you. I smile like a child with a new toy.

Why not us Agatha? Do we not have the right to be happy? Dare I even hope that you will say yes?

As we drove toward Dorchester, I spied upon the Frome two swans with the snowiest of feathers. They danced on the water as if in a waltz, the branches of a weeping willow hung over their embrace, and I longed for you Agatha. I beg you please to consent to be my wife.

I shall cut short my trip — I just want to collect a couple of Guillemots, and anything else that comes my way, from the under-cliff at Beer. I shall return to you the day after tomorrow. I hope you will have had enough time by then to consider my request.

Agatha — oh the roll of your name on my tongue — Agatha.

If the answer is yes, please let me know it is so by placing a vase of roses in the drawing room window. If I see them when I return I shall be the happiest man on earth. Know that I love you always.

Your servant,

William

David was deeply moved by what he read. It was the only letter from William to Agatha concerned with anything other than inventories or household accounts. Something ignited in David's heart; here he felt real love, unquestioning love, the kind of love where you were willing to lose everything.

He must have been wrong about Blake. Perhaps Wilson had never had romantic feelings before, for a man or a woman, perhaps he had just been so consumed by his work that notions of love had simply never occurred to him. Then along comes this war widow, Agatha Turnbull, and everything changes. The letter was so romantic. David could only imagine what had passed between them on the morning he'd left her — a simple kiss on the cheek that shook William from his obsession with documenting the ways of nature to participating in them himself.

Wilson died consumed by joyful love. If Wilson could fall headlong into the romantic abyss, not caring anything of loss or sorrow, why couldn't he? What did William feel, wondered David, in those seconds as he fell through the air, flying like the birds he so adored? Then he thought of Agatha — had she cut the roses from the garden, and placed them in a vase at the drawing room window for William to see when he returned home?

On his way back to the flat that morning David stopped at the florist and bought a dozen pink roses. He left them in water all day. By the evening their blossoms were huge and flouncy with a peach tinge at the base of the waxy petals; their rich, heavy scent filled the room with summer's end.

He took them in to work with him. When everyone else had gone and the doors were locked for the night, he arranged them in a vase, placing them on the table in front of the fake window in the drawing room exhibit. He sprayed them with water to refresh them and they shone under the electric gas light, huge drops of liquid clinging to their blooms like tears.

Pleased with his tribute, David settled into the red velvet armchair opposite the roses with a cup of tea and a copy of *The Telegraph*. He read about the collapse of the world's banks, the media circus surrounding the death of a famous young woman he'd never heard of, and how two African women had been crushed to death trying to see the Pope in Angola. He looked at the cricket report — another English disaster. And tomorrow's weather — cloudy.

The museum grew dark in the sinking evening light and David's eyelids grew heavy over his eyes. He drifted in the blueness of the half-illuminated room, comfortable in the embrace of the chair and the silence.

He woke with a start, unsure of how much time had elapsed since he fell asleep. Darkness covered the great hall, leaving only the capsule of the mock drawing room lit by its fake gas lamp.

David felt a chill come over him, the hairs on his forearms stood up away from the skin and a cold trickle of sweat ran down the back of his neck. The scent of the roses grew in intensity; so heavy was the perfume that he found it hard to breathe in. There was a rustle of silk and the distant sound of sobbing.

She appeared at the edge of the exhibit, dressed in the same black gown as before, the shimmering satin colour of a beetle's wing. There was a delicate cream collar around her neck, the lace repeated at her cuffs. Her face was indistinct but her black hair shone with the same iridescent blue as her dress.

David froze in his chair, afraid to move in case she disappeared. She walked across the carpet — her feet as solid on the floor as any of the museum's other visitors. When she reached the table she picked up the vase of roses and clutched them to her chest, then she moved off towards the back of the museum.

David shook himself from his inertia and sprang to his feet. 'Agatha?' he called after her and rushed out of the drawing room, his feet clicking on the tiles of the shadowy exhibition hall. He saw her turn left out of the butterfly room, just catching sight of the folds of her hem. He hurried past the glass cases of exotic spiders, oversized insects and the silent rows of ancient butterflies. He turned in the direction she had taken and stood next to Bubo, the stuffed owl, both of them looking for her at the end of the corridor. He couldn't see her and wondered if he had not dreamt the whole thing, if she were not just a particularly vivid example of old hag syndrome. Then he was aware of a flickering in the drawing room, as if somebody had walked across the path of the gas lamp.

David ran towards the door of the exhibit but stopped on the threshold as he noticed that the table top on which he had placed the roses was empty. He crossed into the room, looking around him in confusion. He felt compelled to turn. Agatha was behind him to his right, standing in front of the marble fireplace Jeremy had found in the store room. She had placed the vase in the middle of it and was absently rearranging the flowers while gazing at her reflection in the gilt-edged mirror on the wall above it. She was as real as he was; a full solid being of flesh and bones. He could see her face clearly in the glass of the mirror.

David walked gingerly over to her and stood by her side. He could smell the perfume of a thousand roses and the musty tang of wet silk and formaldehyde. He looked at their reflections in the glass. Her face was very beautiful; as white as linen, her lips the same pink as the roses and her eyes flashed with a lilac glow, their startled pupils the deepest black. The virgin lace of her collar had a dark smudge of ink on it just above her left breast. David noticed that his own skin had the same deathly white hue as the vision before him.

Agatha looked at his eyes in the mirror. A spherical tear fell to her cheek.

'I'm sorry,' said David overcome with pity.

She smiled.

'I have a message for you,' she said, her voice had the disembodied clarity of cut glass, 'Adam will be safe — whatever happens in the future — Adam will be safe.'

They stood for a moment and the chill in the room gradually warmed into the heat of a summer's afternoon massaging David's tired body and bringing a smile to his lips. Then Agatha disappeared.

MUSSELS

There it is again. She's sure she can hear it, that it's not just her imagination. She knows she's getting old. No, she knows she is old — she's been old for most of her life — but she's sure it has nothing to do with age. She knows the betrayals of age — sometimes she feels her bones creaking under her skin when she's not even moving, lying on her bed at night — old injuries long healed, now bruising again. In the cool morning air her ankle throbs and her wrist swells with extra fluid, water where there shouldn't be water. The thin white lines are visible on her shiny wrinkled skin. No one else would know what they were or how she got them, they would just think they were signs of aging and disintegration; but May knows. May remembers when they weren't there, when her skin was smooth and shone with youth rather than age.

There it is again. It's so quiet in the bedroom, only the tired ticking of her mother's clock from the dust of the dressing table, a proper clock with clockwork insides — not just a bundle of wire and microchips — from a time when people and not machines made things. It has slowed over the years and has to be wound throughout the day just to keep reasonably accurate time. She forgets sometimes and loses track of the hours, feeling out of sorts with the light outside her window. Not that she has anything to keep time for.

A funny thing, the human need for time — it's usually arranged around food, breakfast by 8, lunch at 12, tea at 6. That's how it used to be anyway, before TV dinners, when everyone sat down together. May stopped all that fifty years ago. Now May's time is arranged around medication — heart tablets at 8 and 8, blood pressure 8 and 3, eyedrops at 4, laxative first thing, memory pills…

Memory pills! As if she wants to remember more.

She's been hearing it for days — the sobbing. Well not days exactly, nights really, in the early hours when the city is asleep. It comes to her at about 4am, the hour she's woken at for as long as she can remember. Old people always wake at this time, her mother did it, wracked with pain and exhausted yet unable to sleep past 4, then back asleep again by 2 o'clock in the afternoon. May knew she was really old the first time she woke at 4 and couldn't drift back off again; more wide awake in the dark than she ever was in the day. After that first time she never went back to sleeping through the night. Even the sedatives only take her this far and she never takes them anymore anyway — Diazepam is a proper drug, Valium by another name — an addiction waiting to happen.

Because she knows how awake she is she's sure that she's not imagining it — the sobbing — if that's what it is.

***

Adam bends his little knees and grabs his thighs with his hands. He looks like an old man playing bowls. He breathes in through his nose; the air is dank, salt-filled, sand and seaweed drenched. It smells like fish tanks and Chinese takeaways.

Adam's nose twitches and a short sneeze blows out a sliver of snot, the colour of peppermint creams. He wipes it away with his already dirty sleeve and shuffles forward, wet sand creeping between his feet and the soles of his sandals.

His sandals sink into the softness below, compacting mussel shells, as he leans forward and peers wide-eyed into the dark hole of the tunnel. Clear water runs down from the inside, over the short lime-green seaweed and the carpet of multi-coloured pebbles on its floor. Adam edges further forward as the flat of the beach, stretching out from the mouth of the tunnel, fills with more and more people drawn by the novelty of the sand.

This is one of the few times and places in the city where you can feel sand between your toes. Just below the Lagoon, as the beach falls sharply away and the tide slips out as far as it will go, the sand seductively calls the locals. *You've only got a couple of hours. Make the most of it — it's like a real beach.*

None of the tourists see it. The ones who walk down from the train and head straight for the first free pebbles they can find. They sit all day in the same spot, walk to the chippy and the bar, buy ice cream and buckets and spades. Their kids might make it to the paddling pool and the climbing frames, maybe even the carousel or the Pier, but they never see the sand.

Adam feels like it's his secret, that even though all the people around him know, he is the only one who comes here nearly every day — even in winter — all these people are part-timers.

The tunnel, in particular, belongs to Adam. Only he knows about the sea monster and the mermaids. Graham told him. Graham saw the monster when he was little and he has heard the mermaids. Graham says that sometimes when you shout *hello* down through the bars of the tunnel the mermaids bang *hello* back from their hiding place deep inside it, where it curls around and turns under the seabed. They don't shout back because humans can't hear mermaid voices, so they bang instead. They don't answer everyone either — you have to be special for them to answer — they have to think you're worth it.

Adam hasn't had the guts to shout *hello* yet. He's only six. He looks down the shaft into the darkness. Inside the tunnel is coated with tiny blue-black mussels. Adam loves the way they hang from the roof like they're waving at him. His Dad eats mussels sometimes, when he takes him out to lunch on Sundays, a huge bowlful soaked in wine. He eats the first one then uses its enormous pincher shell to pull out the others, laying the empty shells one on top of the other on a huge white plate. Adam has fish and chips. They usually eat in silence.

He doesn't know his Dad very well. He's quiet and not like Graham, who plays football with him and talks all the time; but he works with fossils and that's cool — Graham is only a taxi driver.

Today is the day Adam has decided to call the mermaids. He's so close to the tunnel mouth now he could put his hand through the bars. He stares into the darkness, breathes in a huffy little breath and then shouts *hello!*. It's a quiet hello — too quiet — and there's no reply. He screws up his mouth, biting his tiny white teeth into the skin below his bottom lip. He breathes in, deeper, taking in a lungful of fishy air and shouts again, louder this time,

'Hellooooo!'

His shout echoes down the tunnel, he hears it move away from him to the end, then turn and travel downwards, to where the mermaids hide.

When his shout has disappeared, it is silent for a moment but then, unmistakeably, comes a loud watery clang.

Adam's mother and her boyfriend, Graham, sit on the stones near the top of the beach. It's nearly 8 o'clock; Graham will be going back to work soon, the coals on their disposable barbecue are cold. Adam should really be in bed by now but neither of them wants to leave their idyllic evening. Graham looks up at her, this classy bird he met by chance as she was running away. He still can't believe his luck.

The sun, glowing on the horizon, bathes her face in peach-coloured light. She smiles at him. She says she likes him because he's so uncomplicated, he doesn't think too much, he drives his taxi to earn money so that they can spend hours like these, warm uncomplicated evenings in the sun.

Suddenly Ellen's eyes move from his face and scan the beach below. They dart along the tide line, where the water trapped by the ripples of the sand shimmers in the last rays of the sunshine. The expression on her face changes from contentment to concern. She sits forward and peaks her hand over her eyes.

'Graham, where's Adam?'

He turns and looks at the beach. All he can see are seagulls and two teenagers throwing a Frisbee.

***

May's feet shine white in the pre-dawn gloom. She eases out of her bed feet first, feeling for her slippers with wrinkled toes. It was warm yesterday and will be again today, but May would feel cold even at noon in the Sahara. She pushes her feet into the soft sheepskin and waits for the pain in her corns to subside before standing from the bed. She walks over to her dresser, as thin as a bird under her nylon nightie, and peers at the clock. 4.54am. There's no crying now, in absolute wakefulness she doubts her own senses again. Is she being haunted by a memory? Can you hear someone who isn't there — who's never really been there — an almost-child lost decades before?

She shuffles along to her kitchen in the inky light; she fills the kettle and switches it on, staring through the blinds of her 12th-floor window into the silvery dawn creeping upwards through the sky. As the kettle bubbles beside her the first birds wake on the ledges — starlings, seagulls, pigeons — their voices rise in song from their hidden nests. May has always felt an affinity with birds — since that morning years before when they saved her — without the songs of the birds May would have ceased to exist.

She peers at the dawn, pouring boiled water into her teapot and swirling it with a teaspoon. As she taps the spoon on the china saucer she hears the crying. It's early; she's not usually in the kitchen at this time and the sound is loud, distinct — in no way an apparition.

May's hands shake. What should she do? One frail old lady — can she risk investigating? Her heart thuds, she reaches for her angina pill and slugs it down with the milk from the jug. She holds onto the kitchen sink breathing heavily, a wheezy rasp in her chest. The crying continues. Then comes the unmistakeable word, whimpered yet roared. The one word she can't ignore.

'HELP!'

Her door squeaks open, catching on the worn carpet so she has to force it back. Her wrists ache, the copper bracelet her doctor gave her digs into the slackness of her skin. Outside, the corridor is dankly warm, only a couple of the lights are on, the one at the end by the lift flickers in and out, as a moth flutters inside a tubular bulb. The walls swirl around her, longer and wider in her eyes than they really are. May edges along, quiet as a rodent, her palms pressed flat against the cold plaster.

The crying has stopped. She wonders why she is here, scuttling along a hallway with the dawn. She stops outside

Andy's door and lays her ear on it as gently as she can — her whole body trembles. She knows he couldn't be in but even so, fears him opening the door and finding her there — snooping. The only sound now is her breath, the catch of it in her throat, the bubbling in her chest. Then it comes again — as real as the birds. A child's voice, breath catching like her own, sobs caught in a tiny throat.

'HELP.'

The door to number 12A opens and the dog skates out onto the lino, trying to grip the flat surface with its tiny feet. May lets out a frightened moan and pushes herself flatter against the door.

The man comes out of his flat, locking the door once, then again, then hooking a padlock on it and locking that too. He silently turns his head and looks at May. She quietens her breathing but looks at him wide-eyed. He shakes his head and continues fiddling with the locks then bends and clicks a lead onto the dog's collar. He turns towards the lift but then thinks better of it, and man and dog walk slowly towards her, startling her with each tap of their feet.

When the man is level with her, his dog sniffs at her slippers. She feels its cold wet nose and hot breath on her bare skin.

'You ok?' asks the man. His voice is surprisingly soft. She realises she has never heard him speak before. She minds her own business and he minds his — just as it should be between neighbours. She has always been frightened of him though, of the way he looks; his tattoos and his armour of gold chain and the dog — the sort of dog that's made to bite. They are always on the news, dogs like his, attacking children, killing babies with their teeth while the parents sleep drug-filled slumbers in the next room.

Something in his eyes makes her think she can trust him, she relaxes her body, her eyes watery in the gloomy light. She lays her hand flat on Andy's door.

'I can hear a child.'

This time the man tenses.

'A child — you sure?'

'Listen.'

She moves aside for him to place his head against the painted wood. They are about the same height, their heads are close and her blue eyes search his for confirmation, for the last chance of clear-headedness. If she is wrong...

There is a whimpering on the other side of the door, then a sob and a hopeless pathetic cry for help.

The man steps back.

'Shit.'

He looks at his watch then at May. He hands her the dog's lead.

'Stand back,' he says. 'He'll be back soon.'

She does as she's told, grateful that it's out of her hands, and she and the dog shuffle sideways together. The dog looks up at her slack-jawed, saliva dripping to the floor.

The man takes a few steps backwards down the corridor then runs and twists, bashing against the door with his bulky shoulder. It shifts but doesn't open. He does it again — still no budge — then he looks at May.

'Fuck it,' he says and takes a key from his pocket, slipping it into the top lock and turning it left then right. The lock pops and he smiles and pushes open the door.

'I wudn't use it on yours,' he says with a shrug.

They both peer into the darkness of Andy's flat. Anaemic light from the grubby windows filters shadows onto the floor. The open living room is littered with piles of neatly stacked newspapers; they cover the carpets around the walls and the sides of the couch, piled under the coffee table and up against the kitchen door. The flat reeks of old paper — it's a particular smell — nothing else quite matches it, it pricks at the nostrils, depriving them of moisture in a desperate attempt to rehydrate itself. The smell of stale cigarettes competes with it, from over-piled ashtrays on chair-arms and the glass table in front of the sofa.

On the wall opposite the window is a wooden crucifix and a huge framed photograph of two smiling girls in school uniform, the glass is dusty and the girls look out as if through a fog. There are a couple of half-filled coffee mugs on the floor and a litre bottle of Fanta next to a plastic cup printed with a picture of Thomas the Tank Engine. May and the man see this item at the same time and move their eyes to each other.

'Hello!' shouts the man, 'anyone here?'

He pauses — there is only silence.

'Hey, it's not Andy. If you can hear me shout, so I can come get you.'

There's still nothing. May shouts this time, a quivery aged voice.

'Hello dear, tell us where you are.'

The answer comes from behind the bedroom door, quiet and faraway.

'Mum. I want my Mum.'

The door isn't locked, but when they are inside there is no sign of a child. The room is tidy, the empty bed made and the curtains drawn, there's a stuffed teddy on the pillow and a train set rigged out on the floor. The man walks to the wardrobe and flings open the door — but for a few clothes and shoes there's nothing inside. He wrinkles his forehead. The dog strains on the leash pulling May as it snuffles around the bed whining.

'Where are you?'

There's a little knock under the bed and a tiny voice calls out. 'In here. I'm under here.'

The man kneels and feels under the bed, then grabs with both hands and swiftly pulls out a large wooden drawer. The boy is curled foetally inside, wedged in the just big enough space and wrapped in a red wattle blanket. He looks up at them, his mop of curly brown hair stuck to his tear-stained face, the whites of his eyes catching in the ever-brightening light.

'Holy shit,' says the man then looks at May, 'sorry lady.'

The child lifts his head and looks at his two disparate rescuers.

'It's alright dear, we've got you,' says May reaching out with trembling fingers and touching his shoulder. He nods sleepily and sucks his thumb.

'Looks like he been drugged,' says the man. 'We better get a move on.'

He lifts the boy out of his box and stands with him in his arms.

'We'll take him to your place.'

He strides out of the room and the flat, leaving May to follow with the dog.

Inside her flat he lays the boy on May's sofa and puts a cushion under his head as tenderly as any mother would. He looks at May.

'I can't have the po-lice askin' questions. Stay here wit him, give me an hour then call an say you found him in the hall.'

She nods and hands the man the dog's lead.

'What are you going to do?'

'Nuting, am not gonna do anyting. But I can't have the po-lice around so you ain't seen me lady, ok?'

'Ok.'

She sits on the sofa next to the boy and strokes his hair, then looks up at her new friend and smiles, her bright blue eyes radiate warmth in the light of the dawn. The man turns to go.

'Oh, what's your name?' she asks as if she's just remembered she doesn't know it.

'Bulldog,' he says.

'Thank you — Bulldog.'

Bulldog nods and walks away clicking the door quietly shut behind him.

The child sleeps for a while, murmuring and thrashing, his eyelids flickering in REM like a dog's. He's hot and May gets a flannel from the bathroom and soaks it in cold water to make a compress. She places it gently on his forehead. May hears the lift doors open and then lone footsteps and a tune whistled in the corridor. She recognises it but can't name it. She hears a thud from next door and then a dragging sound and the judder of the lift doors.

The child settles and opens his eyes; he has hazel eyes, the pupils are huge, unnaturally dilated. He groans.

'Here let me get you some juice.'

She edges into the kitchen through the beaded curtain, and pours him an orange juice, putting four chocolate chip cookies onto a plate.

When she returns, the child grabs the juice from her and drains it in three gulps then stuffs all the biscuits into his mouth.

'Steady,' says May. 'Lord preserve us, did he not feed you?'

The boy shakes his head; the orange juice has left a thin yellow moustache on his upper lip, he wipes at it with the back of his hand.

'Not much,' he says; his voice dry. 'Sweets mainly and cornflakes.'

He looks at the mantelpiece over the fire.

'Who's that?' he says looking at May's only framed photograph.

'That's my husband, Jack.'

'Where is he? Is he dead?'

'I don't know. I haven't seen him in a long time. I think he might be.'

The child considers this for a while.

'Aren't you lonely, on your own? He left me alone most of the time. I missed my friends and my Mum.'

'Well, I've been on my own for ages now so I don't notice it much anymore.'

'I'll be your friend. My name's Adam. Are you going to get my Mum?'

May looks at the clock. 7am.

'Yes dear,' she says patting his hand. 'I can do that for you now.'

***

Andy wakes to a monumental pain at the base of his skull. His neck is twisted so that his chin touches his chest. As his eyes open he sees blackness above, an uneven corrugated blackness, so black it's almost blue. There's a bright light spreading from his chin, a horizontal line of whiteness that cuts into the lower portion of his vision and is cut again vertically in stripes. It daggers straight into his brain as though he has stared into a naked lightbulb until the glowing filament is all he can see. It hurts, the light, physical pain through colour saturation. White. All the colours of the spectrum reflected at once — cancelling each other out. He can't move, and he's not sure what to make of the light, or the dark.

After a while his head begins to clear, though it still feels like a baby's rattle. In the heavy fog of his mind, impeded by the white, he begins to realise he's in a tunnel — a big tunnel, domed above him, the roof covered in an uneven mass of black pointed stones. They remind him of jet crystals.

Andy's back is wet, from his boots to his shaved head. His skin prickles under three inches of icy water; he moves his fingers in the miniature current and feels the resistance as the water trickles past on its unstoppable journey. The gold of his wedding ring slips coldly down the bone of his finger, lubricated by the wet of his skin under water.

He remembers walking along the corridor after his shift, tired and alone, longing to see the boy, to hold his baked-bread body to his chest and feel the softness of his hair against his cheek. Then sharpness and blackness in his head. Then this.

It smells rotten in the tunnel — of soil and salt swirling together, fish and cabbage, surf and earth. The water runs relentlessly under his back and though he can't seem to sit up he can move his hands, and he grabs at the ground underneath with spadelike fingers. The shells there crack under his grip, cutting into his flesh like razors, the salt and grit bite him and he winces, sensing blinding pain course through his skull.

Mussels.

Andy has worked out where he is. His father brought him here just after his mother left them.

'If you tell anyone, they'll take you away and put you in the prison on the beach. You won't be able to get out through the bars and when the tide comes in, the monsters will eat you.'

If he is where he thinks he is, he knows he won't get out. The water is rising; he can feel it edging up his skin, a blurred line of cold, seeping into his shoes and the folds of his clothes. For a moment he wonders if his father put him here, he remembers his words and remembers that he did tell — Catriona for one, and the prison psychologist later. But he knows his father is dead — was dead — when he told.

He pictures the mussels opening their charcoal shells to greet the tide, to thank it for the coming feast. The bivalves clinging to the uppermost curve of the roof creak in anticipation, sending a storm of steady drops onto Andy's face; they echo as they hit the shallow water below, the sound of a drop sent back to its source.

In the end everything goes back to where it began.

Soon, in less than an hour maybe, the mussels will bloom into orange flesh and feed.

Andy sniffs as a drop curls into his nostril. *How did this happen? I tried — did I not deserve a normal life?*

He remembers the day he left his father alone to die in his pension-fund cottage, with his damaged heart and a bloated liver and not much else. There had been no physical contact between them for two years — since Andy's 16th birthday. Andy had planned to hit him, to part with a hard open-palmed slap across the face; the noise of it played in his head like an unmade memory. In the end Andy didn't even say goodbye, just peeked at his father asleep in his armchair with only the tick of his retirement clock for company, then picked up his suitcase and strode out of the front door. He didn't even shut it behind him, just left it open for the autumn wind to blow in the desiccated leaves from the path.

It stops here. The girls are alright. He never hurt the girls; he never made them feel like he did.

He remembers his accuser Derek Jones. He remembers how Derek was a bully, picking on the kids who were weaker than him, the clever ones, the ones with bad skin, the ones who weren't good at sports. He remembers how Derek used to whip the other kids up into frenzies of humiliation, how they'd pick a victim and chant or push or just growl at him as he went about his daily business. He remembers that Derek reminded him of himself at 12 — all at sea and trying to deflect attention any way he could. Andy remembers his father swelling with pride when he was called into school because Andy had broken a classmate's nose in a playground fight. He remembers the circle of boys surrounding them as he smashed at the kid's face. It was the last time he did anything like that.

My God, he thinks, *Derek was me, trusting little Derek. He was me. He felt like I did. They all did — all the little boys.*

He cries, hot poker tears tearing at his temples as they join their like in the salt water that is about to cover his chest. He can sense others in the tunnel with him, moving up the hollow like a breeze. *Who are they? His victims?*

It ends now.

He readies himself for the rush of water up his nose — it must only be minutes away. He'll not fight it, not try to lift his head or take in the air as it's forced upwards.

He's ready — he even smiles.

Light flickers at the end of the tunnel like a shadow across the moon. There's a wet creaking sound, a metal twisting, loud in the trumpet of the tunnel, amplified in Andy's battered brain. It sounds like a submarine descending, the force of water trying to fill space. Next comes the reverberation of metal on metal, then a moment's silence.

Andy breathes expectantly as the water trickles into his ears. The creak starts up again almost immediately, crunching through his head, the loud clang blinding his ears. He tries to lift his head to see but the salt of his tears and the sea stings his eyes, and he blinks only blurred visions of light and dark. He doesn't know how many times the sound repeats. His heart beats fast.

Is it the monster? Clawing its way up the pipe to find me?

The noise stops. The tunnel darkens. The looming beast reaches out.

Hands grab Andy's legs forcefully above the knees and he feels himself dragged across the floor towards the light, the mussels below him tearing and scratching at his back in an attempt to keep him with them.

'I've got you,' says a man's voice.

Andy lies winded on the beach, the vast whiteness of the sky overhead searing his eyes. There are kites in the sky, starkly red, and the curve of seagulls' wings as they soar together. *Snatched back. Why have I been snatched back?* He can just make out the silver buttons of a police uniform.

'Dad?' he whispers.

They wrap a silver blanket around Andy and lay him on a stretcher next to the mossy concrete of the overflow pipe. They shine lights in his eyes and take his pulse. They secure his head in a neck brace so he can only see as far as his eyes can rotate. It's a strange abstract view of the beach, almost entirely defined by the vast sky and the torsos of the medics and the policeman. He can sense the tide making its way up the pebbles, can sense that it is already way past the end of the pipe. His back is sore from the slashes made by the mussels and the sting of the salt. The paramedic gives him a single sip of water from a baby beaker; it tastes of plastic, adding further unpleasantness to the coating already clinging to Andy's mouth.

The policeman stands over him, tall and imposing against the brightness of the skies. Andy moves his eyes to his face. The policeman studies Andy with a puzzled expression. Andy knows he's been recognised but not yet placed.

'You were lucky, someone called it in. Anonymously. A young girl — said she saw two men behaving suspiciously around the pipe. Don't suppose you know who put you in there, or why?'

Andy blinks. He'll know soon enough.

A flicker of recognition crosses the policeman's face.

'Andy?' he says. 'Andy Watson?'

Andy nods. They all know him — one of the family gone bad.

'I knew your father. He was my superior when I first joined the force. He was a great copper your Dad.' He smiles a nostalgic smile. 'There never was another man like Sidney Watson.'

***

It's Christmas day, about 10.30. May's doorbell rings and she buzzes them up, flicking the door off the latch to leave it open for them as she fetches her coat and the bag of presents from the bed. She's had her hair done and for the first time in half a century, has a smear of pink lipstick on her lips — *Amethyst Sky* (Number 42). As she buttons her coat and pats her hair, Adam rushes in and grabs her around her waist. He's getting taller; his head is at her chest now, just below her heart.

'May! May! May! Merry Christmas! I got a robot dinosaur and loads of Lego, even a Star Wars set and chocolate and *Doctor Who* DVDs and… What did you get?'

'I got you dear,' she says. 'I got you.'

Today is a good day. He has bad ones, but today he is just a child at Christmas. She smiles at his father, David, in the doorway, and kisses Adam's hair.

Adam looks up at her and smiles, then takes her hand.

'C'mon May — if we hurry we can see the swimmers. The water must be *reeeally* cold. I bet they scream when they get in. Do you think anyone will be dressed like a penguin?'

He leads her out of her doorway, chattering as he goes.

'They must be bonker-donkers swimming round the Pier on Christmas Day! Do you like sprouts? Mum's got loads of sprouts! She says I have to eat some to get my ice cream. I hate sprouts — they make you fart — I'm going to hide them in my socks and put them in the bin when she's not looking.'

On the way to the lift, the door at the end of the corridor opens and Cassie snuffles out with a collar of red tinsel round her neck. Bulldog comes out of the flat as May and her new family draw level with his door. She stops and shakes his hand.

'Merry Christmas, Bulldog.'

He ruffles Adam's hair and nods at David.

'Merry Christmas May,' he says and accompanies them to the lift.

'Adam, whatcha get — any guns?'

The lift doors close and floor twelve is silent, save for the cries of the gulls and the decreasing noise of the lift as it rumbles downwards to ground level and the Christmas cheer below.

The Argus June 6th 2009

ADAM ALIVE!

Missing schoolboy Adam Willoughby was found alive yesterday, near the residence of convicted paedophile Andy Watson.

Police are working in conjunction with Adam's parents and the Child Protection Agency to obtain a statement from the 6-year-old.

He was found by Watson's next door neighbour, May Milligan, 88, who heard crying in the corridor outside her flat in Ocean Heights Brighton, at just after 7am, and found the child wandering in a state of confusion.

Milligan gave the boy orange juice and cookies. 'The poor mite was starving,' she said ,'and didn't have a clue where he was. Watson must have drugged him.'

His father, David Willoughby said that he felt as though all his dreams had come true and that he would be forever grateful to Milligan for rescuing his son.

Brighton and Hove police are now questioning Watson, who was found unconscious and lying inside the Hove Lagoon overflow pipe yesterday, after a tip-off from a resident who reported two men behaving suspiciously in the area. The police are eager to question the individual who reported the incident.

Watson was released from prison last September after serving two years of a three-year sentence for the molestation of a 12-year-old boy. Watson was convicted in 2003 for crimes committed whilst he was a PE teacher at Rainer High School in Brighton.

Watson changed his plea to guilty mid-trial when it was revealed that the prosecution would submit video testimony from his former pupil. As a result Watson received a lenient five-year sentence further reduced to four years for good behaviour.

Acknowledgements

I would like to thank the staff and students of the University of Sussex Creative Writing program, especially Catherine Smith, Susannah Waters, Ursula Robson and Karen Hubert. Thanks also to The Booth's Museum, The Old Police Cells Museum Brighton, the Pelirocco Hotel, Grit Lit and Are you Sitting Comfortably ?

Special thanks to Alice's Writing Group and the Rattle Tales Co-operative, a truly inspiring, creative and enthusiastic bunch, and to all the friends who have offered support and reading services over the last couple of years.

Finally, and most importantly, to my husband Rob and our sons, my wonderful Mum and sisters, and my Dad, who didn't get to see his daughter's name in print but is always here.